Benjamin Ricketson Tucker, Félix Pyat

The Rag-Picker of Paris

Benjamin Ricketson Tucker, Félix Pyat

The Rag-Picker of Paris

ISBN/EAN: 9783337428440

Printed in Europe, USA, Canada, Australia, Japan

Cover: Foto ©Andreas Hilbeck / pixelio.de

More available books at **www.hansebooks.com**

THE

Rag-Picker of Paris

BY

FÉLIX PYAT

TRANSLATED FROM THE FRENCH BY
BENJ. R. TUCKER

BOSTON, MASS.:
BENJ. R. TUCKER, PUBLISHER
1890

CONTENTS.

CONTENTS.

Part Third.—The Masquerade.

Part Fourth.—The Struggle.

PREFACE.

Contrary to the usual practice of writers who construct a drama from their novels, the author has constructed a novel from his drama.

This is at least original. It is also easier and safer. The Duval soup is made more easily than the Liebig essence. A play is a work of concentration; a book, a work of elaboration. The largest and often the best part of a drama is not put upon the stage, but a book has no "behind the scenes." The volume gives the author more license, space, and time than the theatre, and, for good as well as evil, the author profits by it.

Thus the drama of the "Rag-Picker" is necessarily only an act, an episode, in the life of Father Jean. The novel of the "Rag-Picker" shows his entire life. The drama is only a picture; the novel is a panorama. The author presents therefore a complete panorama of Paris during the past century, not, like romanticism and its son, naturalism, simply to astound, clutch, and pocket, but to teach, elevate, and moralize; not art for art and gold, but art for man and right,—Socialistic art.

What a man of my time has had an opportunity to see is unprecedented. All the sovereigns of the old world, kings, priests, and masters, giving place to the new sovereign, the People of Paris.

Now, Paris has always brought luck to authors, whether dramatists or novelists. The two greatest popular successes of the epoch have been, in fact if not in right, as a novel, "The Mysteries of Paris," and as a drama, "The Rag-Picker of Paris."

If, then, hampered by the limits of the footlights, the author nevertheless has been able, by dint of condensation, to create a legendary type, he has had ground to hope that with full liberty of action he might make a novel as successful as the drama, according to the axiom that "he who can do more can do less."

FÉLIX PYAT.

THE RAG-PICKER OF PARIS.

PROLOGUE.

Under the arcades of the Palais-Royal, then in all its glory, the centre of all the luxury and all the lust of Paris, of the large *cafés*, the large restaurants, the large book-stores, the large theatres, and the large houses of infamy, — in short, of fashionable Paris, which had not then emigrated to a more northerly part of the city, toward what are known today as the Grand Boulevards, — a rather lugubrious lantern bore upon its glass panes, in big black figures, a number of sinister repute, Number 113, that of roulette, that of *rouge et noir*, that of the large public gambling house, licensed, authorized, and breveted in the year of grace 1828, by the government of the King, for the ruin, murder, and suicide of citizens.

After having traversed the corridor that is found in all the houses of the Palais-Royal, one mounted to the second floor by a side staircase, likewise common to all of them. One entered a bare hall, deposited canes and umbrellas at the office, and finally penetrated to the gaming-room, lighted by Argand lamps placed above the table covered with green cloth.

This cloth had cabalistic divisions upon it, numbered, and separated by red and black lines. The wheel was in the middle, a sort of copper basin fixed in the table, around which a little ball, launched by the finger of the chief croupier, rolled violently, until, its momentum exhausted, it fell into one of the compartments, divided, numbered, and colored likewise, red and black.

At the two ends of the table were seated two sub-croupiers, in black coats and white cravats, shaven and smooth like priests, gloomy and cold like judges, armed with little wooden rakes, taking the money lost or giving the money won without a sign of emotion.

Between the croupiers a circle of players of both sexes, sitting or standing close together, with their stakes before their eyes, noting the decisions of the wheel, placing their bets, withdrawing their winnings or leaving their losses, counting and recounting, piling up and unpiling, rubbing their hands or biting their nails before this green cloth enamelled with gold and silver coins like the yellow and white flowers in a meadow; in short, all the frenzies of joy or of pain, of fear or of hope, all the ecstasy and all the delirium, all the laughter and all the rage, of speculation, of the vilest passion, that for lucre without labor, and of the most grievous disappointment, that of vain effort against fortune.

.Around this altar of human sacrifices, where priests and victims sat together, liveried valets circulated with indifference, fat with the flesh which the players had lost.

Victims! Alas, they were of all ages, except infancy, of every sex and of every sort, in dress coats and in blouses, from the embarrassed workman who played his day's pay to the idle millionaire who played the coupon cut from his bond; from the mother of a family who played her children's bread to the father who played their dowry.

There were sober players, .who won or lost one coin daily, one coin, no more; others who ruined themselves by bold strokes, playing in combined masses like Napoleon I, or in scattered bands like M. de Moltke; others, honorary players, neither winning nor losing anything, but playing on without playing, and because they had played too much; ruined players, whose passion had survived their purse, and who continued a fictitious and mad game, with a zeal, a care, an expenditure of time, and an infinitesimal art, with a patience, a study, and a calculation which might have enabled them to conquer the problem of the quadrature of the circle, but not the fatality of the double zero of the bank.

A misplaced coin, doubtfully fallen astride one of the divisions of the cloth, suddenly brought about a terrible quarrel.

A player who was poor, and therefore the more rabid, a workman who had been losing, and who believed that this time he had won, threw himself furiously upon the croupier, who was already sweeping in the money. He tore his rake from him, and profiting by his surprise, was paying himself with his own hands, when two strong valets intervened and seized him.

Just then a woman of the people burst into the room. On seeing her man between the valets, she cried:

"What, deceiver! Here again! You always come here, wretch, to waste the children's supper! I would rather find you at the wine-shop, as I used to. The idea of throwing our last crust to these thieves, who take everything from us, and leave us nothing, nothing to lose but your ears! Go on, heartless man! Why does the government permit it? Ah, the rascal, the monsters! There is no justice!"

And seizing the rake in her turn, she showered blows indiscriminately upon all, — players, valets, and croupiers, — until they had thrown her, her and her man, out of the door. .

Before entering the room, the poor mother, who had her child in her arms clinging to her neck, had been stopped in the passage-way by the employee in charge of the cloak-room, who had said to her:

"Children are not allowed to enter."

So she had deposited her child in return for a check, at the cane and umbrella office.

Driven out with her man, she had forgotten in the fracas her precious deposit, and was already rapidly descending the staircase, when the child's cry recalled her like a fury, and she claimed her little one.

"Two sous," said the employee.

"Why two sous?"

"Yes, two sous for the check."

"I haven't them."

"Well, then you cannot have the child."

"Ah, this is too much! You are going to steal my little one also? Heap of scoundrels! Go for an officer," said she to her man. "But no, he does not stir. Have you then no heart or soul, no arms or head,—no bowels? You will suffer even our child to be taken from you, coward? Well, look! I am only a woman, but. . . . ."

And in spite of the valets, she leaped like a wolf at the throat of the employee, when, attracted by the noise, some of the gamblers came to the scene, and one of them threw two sous upon the desk to restore peace.

At last the poor mother could go out with her child and her husband.

She seized the latter by the arm.

"You have drunk and gambled everything away," said she, with a cry of wrath that expired in a sob. "Well, you have set a good example. Your daughter, the older one, on whom we counted to help about the house, Sophie. . . . ."

"Well, Babet, what?" asked the father, aroused from his stupor by the name of his daughter.

"Well, she ran away tonight. And it is your fault. There is no supper."

The wheel continued to turn.

Among the most absorbed players, the most reckless of all was a man of great distinction and perfect elegance, sitting, or rather, so carried away was he by passion, standing beside a charming woman, no less elegant, who followed all his movements with a curiosity and an anxiety that increased with the growth of the stakes.

He had just feverishly laid down his last bill, his final stake, his all, a thousand-franc note, the end of a heap.

He had thrown himself upon the red, after having sacrificed ten times to the black. Ten losses in succession, doubling his stakes, and thus losing a fortune, and in the hope, nay, almost sure, that the black would finally yield to the red.

The eleventh time the black re-appeared.

Something like a death-rattle came from the chest of the player.

The young woman turned pale.

"I am ruined," said the man, in a choking voice, with a movement which he tried to conceal under his coat.

The woman rose, restraining his hand armed with a dagger.

Then two gentlemen who had just entered, and had been witnesses of the player's last loss, one with a figure and a bearing equal to those of the ruined player, and with his hat pulled down over his eyes, the other of a more common aspect, and his hat in his hand, made signs to each other, and the latter cried out:

"Gentlemen, which of you, on his way up here, lost a thousand-franc note which we have found?"

All the players stopped. Several looked instinctively in their purses. Others laughed, thinking the question a joke.

Alone, after a short hesitation, the unlucky player raised his voice.

"I, Monsieur."

The other looked at him fixedly.

"You have lost a thousand-franc note, you say?"

"Yes, on my way up."

"Well, if you will go down with us to the janitor, with whom we have left it, we will restore it to you."

They left the room, but, instead of going down the staircase, the man who had before spoken, stopping on the landing, said:

"Here is the note. Look at it. It is really yours, is it not?"

"Doubtless. Thank you."

And the player took the note.

"Very well, in the name of the law I arrest you."

"You arrest me? Why?"

"Because you are a robber."

"I?"

"You."

"How so?"

"This note is Monsieur's, not yours."

"It is mine, I tell you."

"Monsieur's name is on the back of it."

"Ah, yes, but he has passed it to me."

"Very well, then, what name? Don't stir."

The player, caught in the trap, had tried to look at the name.

The officer seized his hand, took back the note, which he restored to the owner, and was about to drag the thief away to the station-house, when the latter drew a stiletto.

At once he plunged it into the heart of the officer, who fell without a cry.

Then, at one bound, the assassin cleared the staircase, escaping all pursuit, thanks to the two outlets of 113, Rue de Valois and Jardin du Palais, more frequented then than today.

The owner of the note then found himself face to face with a young woman, the companion of the player, who had seen and heard all. And lifting his hat that she might recognize him, he said with triumphant coolness:

" Well, my dear, I told you so. Will you believe me now? It is complete. Ruined, a thief, an assassin! Now wil l you leave him?"

She hesitated a moment, and then, with more calculation than frankness, she said:

" Yes, Count."

" Come then," said he, dragging her to the staircase, which they quickly de scended, leaving the police officer in his blood, and entering an elegant *coupé* which carried them at full speed to one of the most splendid mansions in the Rue de-Lille, Faubourg Saint-Germain.

The first player that went out, seeing the corpse, said:

" What? Another suicide!"

And without further ceremony he passed over this occurrence so common in that place, and all night long, and the next day, and every following day, the wheel poured forth its flood of bodies and of millions.

END OF PROLOGUE.

THE RAG-PICKER OF PARIS.

PART FIRST.

THE BASKET.

CHAPTER I.

THE HOTEL D'ITALIE.

On Mardi Gras, 1828, the ill-famed quarter of the Place Maubert still deserved its name, having at that time that morbid charm of the old Paris, so dear to romanticism and the plague, to the friends of the picturesque and of typhoid fever, and which the philosopher must leave microbes and the poets of the Restoration to mourn.

It was still, at that period of religious, political, and literary reaction, at that ill omened and retrogressive period of legitimate royalty and divine right, brought back into France by the invasion, a diminutive of the old Cour des Miracles, a Bohemia restrained by the time, where the degenerate brigands of the nineteenth century continued those of the Middle Ages, just as the dwarfs of the modern fauna continue the giants of the fossil fauna, and the tertiaries the antediluvians.

Nevertheless, they preserved enough of the monster to frighten and shame progress, health, and humanity.

This was therefore the most "conservative" district of Paris, an insult and a challenge to the democratic spirit and to the effort of the Revolution, still rebellious against the law of perfection, deep-rooted in the protecting shadow of the Cathedral, the Hospital, the Conciergerie, the Police Office, and the Morgue, under the favorable influence of those still standing bastilles of every tyranny, physical, mental, and moral, or rather of those nurses of vice and crime, of ignorance and misery, those Catholic and monarchical layers and hatchers of evil, admired and sung by the great deistic bard who doubtless would rather be in Notre Dame with Quasimodo than with Voltaire in the Pantheon.

The natives of this lagging section of Paris, hostile to every Socialistic and hygienic movement, savages arrested in development or fallen back into barbarism, had scarcely anything in common, beyond the fact that they were *sans culottes*, with the heroes of that once republican quarter, the bare-armed of the year II.

Unclean and unhealthy citizens, malefactors and wretches, they were celebrating on the day mentioned a carnival with nothing Roman about it, a Mardi Gras conceived after their own fashion and in their own image, helots making up for their spiritual and material servitude by saturnalia, for their abstinences by abuses, and for their privations by excesses.

Most of them presented the flattened or depressed types of a menagerie or a galley-crew, more abject or more ferocious than their masks; faces and cries of beasts, language of the prisons, gestures of murder, lessons in kicking and club-bing, obscene or cruel games, rude sports, always ending badly, in quarrels, blows, kicks, butts, and bites (man makes a weapon of everything), and even, thanks to the foreign element, in knife-thrusts; costumes in keeping, the horrible not exclud-ing the grotesque; minstrels of the slaughter-house, *turcs de la Courtille*, knights of the muck-heap, and other disguises of the same sort, justifying the vile name *chienlits.*

Such had kings, priests, and their poets, "Genius of Christianity!" made the Sovereign People.

The parish bell had sounded the evening Angelus for these strange believers. It was seven o'clock, the night sharp, bad weather impoverishing the poor, snow falling fast, the violent wind whirling it in eddies or heaping it in flakes which changed their virgin whiteness into mud-puddles beneath the feet of passers-by.

A man in threadbare but stylish clothes, a remnant of opulence, ventured with cautious step into the narrowest and darkest alley of the Rue Galande, and then stopped, undecided, frightened, repelled even by the odious aspect of the place.

The cracked ruins of this infected alley, as dangerous as they were repulsive, threatened destruction, ready to break into fragments under the weight of their overloaded stories; the dirty and reddish walls, covered with a congenial rough coat, reeking with blood and wine, were shedding leprous scales, sweating gangrene, and betraying internal vice, as skin diseases betoken an organic disorder. The cracked and dim window-panes, strengthened by strips of paper, were covered with an opaque layer of dirt which served as a curtain for the mysteries of the Bac-chuses and Venuses of the Faubourg Saint-Marcel.

A stream, the little Seine of this *conserved* Paris, received in its bed all the tri-butary refuse, all the waste-laden affluents, of this dirty swarm, reflecting in its viscous lakes the yellow gleams of the oil-lamps. Rags in the windows, rubbish in the doorways. In the air, vapors of the frying-pan, odors of tobacco, alcohol and wine drunk and given up again, tainted the atmosphere with a fetid and in-jurious steam, which offended all the senses and turned the stomach.

The base has its degrees, and, among the dens or lairs of this sinister alley, the ugliest and most suspicious, the refuge of the worst outcasts, was that which was called, by an abominable euphemism, the Hotel d'Italie, a master-piece of local color, a triumph of art for art's sake.

The man stopped short before this furnished lodging-house, a well-known shelter for the fallen of every race and of every vice. And as if he had found what he sought, he read the sign painted in black letters on a ground glass lantern: *Lodging here by the night, 2 cents.*

His face was lighted with a pale light by the smoky wick which flickered in the transparency.

Perhaps he was thirty years old; his features, contracted and even convulsed with disgust, with horror, with humiliation, with regrets if not with remorse, with every sort of feeling except pity, did not lack distinction or culture.

But nature and second nature, habit, had surely set the stamp of original, hereditary, and cultivated vice upon this very proper face. The eye, that window of the soul, furtive and false, with a pupil too large for the white, became ferocious when fixed, like a feline's. The pointed ear was indicative of the same species. The nose or curved beak, the raised chin, the small mouth, and the sharp nails were no less carnivorous. There was a beast of prey in this man of the world.

Of what world?

No sympathy, no commiseration, not a trace of charity. His whole aristocratic person from head to foot was marked *me.* "When Adam delved and Eve span, Satan was the gentleman," say the English.

Organs develop in proportion to their exercise. The egoistic conscience, exaggerated by the enjoyment of rights without duties; the patrician hand strengthened by fencing; the foot weakened by riding; the forehead narrowed by idleness and raised by pride; carriage, gesture, voice, and mien, — everything about him was proud, haughty, arrogant, insolent even, scornful and vainglorious even in his fall; everything went to show that he was not there in disguise, or as a wanderer, still less as an *habitué*, but as an intruder, one who had fallen, a ruined man, some waif from high society aground in this mire after a hurricane.

From what social sphere had this accidental visitor fallen? Doubtless from the highest. In this gentleman there was none of the emotion common in the *parvenu* who has to resume his station after having risen above it. His top was the opposite pole of this bottom. In fact, his red beard showed the feudalist, the descendant of the ancient conquerors of Gaul, the blue blood of the Frank, of a refugee of '93, of an ex-nobleman returned from the emigration. Apparently born with a silver spoon in his mouth, brought up on an indemnity of a billion francs granted to his family by the Restoration, he must have eaten everything, even honor. He seemed reduced, by reason of miscalculations or misdeeds, through fear or embarrassment or both, to such a pass that he no longer knew where to lay his head, constrained and conducted to this last extremity by necessity.

He hesitated, advancing, retreating, trembling, at the entrance of this hell which Dante did not describe, the Paris of the poor, and he turned away his head as if he were about to commit a crime.

Just at that moment, on the other side of the street, the door of a night-shelter opened.

Then he saw a file of vagabonds more destitute than himself, not having in their pockets even the two cents necessary for the furnished lodging or any fat stored under their skins for the winter season. They surely had not been able to make carnival, and mournfully marched past an indifferent keeper, who counted the heads of these emaciated cattle as fast as they entered a shed, which was once a stable, but had been passed over from horses to the needy recipients of public charity. The stranger saw the keeper gruffly repel the wretches at the end of the line, shouting at them: "That will do, the rest of you!" and shutting the door in their faces after first hanging up the sign: *Full*, as if the building were an omnibus.

The unfortunate surplus, punished for their tardiness and left to await some more favorable turn, threw a look of despair at this word as inexorable as the *lasciate*, envying the lucky ones with the usual vengeful feeling of the unlucky, grinding their teeth and sneering:

"Dogs' weather! Weather for dogs! One would not put a dog outside," and other sorry jests with which every good Frenchman relieves himself when vexed.

These suffering souls scattered at random, cursing and swearing.

"That is the fate that awaits me tomorrow, if not tonight," said the stranger, taking out two cents and throwing away his empty purse. "Let us go in; perhaps I shall sleep. And he who sleeps dines!"

And, as if moved by a sudden determination, he lowered his hat over his eyes; a squall of wind and snow entirely enveloped him and drove him by force into the *cæcum* of the Hotel d'Italie.

He gave up his coin at the door, groped along the passage, and, for good reason, passed by the restaurant of the establishment without stopping. From it came the deadened sound of drinking songs, idiotic laughter, and atrocious conversation, accompanied by the shrill notes of a Neapolitan bag-pipe. At last, passing the rope-ladder which led to the choicer lodgings in the front part of the upper story, he found himself in a large court-yard at the back, a veritable pit, which seemed better calculated for wild beasts than men and was surrounded with gloomy and ill-smelling structures, dens of assassins and burrows of harlots, where swarmed, pell-mell, in unclean promiscuity, the lowest and floating population of the hotel.

There he contemplated with stupor and aversion, but without compassion, the singular companions who were moving about like transparencies in the pale moonlight.

Near him a real swarm of maggots, a group of puny and vicious children, poisonous mushrooms growing out of the civilized muck-heap, were amusing themselves in twisting and biting each other while scraping rabbit-skins. Girls and boys, half naked, shivering, found sport and warmth in brazen words and dirty plays; pullulations of the social sewer, flowers of crapulence and fruits of the gallows, spoiled in the germ, and ripening in this hot-house of debauchery and need for prison crops and scaffold harvests!

Farther on, their alcoholic parents, incurable, eaten to the marrow with corruption, were picking over rags, old iron, and bones, or tying up bundles of old papers, chewing tobacco, drinking, and beating the children, for diversion from work as dirty as their hearts and hands. A few old women whom the others looked up to, the privileged persons of this Gomorrah, were making pancakes in the open air over improvised stoves, thus exciting the envious appetite of the hungry beggars stretched upon rickety benches or seated on dilapidated chairs, who watched these culinary preparations without saying a word, mouths open and stomachs empty.

Suddenly the intruder was pushed violently against the wall by a man who was running away at the top of his speed, followed by the cries and yells of the crowd. All present, rag-pickers, tramps, beggars, thieves, and prostitutes, had left their work or their leisure to rush towards the corner of the court whence the cries came.

The stranger, who had recovered his equilibrium, ran to the spot with the others, and there a frightful picture met his gaze.

A man lay on his back in the gutter, a knife planted in his heart!

A queen of this Louvre, gamey, hideous, with blackened eyes, half drunk, dishevelled, and bending over the victim, was trying to lift up the body, which the mud of the gutter, fitting burial-place, was covering more and more.

The keeper of the hotel came running in, furiously gesticulating.

"Another man stabbed in my house!" he cried. "Who did it? They will surely close up the hotel!"

The fury rose in a frenzy.

"It was that rascal of an Italian," she exclaimed, tearing the knife from the wound, which covered her with a spurt of blood. "Yes, out of jealousy; I would not have him. Then he killed my man. Where is the *biffin de contrebande* that I may kill him in his turn?"

And she fell back upon her dead in the gutter.

Such scenes were of too frequent occurrence in the Hotel d'Italie to cause long-continued excitement. They carried the body of the murdered man into the kennel of his woman, and went about other matters.

The murderer was a naturalized rag-picker. This *biffin de contrebande*, as the girl had called him, this jealous Italian who had come to carry on a two-fold foreign competition with the natives, left behind him unfortunately the apple of discord,—a new wicker basket and a bright steel hook.

They threw themselves greedily upon these precious articles. A hubbub ensued. Each one wanted the property of the fugitive, who certainly would never return to claim it.

Matters were beginning to get warm and knives were being opened, when one of the old women with the pancakes, a fat Minerva, anxious about her pastry, raised her voice in the dispute, crying:

"Idiots! Why don't you draw lots instead of fighting?"

Goddess Reason does not lose her rights, even among brutes. The word was listened to and peace restored.

"Stop! to be sure! she is right!" they cried on all hands.

"A pencil!" solicited the over-ripe Minerva. "Mossieu doubtless has a pencil?" she said to the stranger, who mechanically complied with her request.

They arranged themselves in a circle. Each one wrote or dictated his name. A hundred square pieces of old paper, taken from the bundles, were thrown into the hat which the fugitive had left in the gutter. The stranger alone remained indifferent to the general excitement. He had even turned about already to seek his bed.

"Hey, there, *bourgeois!*" shouted La Sagesse, with an air of raillery. "Then you do not want to win the basket? You are utterly disgusted, black coat!"

Thus appealed to, he retraced his steps, as if yielding to a suggestion or inspiration, or at any rate to a sudden resolution; and, taking from his pocket a glazed and emblazoned card, he tore it in two and quickly threw one of the pieces into the improvised urn. Straightway he tried to take it back.

He was too late.

A sort of Belgian Hercules who was managing the lottery, by the right of might, had shaken the hat and mixed up the names.

"The game is done. Nothing else goes!" he cried, suspiciously, announcing the drawing.

"Bah!" exclaimed the stranger, bitterly. "Why not? Let fortune have her way. This would be a means of livelihood worth keeping."

"The hand of innocence, if possible," again cried the Hercules of the North, laying the hat upon a chair.

A puny, emaciated creature, a mother holding in her arms a child as thin as herself, was pushed forward.

The excitement redoubled, eyes glittered, and hearts beat violently, all heads gravitating to the centre of the circle.

The mother bent over that the baby's little hand might be within reach of the hat.

The child fumbled a moment in the urn and drew out the torn card.

"Garousse," read the mother, and all eyes sought the winner.

"Ah!" exclaimed the Hercules, "it is really the Duke de Crillon-Garousse. Surely Monseigneur has not won. That would be too much luck."

The winner had made a negative gesture.

"So your name is Garousse?" continued the Hercules, ill-naturedly. "You are lucky. The finest name and the finest basket in France."

And spitefully he placed the basket on the stranger's back.

The ill-natured Hercules, with his square Flemish head, avenged himself and the others for not having won the basket. Feeling that he was sustained by the spite which all shared, he tried to pick a quarrel.

"If it is not you, it is your brother. Isn't it so? You belong to the family?" "No," said Garousse, blushing. "There is more than one ass named Martin." "Less ass than fox. I believe you cheated. You put in your name twice." "Yes, he tore his card in two," exclaimed a voice from the mass jealous at seeing its possessions go to the "black coat."

Foreign competition and the national spirit all united against the intruder, and had already attacked Garousse and driven him against the wall to take away the basket, which he was on the point of surrendering, when suddenly the police burst into the court.

They came to verify the crime committed by the Italian, and open, as usual, a platonic inquest over this murder, which was to remain unpunished. The officers, who never visited the place save in a body and were of no use there except to clear it out, saw familiar faces and began a battue. Save himself who can!

In the confusion, Garousse, unknown to all, was able to slip away and gain his liberty.

When he found himself outside, he answered with a Satanic laugh the irony of fate.

"Oh, yes, what luck! I shall never again complain of not being fortunate. I have won the basket. . . . and the street. Free and a rag-picker! Ha, ha, ha! Fate has served me well this time, and well disguised poverty for my Mardi Gras!"

And, with basket on back and hook in hand, he fled from the Paris of rag-bags to the Paris of money-bags.

CHAPTER II.

THE HOTEL CRILLON.

Garousse walked, or rather ran, flew as if he had wings on his back, as if the basket were the cloak of Nessus, in spite of the blinding snow and the biting north wind.

His teeth chattered with cold, hunger, horror, and terror.

On he went, bewildered, like the Jew of the legend, minus the five sous, like the dead man of the ballad, the plaything, the prey of an intense night-mare, the victim, not the punisher, of his passions, of an ungovernable somnambulist's course, of an infernal hallucination, and of his own execration.

Finally he stopped short, saying:

"One must live!"

And going up to a huge pile of filth, a muck-heap which promised rich results, he gave his first thrust with his hook; then, raising it and at the same time his head, he gave a cry, a shriek:

"At my own door. . . . Oh!".

He had read, in letters of gold, beneath a coat of arms: *Hotel Crillon-Garousse.*

A fatal force had led him back to his splendors, as the stag to the spot from which the dogs have started him, as the moth to the flame.

He had returned, insensibly, unconsciously, spontaneously, in a straight line from the Faubourg Saint-Marcel to the Faubourg Saint-Germain, Rue de Lille, to the very threshold of his dwelling, then brilliant and flaming with all the luxury of a fashionable ball.

A line of carriages was passing through the carriage-way ornamented with green shrubbery; their masked occupants were getting out, dressed in elegant or marvellous costumes; valets in magnificent livery were spreading Persian carpets under the carriage-steps and escorting the guests under silk umbrellas, like offerings to social magnificence.

A feeling of supreme revolt took possession of the ducal rag-picker.

"My hotel, my carriages, my servants! Others have them all. . . . No, they are mine. House, friends, women, flowers, diamonds, treasures, all belong to me, to me, the Duke de Crillon-Garousse. This is my masquerade. . . . Well! am I not disguised, too? So much the worse if the women run away from me, the master of this residence, where I have spent fortune and honor!"

And fascinated, dazzled, delirious, dragged on by the illusion of the charm and the music of the ball-room, he said:

"I will go in."

He took one step and remained nailed to the spot.

He had seen his successor. . . and his mistress, arm in arm. Doubly succeeded! This was the last blow, the thrust of the knife. . . . Misery was his sole mistress now.

Ah! to yield one's possessions when dying,—death gives the title to the living, say nature and the law,—but to see one's self succeeded while alive, and by his own fault! That is enough to drive one mad. That is to die twice.

His mistress, this other queen of another carnival festivity, a sylph, a fairy, a pure vision of gauze and roses, was doubtless more beautiful and yet more revolting than the queen of the den of harlots in the Rue Galande. She was a traitor. The one at least wanted, from a feeling of fidelity and savage justice, to avenge her man, the other killed hers.

The charm was broken.

"Impossible," sobbed the wretch, overwhelmed. "I am not a mask, but a man damned by gaming, ruin, debt, and forgery, insolvent, dishonored, betrayed, accursed! This successor is my creditor. This palace is prison, is shame. I should be ignominiously turned out, or arrested. Ah! better still is liberty!"

For a moment longer the ousted man looked at the windows, before which were passing in confusion, as in a magic dream, all the magnetisms of the ball-room, the couples clasped in the waltz, the golden trays loaded with cut-glass, under the chandeliers streaming with light, and the enchanting orchestra covering all these fairy apparitions with its floods of harmony; and then he threw a farewell, a loud groan of indignation and of anguish, at the echoes of the festival, and resumed his course, with lowered head and haggard eyes, fleeing in shame and rage, pursued by the Nemesis of his ruined life.

"*Mauvais biffin!*" said an officer stationed at the door. "He is running away with his booty. I am suspicious. Suppose I arrest him?"

And the bloodhound gave chase.

But the rag-picker duke kept on running, and, having a start, distanced his pursuer, and was soon out of reach, sight, and scent, far from the Rue de Lille, striding along the Quai Voltaire, where the noise of his steps was lost in the rushing torrent of the river, whose flow was swollen by the melting snows. Thus he was able to continue his desperate course towards a future which was the consequence and contrast of his past.

CHAPTER III.

THE QUAI D'AUSTERLITZ.

Still running, lashed like a top by the wind and his emotion, carried away, absorbed, Garousse reached the height of the bridge of Austerlitz.

There, out of breath, in despair, surrendering to fatigue and want, he sank upon a stone bench and took his head in his hands, calling up in his mind his past, present, and future, his grandeur, fortune, friends, and loves, his follies and his fall, everything, in short, even to the last scenes of this carnival *soirée*.

The night grew colder and colder and darker and darker. At intervals the moon emerged from the clouds which eclipsed it, exhibiting against the background of the horizon, in a dissolving view, the monuments of Paris, palaces and temples, covered with a shroud of snow.

Garousse raised his head to view this dismal scene which answered to his affliction and harmonized with the end of his life. Nature's mourning penetrated through his eyes to the very bottom of his heart.

"A rag-picker, I! the Duke de Crillon-Garousse," he exclaimed bitterly. "Enough of such suffering. At least no one recognized me. This misery, this hook, this basket, oh! it is filthy, infamous, impossible. I shall never be reconciled to it after the life that I have led. No, I will not do it; death rather!"

He sprang to his feet with a bound, as if moved by a spring. His mind was made up. He abandoned his basket, threw down his hook, and, with a last gesture, hurled his hat far away. Then, resolutely, he walked to the parapet.

In face of suicide man is a moribund, but a voluntary moribund. Desperate, on the verge of the void, he feels at once the terrors of the agony and the attractions of death. Garousse instinctively allowed himself a respite for this bitter enjoyment, to breathe a last whiff of air, of life, of fright, and of horror.

He lent ear to the splash of the water rolling under the arches of the bridge with gleams which shone with the reflection of the moon and seemed like points of steel bristling to receive him.

The quai was silent and deserted, disturbed only by the distant noise of carriages, the sound of a popular refrain, *Forever wine!* and the staggering footsteps of a drunken man approaching the bridge.

It was a rag-picker, doubtless, for he carried on his shoulder an old sack made of cotton cloth, in his right hand a hook, and in the other a lantern. Dressed in a ragged blouse, on his head a soiled undress-cap, dirty and wet to the skin, he advanced, insensible to the wind and the rain, contentedly singing and chattering.

At some distance from Garousse, seized by a drunkard's whim, he began to contemplate the moon shining at its full.

"Ah, old girl! so you're gettin' up," he said to it familiarly and with the faubourg accent. "Goezh without sayin' that the sun 'zh gone t'bed. The sun and the moon! Ah! ah! what a fine household! When Monsieur get'sh up, Madame goezh t'bed. Misfortune! at that rate if there are ever t'be any little onesh, the comet will have t'step in. Wretches of stars, get away! If it is not shameful for a moon to cross the heavensh 'lone in such weather. You confounded giddy girl, go find your male, with your night-cap, and faster than that. Ash f'me, I will not. . . . Oh! you know very well that you will not s'duce Jean. Away with you! You're not the girl I love. Thash cert'n!"

And when he had thus barked at the moon, the drunken man, whose open face was beaming with good humor and liquor, came back to his passion and his song:

> Forever wine!
> Forever juice divine!
> In it, while life is mine,
> I'll find a source of cheer.

Jean was the name of this robust and hearty man of forty years, a jolly dog of the Faubourg Antoine, broad-backed, bronzed by the open air and by drink, well made, by chance, some child of love, and in good condition in spite of misery, intemperature, and even intemperance, thanks to his out-door life, to Doctor Oxygen, and to carelessness,—an erratic block of Paris. He had the fire and vigor of the country, the sly and Gallic humor of the capital, all the beauty of health and especially of good nature, features as large as his heart,—the substance moulds its form,—in short, the serenity of disinterestedness or of omnipotence, which the ancients called *joviality*, *ab Jove*, after the very Father of the Gods, Bacchus included.

By the grace of this divine son of Jupiter's leg, however, Jean could scarcely stand upon his own. He continued his drunken babble:

"'Sh queer; they say a glass o' wine sustains. Well, I have drunk more'n fifteen, and I can't hold m'self up. A child could knock me down. I haven't drunk 'nough, thash sure. What I need 'sh drop o' brandy."

He stumbled over Garousse's hat, which he picked up with a thrust of his hook and stuffed into his sack.

"Good!" he exclaimed with a shout of joy. "There'sh a beaver for my Sundays."

Garousse turned round abruptly and saw the drunkard a few steps from him.

"Some one coming," said he. "I must end."

He rushed towards the parapet, and bestrode it at a bound.

For a moment he remained suspended between the quai and the river, between life and death.

But Jean, with a violent effort, had thrown himself upon Garousse and seized him by the skirt of his coat; then, as the duke fell back upon the ground, he took him around the waist, and, in a comical tone of surprise and sympathy, said: "Well, friend, where are you going? 'Sh that the way you liquidate?"

"That does not concern you," cried Garousse, struggling.

"But if you are my fellow," said Jean, humanely, still holding him, in fear of a second attempt.

"Your fellow! Filthy beast! Go to bed."

"Thash just what I've been tellin' the moon," said the imperturbable Jean. "You're the beast, to go into the water. Man'sh not a toad. If I were not a man, I'd let you jump and fish you out again, alive for five dollars or dead for ten. What fun, hey!"

"Go away! let me go," resumed Garousse, softened by this good nature; "I have had enough of life. I prefer to die at once rather than die by inches, of hunger."

"Of what! of what! One dies only of thirst. Come 'n take a drop. 'Sh my treat."

"No, let me alone, I tell you; it is my idea. I am tired of suffering."

But in spite of everything Jean dragged him to the stone bench, and began to moralize with his drunken obstinacy.

"There, there," said he, gently. "Come, tell me your troubles. What is it that disturbs you? Poverty? If thash all, I'll cure you. But not by water first; on the contrary, by wine."

And he sang with his hoarse voice:

Of every ill it is the cure.

Then continuing his flow:

"Come, there'sh hope yet. You're not mad if you like water. Duck, away with you! Just change your drink, and if I don't save you, Jean's word for it, we'll plunge in together and I'll pay the toll."

Some carriages went by them, and masqueraders passed in their vicinity.

Garousse, weary of resisting, sank back upon the bench.

"Tick of a drunkard," he muttered, resignedly. "I must not oppose him. I'll wait till he goes away."

The compassionate rag-picker, as if divining his intention, sat down beside him, and resumed his exposition of principles with the effusiveness of intoxication.

"When one has sorrows, my dear man, he must drown 'em; he must drink. But the foam of the grape, the healing draught of Bacchus, a cooling potion. You see, I've been through it. I know how you feel. I too was born to be milord,—·fame that it is, —despair and kill m'self. Well, I have drunk and saved m'self. When I have drunk, my poverty 'sh gone. I have Paris and Bercy. I'm richer 'n happier'n a wholesale wine-merchant. I see everything in beaut'ful colors; all is red and rosy; my rags are velvet, my bones ivory, my old iron bullion, my cotton sack a wicker basket " . . . .

Jean gave a cry of indignation. He had just observed Garousse's basket. " Ah! so you have a basket, you! And more'n that, an elegant one. And new besides. Out upon you, risht'crat! And you complain! Here'sh a pretty fellow, —hash basket 'n wants t' kill himself. What is it, then, that Mossieu desires? A wax candle p'r'aps t' light his way and a plated hook t' pick up his bonds. . . . and the Bank o' France in the bargain."

And crossing his arms, he asked:

" Wha'sh'll I say, then, I who have only a sack, and not a new one either?" Coming back to his fixed idea and to his revelry, he exclaimed:

"I'm choking with thirst. I don't understand why one should kill himself. . . . and by water too. The deluge, wretch, out upon it! And Noah's vineyard and the rainbow. . . . th' little white, th' big blue, th' free red, th' three-six, Mother Moreau, Father Niquet, and Son Cognac, all th' cons'lations of life. Out upon you! you're ungrateful t' the creator. Do's I do, rather. . . Here!"

He handed his flask to Garousse, who refused it with a gesture of disgust.

"Be sens'ble," insisted Jean, without taking offence. "Drink! Drink cash down or on credit, by th' glass, by th' hour, by th' month, by th' year, as you can; but drink always and in spite of everything, and you'll think no more of trouble. You'll live t'be older 'n a patriarch, and fresher 'n more alive 'n Methuselah. . . . and every day Saint Mardi Gras."

The drunken man rose, excited by his own spirit, and, as if to fortify precept by example, emptied his flask.

"I who speak t'you," he continued, in a transport, "see, with a pint o' brandy in my belly and a quid o' tobacco in my mouth, the earth can no longer hold me; it has pavements only for me. . . . and I haven't 'nough o' them; I walk zig-zag, backwards and forwards, from one side of the street to the other; I ricochet like a shell; I am th' equal of the thunder; a wall 'sh not m' master; I could break a throne, I could stop a train, I could overturn the column. I no longer know anything, either cold or hunger, either pain or death, nothing at all. I live then as I have drunk, full to the brim, and I sing with a heart full of joy:

> " Forever wine!
> Forever juice divine!"

Garousse rose in turn, exasperated by impatience, and said in an angry and threatening tone:

" So that is your suicide, you dirty wretch? I prefer mine. Every one to his taste. I like water better than your wine, drunkard. I tell you that I want to die. Make room, or I will kill you."

He seized his hook, and, disengaging himself from the rag-picker, rushed again toward the parapet.

Jean, staggering and clinging, caught him again.

"Stubborn fellow," he stammered, all out of breath. " Die! What a principle! And in my presence! Never! 'Pon my honor, it distresses me. Die! But 'sh forbidden. And your duty ash citizen. Clean your country 's I do, comrade, and come 'n pay your share of th' drink tax."

He tried to lead him away towards a closed wine-shop.

"Shut up before the hour! I protest," he exclaimed; "I'll enter a complaint."

Garousse threw him aside, and in a furious voice shouted:

"Hold! You really worry me. Stand off, or this time I strike."

Jean drew back into the axis of the parapet, and, stretching out his arms, still barred the passage.

" Ah! Monsieur 'sh angry," said he, in a tone of irony. " Excuse me! Monsieur then prefers water t' wine, like the Grand Turk! Ash you please, sultan, and so much th' worse if you don't know how t' swim. You'll be put in the Morgue. . . and in the newspapers, with all the honors due your rank."

The duke shivered as if the cold marble had just touched him. Exposed on the slab, paraded in the press, he! Oh! He had not thought of this outrage upon suicides, of these dregs of the cup.

Jean, seeing that he wavered, redoubled his moral death-dance, and, striking his forehead, cried:

"Stop! I have egzhactly your story in my sack."

"My story?" said Garousse, surprised.

"In black and white and in the 'Officiel.' Precisely that!" replied the rag-picker.

"In the 'Officiel'? It isn't possible," exclaimed Garousse, sitting down again. "Let us look at it; can you read?"

"A little, my nevvy," answered Jean, confidently.

He handed his lantern to Garousse and drew from his sack a bit of newspaper.

"Yes," said he, "I read this while I was drinkin' over there at th' inn; I should have got tipsy, as you say, if they hadn't passed me back the drunkard's glass 'thout rinsing it; thash why I preach t' you so well. Listen:

"'ANOTHER SUICIDE.'"

He interrupted himself to attend to the charred wick of his candle.

"Snuff yourself," said he. "I can't see a thing."

And he continued slowly, reading without slurring his words, stammering:

"'A man in the prime of life has just been taken from the Seine and carried to the Morgue. He should have been taken on a hurdle.' Hm! what sort of 'n animal 'sh that? Well, never mind, I haven't my dictionary. 'A letter found on him proves that he was one more madman unable to endure the trials of life.' Thirst, for sure. 'Better dead than poor, said this crazy coward.' Hear that?"

"Really," said Garousse, shrugging his shoulders, "morality from below followed by morality from above! Go on."

Jean, reeling about in his seat and his eyes fixed on the piece of paper, resumed his reading.

"'There is no greater crime against religion and soci-i-i-e-e-ty than suicide, that son of idleness and pride! Suicide is the brother of murder. Worse, perhaps. It is murder without the risk. The man who commits it is a guilty coward, a deserter, a merchant of wine' — No, theresh no wine there — 'a merchant who goes into bankruptcy, everything that is cowardly and vile.' And so forth and so on. Yes, as much as to say the comrade who does not empty his glass, a pretender, a good-for-nothing, a blunderhead. 'He is' . . . . . but the paper's torn. To be continued in our next. What an oration, hey? What an epitaph! How it strikes home! How pat! The purest of wisdom! What have you to answer, coward? Hey? Drown yourself now, if you want to."

And brutally, as if branding the duke, the rag-picker clapped the bit of newspaper on his shoulder, saying in his rough drunken voice:

"Theresh your mark. Keep it!"

Then he started off, staggering and grumbling:.

"Hm! Hm! The reading has made me hoarse. I'm off to get a drink. Farewell!"

Garousse took the newspaper and read the passage again.

"Yes," said he, bitterly, "fine morality to be read at the table at the Maison-Dorée. Ah! thus the world treats those who wish to rid it of their presence, who, like myself, prefer death to ignoble poverty."

Jean, who had made a pretence of going away, returned to the charge.

"I say!" he cried out to Garousse, "if you're still bent on killing yourself, I'll keep your basket. 'Sh th' only thing I need to bury Rothschild."

With this conclusion he started off again, singing at the top of his voice his favorite refrain:

> Forever wine!
> Forever juice divine!

CHAPTER IV.

THE BANK COLLECTOR.

Garousse walked back and forth with long strides, turning and twisting on the quai like a tiger in his cage. He seemed to be revolving in his over-excited brain an idea even more frightful than suicide.

"'Everything that is cowardly and vile,'" said he, repeating the last phrase of the newspaper article. "Well, no! Neither cowardice nor villainy, neither water nor wine, neither the mud of the street nor the hurdle of the press. If I do this, I shall be an object of terror. Better an object of terror than of shame. Away then with the thought of another suicide; crime's the thing! Yes, a curse, a curse not on myself alone, but also a curse upon others!"

He looked steadily before him, in a fit of dizziness, his hand stretched out as if to recover all his losses, riches, pleasures, loves, his head on fire, his eyes bloodshot, seeing everything in red.

Prey to a spasm of homicidal madness, he brandished his hook as if to strike a hoped-for victim.

"What do I see?" he cried, hiding suddenly in the dark angle of the wine-shop. "Oh! Providence of evil, you serve better than the Providence of good."

And he did not stir, crouching behind a part of the wall which screened him from the street-lamp.

Two bank collectors, dressed in blue uniforms with brass buttons and wearing on their heads the three-cornered hats looked upon as an essential of their profession equally with their honesty, were rapidly approaching, completing their route and talking.

One of them carried on his back a heavy money-bag, and an enormous bankbook, held by a strong but small chain, stuck half-way out of his front pocket.

"What a day!" said he to his companion. "I have been delayed by the weight of the receipts. Let us double our pace. Do you know that we carry on our persons half the wealth of the house?"

"Yes," said the other, "it is heavy and tempting. But here we are in Paris. Suppose I leave you and go home? There is no more danger now?"

"No. Thank you, and farewell till tomorrow. As for me, I am going to get rid of this load as fast as possible in order to go home myself. My wife must be anxious."

"Think of mine, then! She is in confinement, you know. One mouth more to feed."

"I know that," said the collector with the big bank-book; "but bah! when one has health, what matters it?"

His honest face beamed. He continued:

"I have a little girl, Marie, a love of a child. She is as big as a cent's worth of butter and gives me a hundred thousand dollars' worth of joy. Oh! I am happy. You see, Louis, a child is the joy of a house."

"Or its sorrow," said the other, shaking his head.

"Yes, but when one has heart together with health and work " . . . .

"He has all, you are right, Jacques. That's what I meant."

"Be off, then; let me detain you no longer. Good evening, Dupont."

"Good night, Didier."

Thus they separated, each going in his own direction.

He whom his comrade had just called Jacques Didier continued on his way, apart from the other, and directing his steps towards the lamp in front of the wine-shop.

He walked. briskly, thinking of his day's work done, his duty fulfilled, his family's bread earned, and rest by his humble fireside with his young wife and his little Marie.

Suddenly, as he reached the wine-shop, at the corner of the quai, a threatening form emerged from the shadow of the wall, and a terrible voice hurled these words into the silence of the night:

"It is over! Blood. . . . gold!"

Jacques Didier stopped short with a cry of distress.

"Help! help!"

He had received a stunning blow. Blood spurted from a small but deep hole in his temple.

Fatally wounded, he staggered a moment; his outstretched hands seemed to grasp at some means of salvation and clutched in the empty air; then, uprooted, losing his footing, he fell at full length, like a tree.

Garousse, frightened but determined, threw down his bloody hook and leaped upon his victim like a vulture on its prey.

Didier then made a last resistance. With his failing arms he surrounded the precious money-bag, and like a faithful dog defending to the last his master's property, he gave, in spite of his death agony, a final sign of energy and honor.

The assassin had to use all his strength in plundering the unfortunate Didier. Death came to the aid of crime against the duty that still defended the coveted receipts. The man of duty at last let go his hold with a plaintive groan.

With his foot on the money-bag, Garousse took hold of the bank-book, fastened by its chain to a button-hole of the uniform, and tried to tear it away.

At that moment a sound of hurried steps fell upon his ear. Frightened, he dropped the chain, which had held firm, and quickly, to make an end, he rummaged the bank-book lined with bills and stuffed the bundles into his pockets by the handful; then, his infamous task ended, he was about to flee, when Jean, recalled by the cries, came running up with an uncertain gait, calling out:

"Well, what's the matter there?"

And throwing down his sack in order to run faster, he fell upon Garousse just as he was picking up the money-bag.

"Assassin! robber! false brother! To dishonor the profession! Help! Wait!"

Garousse tried to release himself from Jean's grasp. .

"Will you be silent, you rascal?" he said, in a hollow voice, while Jean screamed like a dog at a wolf.

A short struggle ensued between them, near the inert body of the bank collector. The guilty man saw that he was lost if the combat lasted. He made a desperate effort; his iron hand seized the rag-picker's throat; and, with an irresistible strain, he threw him down by the side of the poor Didier.

"Ah! brigand!" exclaimed Jean, with a choking voice. "What a wrist! What a throw! I shall not soon forget it."

Garousse freely picked up the money-bag. For a moment he looked at the two men stretched at his feet; then, slapping his pockets stuffed with bank-notes, he burst into a diabolical laugh.

"Neither cowardly nor vile," he cried. "Blood and gold. Now I have the wherewithal to live respectable and rich, and so I will live."

The storm had redoubled in fury, drowning in its continuous roar the echoes of this double struggle. Nature seemed no longer indifferent to this human tragedy; the night made itself the murderer's accomplice, an English night: Paris disguised as London for its carnival. One could not see ten steps before him. The assassin disappeared as if he had plunged into the earth. No one but the rag-picker had seen or heard him.

Jean got up painfully.

"Good God!" he repeated. "What a throw! What a wrist! It has sobered me."

In fact, a new expression had replaced his bewildered look. He was transfigured. He seemed awakened from the bestial sleep of Circe, returning by the way of Damascus, converted by a revelation, possessed by a vision and an inner voice which cried out to him: "Jean, you are guilty also! What have you done with Jacques?" . . . what the mystics and Biblicals formerly called a divine miracle, but which was only the natural awakening of the moral sense, of social duty. In the corpse of his fellow Jean had found again his conscience.

The rag-picker, still dazed by his fall, gathered himself up and took his head in his hands in order to drive away the last fumes of the alcohol.

A voice which seemed like a death-rattle, so slow and feeble was it, recalled him to reality.

"My wife! My child!"

Jean again saw Jacques lying before him, clasping his hands in an impulse of ineffable affection and breathing a last farewell to all that he loved.

"Oh! poor, poor man!" murmured the rag-picker, in the heartfelt tone of a Good Samaritan. "His family! Nothing else was lacking!"

He bent over the dying man covered with blood.

"His wife! his child!" he continued; "it is enough to break one's heart."

And suppressing his emotion in order to console the unfortunate money-carrier, he said:

"Rest easy. Some good soul perhaps will look out for them. I at least will do what I can. Your name, friend?"

And Jacques, with a last unfinished gesture, pointing to the bank-book hanging to his blue coat, ejaculated:

"Berville Bank. . . . Jacques Didier. . . . I defended it . . . but . . . Oh!"

All was over. The body stiffened and stretched out, forever motionless, inanimate. The victim of the Duke Garousse had just expired in the arms of the rag-picker.

The measured and sonorous tread of a patrol then mingled with the noise of the squalls, unchained and furious, which blew down chimneys and tore off roofs in a dismal whirlwind. It rained tiles; blinds opened and closed again, grinding on their hinges and slamming against the walls.

In the uproar of this nocturnal tempest Jean neither heard nor saw the guard. He detached the bank-book, which bore in gilt letters the address of the Berville Bank and the name of the bank collector, Jacques Didier. Trembling and agitated as if he were the author of the crime, Jean examined the bank-book to see if it was really empty, and, reassured, put it under his blouse.

"And he has killed him, the scoundrel," he exclaimed, shaking his head. "A poor devil of a man of the people like ourselves. God! is it possible that we should eat each other thus? Worse than the wolves! Ah! the Cain! It was worth while, indeed, to stop him from killing himself that he might kill another! The bad saved at the expense of the good! It is my fault."

Indignant at himself, he dealt his chest a rude blow; then he continued:

"That's what comes of being drunk. I should have let the bandit drown, or at least I should have aided the other! I should have had legs, arms, a head of my own, and eyes to see! I should have been a man, in short, not a brute!"

And, folding his arms, he added in a terrible voice:

"I have drunk the blood of a man!"

Then, falling on his knees before the corpse, bareheaded, with the respect of a Parisian for death, he extended his hand solemnly, and said:

"I renounce wine forever. That shall be my penalty. No, not another drop! I swear it here over the body of this unfortunate, killed by my drunkenness as well as by this brigand's hook. I am his accomplice."

Still the patrol approached.

Jean rose and noticed at last the sound of the guards making their round, queer police, announcing with their heavy resounding steps their useless arrival as powerless for the prevention of the crime as for the arrest of the criminal.

"I must not stay here," exclaimed the rag-picker, hurriedly. "There's nothing to be gained by the side of a corpse. And my sack?"

He ran against Garousse's basket.

"Ah! his basket! An entirely new one, too! And to steal when he had that! A vicious rascal, indeed! Yes, to bad hands the good tools."

While making his reflections, he put the basket on his back and picked up the hook stained with Didier's blood.

"Mine the inheritance," he concluded, "and with it to do my best to help the wife and child of this poor fellow. . . . Ah! if he had carried only rags, as I do! But the other,—if ever I find him again. He was not worth even this sack,— yes, to be put into it!"

And, taking his old sack, he threw it into the basket.

The forms of the soldiers were becoming visible in the darkness, a few steps away.

Jean put out his lantern and crouched down.

"The patrol!" he exclaimed. "High time, I should think!"

But he had just been seen and hailed.

"Who goes there?"

"A dead man," said he, as he stole away. "Too late, snails, good evening!"

The patrol came into full view at the corner of the wine-shop, keeping step with regulation indifference, and halted under the lamp that lighted the body of Jacques Didier. . . .

CHAPTER V.

THE BERVILLE MANSION.

Midway of the Rue du Louvre rose a heavy and cumbrous freestone structure, high if not grand, whose ponderous aspect and strong-box solidity indicated the establishment of a *bourgeois* master-Plutus, preferring rough stone to mouldings and placing security and comfort before taste, style, and art.

On a clean black marble tablet, fastened to the wall, appeared this simple inscription in shining and well-kept silver letters:

BERVILLE BANK.

The lower part of the edifice — ground-floor and second story — was divided symmetrically, by doors containing slides, into a cashier's office, counting-rooms, and manager's office. Much order and no luxury, everything necessary, nothing superfluous, a massive and substantial whole. The upper part — three stories — served as the private residence of the owner, M. Berville, recently left a widower, with his only son, Camille, a school-boy of nine years, and his cousin, Mlle. Gertrude Berville, who, on the death of her relative, had assumed the care of the house.

The banker, a man of mature age, already fat, with an apoplectic look, at the zenith of life and success, was, like almost all Parisians, from the country, which is ever recruiting Paris with its best blood. Which makes Paris really France.

M. Berville, then, had come from Bourges, where he had succeeded, to Paris, where he succeeded better still. Ambitious only for wealth, industrious, exact, trained for his business, as precise and orderly as clock-work, he was born a specialist and strong consequently in his single capacity of calculating profit.

To a certain extent he shared, no doubt, the ideas of his class and age. Voltairean in religion, liberal in politics, constitutional in principle; but at bottom his creed was his cash-box, the charter his ledger, the Constitution his coin; his figures were his principles, his business his honor; and his opinions, more metallic than religious and political, all passed through his strong-box before reaching his head and his heart. Interest was his real passion, dominating everything in him, — religion, society, and even family, so dear to the *bourgeois*. His country was his pocket. His France stretched from the Bourse to the Bank, and the future of the nation was the end of the month. In short, he counted as he breathed, as the bird flies and the fish swims, by birth and training a perfect banker.

Like father, like son, says the proverb, — an error. Like mother, like son, — that is the truth. Washington's mother was worthy; Bonaparte's mother was base. A wise law of nature which seeks variety in human unity, and in the absence of which the world would always be one and the same man. Berville's son, then, stood as the contrast of his father and the image of his mother. For, by another law of nature no less wisely ordered for the variety and progress of the race, by the very attraction of opposites, the man of money had married a woman of heart.

Catherine Berville, a beautiful and good creature, belonging to the same class as her husband but of city and republican stock, a daughter of the French Revolution, a pupil of the philosophy of the great century, that of Rousseau and Voltaire, the century infatuated with humanity, had learned to read in "Émile." She had broken with the Bible, giving her son a Roman name. Democratic although *bourgeoise*, and of the people although rich, she was the Providence of the neighborhood. The poor called her the good lady.

But her tender affections and her lofty aspirations had been speedily checked by the marital arithmetic; she had concentrated all her woman's heart in her child. She was nothing but a mother, but completely a mother. Her son was her life, her faith, her law, her gold; she lived only for him; to her he was the Divine Child! At Bourges, a lady of charity, by precept, example, and practice, this Cornelia had taught him humanity; she had taught him to write by dictating bread tickets to him, showing him the poor and saying to him: "Their bread makes your cake." At Paris, under the influence of the change of air and life, deprived of her benevolent habits and above all of her son, who had been left at school in Bourges, as indifferent to pleasures as to business, she soon declined and succumbed, suffocated by the verdigris atmosphere in which her husband prospered. She died, leaving the best part of herself, her greatest wealth, her heart, to a child made in her own image, — the work *par excellence* of woman, a child destined to become a man worthy of the name.

Camille, in fact, was more than a resemblance, he was a survival of his mother. "That boy will never bite at a bargain," said the banker, thinking of his heir and looking at his offspring with an air of stupefaction.

Full of fun and feeling, impulsive, charming and excellent, Camille pleased everybody except the author of his being.

A precocious, passionate, spontaneous child, the pet of his mother, the terror of his father, a Gavarni, he, thanks to the memory of his mother's love and to his filial piety, preserved the respect of himself and of others, kept himself unbroken and undamaged, and maintained his originality and his purity even in school, in that promiscuity of the boarding-school, as harmful physically and morally as that of the convent, of the barracks, of the hospital, and of the prison; in which children rub against each other, wearing each other away like pebbles on the shore, staining each other like plums in a basket; from which most of them come out dry or rotten fruit, deprived too early of their mothers' teaching, of woman's moral nursing, of the influence of the family which suffers no less than the child, as ill reared as taught, all formed after one pattern like their dress coats, all cast in the same mould, having lost, to the detriment of society itself, independence, initiative, individuality, personality, and liberty.

Through his mother's influence Camille escaped this deformation. A liberal school-boy at the Jesuitical epoch when the school resembled the ecclesiastical seminary, he was even then secretly reading Béranger instead of Loriquet. Rebellious against the clerical and royal spirit, he got expelled from school for two offences. He had taken a drink of the wine while serving the mass; and, like the people, he had described as malodorous the huge *fleur de lys*, emblem of the big king, Louis XVIII., which that "fat hog" had brought back from Ghent with the Charter and placed everywhere, even on the school-boys' buttons.

Camille had then come back to his father's, dismissed and recommended with this complimentary remark promising well for his future: sacrilegious, seditious, incorrigible, an utterly worthless scamp.

"The child is father of the man," says the English proverb, with humor and sagacity. We shall see its truth.

Mademoiselle Gertrude Berville, who affected to call herself *de* Berville, was different.

Already an old maid, irreproachable, impeccable, as stiff and starched as a dragon-fly, always looking as if just out of a band-box, pretentious and affected like every woman who reads Balzac, steeped in devotion and nobility, she was as singular as the two other members of the family, of whom, however, she was sincerely fond; for beneath her ridiculous ways of a Berri woman wedded to God and the king she was not without heart or mind. Perverted by a false ideal and an intense need of authority, she divided her time between her domestic reign and the worship—with strictly honorable intentions—of an abbé, her confessor, of whom she took as good care as of her dog, going every morning to mass in an equipage which she ordered harnessed simply to take her across the street from the house to the church and back. In all things and for all things Mlle. *de* Berville liked the grand style.

At Bourges, the cathedral town *par excellence*, she did not go out of the church; she was wholly devoted to the chapel of Mary, to the month of Mary, to the flowers and robes of Mary. . She was called the Holy Virgin's maid.

The influence of the Church in the provinces, especially in a cathedral town like Bourges, is extraordinary. The Church fills the same place in the minds of its patrons that its temple fills on the pavements of the streets. At sunrise the stone leviathan covers with its deadly shade one-half the city, and all its souls through-

~out the day. Its bell is heard for five miles around. Its towers may be seen at a distance of twenty miles. Its power is proportional to the *ennui* of its flock. *Ennui*, that bane of the provinces, that rust of the heart, which takes possession of the inhabitants of these dead cities as the grass takes possession of their streets, —*ennui* delivers them, especially the women, body, soul, and possessions, to the Church, which exploits their idleness, the two cardinal passions of the human soul, hope and fear, and even their need of social life. In the provinces, where a department is still called a diocese, the Church has no competitors as in Paris, no offsets like the great theatres, the concerts, the museums, the meetings, and all the distractions of the capital.

The Church alone has this grandeur and this variety. Such as they are, it offers the multitude festivities, music, painting, decorations, costumes, all its spectacular effects, free of charge. It breaks the monotony of isolation by gatherings, and the prose of daily life by ceremonies. Thus it meets more or less the individual need of collective life. While the man, rich or poor, is with his fellows in the wine-shop or the *café*, the woman has only the Church in which to seek her associates, whether in silk or woollen, and satisfy her instincts of art, of the ideal, of curiosity, and of society. This explains why women were the first, as the Bible says, and will be the last, to see *God*. That only is really destroyed which is replaced; and so far the Holy Mother alone holds her children in her bosom from their birth until their death and even afterwards.

Gertrude Berville, left an orphan with a pious guardian and a large fortune, had been speedily captured by the priests, who had called her angel and then saint, and overwhelmed her with caresses and blessings, receiving in return her entire affection both as a child and as a rich and devout young girl.

Baptized, confessed, communicated, confirmed, and canonized in advance by them, in hope of inheriting her property, she had passed through all the sacraments except that of marriage; and doubtless she would have ended by that of the Order, but for the death of her cousin, which had restored her to the family. Neglected by the stronger sex in spite of her dowry, she had not given herself to God without a sigh or a desire for man. She had not yet taken the veil, clinging to the vague hope of a spouse less polygamic and more earthly than the husband of all the female saints in Paradise.

Already past the age of thirty, slim and frail physically, long rather than tall, pale rather than hale, slender but not graceful and beautiful but not charming, elegant without *chic* and coquettish without the power of captivation, precisely as an effect of celibacy so contrary to nature, especially in women, who more than men are observant of nature, she was still thin at an age when she should have been stout, and slim when she should have been plump. Youth without lustre and maturity without power, there was something of the faded rose and shrivelled apple about her which inspired regret rather than desire.

Lettered moreover, well informed, as arch and cunning as a cat, devout without austerity and feminine without frivolity, capable of exaltation and enthusiasm, she had nothing in common with the Berville race save the spirit of despotism and economy, accompanied, however, not by greed or severity, but even by generosity; ridiculous certainly, but interesting in spite of prejudices and faults due rather to her surroundings than her person, and of which she was a victim rather than a guilty cause; in short, superior, far superior, to her constitutional cousin, whom she regarded as a well-bred man, who for a moment had thought of marrying her for the sake of domestic economy, but who, finding her sufficiently devoted without it, had abandoned the design without sorrow either on her part or on his own.

Such was the Berville trinity seated at table on Mardi Gras, 1828, at a Carnival dinner given to all the celebrities of Parisian *bourgeois* society.

The Paris of Berville was not that of Garousse or of Jean.

We then had three classes in France. The Restoration had reconstructed the orders which the Revolution had torn down, — Nobility, Clergy, and Third Estate. It had even divided the Third Estate into two parts, the *bourgeoisie* and the plebeians, which, united, had made the Revolution, and formerly France itself through Jacques Cœur and Jeanne d'Arc, and which may ruin everything, both Revolution and France, by their disunion.

The One and Indivisible of '92 no longer existed, then, in 1828, any more than it exists in 1886. Let us hope for it at the centenary.

There were then the feudalist, the *bourgeois*, and the proletaire; De Garousse, Berville, and Jean; carnivora, ruminants, and stereovora; three faubourgs, — Saint-Germain, Saint-Honoré, and Saint-Antoine; palace, mansion, and garret; three social strata corresponding to the three *racial* strata, the Frank, the Gallo-Roman, and the Celt, composed or rather superposed in the alloy which constituted France, and which is still better represented by a mixed railway train containing first, second, and third-class cars.

In this social chemistry the two real elements of the nation, the *bourgeoisie* and the people, were still held together by the common hatred of the *carabas* and the *calotins,** and of their Bourbon princes again enthroned by the foreigner.

The *bourgeois*, through envy of the nobility, disgust with the priesthood, and fear for their national possessions; Bonapartists on half-pay, in the rancor of defeat and hope of revenge; Orleanists, struggling against their elders; the people, moved by their love of country and liberty, — all were as one, forming what was called the liberal party.

Undoubtedly a philosopher could already have discerned in this coalition a fatal cause of rupture, though latent then and destined not to manifest itself till after the victory, the revolution of July.

---

* *Carabas* and *calotin* are derisive epithets applied to the nobles and the priests respectively.

Those seated at the Berville table on the evening in question, in a dining-hall where everything was rich and abundant, with provincial solidity beneath Parisian refinement, all belonged, whether guests or hosts, to this class and this party.

They constituted the flower of liberalism, the pleiades of the opposition, financiers first, lawyers, soldiers, literary men, artists, all the celebrities of the *bourgeoisie* of the day.

At the right of the host was seated his friend, his master, the great national banker, Jacques Laffitte, in a dark blue coat with brass buttons, the promoter of the Foy subscription, the treasurer of the party, the quarter-master of the army, destined to be minister of the revolution and to lose his fortune in victory. By the side of Laffitte, his *confrère* and rival, Casimir Perier, who was to supplant him, and his *protégé*, the young little Thiers, who was to betray him. Farther along was the historian of the cause, Sismondi, the surest and also the soundest of our historians, and his young and brilliant pupil, Lieutenant Carrel, the pen and sword of the party, the rebel of Bidassoa and the republican of the "National," who was to fall by the bullet of a thief. Then David d'Angers, the sculptor of Barra, and the astronomer Arago, predicting the return of a red comet.

Near them the lawyer of the middle class and the middle king, Dupin, in heavy iron-tipped shoes, more rustic than Roland and more crafty than Pathelin, still hot with the Orleanist protest against the birth of the Count de Chambord, and already meditating the will of the Prince de Condé.

And the Bonapartist general, the Corsican, Sebastiani, destined to be less famous for his deeds than for his phrase, "Order reigns at Warsaw," and for his poor dead daughter assassinated by the hand of her husband, the noble Duke de Praslin.

In the middle, opposite M. Berville, in the place of honor, sat the eldest, the venerable patriarch of the Revolution, the ex-Marquis de La Fayette, *en cheveux blancs* (in the words of the poet Delavigne), who had cut off his particle together with his cue on the night of the Fourth of August and had since called himself *Lafayette* for short; the "hero" of Two Worlds, a would-be Washington, a miscarried Cromwell, a gallant Warwick, dethroner of kings and courtier of queens, still, in spite of his age, treating all the fair sex as Marie Antoinettes, and, placed near Mlle. Berville, dominating the whole company by his high stature, his great renown, and his all-powerful authority.

At the left of Berville was Benjamin Constant, a beau of the Consulate, a skeleton, with three garments to fill him out, who, like a certain Greek, would have needed lead in his boots to hold him before the wind, his head covered with long hair, now gray but formerly light, which fell over his shoulders and curled angelically, in the style of Bernardin, the author of "Virginie," his chin buried in a Directory cravat, in the style of Talleyrand; in short, all that had been left of him by his fat mistress, daughter of a Genevan banker, wife of a German baron, and mother of a French duke, Mme. de Staël. Such as he was, he was the tribune of the opposition. The King's body-guards had demanded satisfaction (*raison*) for his last speech, and he had answered them that they undoubtedly stood in great need of reason (*raison*), but that he had not so much that he could spare them any. Which had amused France.

Then there was the deputy Manuel, still covered with glory by his expulsion from the Chamber by the *gendarmes* who had laid hands upon him after the national guards on duty at the Palais-Bourbon had refused. Which had made France indignant.

Then his friend Béranger, his forehead already bald, a real alabaster globe above his two handsome, delicate, soft, radiant, sparkling blue eyes, who had just lampooned in song the *Carabas* and the *Hommes noirs.** Which had set all France singing.

Without counting the newspaper writers of the "Constitutionnel" who enlightened her, Jay, Jouy, Jal, and even the publisher Touquet,—in short, all the stars of the political and literary firmament, all the glories of liberalism, all the forces of that opposition which was turning towards conspiracy to end in Revolution. Brilliant stars then, obscure today, which have had their influence, shot across the heavens, and disappeared in the limbo or become nebulous in the galaxy of history, from which the novel rescues them for a moment for its use if not for its pleasure.

After the period of silence with which a grand dinner usually begins, there was a running fire of raillery, anecdote, political, literary, and financial gossip on all the subjects of the day, barring the fashions, woman not being represented at this table of black coats, save by Mlle. Berville, who represented only the reaction and the kitchen.

Witticisms were showered on the Bourbons, the king *a l'engrais*, Louis XVIII., and his honorary mistress, the hunter, Charles X., and his Jesuit confessor, the Miraculous child and his immaculate mother, and especially the responsible ministers, their legislative projects and administrative policies, the double vote, right of primogeniture, law of love, law of sacrilege, tickets of confession, abolition of civil marriage,—in short, all the clerical and royal pretensions contained in the ominous Article 14 of the granted Charter.

The scandals and crimes of the clergy, high and low, of Archbishop Quélen and Father Mingrat, were no less bombarded.

All this political and religious artillery, varied with financial petards regarding bonds and discounts, conversions and loans, rise and fall of prices, heavy stocks, the latent crisis, suffering commerce, canals, roads, imports and exports,—all was of the opposition.

While biting the legitimate dynasty, they never failed to set their teeth in bet-

---

* The priests.

ter meat. Upon the artistic appearance and the flavor of each dish they congratulated Mlle. Gertrude, who, the only woman at the banquet, with her abbé beside her, was the target of the male sex and threw her grain of feminine salt into the conversation.

"Well," she replied to Benjamin Constant, an epicure who, while eating the king and the priest, regaled himself and complimented her on a *languet de Vierzon,** "will you always speak evil of religion?"

"A monk's dish!" exclaimed the delighted orator.

"You are right; I hold the secret directly from the convent of the Benedictines. Ask my cousin, M. de Berville."

"Berville, if you please, cousin."

"Yes, the last monk whom your frightful '93 expelled from the convent left the receipt to my aunt, the mother of my cousin de Berville."

"Berville, cousin."

"You see, the Church has done some good."

"Ah! if it had done nothing but give banquets!" said the orator, laughing and licking his chops.

"Your Revolution has not done as much, has it?"

"That is Voltaire's fault."

"To say nothing of the burnt almonds of Bourges, and the pastries of Linières, and the *case-museaux de Mehun,* all products of the convents of our religious Berry."

"That is Rousseau's fault."

"And the liquor of Chartreux, and the gingerbread-nuts of Reims, and the feet of Sainte-Ménéhould, cousin," added M. Berville, who liked to tease her.

"Your guillotine has killed cookery with the rest. No more Vatels; I am going to discharge mine, first because he swears, which I do not like, but especially because he has a notion that he will not make the white sauces which I like," said Gertrude, laughing.

"Ah! if our poor defunct were here, what a lesson in equality she would give you, cousin."

"Yes, the dear republican who called Our Lord *Sans-Culotte* and God *Citizen* . . . . who sang her child to sleep with the Marseillaise. That God may forgive her is my daily prayer. The old Christmas hymn and the blessed bread would have been better."

"Yes, we do justice to the Church, but at the table, not of communion, but of Mardi Gras," said Constant. "This fine *languet* makes up for the insipidity of the host."

But the coarse *bourgeois* wit of the sceptical banker, his swaggering incredulity

---

*This phrase and another occurring a few paragraphs farther on, *case-museaux de Mehun,* are not to be found in the dictionaries, and are unknown to such French cooks as I have been able to consult. They doubtless describe dishes or products peculiar to the places specified in them. — *Translator.*

and vulgarity, redoubled when the poultry was served, a turkey truffled ministe-
rially which he invariably called a Jesuit, offering Monsieur the abbé the rump,
which he pitilessly called a bishop's cap, and accompanying it with some pastry,
which, to cap the climax, he described as nun's wind.

There was only a shout of laughter.

"Respect for the child," said Gertrude.

"With the mitre," said M. Berville savagely to the poor martyr, "you cannot
fail to succeed the archbishop of Paris, and even become cardinal-minister, like
Dubois, or at least king's confessor, like Father Cotton. And, speaking of confession, have you read Paul Louis's latest pamphlet on celibacy?"

The abbé, stout and fat, Gertrude's spiritual director, did not breathe a word,
but closed his ears and opened his mouth, as much as to say, like his Cardinal
Mazarin, "Let them sing, they will pay for it!" and took his revenge upon the
banker's larded truffles, gluttony being the most venial of the seven capital sins.

Benjamin Constant, as gluttonous as he was thin, came to the aid of the priest
out of sympathy with his vice, saying that the Church had civilized table manners
as it had civilized morality, politics, and literature, — *Alma parens*, holy mother of
all knowledge!

And straightway the conversation took an upward turn.

"Well and good," said Mlle. Gertrude, "you, a Protestant, do more justice to
Catholicism than these freethinkers like my cousin de Berville. You are at least
Christian. But these Voltaireans, these infidels, these atheists, like my charming
neighbor, Béranger". . .

"I beg pardon, Mademoiselle," said the poet, "I an atheist! You forget the
'God of the good people.' I an infidel! Not to 'Lisette.'"

"It is true. But you do not recognize as we do the glory of the century, Monsieur the Viscount de Châteaubriand, the illustrious author of the 'Genius of
Christianity'". . .

"And of 'René,' the incestuous."

"You do not like our modern literature so original and so new". . .

"New, humph! as new as the Middle Ages."

"So Catholic, so monarchical, so national". . .

"Like Pitt and Cobourg."

"Ah! I can see them all gathered in their *coterie* at Abbaye-aux-Bois, at the
beautiful, noble, and pious Madame de Récamier's."

"Ah! yes, the Magdalen of the Directory, but little repentant! No, indeed!"

"Radiant constellation, of which Viscount de Châteaubriand is the sun, and the
planets Viscount d'Harlincourt, Chevalier de Lamartine, Baron Taylor, Count de
Vigny, and the son of the happy Vendean, the young Count Victor Hugo."

"Yes, all counts. . . the Gotha almanac. . . all nobles, and Apollo was a shep-
herd. . . . stay, you forget Dumas, the Marquis de la Pailleterie, a negro marquis,
and the printer Balzac, who has also become a noble author, — Honoré de Balzac."

"Just as my cousin is de Berville," said M. Berville.

"Oh, speak not so ill of the noble particle," said Gertrude. "Are not you your-self, dear poet, noble also, M. de Béranger?"

"Oh! oh! if my father, the tailor, could hear you in his grave, he would be ca-pable of recrossing his legs."

"No matter! you, a poet, you, the singer of 'Lisette,' admire at least the child of genius celebrating in song the child of miracle, the poet of the 'Ode to the Duke de Bordeaux'! What poetry! 'the flower of the grave.'"

"Humph! the flower of the grave! what a perfume! the odor is unpleasant."

"And the 'Ode to the Column,' great patriot, what do you think of that?"

"Yes, there is something for all tastes, except mine. You see, Mademoiselle," said Béranger, seriously, "I am only a song-writer, but a Frenchman; and all your poets are only foreign troubadours, English and German minstrels, sons, and, I fear, fathers, of invasion. Wellington and Blücher have invaded and abandoned us; but they have left us their fellow-countrymen, Scott and Goethe! Voltaire and Rousseau are conquered, like France. We are, I repeat, invaded and occupied. Are we going to progress backwards, advance toward the rear, retrace our steps, return to the Middle Ages, and relapse into childhood, the second, the ugly child-hood, that which precedes death? I have said: 'Kings never will invade France.' I was wrong. With this poetry they will regain it. You will not make citizens with René and citizenesses with Atala. And to save ourselves, to restore us to the path of progress, a second revolution is needed."

"We will make it; we shall see the Republic again!" cried Carrel, raising his head filled with enthusiasm.

"Yes, we shall have the 'best of republics,'" said La Fayette, diplomatically.

"We shall have the citizen-king," insisted the little Thiers, with his owl's head and his rattle voice.

"Yes, yes, the golden mean," added Dupin.

"And then all will not be ended," said Sismondi, shaking his head. "The Re-volution perhaps will go farther and faster than they would like to have it. Let us remember! The taking of the Bastille caused the taking of the Tuileries. The taking of the Tuileries will cause the taking of the Bank."

At this word Bank, M. Berville stopped laughing and teasing his cousin. His interest, in the absence of intellect, comprehended the historian Sismondi and checked the sage.

"Yes, not so fast and no extremes! Let us be positive!" said he. "I am very willing to subscribe to the 'Constitutionnel,' but for the Constitution. I desire the Charter, but not the Republic. I am for the golden mean, as M. Dupin says. Frankly, I do not like priests or nobles, as my cousin well knows; but I like demo-crats no better. I say more; I even prefer knights to citizens and 'short-robes' to *sans-culottes.* Anything rather than demagogues who have neither house nor home nor faith nor law ". . .

"Very good," exclaimed his cousin, laughing; "soon you will call yourself de Berville. Bravo, and thank you, my cousin, for thus defending religion and royalty."

"They are necessary for the People," said Berville, with a sagacious air.

"So, then," replied his malicious cousin, "you deny the nobility from pride."

"As you desire it from vanity. Yes, my dear vain cousin, no more nobles. All Frenchmen are equal before the law."

"That is just what the People say to the *bourgeois.*"

"They are wrong."

"And you right?"

"Undoubtedly the People are at least our equals. I even maintain that the most insignificant workman who calls himself a slave is freer and happier than I ". . . .

"Yes. *Les gueux, les gueux sont des gens heureux,*" hummed Béranger.

"Allowances, fees, wages, salaries, — the same thing under different names. Really the employee has neither responsibility nor care nor supervision nor obligations. I am not his master, I am his steward."

The young Berville, who had listened to all this long conversation without going to sleep, thanks to the nun's wind and other holy *bonbons* of the great confectioner of Rome, at this point addressed an indiscreet question to his father between two mouthfuls of gingerbread-nuts:

"Say, then, papa, why don't you become a workman?"

The guests smiled.

The father, nonplusssd, evaded the question.

"There, Camille, children of your age should be seen and not heard. Gentlemen, I may seem paradoxical; but really I declare to you that the meanest of my employees is more independent than I."

"Oh! oh!" exclaimed Carrel.

"Take, if you will, the lowest of all my collectors, — Didier, for instance. I take him because he is steady. He earns eighty cents a day, and for doing what, my God? He goes, he comes, he receives, and he carries. A terrier would do as much. His life is assured, and, as he is honest, he is more than rich, — he is happy."

"Why don't you change places with him?" asked the *enfant terrible.* "He would ask nothing better."

And the guests shouted.

The father, now indignant, was about to resume his argument after an angry gesture at the child, when behind a valet a man of mature age entered cautiously, and with an air of embarrassment and anxiety approached the banker's chair.

It was the cashier of the establishment.

"Monsieur," said he, in a hesitating tone.

And in a low voice the following conversation began.

"What do you want, Brémont?" said Berville, testily.

"To speak to you in private."

"You know very well that I do not wish to be disturbed when I am at the table."

"Excuse me, Monsieur, but "...

"And how happens it that you are here at this hour? Why come back?"

"I have not come back; I have remained."

"Why?"

"I have been waiting for the collector, who has not yet returned."

The banker leaped from his seat.

The conversation ceased, and all eyes were fixed on Berville, erect and petrified.

The sinister finger tracing the fatal handwriting on the wall at Belshazzar's feast amid the noise of thunder had no greater effect upon the king of Babylon than the words of the cashier produced upon the banker Berville.

Presentiment, that shadow of misfortune, which precedes it instead of following it, passed over the moist brow of the financier, who, erect as a statue and pale as death, left the dining-hall with Brémont, without an excuse or a bow to any one.

The guests, who had seen him turn pale, watched him go out, some with surprise, others with suspicion, his rivals with joy, no one with pain. And then, looking at each other without saying a word, all went out one after another, leaving Mademoiselle Gertrude, threatened with celestial wrath, lone and dejected, in the middle of her wasted dessert and her empty dining-hall, all abandoning the house, as rats abandon a sinking ship.

As for the Berry banker, the miracle which changed Nebuchadnezzar into a wild beast was no longer necessary. It was done.

.   .   .   .

No more festivities. All is silent, dark in the Berville mansion, except in the director's office.

The banker and the cashier, anxious and mute, are shut up there.

They are waiting.

The clock strikes one in the morning.

"You see," exclaimed the banker in a tone of anguish, "my ruin is complete. He will not return."

And walking up and down the room in agitation, his hands clinched behind his back, he continued:

"How imprudent you have been, Brémont! To entrust a collector with such a sum! Three hundred thousand dollars! It is enough to tempt honesty itself."

The cashier, trembling, tried to excuse himself.

"But Didier really is honesty itself. During the fifteen years that he has been in your service he has not deserved a reproach, and that is why I selected him. Probity, activity, morality, he has everything in his favor, everything!"

"Even my collections!" exclaimed the banker, ill concealing his growing irritation.

"I acted for the best. And what should I have done?" observed the cashier. "I had no orders" ....

"No orders, no orders. . . . you had the orders of good sense; you should have taken the responsibility of sending some one with him."

"That is what I did, Monsieur; Louis Dupont went with him, and I wonder" . . . .

"You sent some one with him? . . . . . . All is explained! Shared between them!"

"But, Monsieur, I scarcely understand you."

"I understand myself only too well."

"Their route was a long one, extending outside of Paris," ventured M. Brémont. "Perhaps they could not find a carriage to bring them back."

M. Berville stamped his foot.

"Say rather that they have run away together!"

"Jacques and Louis?" replied the cashier. "Impossible! I would answer for their honesty almost as quickly as for my own."

"Be silent," cried the banker, "or I shall believe that you are their accomplice." The cashier started, and, in a voice choking with indignation, said:

"I! Oh! Monsieur!"

The master perceived that he had gone too far, and, recovering himself immediately, he said in a softened tone:

"I beg your pardon, my dear Brémont. My head is no longer my own; I am carried away by my distress; this blow strikes me unexpectedly. Come, let us be cool, let us reason. At what hour ought they to have returned, allowing for all possible and even impossible delays?"

"I repeat that the route was a long one," said the cashier, scarcely recovered from his emotion. "The largest sum to be collected, exceeding all the others combined, was outside the city. Bad weather and mischance, the foreseen and the unforeseen, would very likely detain them till ten o'clock, perhaps till eleven, at the latest till midnight."

The banker pointed to the clock, which indicated half past one.

The cashier made no answer to this gesture, more eloquent than any words.

The two men looked at each other in despair, and for a few seconds silence prevailed, disturbed only by the ticking of the clock, whose golden hands turned as inexorably as fate.

The half hour struck.

"Where does Didier live?" suddenly asked M. Berville.

"Rue Sainte-Marguerite."

"What street is that? Is it far?"

"Far enough. In the middle of the Faubourg Saint-Antoine."

"A devil of a distance! And Dupont?"

"He lives near here, Passage" . . . .

The banker prevented him from finishing.

"Run and find him. Quick!"

M. Brémont went out upon this errand.

Left alone, M. Berville could not sit still. He rose, walked back and forth, then sat down again only to rise once more, impatient, enervated, exasperated, tortured by anxiety.

"I wish to know where I stand; this uncertainty is killing. . . Over a quarter of a million," said he slowly, folding his arms. "More than I possess! Oh, it is horrible! This Didier is surely a robber; but he cannot be alone; that is out of the question. And this imbecile of a. Brémont who does not return with the other! Undoubtedly all three have an understanding."

He listened anxiously to the street sounds, awaiting the cashier's return. A carriage, arriving at full speed, stopped in front of the house.

A minute later the cashier reentered the office, accompanied by Dupont.

"Where is Didier? Whence come you?" burst out M. Berville.

The collector stammered, astonished and frightened by the master's question and the absence of Jacques.

"Didier! What! He has not returned? I left him at ten o'clock at the Quai d'Austerlitz."

The banker exploded.

"Confounded beast! . . . . traitor! . . . wretch!" . . . .

And he seized his employee by the arm, grasping him tightly and shaking him. "Why did you leave him?" he cried.

"Monsieur, the collections were made. . . . the day's work was done. . . . . I was anxious. . . . My wife is sick. . . . She has just given birth to a child."

"In the name of God, what's that to me?" swore the banker, pushing Dupont away in a mad fit of anger. "But this will not be the end of it. I will have you all imprisoned."

He paced the room for a moment like a wild beast in its cage, his look recalled to the clock as it struck two.

"Ah! you strike my ruin," said he. "To have worked so hard to establish this house . . . destroyed by these monsters! Robbed! Ruined! A den of thieves!"

Then, seized with a fit of madness, he leaped at the clock.

"You shall strike no more," he cried.

And he dashed it upon the marble hearth, breaking it and trampling on the pieces. Then, his nerves strained almost to bursting, he vented his rage upon himself, tearing out his beard and lacerating his face.

M. Brémont and Louis, overwhelmed, looked on in fear at their master's despair. Finally he stopped, with foam on his lips and his eyes starting from their sockets, and planted himself in front of the collector.

"Clear out, you scoundrel! I dismiss you. . . Or rather, no, I keep you. You shall be imprisoned in La Force, there to await the other, with your fellows, bandit!"

And, addressing M. Brémont, he added:

"An officer! Go get me an officer! Not a word. It is my will!"

The cashier started to obey this peremptory order.

"No, stay, you too!" exclaimed the banker, stopping him at the door. "You shall not go out either."

And he began to scream at the stairs, calling the janitor.

"Plumet! Plumet! Bring me the police. Do you hear me?"

The janitor, waking with a start, hastily dressed himself and obeyed passively, like an automaton, without knowing why.

Soon an officer made his appearance.

"What is the matter?" he inquired.

"Here I am, surrounded by fools and knaves, who have robbed me and allowed me to be robbed," cried the banker, beside himself.

The officer, ever ready, went straight to the point, and, designating the cashier and the collector, asked:

"Which is to be arrested?"

"The other first!" exclaimed the banker.

"The other?" echoed the officer, with a look of surprise, searching the room with his eyes.

He was looking for the third, almost suspecting the employer's sanity.

"Yes," explained the banker, coming back to his senses, "another: Jacques Didier, who has not returned his receipts. It must be ascertained what has become of him. He must be found and arrested."

"Is he married?" asked the officer.

"Undoubtedly."

"Indeed! Where does he live?"

"Faubourg Saint-Antoine."

"Surely he must have first gone home. We must start at once. Perhaps we shall catch the bird in his nest before he flies again. The paired robber always returns to his home to carry away his female."

"You think so?" exclaimed the banker. "Let us be off."

And, taking his hat, he opened the door.

Alarmed, with eyes and ears wide open, two human forms then faced him, — his cousin and his son.

"What are you doing there?" cried the banker.

"Berville, my fortune is yours," said Gertrude.

"Fool, keep your pear for your own thirst."

And he pushed her aside brutally.

"And I tell you that Jacques is no robber," exclaimed the *enfant terrible,* stopping his father.

But the crazed banker overturned his son as he had overturned the clock; and, at the risk of his life and in spite of his weight, he cleared the stairs four at a time, followed by the others.

CHAPTER VI.

THE DIDIER GARRET.

A moment later M. Berville, his cashier, the collector, and the police officer, were being driven rapidly in the direction of the Faubourg Saint-Antoine.

On the way the four men could not exchange a word. The cab, going at full speed, made a deafening noise.

They stopped at last in an uninviting street before a sorry-looking house.

"This is the place," said M. Brémont, opening the cab-door.

M. Berville cast an indignant glance at the Rue Sainte-Marguerite and the entrance of the house.

"Why, this Didier lives in a hovel!" he exclaimed. "And you knew him, Brémont?" •

The officer, too, made a significant grimace. •

"Find the treasure in there! We are foiled!"

"But," observed the cashier, "the laboring class is obliged to live in low quarters; at a dollar a day one does not live where he likes, but where he can. Poverty is not a crime, Monsieur."

The banker made no answer.

They all entered a dark passage.

Reaching a staircase as steep as a ladder, M. Brémont stopped in embarrassment.

"I do not know the floor," he said, casting his eyes about for the janitor's lodge.

"The top story, I think," said Dupont.

"No matter, let us go up at any rate," said the officer.

"Yes, and without delay," exclaimed the banker.

A door opened at the top of the house, and a light appeared.

At the same time a woman's voice was heard, a voice of gentleness shaded with anxiety.

"Is that you, Jacques?"

The officer shook his head.

"Not returned!" said he, simply.

M. Berville stifled a cry of despair.

Brémont and Dupont looked at each other in consternation.

The four men rapidly ascended the stairs. As they reached the last step of the fifth flight, they saw the wife of Jacques Didier.

The attic room was so orderly that it seemed large and so clean that it seemed luminous; not a rag, not a thread; not a straw or a grain of dust; a cleanliness, not of the surface only, but of the depths; the nooks and corners that never come into the middle of the room thoroughly searched with the duster: the brasses worn with rubbing and shining as if new; everything in place, nothing dragging; Jacques's spare pantaloons and shoes drying on a chair before a remnant of fire; a table set for two persons, perfect in its neatness, awaiting the ragout stewing on the stove; but the crown and centre of all these great and little cares was a pretty white cradle for the rosy-faced baby.

Ah! the amount of courage and virtue that such a woman as Louise Didier expends in struggling with fortune is inexpressible!

Always neatly shod and wearing on her head a linen cap that added to her thoroughly feminine look, anxious at this moment and more than anxious, alarmed, Louise lighted a second candle, the first having burned out; she was starting up her fire and ironing her baby's linen to distract her thoughts while waiting, when she heard the noise on the stairs, opened her door, and hailed her husband.

She seemed about thirty years old, with features as regular as her life, surrounded with light hair, and possessing the bloodless and touching grace of the women of the people made prematurely pale by the hard labors of the house and shop through lack of air, food, and clothing.

Mme. Didier started back in surprise upon the entrance of the four men, half in fear, half in shame, scarcely dressed as she was in a short skirt and a white sack, half open to nurse her child.

"What is the matter?" she asked, seized with a fearful presentiment and modestly covering her bosom in presence of these strangers.

"Where is your husband?" asked the officer, brutally.

"I am waiting for him. He has not yet returned. But what do you wish of him, gentlemen?"

"I wish him to return me three hundred thousand dollars," cried the banker, containing himself no longer.

"Three hundred thousand dollars!" exclaimed the poor woman, clasping her hands. "What would he do with such a sum, great God? If he has it, he will return it to you, you may be sure. Three hundred thousand dollars!"

The officer confronted Mme. Didier.

"Come, no nonsense!" said he, staring at her. "You know what the trouble is. Your husband has stolen!"

"Stolen! My husband!"

"Yes, stolen my fortune!" said the banker.

"It is not true! You lie!" cried the young woman, straightening up like a lioness struck with a lash.

"Wretched woman! you forget to whom you speak!"

" And how about you, then?"

" Alas! everything accuses him," said the cashier, intervening.

" But I tell you it is not true!" repeated Mme. Didier. "Look, hunt, ransack everything; here is our furniture,—cupboard, clothes-press, commode, everything that closes " . . . .

And she threw everything wide open.

" No difficulty in finding three hundred thousand dollars there. Your fortune is no more there than Jacques is," she continued.

The banker and the officer had soon examined the whole room.

" No, nobody!" said M. Berville.

" Only an infant," said the officer, in turn.

In fact, in the midst of this household of workers, clean and orderly, they had seen the muslin-covered cradle where slept a new-born babe, the jewel of these poor people,—Marie.

Disturbed by the noise, the child began to cry desperately. The mother, thus called by her daughter, took her in her arms as in a cradle to pacify her.

This touching picture calmed the banker's fury for a moment.

" Tell me, Madame," said he, almost gently, "does your husband often come home late?"

" No, Monsieur," said the mother. "That is why I am anxious. He should have been here at eight o'clock, as usual, or at nine at the latest. See! his supper is there on the stove, waiting for him."

" Does he sometimes play?"

" With what?"

" Does he go to the wine-shop?" insisted M. Berville, while the officer still rummaged about in all directions.

" Never," protested Mme. Didier, "and I do not know what this means. He, always so exact. . . . Oh! my God, if any misfortune has befallen him!"

" Pshaw!" cried the banker, with an air of importance and raising his voice again, his momentary calmness exhausted; " it is my money that misfortune has befallen!"

In the meantime doors had opened on the landing, and the neighbors were approaching curiously.

Mme. Didier turned to them, quivering with indignation, and called them as witnesses to her husband's honor.

" Come in, enter. They say that Jacques is a robber," she cried, in turn. " Is that possible, tell them?"

All, men and women, shook their heads, and a unanimous, energetic " No," almost threatening to the accusers, answered her question.

But a noise from the street came up the stairs, growing louder and more distinct. Some of the neighbors leaned over the bannisters and jumped back, frightened.

"It is he?" asked Mme. Didier, with a gleam of hope.

There was no answer.

"What is the matter?" she continued.

"Nothing good," murmured a member of the group.

She rushed to the stairs, pressing her child to her bosom.

"Go no farther, poor lady!" said a man who was hurriedly ascending.

It was Jean.

But, borne on by her impulse, the unfortunate woman violently pushed him aside.

Banker, collector, cashier, and officer followed her.

Some municipal guards appeared, bearing a torch.

"Arrested! at last!" cried the banker, deceived by appearances.

But suddenly the body of Jacques Didier came into view upon a stretcher.

"No! dead!" said the poor woman, with a terrible cry.

"Ruined!" exclaimed the banker, leaning against the wall to keep from falling.

"Murdered! Murdered!" repeated the widow, throwing herself upon the stretcher.

"Dishonored!" he responded.

"My husband! My baby!"

"Oh! My God! My God! restore my uncertainty!"

And a flood of blood rushed to the banker's neck and head.

"You see that we are not all knaves or fools," said Brémont, gravely; "you sought a robber and you find a victim."

The banker heard no more; his apoplexy stifled him; and, stammering these incoherent words: "Maturity, end of the month, bankruptcy!" he sank at the head of the stairs like an ox felled by a club.

The widow, raising her head, saw the miserable man fallen near Jacques at her feet, and with a movement of sublime compassion she exclaimed:

"Ah! poor Monsieur!"

Then, quickly entering her room again and depositing her baby in the cradle, she was the first to go to the banker's aid, moistening his temples with salts and water.

"Ah! he would not do as much," said the cashier, deeply moved and looking at his employer, who was recovering consciousness. "A strong-box is not a heart!"

All hastened around the banker. The cashier aided the guards to bear him away.

It is said that the name Calais was found in the heart of Queen Elizabeth. The word bankruptcy would have been found in that of the banker.

While they were going out, the widow came back to her own sorrow and her own dead, distracted for a moment by that feeling so keen among the masses,— solidarity in misfortune.

Kneeling by Jacques's side, she felt of him, called him, kissed him, tried to re-store him to life, to impart to him her own.

"Ah! his poor blood! Dumb, dull, cold, dead!"

And, despair giving her tenfold strength, she took the body in her arms and laid it on the conjugal bed.

Unperceived by her, Jean had remained a witness of this desolation. At all risk he had rejoined the patrol and guided it to Didier's address. Agitated, he descended to the story just above the ground-floor, where the janitor's lodge was located.

"Have you anything to let here?" he asked the janitor, abruptly.

"Yes, a loft," answered the latter, sleepily. "But why?"

"Nothing. I simply wanted to know. I will come back."

And he descended, or rather jumped down, the rest of the stairs, wiping two big tears from his beard as he reached the street and saying:

"Really, I didn't think I knew how to weep. Ah! yes, I will come back, by tomorrow at the latest."

CHAPTER VII.

AT THE PAWN-SHOP.

The next day the entire press reported the double tragedy of the Berville mansion and the Didier garret. The authorities were congratulated on restoring the body of Jacques to his widow, instead of sending it to the Morgue, as is the rule. Right-thinking journals, well cared for out of the secret funds, did not fail to affirm that it was a great consolation to the poor woman in her affliction to be able to bury her husband at her own expense.

It was necessary, then, to pay for burial in any cemetery save that of the criminals, which receives its bodies from the Morgue and from the scaffold, scoundrels and outcasts, murderers and suicides, the whole offscouring of civilization, no less good than Providence, that other Divine.

An immense current of interested sympathy was formed. . . . for whom? For M. Berville. And everybody repeated after his newspaper: "The poor man!" As for the widow, there was no further question of her; she was left to herself. For she had no stockholders, no person interested in her safety.

What is the ruin of a woman of the people? That of a banker is quite another thing!

The principal creditors and stockholders of the Berville Bank granted a renewal of their claims for a fortnight, thus permitting the banker to double the cape of maturity, the end of the month. This mark of confidence and prudence did not fill the treasury; but at least M. Berville had a breathing-spell before the inevitable crash that awaited him on the fifteenth of the month, the wealthy classes' day of settlement and the limit of the conceded delay.

That of the poor, the petty rent-day, as it is scornfully called by the proprietors, was near at hand with no prospect of indulgence. Consequently the pawn-shops were never empty. The central office, in the Rue des Blancs-Manteaux, was crowded from morning till night. The entire laboring and consequently needy population of Paris came to this shrine of Saint Necessity to pledge their poor offerings at the headquarters of philanthropic and official usury.

A woman dressed in black made her way into the office of pledges and redemptions.

Undecided or ashamed, she looked on for a mome nt at the continuous and varied procession, by turns ludicrous and pitiful, of those coming and going.

She did not notice the presence of a man in a blouse, who had entered behind her and was sitting in concealment on a bench in a dark corner of the room.

Summoning all her courage, she finally took her place between two railings, running in front of the grated windows.

The clerks, bending over their registers, noted the pledges, took strict account of the names, addresses, and professions of the borrowers in order to strip them as much as possible, delivered them their pawn-tickets, and handed them cards against which the cashier paid them the sums loaned.

The attendant went back and forth, taking the packages and carrying them into an adjoining room, where they were estimated in a loud voice.

The woman dressed in black was the last of a line of thirty persons, arranged in single file as at the ticket-office of a theatre, all having packages or articles in their hands.

A girl dressed with the elegance of an interloper, with a fine India cashmere on her back and a short silk mantle under her arm, then entered as if perfectly at home and went straight to the window without heeding the procession.

" At the end of the line!" cried the crowd.

Not disconcerted, the beauty slipped a coin into the attendant's hand and advanced.

" At the end of the line! at the end of the line!" the voices repeated, louder than before.

" It is an outrage!" exclaimed a Hercules with a husky voice.

" What do you expect?" answered the attendant; "it is a custom."

She was already at the window, on the other side of the railing, handing in her shawl.

" Ah! this has been here before," said the clerk, not examining it very closely; "number 66, ninety dollars."

" I need a hundred."

" Then complete your security, my dear."

She took off her lace veil.

"Oh!" exclaimed the Hercules, " it is Sophie."

" My daughter! Sophie! Sophie!" cried in turn a woman at the head of the line, "give me a dollar."

"What does this crazy creature mean?" said Sophie, superbly.

"All right! One hundred dollars," said the clerk, receiving the veil. "Forty cents to be deducted for the wrapping."

Sophie threw down the forty cents, received the hundred dollars, and, putting on her mantle, went out, as proud and irresponsible as Queen Victoria.

"Number 67. Come, be quick," cried the clerk from his window, the space in front of which was left vacant for a moment.

And the denied mother, a poor madonna with a poor Jesus clinging to her neck, who, either from shame or fear, had hesitated a moment before opening her bundle, with a trembling hand laid a heap of rags upon the counter in front of the window.

They were the woman and the innocent who had presided at the lottery of the basket at the Hotel d'Italie.

"We cannot lend on those," said the attendant, pushing back the needy woman's collateral.

"I am in such need, good people," she murmured. "Only twenty cents. I have nothing but these things, and no bread."

"You know very well that we do not lend less than sixty cents," said the clerk.

"Monsieur! I beg of you," said the poor woman.

"This is not the charity department; go to the board of public relief."

"Come, my old woman, make room for the others!" said the attendant.

The unfortunate creature left the railing and went away, saying in an undertone of despair:

"Nothing left, nothing! Ah! such heartless people as my daughter!"

She passed by the woman in black; the latter stopped her, and, quietly slipping a few copper coins into her hand, said, in a voice of ineffable sadness:

"For the little one."

"Oh! thank you!" exclaimed the other. "God bless you! This saves us . . . till tomorrow."

And she passed out, pressing her baby, who also uttered his moan of thanks, more closely than ever to her breast.

"Number 68," cried the clerk.

A drunken and dissolute man, another acquaintance of the Hotel d'Italie, the Hercules of the North, asked by the attendant to lay down his collateral, fumbled for a moment, and then, with herculean wit, said:

"One moment, and I will show you, governor. . . . I have been robbed. . . . . One would say that 'my aunt' has nephews and all sorts of relatives. What a family! It is enough to stifle one! It makes one hot. . . and thirsty. Ah! but don't push so in the rear. Say, easy there, relatives!"

"Well?" said the attendant, getting impatient.

"Yes, well? what do you want, young fellow?"

"What have you to pawn?"

"Myself!" answered the Hercules. "I weigh two hundred . . . . not easy to support, and the government is bound to restore articles in good condition!"

"Will you clear out?" said the attendant.

And he gave him a rude shove.

"Take care . . . fragile! You are answerable for breakage. I come to put myself in gage, I tell you."

"In cage, you mean," said the clerk, intervening.

Then, calling the officer on duty, he said:
" We have had enough of this. Officer, take Monsieur into the jewelry room."
The drunkard tried to resist.
" I tell you that I wish to be *hung up.*"
" That's what we are going to do with you," retorted the clerk. " Next ! "
The officer led away the obstinate man, who still went on jabbering:
" You will give the ticket to my wife. She will come to redeem me, — the tall beauty who just went out without her cashmere. She loves me like a beast; consequently I do as I please. When one is a fine specimen of a man, he ought to live on his physique, eh ? "
The door closed upon him.
" Number 69, a clock . . . Ah ! we are deaf with them, two dollars," cried the clerk ; "number 70, a set of teeth, not new, sixty cents."
M. Brémont, M. Berville's cashier, hesitating and mortified, offered a set of diamonds which had belonged to Mme. Berville.
" Number 71, six thousand dollars."
Then came the turn of a man of military bearing.
" Number 72, a sword, three dollars. No, it is a sword of honor, with the name upon it : only two dollars and forty cents."
The valuations continued.
A gentleman, decorated and serious as a diplomat, was at the window.
" A necklace of the order of the Golden Fleece . . . an imitation. Number 73, one dollar."
A workingman, in the prime of life, handed in the implements of his toil, saying in a discouraged tone :
"No more work. . . No need of tools ". . .
" Number 74, a hammer, nippers, etc., eighty cents."
"Not a dollar ? "
" No, we have too many of these traps. Eighty cents. . . will you take it ? "
" I must."
" Twenty cents for wrapping, you know ? "
The workingman bit his moustache and grumbled as he passed to the cashier's office, where he was given but sixty cents.
A freshly-shaven individual, looking like a clergyman, advanced a picture.
" Number 75, a Raphael, ' The Holy Family,' a copy. We cannot take that. Ah ! yes, the frame is copper ; a dollar and forty cents."
" That is not much for my poor little ones, Monsieur."
"Or your mistress," muttered the workingman on his way to the payment office.
And he added, laughing :
" See, the Good God ! the Good God also pulls the devil by the tail."
A musician took his place before the window,

" A violin," said he.

" Try it," said the clerk.

The artist began to play the "Marseillaise."

" Stop, or I arrest you!" exclaimed the officer, just then coming in again.

" All right. Number 76, six dollars," continued the appraiser.

A sculptor passed in several busts under the head of objects of art.

" Number 77, Charles X, Napoleon I, and Louis XVIII. Three plasters, not much difference! a dollar, forty cents, twenty cents, — in all, a dollar and sixty."

The Hercules had returned behind the officer.

" Louis Eighteen," he cried, with his massive wit, " Louis Eighteen! I prefer eighteen louis! Where is Sophie, who has twenty-five? I must have her."

Again the officer put him out.

" Ah! Number 78, a silver watch with its chain, and a second-hand wedding-ring, five dollars."

The tired clerk raised his eyes upon the person offering them.

It was the last comer.

" Your name?"

" Madame Didier."

" Residence?"

" Rue Sainte-Marguerite."

" Business?"

" Seamstress."

" Have you your husband's authorization?"

" I am a widow, Monsieur."

" Then a death certificate is necessary; two licensed witnesses must answer for you and sign upon this register."

" Two licensed witnesses?"

" Yes, two merchants of your neighborhood."

" But I have nobody, Monsieur. I cannot make my position known to everybody. It is impossible."

" I am very sorry, but it is indispensable."

" Then give me back my things; I will go to a second-hand dealer."

" No. The pledge is seized. Here is a receipt."

" Seized!"

" Yes, until the formalities are complied with. It is the law in your case. For loans of more than three dollars, regular papers are required and the testimony of two honorable persons."

The man who had entered after Madame Didier and remained hidden in the corner, rose suddenly and spontaneously offered himself at the window:

" Two honorable persons? Here is one at any rate!"

" You know Madame?" asked the clerk, with a look of disdain.

"I should say so; I live in the same house."

"Who are you?"

"Jean, dealer in rags."

"Wholesale?"

"Wholesale and retail."

"Let us see, are you established? Have you a license?"

"You mean a basket?"

The clerk became angry.

"Confounded *biffin*, away with you! Clear out, and be quick about it! Who ever saw you?"

Jean did his best to restrain himself.

"I tell you that I am the witness of this poor lady; and, since you will not lend to her, you at least will restore her property."

"What? You are doubtless in conspiracy". . .

Madame Didier took the rag-picker by the arm.

"Thank you, Monsieur Jean," said she, alarmed. "Make no scene. I prefer to abandon these articles. Oh! these wicked men!"

"The regulations apply to all," concluded the clerk. "And no comments, or else". . . .

And he pointed to the officer, who stood ready to intervene.

"Miserable quill-driver!" exclaimed Jean, grumbling, swearing, storming.

Nevertheless he suffered the widow to lead him away.

"Now, there you are, stripped," said he, on reaching the street. "And they call that the Mount of Piety! I was not acquainted with it, but I shall remember it."

The widow started to go, after a final expression of thanks.

"No," exclaimed Jean, "this must not be left so. You have been robbed as if this were the forest of Bondy. Mount of thieves, away with you! Oh! I wish". . . .

"I pray you, for pity's sake, do not make my pitiful situation public. I should die of shame as well as pain."

"Well," answered Jean, "I will be silent. . . . But on one condition, — that you permit me as a neighbor, and without regarding it as of any importance. . . . Within the last week I have saved a dollar". . . .

"Never! Thank you again, and farewell, Monsieur Jean."

"But I tell you that it is 'for the little one,' as you said just now to the woman who was poorer than yourself."

And he dropped the coin into the widow's pocket.

"You may return it when you can; it is you who oblige me. The money is well placed. Perhaps I should drink it up. It is agreed? For Marie! *Au revoir*, Madame Didier."

And he slipped away as if he had robbed the widow.

Stop, honest Jean; you are not the robber; the robber is the Mount of Piety!

The poor mother, surprised and deeply moved, could not restrain him or recall him to return his money.

"Worthy man! when I can! But it is impossible. He does not know my situation. Rent tomorrow, bread today. Oh! it is all over! Poor Marie, in losing your father, we have lost all."

And with lowered head, ashamed of this forced loan, the first of her life, she went back to the quarter in which she lived, hurrying away as fast as possible from the headquarters of usury where all Paris "on the nail" can satisfy both Heraclitus and Democritus, giving them something at which to laugh. . . and to weep.

CHAPTER VIII.

CANAILLE & CO.

Everything here below has its parasite : wealth has flatterers; want, usurers. Fortune and misfortune, everything is exploited, — misfortune especially!

Widowed, exhausted, emaciated, Louise Didier was also an object of prey. What was she to do? What was to become of her? Should she prostitute herself or kill herself? A dilemma without a difference.

Crushed by her condition and by society which created it, she bent her head, dwelling in despair upon her famished little girl and upon the rent-day which was approaching to complete their ruin. She had no hope left save in death for both mother and child.

But on reaching the Faubourg Saint-Antoine, an idea struck her as her eye fell upon a three-story house which bore three signs.

The first and most complicated was phrased in the following obliging terms:

PROVIDENCE.

Pawn-Tickets Purchased, Redeemable on Easy Terms.

Sales on Instalment. — Very Easy Payments.

The second, more laconic but no less benevolent, read simply:

SALVATION.

Intelligence-Office for Women.

And finally the last, thoroughly Christian:

THE GUARDIAN ANGEL.

Mme. Gavard, First-Class Midwife, Holding a Diploma from the Faculty.

This house, with its three signs and three trades, one for each floor, was inhabited by M. Abraham Gripon, his wife, and his sister-in-law, Mme. Gavard.

Gripon, an Israelite of low Judæa and one of the most circumcised, bought, sold, loaned, and discounted providentially at five per cent., not per week, but per hour.

His wife, by way of salvation, kept the intelligence-office, and lodged, fed, and clothed girls coming from the country in search of a place in the grace of God.

This industrious and well-matched couple had given birth to a perfect little Jew, Ismaël Gripon, no less an enemy of pork than a friend of gold, who already filled his family with the finest hopes.

His father destined him for high Judæa, for the lofty career of a stock-broker, with the upper grade of thieves, where he could steal with more freedom, honor, and profit than his ancestors.

Mme. Gavard, old Gripon's sister-in-law, angelically practised abortion and even midwifery at accommodating prices.

In the neighborhood the three signs were thought to contain many words for the expression of few truths; and the entire holy Gripon-Gavard family of providential money-lenders, salvation-securing employment finders, and angel-making abortionists, this complete Noah's Ark, had been popularly baptized under this typical firm name: *Canaille & Co.*

Even at that epoch such offices as these were the cut-throats and cut-purses of labor.

The widow Didier took her dollar from her pocket and entered the den. Going up one flight, she stopped before the door of the intelligence-office.

She rang timidly. An old woman in spectacles, her head adorned with curl-papers, opened the door and scanned her with a sneaking and inquisitive air.

"What do you want?" she asked her.

"Work," answered Mme. Didier.

Mme. Gripon pointed her sharp nose upward and scratched her ear for a moment with the end of her pencil, asking herself undoubtedly what she could get out of this woman who seemed to her already consumed by poverty and sorrow.

"Come in," said she, finally.

Louise was ushered into a cold-looking room, furnished with benches upon which were sitting seven or eight women, in search, like herself, of a social position.

"Wait," continued the old fairy of *salvation.* "You will take your turn." And she called a customer.

Then, making a sign to a spirited, shrewd, and buxom young woman, she retired into a little closet with a glass door.

"You know," said the customer whom she had called, speaking volubly, " I do not like your place. An old bachelor with nothing at all; decorated, but without four cents to his name; an old soldier, retired on a pension, who pawned his sword yesterday!"

"My dear friend," said Madame Gripon, superbly, "you must be resigned to service in the army. Your early education was too much neglected. The clergy, the magistracy, and finance, impossible!"

"Why? Why? Especially as I must have what I want."

"Hm! hm!"

"And I tell you that I want a good handsome place for my money!"

"Indeed!" said the employment-agent, sharply, showing her teeth almost to the point of betraying herself, "do you think that I am going to give you, for your paltry two dollars, a place as governess at the Louvre or as niece to a priest?"

"Then how much do you want?"

"Well, sign a couple of little notes for me . . . . oh! a small matter . . . . four dollars each ". . . .

"And then?"

"Why, I will get them discounted down stairs, at M. Gripon's; but take care! with him there is no trifling. When the money is due, it must be paid. On these conditions you shall have the place that you desire. Is it agreed?"

"Yes."

Mme. Gripon drew up the papers, had them signed by her customer, and in exchange handed her an address.

"The abbé Ventron," read the stout girl. "Very well! That suits me; *au revoir !*"

The agent called another customer.

"So," said she to the new-comer, "you will not work at the place to which I sent you?"

"Why, Madame, it is a bad place, a disreputable house."

"Well? You are not a policeman, I suppose."

"Never, I cannot" . . .

"Never!" repeated the old woman, "we shall see. What! you come to Paris without a cent! I give you board, lodging, and washing, in short I support you from head to foot, and after that you raise objections!"

"Madame!"

"There is no Madame about it. You should have refused in the first place. There is a prison for swindlers, my dear. Choose."

The unfortunate girl hesitated a moment, and then, overcome by fear and hunger, faltered:

"I will go."

"Next," cried Mme. Gripon.

A poor girl, far advanced in pregnancy, came in her turn.

"You here again!" exclaimed the old woman, indignantly. "And in the same condition! Incorrigible!"

"Oh! if you knew!" said the poor creature. "I have done wrong, it is true, but the son of my employer ". . . .

"Then you have been discharged?"

"My God, yes, Madame."

"And you come back to me! Always the same story. Upon my word, I am your milch cow," screamed the old woman, striking her flabby breast.

She continued in the same tone:

"Well, once more I will relieve you of your difficulty. You will go up stairs to Mme. Gavard. I will pay your board. But after that you are mine."

"Oh! I will be entirely, eternally grateful to you."

"Pshaw! that's all nonsense. The question is whether you will be submissive and practical."

"I will do anything you want me to."

"Good! that's the right sort of talk, at least. Here is a word for Mme. Gavard. All ready!"

It was Louise Didier's turn.

"This is the first time that you have been here, isn't it?" said Mme. Gripon; "then pay me sixty cents for your registration. It is the custom of the house."

Louise handed her her dollar, which the old woman kept in her hand.

"What do you want to do?" finally asked the latter.

"I do not know," confessed the widow. "This is my situation. I have just lost my husband. I am left alone with my little girl, and I am a seamstress without work."

"Ah! you have a child," interrupted the agent. "That is embarrassing. Never mind, go on."

"I should like to get sewing to do at home. It is impossible to find any immediately, and I cannot wait. So I should have to work at a shop. But there is Marie."

"Yes, the little nuisance."

The old woman gave her victim a piercing look.

"It is not at all easy to find a situation for you," said she, pocketing the coin.

"I could be a housekeeper," ventured Louise.

"And the child?"

"I could put her in charge of some one else for a few hours. Undoubtedly some neighbor would take care of her."

"On that point consult Mme. Gavard, on the floor above. Perhaps she can be useful to you. She is a sensible and obliging woman". . .

"The midwife?"

"Yes; she would relieve you of the little one. Who knows? She might even make it an object for you."

"What do you mean?"

"Oh, that's all right; she will explain all that to you better than I can. Let us talk of our affairs. I will give you an address. The charge is forty cents. Does that suit you?"

"Since that is what I came for. What is it?"

The agent turned over the leaves of a thick, greasy book, mumbling:

"I hope that you will not play the prude. Money has no odor. I am going to send you to Mlle. Sophie, a ballet-dancer or something of that sort. You were not born yesterday, I take it. It is No. 24 Rue Notre-Dame-de-Lorette . . . . and *des Lorettes,** you understand?"

Mme. Didier remembered the girl with the cashmere, and revolted.

"No, Madame, give me another address."

The old woman was nettled at this refusal, and a wicked smile crept over her lips.

"As you please, my dear lady. You talk sensibly. But you will have to pay me, not forty cents, but two dollars. Then we will see about getting you a place in some higher sphere."

"Two dollars!" exclaimed the widow, in the same tone that she would have said two hundred dollars.

The agent understood.

"That ends it, then; good day."

"And my dollar?"

"Costs, my beauty. Registration, sixty cents; address, forty cents; total". . .

"It is a robbery."

"Ah! do not repeat that, or I will have you shut up. The operation is legal, under the authorization and protection of the police."

Mme. Didier, in consternation, turned her back to quit this den in which she left Jean's savings, her last coin and her last resource.

The old Gripon, reconsidering, recalled her.

"Listen," said she. "You are too silly altogether. Do people return money? 'What is good to take is good to keep,' says the proverb. Now that I think again, I have a place for you. A marvel. Rich people who are temporarily diminishing their retinue. A place as cook or head-servant". . . .

The widow snapped at the bait.

"Alas! I have nothing left," said she.

"Nothing at all? Really?"

"Not a cent!"

"Not even a pawn-ticket? My husband would take that of you. You could redeem it within a month. Ten per cent. interest, or a little more, as at the Mount of Piety."

"I have this," said Louise, taking out her certificate of seizure.

"Oh! bad! very bad!" exclaimed the old woman.

And, pretending a sudden sympathy, she added:

"But never mind, I will take it of you. To tell the truth, I am interested in you. I pressed you only to test you. We will get back your articles. We are licensed; that will be sufficient. I give you, or rather M. Gripon lends you, two dollars on this paper. There, sign that."

---

* *Des Lorettes,* of the Lorettes. *Lorette* is a term applied in Paris to a woman of pleasure occupying a position between the grisette and the kept mistress. Many of them live in Rue Notre-Dame-de-Lorette. — *Translator.*

Louise hesitated, and then signed.

The greedy old woman took two dollars from her cash-box and showed them to her.

"I keep this money and find you a place; is it agreed?"

"Thank you. But when and how shall I again get possession of these articles, which I prize?"

"Tomorrow, if you like, by paying two dollars and ten per cent. for the week. You understand?"

"It is well. And the place?"

"In a moment."

And the agent, adjusting her spectacles, looked at her attentively.

"You have an intelligent air," she said. "Wait."

Then she turned over the leaves of her book of addresses, and her eyes rested upon three lines written in red ink.

"Let me read once more this police note," said the agent, aside.

The note read as follows:

"Learn from the servants for whom you may find employment there all that goes on in this house, where many liberals are received."

After reading this, she closed her book.

"Say," said the Gripon, "you will come to see me often, will you not? We shall soon be two friends, and you will see that I will enable you to earn a great deal."

And, to trap her more surely, she added:

"Your little one shall lack nothing."

"Ah! so much the better," said the poor mother.

The agent imposed silence upon her with a gesture.

"Here is the address. . . . A godsend! . . . Upon my word, two dollars is nothing for it; I lose by the transaction."

Louise was all ears.

"Berville mansion, Rue du Louvre," read the Gripon.

"Oh! never, not there," cried Louise Didier, in a tone of mingled repugnance and fright.

"Ah! but this is too much," exclaimed the Gripon, rising in astonishment and indignation.

"No, not there! I do not want that place," repeated the widow, energetically.

"Not there!" cried the agent, containing herself no longer. "Why, you confounded ninny, you don't know what I offer you. It is more than silver, it is ingots of gold. You would be in the service, not only of the banker, but of the police, of the government. Idiot, there is a fortune to be shared."

She stopped, choking with anger and already regretting having said too much, and then continued:

"You will die of hunger, beggar, you and your". . . .

But Louise, without hearing more, had run out of the little closet into the hall
and thence into the street, away from the Gripon-Gavard, Jew and Christian den,
authorized and honored by the State and stigmatized by the People in three words
with this brand: *Canaille & Co.*

CHAPTER IX.

IN PARADISE.

The furious Gripon, stammering and grimacing, was still threatening the widow with her fist, when the door opened again before a woman dressed in puce-colored silk, a white apron, and a lace cap.

In this frightful three-story house, with a crime for every story, where for no other cause than hunger and thirst for gold, *auri sacra fames*, without preference of faith or race, circumcised and baptized, saviour of the damned and massacrer of the innocents, with leave and even on account of the Rue de Jérusalem, crime mounted, grew, and increased, spy, robber, and assassin, from the first to the third, there, we have said, at the top, at the very summit of this three-fold commerce, the midwife was proudly located, nearest to Heaven for which she labored all day long, by the day and by the job, at home and in the city, undertaking at a fair price anything that had to do with her profession.

She was another Gripon, younger, her pupil, a second edition, augmented, not corrected but aggravated, Mme. Gavard, the "maker of angels," the outfitter of Paradise, a monster prosperous, perfect, and patented!

"Well?" said she, in a tone of interrogation and surprise. "What is the matter with you?"

The old woman was choking.

"What is it?" again asked the Gavard.

"A horror . . . an abomination. . . Ah! my poor sister. . . You see. . . it is enough to disgust one with the profession."

"So serious as that?" exclaimed the midwife.

Mme. Gripon, calming her exasperation, was able at last to explain her professional mortification.

Raising her hands toward the ceiling, she said:

"Would you believe that I have just pitched a goose out doors ". . .

"Without plucking it?" said the midwife.

"No," replied the other.

"Oh! that's all right, then; I was going to say". . .

The employment agent continued, hissing like a viper rather than speaking:

"A sort of widow, a pauper . . . . more stupid than her hands . . . . a good-for-nothing . . . would you believe it? I offered her a place at the Bervilles', an address recommended by the prefect of police . . . . a real *chopin*, and we were to share ". . .

"And she wants the whole?"

"Oh, no. She refuses."

"Ah! Madame is honest!"

"Yes, too silly to accept," cried the Gripon, with redoubled rage.

"Pshaw!" said the midwife, trying to quiet her with a gesture. "Imbeciles are a necessity; without them, my God, how should we live?"

" Yes, but there is no need of too many of them. . . . To be imbecile to such a degree as that! She, the only one of the lot whom I did not want to victimize. That will teach me! Fortunately I shall get her watch and ring. With those I shall secure my revenge! She will find herself in a fine fix. I shall not let her off for less than ten per cent."

"Ten? That is the usual rate. You treat her as a friend," said the Gavard. "But let us leave her case for another and better one, that of the girl whom you sent up to me; I have come down in regard to her."

"Ah, yes, I had forgotten her."

"What are we to make out of her?"

" A good thing. Listen. Placed with *bourgeois*, in a family of magistrates, she is with child by the son of the house ". . .

" And we could threaten them with a great scandal?"

"Exactly."

"You believe it will succeed?"

" Why not? They are pious and rich. They will be frightened and will shell out. Be easy, I know these people. We have only to go and say to the papa: 'Monsieur, your young man, the State's-attorney's substitute, is going on at a great rate, my faith! But for us you would be the subject of a scandal that would pull everything down about your ears. Your former servant is with us, and wishes to give publicity to the story with which you are familiar. Enough said. Pay, and the mother will keep quiet, and so will the child.' And thereupon, without being seen or known, we pocket the money, and good evening!"

"Well, well!" observed the midwife, "but these are magistrates. We shall have to look out for ourselves."

".No danger. Are we going to send in our cards? We are not such geese. Just have your boarder write a word that will be understood, and we will start."

"All right," approved the Gavard. "Who risks nothing ". . .

And she went up stairs again.

A few minutes later she came down, holding in her hand a sheet of paper covered with bad writing.

"There, will that do?" she asked her sister.

The old Gripon read attentively:

I declare that it is in consequence of my misconduct with a *valet de chambre* of the establishment that I have been discharged by M. Bardin.   My pregnancy is this servant's doing. This is the truth.   Anything that I have said about M. Bardin or his son is simply falsehood and calumny, for which I humbly ask pardon.

"A little too correct, but that's nothing.   It will do as it is, and we shall get fifty dollars, at least."

"No more than that?" said Mme. Gavard.   "We shall see."

The two women went out quickly.

As they passed by Abraham Gripon's shop, they opened the door, and the young woman said to the old Jew, with a wink:

"We are going out on urgent and profitable business.   A first-class case of confinement.   You will look out for matters up-stairs, will you not?"

"All right," said the usurer, "I will keep the house with Ismaël.   The child will repeat his four rules."

"Two and two make five," cried Ismaël, "and two from four leaves three."

And the family burst out laughing.

As they walked along, the two women began to talk like the two good sisters that they were.

"Let us agree carefully about our facts," said the Gavard, lowering her voice. "Shall we send the child to the Board of Public Charities?   Or ". . . .

"That will depend upon the *bourgeois*.   We will give them to understand that foundlings may be found again, while ". . . .

"Yes, but then it is more expensive."

"Undoubtedly.   We must push the matter to the extremity," insisted the Gripon.   "And with the Italian whom you took the other day ". . . .

"I have a market for my products ; you are right.   Paolo has made a bad stroke at the Hotel d'Italie.   I have confessed him a little.   I hold him.   Each day makes its 'angel.'   Things are progressing famously now, and I am overrun with business ; frankly, I needed somebody."

"Then it is agreed ". . . .

"In Paradise !" said the Gavard.

"Hush !" whispered the employment agent.   "There is my widow."

Louise Didier was in front of them, sinking upon a step under her load of sorrow, fatigue, and want, reduced to the last extremity.

The Gripon pointed her out with a gesture of contempt.

"It is good enough for you," she said.   "Die or beg !"

And she passed by, leading the midwife after her, who approved her words with a wicked smile.

"Beg," repeated the exhausted widow, when the two knaves had passed. "Truly, I cannot die here and leave Marie alone, her father dead.   Oh, bread ! bread !   No false shame !   That would be pride.   Yes, for my child."

At that moment a fashionable lady, holding a schoolboy by the hand, approached. It was Mlle. Gertrude de Berville and the young Camille, seeming rather to be fleeing from this populous quarter than returning home after the performance of some good deed.

It must be stated here that Jean, who followed the widow like her shadow, nevertheless had left her to find the honest Brémont and induce him to help the wife and child of the deceased.

"I saw that you were afflicted as I was by the death of Jacques," he had said to the cashier, "and I come to ask your aid for his poor family. It is very annoying to me to beg, seeing that it is not my trade, but I can do nothing myself, and it is useless to attempt the impossible."

Brémont, pressing his hand, dismissed him and went at once to recommend the Didiers to Gertrude.

Thus it was that the pious old maid and the hearty child found themselves together at this hour in the Faubourg Saint-Antoine.

"Oh!" said Gertrude to Camille, "I begin to regret my carriage. The idea of going to such a place on foot! But then, we owed a visit to the widow of this poor Didier. She is not at home. So much the worse; our duty is done."

"But suppose she is in want?" said the child.

"We have left her our address. She will know very well how to find us, never fear!"

Louise Didier had heard nothing of this rapid conversation. Not knowing Gertrude and unknown to her, urged by hunger, making up her mind and lowering her head, she advanced in a supplicating attitude with outstretched hand, and said in a low voice:

"Pity, Madame . . . if you". . . and her voice stopped, her hand fell, and her tears began to flow. "I never can," she said.

Gertrude drew back as if frightened.

The child, affected, was already hunting in his purse for money.

Mlle. Gertrude saw his movement, and stopped him.

"No, Camille, we must not encourage begging on the public streets; it favors vice or laziness. Be generous only where you know the circumstances, my child; there lies the merit of generosity. Let us give only to the good poor of our friend the abbé Ventron". . . .

The old maid had very hurriedly expressed her doctrine of formal charity, doubling her pace to get rid of the very sight of the poor woman.

Surprised at not being pursued and annoyed, she looked back and saw the wretched woman sinking back upon the stone, overcome by shame and despair.

Retracing her steps, though not her doctrine, and without contradicting herself by the gift of an obolus, she nevertheless had a pharisaical word for the satisfaction of her conscience.

"If you are in need, why do you not apply to your parish-church or to the Board of Public Charities?"

And, believing herself acquitted of responsibility by this good advice, she passed on, leading Camille after her.

Unconvinced and mutinous, remembering the bread tickets, the child repeated: "Poor woman! Oh! it is not good, Gertrude; no, it is not good. Mother would have given her something."

And he threw back, toward Louise, his little purse, which a *professional* picked up.

CHAPTER X.

AT THE PARISH-CHURCH.

The widow had doubtless shed all the tears in her body, for she wept no more. She gave a dry cough, a long shiver, and a sigh.

"These rich people," said she, "they do not know! Oh! how hungry I am. . . and cold!"

Not a cry of revolt, not a word of hatred.

Before begging, she had tried to borrow at usury, but in vain; then she thought of getting a loan as a favor, but she did not know Dupont's address, and, as for the baker, she was already in his debt. She was in a corner.

"To die or to beg," she continued. "To die! to rejoin my poor Jacques, that would be so good. But no. What would become of Marie? I cannot take her with us into the grave. I have no right to do so. Well! to beg? Yes, but no longer in the street. The parish-church, the Board of Public Charities . . . . the lady is right; that is less distressing. Come, courage! to suffer, always to suffer, but bravely, such is my life henceforth."

Feverish, with death in her heart, determined however upon all sacrifices, not for herself, but for the fruit of her love, the noble woman resumed her painful journey from one station to another.

She was in front of St. Paul's Church; she crossed the threshold and made her way into the nave.

They were saying mass.

A Swiss, a burlesque remnant of the temporal power, all covered with velvet and gold, carrying a cane, sword, and halberd, a soldier of the good God of armies, proud of his position and consequently haughty, attracted the attention of the widow.

She advanced toward him, and, with an effort to put firmness into her voice, said:

"I should like to speak to Monsieur the priest."

"To Monsieur the priest," repeated the Swiss, astonished at the enormity of the request.

"Or to a vicar," continued Louise, seeing her mistake.

"For a mass?"

"No; for help."

The Swiss turned upon his heels.

"Speak to the beadle," said he, with a disdain that bordered on disgust.

The widow obeyed, and was sent by the beadle to the sexton, who sent her flying to the church-warden, very busily engaged just then in twirling his silver chain with his fingers.

"Monsieur". . . .

"Well?" exclaimed the sexton's subordinate, without raising his eyes.

"To whom should I apply to solicit ". . . .

"To me, first."

"My husband has been killed . . . I have a little girl . . . no work . . . rent-day is at hand ". . . .

"Have you your last year's certificates of confession? Monseigneur Quélen's charge requires one every month."

"I received the sacrament only at Easter," ventured Louise Didier, "and ". . . .

"At Easter! Well! you shall have your help at Trinity."

"But I follow my religion strictly," insisted Louise. "My daughter is baptized."

"The only point left for you to fail in," exclaimed the beadle, with horror.

"In future . . . since it is necessary ". . . .

"Pshaw! pshaw! we have our poor who come to mass every morning, confess every week, and receive the sacrament once a month at least."

"But, Monsieur, generally I am at work."

"Work, then, and leave the aid for the faithful who do not work. Moreover, you have only to write to Monsieur the priest; he will answer you."

And the church rat, satisfied at having staved off an applicant in accordance with his instructions, resumed his interrupted occupation, twirling his chain with an increasing interest.

The widow went out of this other den, not of Jews, but of Christians, where the Catholic, apostolic, and Roman Gripons rarely lend, always take, and never restore money.

As she reached the portal, she met the Swiss, striking the flagging with his heavy gold-headed cane, before Monsieur the priest who was collecting: *For the poor of the parish*, with a very pronounced and very conclusive *If you please.*

CHAPTER XI.

Determined to struggle against fate to the end, the widow started for the department of Public Charities, the last station of her cross.

Private and religious charity was refused to her; Louise was about to have recourse to public charity, to civil beneficence, to social and official aid, hoping to finish there her Golgotha of pain and shame.

She inquired the way to the Charity Office, reached there, and was at last admitted into a waiting-room, a Calvary full of the scum of civilization, of a detritus of both sexes or rather of no sex, of shabby and decrepit old people, so old that death seemed to have forgotten them, so ugly that they seemed to have frightened death away.

There Madame Didier again had to wait her turn amid this needy crowd, which, by no means disposed to share and embittered by fear of want, already repulsed her with eyes, gesture, and voice, as a competitor, an enemy, coming to cut down the shares of the *habitués.*

"She is not a *mendigotte,*" the word was passed round.

An attendant, a good fellow like his chief, whose duty it was to keep order in the room, noticed the widow as she advanced, trembling and with lowered head.

" A new one!" said he, "and timid. . . Come with me. Silence in the crowd, do you hear, subscribers? Otherwise your incomes will be cut off."

The threat had its effect. Needy and lazy, parasites and pariahs, beggars pro. fessional and beggars occasional, all became quiet. The recriminations died out in a sullen growl.

Louise Didier followed her escort toward an office situated at the end of a gallery.

There she found herself before a stout gentleman seated at a double desk. Opposite him was a young secretary, with pen raised and eye attentive, ready to write at his chief's dictation.

The poor woman could not have felt a more poignant emotion in presence of an examining magistrate.

She lifted her eyes humbly upon the man who was about to decide her fate.

The kind face of the chief inspired her with confidence.

"Monsieur," said she, "I come to you in despair". . . .

And in one outburst of frankness she told the story of her misfortune, omitting no detail, insisting on her child who was "dying by a slow fire," to use the popular expression. She finished by soliciting immediate aid.

The chief of the department had listened with a certain benevolence.

"Undoubtedly. . . I do not say no. . . Didier? . . . To be sure. . . . I read of the crime in the newspapers. But, by the way, why do you not apply to your husband's employer . . . M. Berville, I believe?"

Mme. Didier shook her head without replying.

"Nothing to be done in that direction?" said the chief of the department.

"Ah! that astonishes me. Died in their service!"

The distressed widow cut short these reflections.

"I have neither the power nor the desire to apply elsewhere than to the Board of Public Charities. I am unfortunate. Is not that enough, Monsieur?"

"In principle, yes. In practice, no. We have to deal every day with individuals—I do not refer to you—who positively live on public charity. With them it is a real profession, and a lucrative one, I assure you. I know some who regularly collect their revenues from the parish-church, from the Department of Charity, from a hundred benevolent persons, here and everywhere. We are duped every minute by idlers who know all the tricks of beggary and get a better living at it than any workingman. Under these circumstances we are forced to be extremely distrustful and circumspect. Generally the really needy do not ask; the genuinely poor are proud."

"I have a child," replied Louise Didier, wounded by these observations. "It is for her, not for myself, that I . . . beg!"

"Well, it is your right. I wanted to make you understand that you ask an impossible thing. Immediate aid! But you must remember that, even with exceptional celerity, it takes at least a week to go through all the formalities required in such a case."

"What formalities?"

"You do not know, then, that we shall have to write to the mayor of the place where you were born, and then make inquiries at your residence?"

"Why?"

"We shall go to M. Berville's house and yours. Your neighbors, and especially your janitor, will be questioned in regard to you."

"But, Monsieur, I shall no longer be able to take a step in the neighborhood."

"Ah! my lady, we can have nothing without pain. You will have to make up your mind."

"And how much shall I obtain by means of this humiliation?"

"About two dollars a month, or even two and a half. Sometimes we give as high as three, where there is great poverty and a large family."

"Ten cents a day. Well, that would help me!"

"You consent! Do not forget that you will be under our supervision; we are

obliged to have a special police by way of precaution.   You will have to call here
at regular intervals."

"My God! my God!"

" Let us see, where were you born? "

"Near Epinal, Monsieur, at " . . .

"In Vosges! You should have told me that at the start.   That department has
no treaty with the Paris Board of Public Charities.   They would not repay us,
and therefore" . . . .

"Therefore?"

"We can do nothing for you; beyond giving you a few bread-tickets perhaps."

"Thank you, Monsieur."

"Unless you wish to return to your native place by stages."

"Yes, Monsieur," she said, with proud irony, "thank you for your information;
I am in a hurry to return, and am going to take the post. . . . for I am hungry
. . . . a glass of water for me" . . .

She did not finish, but fainted.

The attendant gave her the glass of water of the Gospel.

The widow recovered her senses and went out, bowing to the astonished chief
of the department.

Then, again escorted by the attendant, she passed a second time through the
waiting-room.

The beggars, male and female, divined her failure in the confusion which covered her face.

Exclamations of spite and satisfaction were exchanged.

"The blonde is upset! "

"The young woman got left! "

"The beauty is done for! "

The attendant had pity on her, and as she disappeared in the stairway, he recalled her and said:

"Stay, go mingle with the crowd there.   Talk with them, and you will find out
where soup, linen, and even pennies are distributed, morning and evening, at the
houses of the 'good heads,' as they call them."

Then, looking at her with a complacency and an absence of moral sense peculiar
to his philanthropic business, he added:

"But no. . . . listen a moment.   You are not smart.   To beg here is to waste
your time, as pretty as you are."

The widow went away, bedaubed with this last insult.   A handful of mud after
the thrust of a knife.

•   •   •   •   •   •   •   •   •   •   •   •   '   •   •   •   •

Thus religious and civil aid, the assistance of Church and of State, of God and of man, one of the two (which of the two?) made in the image of the other, the en-tire official and officious almsgiving machinery, failed a woman in the most sociable of societies.

Behind the dirty cart of a dirty knacker, drawn by a dirty horse and loaded with a dead jade, its four feet in the air and its neck hanging and bleeding, follow a file of beasts old and valueless, utterly worn out, with nothing but skin on their bones, walking carcasses, some lame in the left foot, others in the right foot, some even in both feet. They walk or rather are dragged to the slaughter-house, whipped toward death, unconscious and docile beasts, who, serving man all their lives, now go to receive the finishing stroke and furnish after their death the leather with which to bridle and lash their fellows.

Sad emblem of the poor man who, in spite of the right professed by modern so-ciety, gives all his life to clothe, feed, and defend the rich man, and, dead, gives also to science even his body to cure him.

In the bosom of the Tiber of ancient Rome, on a deserted island, the pagan slaughter-house guarded by Cæsar's soldiers, they landed the old and useless slaves, there to die of hunger; but at least after having sufficiently fed them, as horses are fed, during their lives of service, and without subjecting them, as the modern slave is subjected, to the torture of Tantalus, starvation in the midst of abundance, hunger at the doors of Paris restaurants.

Animals, you have no reason to envy the "king of creation"; slaves of Rome, you were tortured less than the "sovereign people" of France!

Even in Rome, when Paganism was at its height, death was only for invalid old age. In Paris as in Pekin, amid European civilization as amid Asiatic barbarism, death even for children!

CHAPTER XII.

AT AUCTION.

Jean, who was neither a deputy, nor a peer, nor a judge, nor a priest, and as little of a deist as a royalist, had kept his oath, faithful to his conscience, to the promise which he had given himself over the body of Jacques.

He drank no more, ate little, slept still less, and worked a great deal, watching incessantly over Didier's wife and child.

"I will do what I can to aid them," he had said to the dying collector.

But what can a rag-picker do for others? Scarcely can he do anything for himself!

He did more than he could. Every night a double basket, beginning early, finishing late, leaving his hole before twilight, returning to it after daybreak, the first and the last of the night-walkers. He went to the muck-heap with the same ardor with which he formerly went to the wine-shop.

Hence, on the night preceding the third day after the murder of Jacques, Jean had gone out and come in twice with two full baskets.

He had gone out a third time.

Having taken quarters in the very house where the widow lived, a benevolent spy, he never abandoned his watch except to help her.

"Poor woman," he continually said to himself, "she has nothing from the banker and what from the rag-picker? If I were rich, if I only had enough to pay the rent and the funeral expenses. What a life, or rather what death! All day on the run! All night on the watch between a corpse and a cradle! And on top of all the rest the police pestering her with their inquests and visits. They would do much better to catch the guilty than to mangle the victims."

He was thus soliloquizing during his third trip, when he had a singular meeting beside a pile of dirt.

An individual, tolerably well-dressed but suspicious in appearance, had stopped there before him and thrown a bundle into it.

Jean, suddenly coming up, thrust his hook into the heap, when the individual, who had started as if to retreat, noticed by the light of the lantern the rag-picker's basket, stopped short, and, seized with an irresistible fit of curiosity, said to Jean:

"Where did you get that basket, I should like to know?"

"That doesn't concern you, friend," said Jean, in little humor for talking, especially on that subject.

And again he plunged in his hook.

"Oh! what's this! an infant!"

His hook had torn open the bundle, which contained a still-born babe.

"Another crime! Police! Police!" he cried with all his might.

Then the individual wheeled about as if to run away.

"What! the coat fits you? Stop!"

And Jean seized him, shouting at the top of his voice:

"Police! Where are they? Sleeping with servants or hidden in doorways? Hurry up; don't be afraid! It's only a dead baby!"

An officer came at last.

"What is the matter?"

"Here, see what I have found," said Jean, still keeping a firm grip upon the individual. "This is the gentleman who threw that there."

"No, no," cried the individual, struggling, gesticulating, and swearing in Italian.

"Your name?" asked the officer.

"Paolo, an employee at". . . .

And he stopped short.

"Where? Tell me, or I arrest you."

"At Madame Gavard's."

"What does she do?"

Again Paolo hesitated.

"She is a midwife."

"Indeed!" cried Jean.

"Well, let us be off, then. To the station-house, everybody," decided the officer.

"To kill a child, there's a crime for you! We know what a grown man is, but a child we cannot know," said Jean to himself, thinking of the little Marie as he carried the poor body to the station-house.

Then he returned to his work, and in a frenzy threw the rags into his basket.

At last, reaching home again, overcome with fatigue, he threw himself upon his pallet, where he slept until late in the morning.

What was going on in his neighbor's room during his morning slumber?

She did not sleep. She had been, not wakened from her sleep, but shaken from her stupor by a veritable invasion of her room.

Janitor, proprietor, process-server, auctioneer, auctioneer's clerk, second-hand dealers, and buyers, who came, in the name of justice, to execute the law!

Ravage followed invasion.

The process-server brought an execution for the last quarter's rent, the payment of which had been delayed in consequence of Louise Didier's confinement.

The auctioneer immediately took possession, sitting down rudely in the arm-chair in which Louise had passed the night and from which she had just risen with a start.

The clerk asked her for the keys to her furniture, opened the different pieces, took out the linen and anything that he found, laying everything pell-mell, upside down, in parcels, on the table, where the auctioneer took note of the lots of the poor establishment.

The proprietor reviewed each article with an anxious eye, coldly calculating whether the whole would suffice to pay the rent.

The public subjected to the same careful scrutiny all the articles to be sold, weighing them, estimating their condition and value, the women especially admiring their cleanliness.

The auction began with the bed coverlet.

The auctioneer picked it up roughly, revealing, stiff upon its couch,—this at least unseizable,—the pale corpse of the bank collector.

Louise, stifling a cry, covered Jacques's face with her handkerchief, the body having been left there for the inquest and now awaiting burial.

"A woollen blanket, very clean, without a hole or a stain, in good condition! A dollar, did I hear that bid?" cried the auctioneer, quickly recovering from his astonishment.

"Dollar ten," said the proprietor.

"Dollar twenty," said an old woman, enviously.

"Dollar forty," cried a second-hand dealer, the Jew Gripon.

"Ah! if Canaille & Co. are here, we are done for," said the old woman to her neighbors. "It's a pity."

"Dollar fifty," rejoined the proprietor.

"Dollar sixty," said the old woman.

"Dollar eighty," answered another second-hand dealer, with an Auvergnat accent.

"One Auvergnat is worth two Jews; there's no hope," said the old woman, in a rage.

And there was silence for a time.

"Dollar eighty," repeated the auctioneer, having an interest, like the proprietor, in getting a high price on account of his percentage; "why, that's nothing at all! don't you see that it's almost new?"

"Dollar ninety," pushed on the proprietor.

"Two dollars," exclaimed the Auvergnat.

"Disgusting!" cried the old woman; "I drop it entirely."

Again there was silence.

"Two dollars . . . no one says a word? Once, twice, going, going, gone!" said the auctioneer, letting fall a black and white hammer with an ebony handle and an ivory head.

Louise had not left her husband's side; she stood erect, petrified, the statue of grief.

The sale went on.

She looked at this crowd in her orderly home, upsetting, depreciating, profaning its chaste and sober interior, everything that she had that was private, precious, and dear in her domestic life, these poor nothings in order which had cost her so much toil and care, these small treasures of her past happiness, these solemn witnesses of happy days, these gifts associated with joyful memories, some paid for by her labor, others surprises of her husband for her birthday, even to her wedding-wreath, the entire museum of her love ransacked, scattered, disparaged, sold at a reduction, at a contemptible price, in presence of herself and her dead husband.

She felt herself becoming mad, unable longer to stand, as if they had torn, sold, and carried away the shreds of her heart.

"A cradle," cried the auctioneer.

At this word she leaped like a lioness toward her child.

"Do not touch," she cried, and, throwing herself upon Marie, she lifted her from the cradle, suddenly wakened by the noise, moaning and wailing in her mother's arms.

"Make your child keep quiet," said the auctioneer, continuing:

"A wicker cradle, trimmed with muslin, very clean. Forty cents. Keep the child quiet, I tell you, or go out; we can hear nothing."

To quiet the child, the mother gave her her breast. Alas! there came from it only a thread of reddish serum. Suffering had turned everything . . . . no more milk, nothing but blood!

The child cried with hunger and shook convulsively.

Then Louise Didier, as if impelled by an extreme resolution, went out suddenly with her daughter hanging on her neck.

"Good enough!" said the satisfied auctioneer.

"A cradle, forty cents". . .

"Fifty," cried a young wife, who seemed to have a pregnant woman's desire for the article. And the auction went on briskly.

Jean, awakened also by the noise of the sale, had come down from his garret to the chamber; and, seeing the door open and the room full of people, he entered and stood for a moment dumbfounded by what he saw and heard.

"What's the matter? What's this? What! What! An auction here!" he cried at last to the janitor.

"Well, what of it? You see for yourself. You can hear as well as I. We are selling everything to get the rent. What then?" answered the janitor, indifferently.

Still a warm dispute was going on for the cradle.

"And Mme. Didier?" said Jean, alarmed.

"Gone out."

"And the child?"

"With her."

"And where?"

"Faith, I don't know."

"When?"

"Just now."

Jean asked nothing more, but started like a ball, leaping down the stairs and rushing like a madman into the street after Mme. Didier. . . .

"A pretty little cradle," continued the auctioneer. "See, ladies, all white, fresh, and trimmed, at only a dollar. It's no price at all; it's worth double the money."

"Dollar ten," said the young woman.

"Dollar twenty," answered the proprietor.

"But you are a bachelor; you have no need of that."

"Dollar thirty."

"Dollar forty," said the Auvergnat.

"Dollar sixty," said the Jew.

"Are you going to have a baby, like me, old Auvergnat?" cried the exasperated young woman; "and you, old Jew, can your old Rebecca still make little Jacobs?"

"Dollar eighty," answered Gripon, without laughing.

And there was another period of silence.

"Once, twice. Dollar eighty! No more amateurs? For the third time. Dollar eighty! Sold!"

The sale concluded: all the furniture,—clothes-press, chest of drawers, cupboard, table, chairs; all the linen, —sheets, table-cloths, shirts, napkins, handkerchiefs; all the household implements, —shovels, tongs, broom, dustbrush; all the humble utensils of the poor woman's kitchen; all the wearing-apparel, — garments, shoes, caps;—everything passed under the fatal hammer, everything was struck and coined into money for the pocket of the proprietor, the official, and the second-hand dealer.

The spoils were divided in the interest of those three harpies, — property, the law, and usury.

As for the creature who had acquired and accumulated it all by dint of labor and economy, nothing was left for her but her weeping eyes. And as for her sisters in poverty who hoped for bits of her effects, they had to buy them on the instalment plan from the three monopolists.

The proprietor held out against the Auvergnat and the Jew and arranged with them to surrender, in consideration of a premium, all that he had bid in,—in short, he was repaid and more.

The Jew and the Auvergnat, hand and glove together, sold to advantage all that they had bought—coverlet, cradle, furniture, linen, etc.— to the old and young wives, who paid double and triple according to their necessities. Then all was over,—the furniture removed, the room evacuated, the door closed; and each retired, speculating and commenting upon his profits and losses, more or less content.

Meanwhile Jean had overtaken Madame Didier with his eyes, and was following her as if he were her dog.

CHAPTER XIII.

RETURN TO THE BOARD OF PUBLIC CHARITIES.

In the Public Charities building a bare and gloomy room, divided into two by a wooden barrier, was devoted to the reception of abandoned infants.

Unfortunate or degraded mothers, indifferent or constrained relatives, midwives or simple commissioners, came to this human pawn-shop to pledge forever their own children or the children of others.

On this first day of April poverty had driven a number of unfortunates to this ante-room of the hospital for found, or rather lost, children.

The aspect of the room was terrible from the very variety of its phases of despair and shame.

Some of the women, silent or excited, resigned or maddened, with eyes moist or burning, offered for the last time an exhausted and withered bosom to the fruit of their love, while awaiting the supreme and frightful sacrifice of Carthage to Paris.

By the side of the mothers were step-mothers, with eyes dry and hard, sneering at these mute sorrows which condemned them. Some brought their children to save them, others to lose them. These, unfortunate, were no longer able to feed their poor offspring; those, rarer and more miserable, were no longer willing to do so!

"Poverty is not a vice," said Voltaire; "it is much worse." Yes, it is a crime, a social crime! Where were the responsible authors of these miseries? For, when a woman falls, it is because a man has pushed her. In love there is no fault without an accomplice, and the accomplice here is the real author. And the law, as immoral as the prostitution which it creates, maintains, and regulates, prohibits search for the original criminal in forbidding inquiry as to paternity.

Yes, most of these destitute creatures had committed their "fault" perforce, driven to it by poverty! Their babies had no father. . . . No father! O law of nature! O so-called civil code!

On the bench, between two midwives, in a hurry to finish their professional duty, a man in the prime of life, the workingman of the Mount of Piety, dandled an infant feverishly upon his knees. In his whole person there was something tragic, an immense sentiment of tenderness mingled with indignation and even with rebellion.

In front of him a vixen, abominably drunk, was constantly on the point of dropping her offspring, which, all covered with pustules, seemed to have an alcoholic head.

The clerk in charge of this infernal office registered the abandonments, talking to the women in a supercilious and wearied tone. He was in a hurry to get through. . . . and while the mothers stifled their sobs and embraced their crying babies, he looked at the clock and rolled a cigarette.

From time to time he stormed.

"A little silence! Whose turn next?"

The habit of following this diabolical calling had hardened the bureaucrat against emotion. Through handling iron the blacksmith gets callous hands; this clerk had a callous heart. He wrote rapidly, unmoved by the mothers' tears falling under his pen and moistening the fatal registry.

The midwives came first, no one disputing this privilege with them; then the liquor-soaked woman advanced to offer her bud.

"Here'sh a present I make you," said she to the clerk. "Soon you will have a pair."

The bureaucrat turned away to avoid breathing the odor of brandy which the creature exhaled.

"Pooh!" he exclaimed. "Why don't you keep your child?"

"Can't. My husband drinks disgustingly."

"And you?"

"I, never. Besides, my husband beats me, and my milk spoils. Understand? It is to save the brat."

"All right; hand it over!"

"There you are. Good luck, little glutton, you will suck at the municipal bottle. Don't deprive yourself! get full, like papa."

"And mamma," said the clerk; "she ought to be condemned to water."

"To water yourself! Oh! it's poison. . . . not good even for drunkards."

"Another! and quickly!"

And as the mothers naturally did not hurry, and looked at each other with terror, the clerk hailed the workingman.

"Say, you there, come forward. A man. . . . this is a pretty how-do-you-do!"

The workingman started under the insult.

"Confounded clerk, attend to your scribbling," he cried. "Ah! one of these days, and before long too, we'll give it to you."

"Threats!"

"Until we can do better. To think that we have to pay all these quill-drivers for bullying us!"

"Go on, I hear," said the clerk, "you are a red. . . . or rather a loafer."

"Yes, a forced loafer; I am out of work, and I have only my arms with which to feed my child. I am not in the same case as you, who have enough to feed the child that perhaps you do not possess or that you lay in the nest of others."

"Enough, we know the tune. Your name?"

"Brutus Chaumette."

"Good, the name goes with the principles. You are a spirit of the great epoch, it seems."

"Yes, republican from father to son."

"Well, this shall end the race. We will bring it up differently. It shall be a royalist."

"We shall see."

"You had better take it back. Why leave it with us?"

"Why? Because her mother is dead, and I cannot give her suck, and I wish her to live."

"What is her name?"

"Marianne."

"Oh, that's promising! Here, put your name at the bottom of this sheet."

The workingman signed, kissed the little girl, and then went out, turning back toward the clerk and shaking his fist at him.

The bureaucrat, while filling out Marianne's registration paper, gave a lecture on morality *ad hoc* to the poor women whom he was under instructions to treat harshly in order to turn as many of them as possible away from the budget of Public Charities for the benefit of the budget-eaters, the biggest, fattest, and most insatiable of beggars.

So the official, faithful to this order of exclusion, growled away as he scribbled:

"Ah! I know you, my wenches, and it will be vain for you to deny what I say; only unnatural mothers come here. . . . No excuses! Without work? . . . . . ta-ra-ta-ta, without work, yes! When people make children, they must keep them. No pleasure without pain. Indeed, that would be too convenient. They come from the country to Paris, believing that larks are going to fall all roasted into their beaks. . . . Think of it! . . . . And what happens? They do not work, they allow themselves to be inveigled. . . . they commit a *fault*, as you call it. After the performance comes abandonment. They are left alone. . . . the man goes and the kid comes. . . . Then they whine and cry poverty; and then at the last they bring up here as at "my aunt's." Ah! but, you know, it is not the same to the end. Here they pawn, but they cannot redeem. A child found for the Public Charities is a child lost for the mamma. A warning to such as have hearts. There is still time."

This harangue, ingeniously drawn up and learned and recited by heart, had on this occasion, as it always had, an excellent result for the administration; three or four women, the best of them, rose and went out, taking their babies. But patience: poverty does not lose its rights; mothers and children will be found tonight drowned in the Seine or hanging to some nail or suffocated in their room. Ah! these suicides are murders!

The pitiless clerk, undoubtedly decorated for this, went on with his task, registering social conditions, passing the abandoned little ones to a woman in waiting, and in exchange handing the unfortunates papers to sign.

At four o'clock in the afternoon the room was empty. The clerk resumed his ease and lighted his cigarette.

"Ah! it's over," said he, stretching his arms carelessly. "No damage. A dog's life. Always the same thing. What a bore! Oh! if there were no perquisites!"

At that moment two new faces appeared in the room. The first, Mme. Gavard, made her entrance superbly with an infant under each arm.

The clerk was as polite to her as he had been rude to the others. A smile spread over his entire face. He even forgot his cigarette.

The midwife advanced straight to the desk, sure of her business and of a cordial welcome, as an *habituée*, even as a friend, almost as mistress of the establishment. Why? Administrative mystery.

"Here are two for today," said she, depositing her double burden on the table and then extending to the clerk a hand which did not seem empty.

The girl charged with verifying the sex approached complacently and said in a loud voice:

"Male sex."

And, without further formalities, she carried the infants into an adjoining room.

"Just born, at my house, no name, father and mother unknown," said the Gavard, expeditiously.

"All right! sign, please," said the clerk.

The midwife signed, and went to sit down and talk with the examiner, who had come in again.

"No one else . . . no . . . yes, there is! What is it that you want, you there?" cried the clerk.

He had just noticed a dark shadow at the rear of the room, the woman who had entered behind the Gavard.

He went on scolding:

"Ah! you don't hear then? Is your business for today or tomorrow?"

The woman thus appealed to dragged herself toward the desk.

She was hardened to all outrages, and had already, on revisiting this hell, met one insult more as she entered, from the jovial attendant of the charity office, who had said to her in passing:

"Back from Epinal already?"

But she was no longer sensible or conscious of anything except the desperate act which she came to perform.

"I beg pardon, Monsieur," said she, "but". . . .

"No buts. We will put this through in two times and three motions. Besides, it is purely an accommodation on my part. Shall we say, then, that you abandon your child?"

"Yes . . . it is necessary ". . . .

"Naturally. . . And of course it is yours, at least?"

"Oh! yes," burst out the mother; "Marie . . . farewell! I shall die."

"Oh! that's the usual racket; come, pass the child to Madame."

The woman in waiting, the cynical examiner, seated on a camp-bed covered with haircloth, rose listlessly and took the baby, which began to cry, being frightened and hungry.

"Bah! you will see many others," said she, stretching the little one on the hard bed and unswathing her rudely, as one opens a bundle to verify its contents.

The mother had fallen on the bench.

"What's your name, Mam'zelle?" asked the clerk.

"Madame Didier," answered the widow, proudly.

The bureaucrat turned to the examiner.

"What? . . . male?" he asked.

"No, Monsieur, it is a girl," the mother hastened to answer, wounded by this brutal question.

"No one spoke to you," said the clerk; "you saw well enough that I addressed myself to the *searcher.*"

"Feminine sex," said the latter, rolling the child up in its linen.

"Oh! you will hurt her," cried the mother, as if she had felt the shock herself.

"That's not your business now," answered the clerk, who went on filling out the registry blanks until he reached the heading: *Motives.*

"Why do you abandon your child?" he said, repeating the question which he had put to the workingman a little while before.

"Why do I abandon her?" repeated the widow, with a look of surprise.

"Yes; answer!"

"Because I cannot do anything else, Monsieur; because I have no more milk," said Louise, staggering as if she had been drunk; "because it is my blood that flows ". . .

"Blood . . . or wine."

"Oh! wretch," murmured the widow, falling back on her bench; "have I, then, committed a crime, that I should be punished in this way?"

The clerk did not hear or did not want to hear.

"Received!" he cried to the girl, who disappeared with the child through a low door-way on the other side of the barrier.

And he continued in a tone of doubt:

"Then you say this child has a father?"

"No, Monsieur."

"That's it, she has no father."

"She no longer has one."

"I understand; he is traveling. Known?"

"He is dead," replied the widow; "murdered at night while defending his collections. And if you doubt it, come with me. He is at our house . . . this is the third day, and I have no money to pay for his burial."

"The devil! look out for disease in the house," said the clerk. "Murdered . . . stay! we will put down this detail!"

And he mentioned this "detail" on his register, interested by the peculiarity of the circumstance; then, handing a sheet of paper to the widow, he said:

"Sign that . . . good! . . . Now, I must tell you of the regulations. Your daughter will be sent into the country in the course of a fortnight. You will not know where she is, do you understand?"

"But, Monsieur," cried Louise, horrified by this atrocious revelation, the crown of this scheme of official charity invented by the believers in the family . . . "but it is impossible. I swear to you that I will take the child back right away, as soon as I can find a way to earn my living. Oh! it will not be long!"

The bureaucrat shook his head impatiently.

"Take it back . . . You will not see it again, I tell you. The most that can be granted you, if you get work and behave yourself, is an occasional bulletin of life . . . or of death, as the case may be; and it is rather the latter that you should expect. There's not one in five that . . . But that will do. Go; good evening."

The mother gave an inexpressible cry. She rushed to the railing and leaped over it, crying with love, fright, and fury:

"My child! Give me back my child! I take her again."

"You have signed! Stop!" cried the bureaucrat, but he could not prevent her.

Mad and strong with grief, she opened the low door through which Marie had disappeared in the examiner's arms, and found herself in a large, dismal room, recalling the infants' limbos of the Æneid, filled with poor little creatures, consumptive and timid, some stretched upon benches, others stuffed into coarse cradles, all guarded and watched by Sisters of Charity, most of whom were old and whose repressed maternity had turned, by a sort of physical and moral allotropy, into poisoned gall. Parodies of motherhood, caricatures of womanhood, jailers of childhood, guardians of this orphans' morgue, they glided about like black spectres, with rods in their hands, ill-tempered and awkward, distributing among their angels consecrated box, holy water, and whippings, instead of caresses, cakes, and toys.

Louise uttered a groan.

"Where is Marie?" she cried, in anguish, looking about among the mass.

"Find her," said a sharp voice.

"Lost! I want her; she is mine! She is my child!"

A wail answered her.

Without heeding the fright and indignation of the good Sisters, the mother ran to a distant cradle, whence came a familiar plaint, which had moved the mother to the heart.

"You!" said she, grasping and clasping her with frenzy. "Not take you back, not see you again! She live without me and I without her! Never! never! we will die together."

On returning to the office, she found herself face to face with Jean, who cried out to her:

"No, you shall live together."

Jean, who had, as we know, caught sight of her and followed her to the Public Charities building, had then gone almost at one bound to the Berville mansion, where, fortunately, he had found the good and honest Brémont.

Then he had returned quickly, in a perspiration, with joyous heart, pockets full, and hands loaded with a cradle and other articles.

"I arrive in time, and with all that you need; you have taken her back, that's the main thing," said he to the stupefied Louise; "put Marie in this cradle, and come; I will carry everything home. Thanks to M. Brémont, a worthy man, you will pay rent, funeral expenses, and all. Let us leave here, and quickly!"

And he led away Louise, who had to lean upon his arm in order to walk and was unable even to thank him.

As they went out, three personages entered, two of whom seemed to be subordinates of the third.

They advanced with covered heads and an air of authority; and the chief said in an imperative tone:

"Madame Gavard!"

"That's my name, Monsieur," said the midwife, in surprise.

"You are really Madame Gavard, midwife?"

"Yes, Monsieur," said she, growing alarmed.

"Then, in the name of the law, I arrest you," said he, showing his scarf.

Upon a signal from the police official, his two subalterns surrounded the Gavard, now fairly thunderstruck.

"Why? For what?" she cried.

Without answering her, the official went straight to the clerk and said to him:

"In the name of the law, I arrest you too, Monsieur, as an accomplice."

CHAPTER XIV.

THE HOTEL MEURICE.

We will now pass from the East End to the West End of Paris, from the poor quarter to the rich quarter; for in Paris as in London and in every place where west winds prevail, carrying all vapors and miasma to the east, wealth naturally occupies the healthiest part of the city, the western part.

In the Rue de Rivoli, therefore, in the Hotel Meurice, then as now the most sumptuous hotel for travellers of high position, and in its finest suite of rooms, the suite on the second floor with a balcony, facing the garden of the Tuileries and commanding a view of the Faubourg Saint Germain, were two guests, who had arrived two days before, with heavy trunks apparently new, and had established themselves as patrons with full pockets.

One was the valet and the other the master; they seemed to be of the same age and resembled each other in size and complexion; both had a rich look and a haughty air, making it impossible to tell which was the master and which the valet.

The suite which they occupied consisted of sleeping apartments, parlor, and dining-room, coupling Parisian luxury with English comfort, and including all the superfluous features necessary to the *habitués* of the house.

Carpets, curtains, and furniture, — all were of silk and velvet, stuffed, thick, soft, dark, padded, upholstered, and close, made in short for the eyes, feet, and backs of aristocrats; shielding their delicate senses from light and noise, deadening the glare of the day, stifling the sound of steps . . . and a good fire in every room to keep away the chill and the dampness. What a bill to pay!

Already the master, on inscribing his noble name on the hotel register, had paid for a fortnight in advance, without calculation, at the maximum rate, with a generous fee for service.

On the morning of the second day after the arrival of the two new comers, they had ordered a fine breakfast served in their dining-room at an early hour.

Two plates only were laid on a table loaded with silver and glass ware elaborately chased and cut in forms of flowers and fruits, pell-mell, *à la Russe*, with poultry, fish, and venison with truffles, vegetables and fruits out of season and reason, green peas and red strawberries in winter, June products in March, in Lent, two days after Mardi Gras, on the very morrow of Ash Wednesday.

The Basket. 85

Every day is carnival for the rich, as every day is fast-day for the poor. And as the poor man has no summer, so the rich man has no winter. He carries the sun in his pocket, in his purse.

. The valet was superintending the service performed by other valets, those of the hotel, who looked out for him as solemnly as for the master.

The master was still stretched upon his featherbed, though not asleep; for the whisperings of a bitter-sweet conversation could be heard, proving that he was awake and not alone.

A ring of the bell, coming from the chamber, proved it still more conclusively. The valet, answering it quickly and coming back likewise, said to the waiters in an imperious tone:

"Serve the breakfast!"

The door of the chamber then opened, allowing a charming couple to enter the room arm in arm, the woman in all the splendor of beauty, fashion, and pleasure, the man in all the strength and joy of a well-spent night and the hope of a well-served meal.

They took their places at the table, and all the hotel servants went out; the valet was following them, when his master said to him:

"John, has the tailor come?"

"Not yet, Monseigneur."

"Ah!" exclaimed the master, in a tone of irritation; "as soon as he arrives, show him into the parlor and let me know; I expect him. Now go!"

"Yes, Monseigneur."

And the valet bowed and withdrew.

The couple, left alone, attacked the viands with a keenness of appetite which a good night imparts to the young, devouring side dishes, principal dishes, sweetened *entrées*, obelisks of asparagus, and then the dessert, with its pastries large and small, with its ices and jellies melting in the fire and flame of the choicest brands of wine, Madeira, Bordeaux, champagne, coffee, *pousse-café*, cordials. . . . and tea to digest the whole. A meal for two rich people, the price of which would have kept a hundred Didier families alive.

The conversation, begun in bed and continued at the table, gradually became animated, and finally, under the influence of Comus and Bacchus, multiplied by Venus, passed from gay to grave, from lively to severe.

Heads seemed excited no less than hearts. Teeth and forks at rest, they were at their last cup of tea, when Monsieur said to Madame:

"Well, my dear, you see my position. What is your decision? A conclusion must be reached. Whom do you choose?"

"Why choose?" she answered, with an adder-like movement.

"Because I want you for myself alone as before," said he, passionately.

"Impossible," said she, with a cold coquetry; "I have engagements now,"

"What! in spite of our child?"

"It is not my fault if you have not been able to keep your promises. For my part, I have other ties."

"Do not speak of them," said he, in a threatening tone; "break them, and come back wholly to me, I pray you, or" . . . .

"Or what?" said she, defiantly.

"Or I kill myself in your presence."

"Ah! no nonsense. You ask for too much, indeed. Remember that he wishes to marry me, exactly that! To become Countess de Frinlair is a fine chance, isn't it? And you would think me a fool to lose it."

"The wife of Frinlair! Never!" said he, in a voice full of hatred, envy, jealousy, wrath, and revenge.

The fury of the one increased with the cynicism of the other.

"Well, why not? Each one for himself!"

"But I am richer than he."

"Yes, but you will not marry."

"I pay only the more on that account."

"But you owe so much! Do you know that you are running great risks here, imprudent man?"

"There is nothing that I would not brave for you, so much do I love you."

"Suppose some one should inform against you! In your place I should be afraid of Clichy."

"If I go there, I shall be like Ouvrard; my prison will be a palace. But Frinlair is tracked, and unless he has promised you an allowance" . . . .

"Let us see, how much have you?"

A light and discreet knock at the door interrupted the conversation.

"Come in," said the master.

And the valet, entering, announced the arrival of the tailor.

"Very well; let him wait in the parlor. I will be there presently."

The valet gone, the bitter conversation was taken up where the interruption had broken it off, and rose rapidly to the pitch of violence.

Bitten to the heart by jealousy, in the sensitive spot, pride, the gentleman grew more and more enraged, as he sipped his brandy.

"So you will not leave him?" said he.

"Not without knowing whom I take back!"

"You ask me how much I have?"

"Yes, and you do not answer," said she, with an air of doubt, suspicion, and bravado; "let us see."

"Well! I have all that is necessary for you, traitress," said he, frantically. "I have gold to pay you or lead to punish you."

And suddenly, drawing a pistol from his pocket, he placed it squarely against her heart and fired. Without a cry or a gesture, the report stifled by the proximity of the weapon to her body, the woman sank back over her chair, dead.

Without even looking at his victim, the assassin reloaded the weapon, put it back in his pocket, went out, locked the door, and walked straight to the parlor, glutted with all the pleasures of man and of the gods, lust and revenge, cooled by his crime and calm in his ferocity.

Led back to his mistress by passion which had overcome his prudence, he had killed her through jealousy and prudence, which in turn had become stronger than his passion.

In the parlor the tailor was waiting with the valet, having taken from its wrappings a full suit cut in the latest fashion and spread it on the divan.

"You are behind time," said the master, severely.

"Monseigneur was in such a hurry," said the tailor, respectfully. "Will Monseigneur try it on?"

"I have no time."

"When shall I come again, Monseigneur?"

"I will let you know."

"I think no alteration will be needed; but if perchance" . . . .

"The bill?"

"Oh! there's no hurry, Monseigneur," said the tailor, while presenting the account as quickly as obsequiously.

"How much?" asked the master, without looking at the price any more than at the clothes.

"Seventy-five dollars, Monseigneur."

"It is receipted?"

"Yes, Monseigneur."

"All right."

Then he looked at the suit as if examining the cloth, placed the bill in the pocket of the coat, opened his purse, paid cash, and dismissed the surprised tailor, charmed at having a customer as prodigal as he was easy to satisfy.

"John," then said the master to the valet, "I am in a hurry; Madame is waiting for me; I have no time to try these on, to undress and dress again; try them on yourself, and right away."

"I! Monseigneur," said John, surprised at this queer order.

"Yes, I tell you! Besides, there's no large mirror in this beggarly parlor; I could not see myself from head to foot; you are just my size, and I can see them better on you! Come, be quick!"

Thereupon John felt a valet's last scruple at donning his master's effects.

"I beg pardon, Monseigneur," said he, blushing almost like a virgin; and he took off his coat, vest, and pantaloons and replaced them with the new suit.

When he was completely dressed, the master, at a distance, surveyed him from head to foot as if to judge of the effect, as an expert looks at a picture.

"That fits well. . . . except in the neck. There's a slight wrinkle there!"

And approaching as if to make sure of the fault, he quickly took out his weapon and fired full in the face of the poor John, who fell stiff, dead and disfigured.

Immediately, without loss of time, he in turn threw off his clothes, dressed himself in those of the valet, put the weapon in the right hand of the dead man, and, as he rang the bell, called for help with frightful audacity. To the servants who came running in answer to the hubbub, he said with sobbing voice and his hands over his face as if to wipe away his tears: "My master, my poor master! He has killed himself together with his mistress, she in the dining-room and he here. . . . see!"

Then, thanks to the surprise, the tumult, and the bewilderment of all, he left the scene of his double murder,.applauding his success and saying to himself: "All the crime necessary, but nothing superfluous. . . . I have paid the hotel bill."

And, to avoid having to reenter the rooms, he went away with every chance of impunity and security.

The next day, in the local columns of the "Constitutionnel," the following paragraph appeared, to the great joy of the Liberal opposition:

It is known at last what has become of one of the highest livers of the aristocracy and purest blue-bloods of the noble *faubourg*, the criminal madman who, after having dazzled Paris for so long, disappeared in an abyss of debts with a charge of forgery hanging over him. Instead of ending his life of scandal and crime at Clichy or Brest, this swindling courtier, this very high and very powerful lord and bandit, the Duke Crillon-Garousse, committed suicide yesterday with his mistress at the end of a Mardi-Gras breakfast in Lent, in the finest apartments in the Hotel Meurice, Rue de Rivoli.

CHAPTER XV.

BARON HOFFMANN.

All is flux and reflux in this life. In Paris especially "destiny and the floods are changing" according to Béranger. The current of sympathy for the banker Berville which the assassination of the bank collector had created on the first day had disappeared on the morrow, or rather changed into an exactly opposite current.

The world also is a banker, demanding the return with usury of the benevolence which it lends.

So inconstant opinion had already turned, and the wind of injustice blew upon the unfortunate.

A real fire of straw is human sympathy,—all flame for an instant, and only ashes afterwards. "Oh, my friends, there are no friends," said the Greek proverb. "Heaven defend me from my friends, I will defend myself from my enemies," says the English proverb. "Prompt payments make good friends," says the French proverb.

Berville's friends therefore were the first to believe that his misfortune was his fault,—worse, his crime; that he had shown extreme imprudence, bordering upon or rather screening deceit, theft, and murder. Once entered on this path, friendship and imagination never halted; hints became charges. The story of the Duke d'Orléans procuring the assassination of the broker Pinel was recalled. In short, as often happens, especially in France, where fancy is queen and imagination overpowers reason, to the idlers who are weary, to the wicked who amuse themselves, and to the fools who swallow everything, in a word, to the changeable, malignant, credulous, and sensation-loving mass, the unfortunate was the culprit.

"It is worse than a crime, it is a mistake," said Talleyrand. With us failure is always both a mistake and a crime. It was a Gaul who cried: "A curse upon the conquered!"

M. Berville had fallen a victim to this fatal reaction. Around him isolation had succeeded eager attentions. The rare faces which he still saw grew longer. The very stockholders and creditors who at first had aided him, who had given him a footing and granted him delay, believing no longer that he could recover himself, were now the first to bury him.

It is pretended that wolves do not eat each other. A mistake; they bite the wounded.

The third day after the disaster the banker and his faithful cashier were shut up together at an early hour in the office with which we are familiar, the clock not replaced.

Under the weight of these charges which reached his ears (there is always one friend left to bring good news), the banker had no more recovered health than fortune; the congested brain had lost its natural clearness, even in the matter of accounts. Bankruptcy, "hideous bankruptcy," as Mirabeau called it, possessed him, showing him all sorts of horrible images, — seizure, execution, auction, published shame and ruin, house for sale, and the hands of the law upon his books and upon his honor.

Now comatose and now convulsive, he spent whole hours in examining and balancing columns of figures, which all cried in his ears the same word, failure, and assumed before his eyes shapes of claws and teeth ready to tear and devour him.

"Enough of suffering! I want no more of it," said he to the honest Brémont, who had just added up the debits and credits. "There is no hope!"

The cashier answered only by a sad sign of assent.

"Delay would only make the disaster worse."

"Yes, for those who at first held out their hands now withdraw them." ·

"To borrow is not to pay, my good Brémont, and it is better to refuse. That will shorten the agony by a fortnight. I had rather leap out the window than tumble down stairs. I desire to end the matter at once."

And he rose, as if he had come to a final decision.

"Put out the announcement of suspension. Go on."

Brémont rose in his turn and went out in despair. His master's honor seemed to him his own. There are still these poodles among those whom his master called knaves.

Then the banker took a box of pistols from a drawer, and seized paper and pen, doubtless to write his last directions.

Just then he heard a knock at the door.

"Who's there?"

"I," said a woman's voice, and Gertrude entered, even paler than usual.

"What do you want, my dear Gertrude?"

"I have just seen Brémont, who informs me of the suspension of payments."

"Yes, the end has come."

"But, my cousin, it is madness."

"No, all is over . . . hopelessly ruined!"

"But could you not delay, renew? You have had offers . . . . and with an arrangement whereby you could pay in instalments. . . . I have already told you, Berville, that my property is at your disposition."

"Thank you, my friend," he answered, affectionately. "Thank you, it is useless, insufficient! You would ruin yourself without saving me! Keep all for yourself and Camille; he will need it after me."

"After you!" exclaimed Gertrude, noticing the weapons. "What do you say? What are you going to do? Ah! Monsieur, why this weapon? A suicide, great God! You are only unfortunate; do you want to be guilty? I say nothing to you of God; you do not believe in him! But your duty as a father! Your poor child!"

"I leave him to your affection; he will not lose by the change," said he, with genuine emotion; "go find him . . . no, you will kiss him for me. . . . Adieu."

"I shall not leave you, madman."

"I beg of you to go. Nothing will shake my determination. Life is intolerable to me. Go, I tell you, unless you wish to be a witness of my death."

Brémont came back, with a card in his hand.

"Have you put out the placard?" said Berville.

"Yes, Monsieur." answered Brémont.

"You hear, cousin, it is settled. Go now, both of you."

"A person who handed me this card for you desires to speak with you," said Brémont.

"Another creditor who wants to aid me; doubtless an impatient undertaker! Who is he?"

"A stranger."

"You know very well that I do not wish to receive any one."

"I told him so; but he insisted obstinately and handed me his card with a pressing word penciled upon it."

"'Baron Hoffmann,'" the banker read aloud. "I do not know him . . . . and 'on important and pressing business.' Important! What is there of importance to me now? Send him away!"

"Who knows?" said Brémont.

"Yes," added Gertrude. "I have prayed so much to God in your behalf."

And the banker, like the drowning man who instinctively catches at every straw, said:

"Let him come in!"

Gertrude quickly covered the weapons with the table-cloth.

Brémont opened the door and said:

"Come in, Monsieur."

A man of about thirty years, with a distinguished air and correct deportment, in *bourgeois* dress of white cravat and blue brass-buttoned coat, such as the rich of that day wore, entered and bowed, with perfect politeness, first to Gertrude and then to the banker.

A general rule. From policy as well as from politeness, if there is a woman in a house, every visitor who wishes to be welcome should bow to her before the man.

The new-comer seemed too courteous and too sagacious to violate this rule. Brémont made haste to give him a seat.

For a moment there was silence.

" To whom do I owe the honor of your visit? " said the banker, impatiently.

" Frankly, Monsieur, and saying nothing of sympathy, I make you this visit as a matter of self-interest," answered the unknown.

And as Gertrude and Brémont made a show of going out, he added :

"Oh! I can speak before you all ". . . And continuing: "I am a stranger to you, unknown even, Monsieur Berville; but with you it is different; you are known to me, at least by name, as you are to all Paris, especially since your misfortune."

" Alas! yes, too well known ! " exclaimed Berville, with a sigh.

"But, Monsieur, that which has made you known to me has also aroused my sympathy."

" Thank you, Monsieur, for your kindness."

" And I come to give you a proof of it . . . by asking you to accept it."

" What does it concern ? " asked the agitated banker.

" It concerns your salvation, I think."

"My salvation? How? Speak."

" And my interest also, as I have told you."

" Well, Monsieur, pray go on."

" We no longer live in the golden age, I believe," said the unknown with fine irony, "but in the age of paper. I am not a knight, but a capitalist. I do not come, I am ashamed to confess, purely to oblige you, Monsieur Berville. You do not see a Don Quixote before you, but rather his matter-of-fact squire. In short, I come to you, I tell you again quite plainly, in your interest and mine. I know your indisputable honesty and shrewdness. And if you wish to take me as a partner in your bank ". . . .

"What! Monsieur, in my present situation you would like to ". . . .

" Have the honor and advantage of aiding you and putting you on your feet again. I believe I have nearly the amount that you have lost! Three hundred thousand dollars, the papers say, do they not? If, then, you are willing, I will share in your losses in order to share in your profits. I put the amount at your disposal . . . this very day."

It was Providence in person. Gertrude clasped her hands.

"Monsieur, such a service. . . . gratitude stifles my voice," said the banker.

"No thanks. You owe me nothing. I do not render you a service; it is simply a matter of business. I repeat, I am your partner. Losses and profits! "

The trio who listened were mad with surprise and joy. They could not recover; amazed, hallucinated, duped as by a dream, scarcely knowing whether this was fraud, farce, or phantasmagoria. They were transported with hope. All three madly embraced each other in presence of the stranger.

Gertrude especially, fascinated by the generosity and delicacy of the offer, by this unforeseen, unhoped-for, unexpected aid, which shone the more brightly be cause veiled by egoism, gave thanks aloud, first to God for this token of grace and then to the baron, whose title, of course, she had remembered.

The cashier was also charmed, although less piously.

As for the banker, who had at first cried: "Saved!" and who had accepted every thing suddenly, without even an idea of a reference or even of reflection, as the falling man grasps a branch, the stroke of joy was too much for him after that of pain. His cheeks became purple, and the reddish petecchiæ which spotted them became viclet. He had only time to cry to the cashier:

"   e down the placard!"

And he fell back on his chair, served with a second summons by the great creditor.

But there was no immediate execution. Death still granted a delay, long enough at least to allow everything to be regulated according to the desire of the baron and the banker.

M. Berville was on his feet again in time to establish the baron in his place as his partner and thus meet his obligations, restore honor to his business, avoid bankruptcy, and save his credit, his reputation, and his bank, which then became the bank of Berville, Hoffmann & Co.

The baron, thanks to the aid of the diligent cashier and to his own aptitude, in twenty-four hours became familiar with the business and was initiated into the secrets of the ledger as well as of the note-book. Man learns nothing so readily as robbery. One would have said that he had had all his life no other merit.

"He will be worth two Bervilles," thought Brémont.

In his partner, then, the banker had found at least his equal. All was saved,— the bank and honor. The proverb says; "As one makes his bed, he must lie in it." Let us add: Each finds his honor where he left it. The banker had put his in a bag! He found it there, without asking too particularly what bag. Money has no odor. *Non olet,* as Vespasian said, an emperor whose name on this account has been given we know to what.

But if the baron had succeeded in the bank, he had no less succeeded in Gertrude's heart. He had won that likewise, at one stroke.

He had literally bewitched her. His distinction, his courtesy, his gallantry even, the singularity of his intervention and of his name, and above all his title of baron, had subjugated her, taken her by main force, like an irresistible rape. Love had entered this weak heart through two of its broadest doors, — gratitude and pride. Everything comes to those who know how to wait, who can wait. Finally, like Archimedes, she had found.

In fact, the banker's partner had confessed to Berville that it was with the keenest interest that he had seen Mlle. Gertrude in society, at an evening party given by Laffitte; which explained to the banker the baron's chivalrous generosity. Hoffmann had even added that he would be happy to be connected with the house by one tie more and to rise from the bank to the family.

Consequently, feeling that he was about to die, Gertrude's cousin had summoned her to his death-bed, had confided to her the intentions of his partner, had urged superior considerations and pressing circum stances, and, in the name of all the proprieties, the interest of the banking-house, the future of his son of whom she was to be sole guardian, under the same roof as a bachelor, had adjured her to accept the baron's offers were it only out of gratitude for past services and in the hope of services to come, saying, with all t he emotion of which he was capable in his last hour, that he thanked her in advanc e for her devotion to his interests and that he should die happy if, by the sacrific e of her liberty, she should assure the future of the family and the honor of the house.

So much effort was unnecessary to victory. The fortress was captured, and made a show of defence only to surrender more gracefully. Age had undermined the walls, and, the prayer of the dying man aiding, without further discussion of financial conditions, money lifting all obstacle s, granting all dispensations, delays, banns, and publicity ("there are ways o f compromising with heaven"), and the religious marriage being of the most importa nce to Gertrude, reserving the civil ceremony for a later date, the marriage of love and interest between Baron Hoffmann and Gertrude *de* Berville was therefore resolved upon in presence of the dying cousin.

In this forced precipitation of marriage and burial one upon the other, there was something rational no doubt, but also somet hing forbidding which oppressed the heart of the old cashier and, though possib ly in a less degree, that of the old maid as well.

The marriage took place at Saint-Roch, at night, by special permission, and consequently at greater cost and profit to the priest, Monsieur the abbé Ventron.

From that time, then, the Berville-Hoffmann fortune and family were indissolubly united and made but one for life and death.

On the same evening, in spite of all the art of the great physician of the opposition, the famous Doctor Dubois, a third and last attack of apoplexy supervened; and cousin Hoffmann closed the eyes of cousin Berville, who died in the odor of glory and peace.

And the next morning the " Constitutionnel " announced the death and funeral of the Liberal banker, devoting to him a dithyrambic obituary in marked contrast with that of the noble Duke de Crillon-Garousse.

CHAPTER XVI.

AT SAINT-ROCH.

Twenty-four hours later, at noon, the bell of Saint-Roch tolled a prolonged knell. The front of the church was hung, from cornices to base, with black draperies sprinkled with silver tears, and a large escutcheon bearing for device a capital B, also of silver.

In front of the steps stood a file of mourning coaches similarly caparisoned, escutcheoned, and lettered, official coaches of the family and the clergy, followed by private equipages in black and crape liveries even to the horses and whips.

Around was a crowd of curious people who watched the spectacle, mourners who laughed at their godsend, undertaker's employees indulging in merry jokes over this fat corpse,—in short, all the grief of pomp, all the formal sorrow, all the dismal and savage, grotesque and lugubrious ostentation of first-class Christian burials.

Let us go with the crowd into this Catholic temple, Pagan—I beg Jupiter's pardon—Jesuitic in its architecture.

Here, in fact, we no longer find Gothic art with its fugues and pinnacles, as at Notre-Dame; or even the art of the Renaissance still so spiritual in its juvenile grace, as at Saint-Eustache; or even the stiff majesty of the false art of the Great King, as at Saint-Sulpice. No, we find the senile sensuality of Louise XV, carnal and pietistic art, Pompadour and lewd art, with hearts of Jesus and Mary spitted, flaming like fire-pots, larded like calves' livers, and garlanded with roses and ribbons like the newly-married.

In this temple, where the services are no more Christian than the architecture, and which is so fittingly dedicated to the God who knows not where to lay his head, to the *Ecce Homo* whose poor are members and whose rich are accursed, to the carpenter's son who was born on the straw of a manger and who died on the wood of a cross, there were then in progress two funeral as well as two baptismal services.

One baptism in cold water for an elect of heaven, a child of the poor; another in tepid water for an outcast of heaven, a child of the rich.

As for the two burials, they offered no less a contrast in their solemnity.

For one, in the centre of the broad nave, before the divine altar and before the

evangelical pulpit, stood an immense catafalque draped with Lyons velvet, ornamented with plumes and silver fringes and tassels, and lighted by a triple row
of tapers, a mass of silk and fire. Beneath this splendid dome, in the midst of incense, between the banner and the cross veiled with black, God himself in mourning for man, rested, in a double coffin of oak and lead, an embalmed body, covered
with a pall of damask and a shower of crowns, wreaths, branches, and bouquets.

Around this monument of human vanity and pious commercialism stood the
relatives, the friends of the family, ultramundane society, thoughtless, frivolous,
wearied, and absent-minded, men and women, gathered there out of propriety, especially to see each other and well acquitting themselves of their task, thus paying
their respects to each other much more than to the deceased; black coats and
black dresses struggling to surpass in luxury of mourning, rubies giving place to
diamonds.

At the head of the coffin, more hypocritically if not more religiously, stood the
clerical *officiants*, first the choristers, singers of the Devil as well as of God, in the
morning at church, in the evening at the opera; then the priests, and, first and
fattest of all, Monsieur the parish priest, the abbé Ventron, though not thoughtful,
yet profoundly absorbed, calculating and storing in advance in his heart the product of these obsequies before putting it into the poor-box.

Breviary in one hand, aspergillum in the other, dipped in a silver holy-water
basin, he whimperingly and with an air of grief intoned, in a tongue which not
one believer in ten understood, in Latin, the *De Profundis*, which the opera-singers
sang in chorus without understanding it any more than the listeners.

An odd, a barbarous thing, that priests should sing when others weep.

What said this *De Profundis* in Latin? *Domine ad te clamavi, exaudi me!* In
English; From the depths of the abyss, O Lord, I have cried unto you, hear me!

Ah! if this fat priest of a lean God; if this priest of his Christ had been faithful
to the human idea of the *first sans-culotte;* if he had himself understood what he
sang; if he had touched, beneath its mystical form, the real meaning of this psalm;
if he had applied to the facts of this world the chimeras of the other; if he had
grasped the actual significance of this recourse of man to God, of earth to heaven,
of the fallen, of the damned, to their lord and master; if he had not had, like his
golden crucifix, like these metal idols, insensible, blind, and deaf, eyes not to see,
oculos habent, ears not to hear, and a heart not to feel; if he had not had only a
stomach and an abdomen, like the whole egoistic and vain crowd that surrounded
him without listening to him,— what would he have heard, understood, and felt?

In this *De Profundis*, that psalm of psalms, that innermost and most intense cry
of Christian faith, that summary, that most fervent outpouring of all the hopes
and all the fears of the Middle Ages, that most complete and moving hymn of spiritual sorrow, a true canticle of the miseries of the human soul, a sublime invoca-
tion of the believer to his *God*, he would have heard other lamentations, perceived
other sufferings, seen other abysses.

He would have felt, beneath ideal sorrows real sorrows, beneath imaginary limbos the present, living torments of an earthly hell.

He would have heard, no longer the clamor of souls anxious about their salvation on high, but of men anxious about their life here below. He would have seen
the modern Job stretched upon his muck-heap. He would have heard beside the
body of Dives thousands of Lazaruses crying from the depths of the abyss: *De
Profundis*, O Lord, hear us!

And in this monster chorus of the victims of the rich, in this infernal harmony
of the accursed, so infinite, so general, and so continuous that it is no longer even
heard, he would have distinguished the cries of the shop, the hospital, and the prison, the voices of men crying: "O Lord, we have given you our arms, our sweat,
our blood . . . . and we have no clothes, no shelter, no food! O Lord, hear us!"
the voices of women crying: "We have reared our sons for your defence and our
daughters for your pleasure . . . . and we are alone in weeping over our dead sons
and our dishonored daughters. O Lord, have pity on us!" And among these
feminine voices the youngest saying: "Our hearts, made to love, have not known
the holy joys of love, dried up in poverty or spoiled in debauchery. O Lord, have
pity! hear us!" Then the wails of children crushed in their flower, and the sighs
and groans of the aged, alone and in despair, no longer even crying: "O Lord,
hear us!"

Yes, he would have listened to all these growing clamors, rising incessantly *en
masse*, like the dead in Michael Angelo's "Last Judgment."

He would have seen these prayers, left unanswered, change into gnashings of
teeth; these laments into threats; these sorrows into furies; these cries of misery
into cries of revolt, into a song of war; the "Marseillaise" of despair, an immense
and terrible chorus louder than thunder, animating, guiding "avenging hearts
and arms"; the cry of the Revolution once more starting forth to break sceptres
and crosses, crowns and mitres, altar, throne, and strong-box; to force all the Bastilles left to be taken,—those of the master and the priest as well as those of the
king; to scale the Louvre, Heaven, and the Bank, and to bury the Lord, in his
turn, beneath their ruins.

That is what, instead of singing in Latin, the officiating priest of Saint-Roch,
Monsieur the abbé Ventron, had he remembered the love-feasts of the catacombs,
would have said in good French to his faithful living beside the body and soul of
his faithful dead.

At the same time that the rich parishioner occupied the centre of the nave, in
another direction, thanks to Brémont, under the lowest wing of the same church,
at a side entrance, stood, as if banished, on a trestle almost bare, a coffin made of
four badly-joined deal-boards scarcely covered with serge, between two dimly-
burning candles; and beside it a poor widow on her knees, perfect image of the
Mater dolorosa, holding in her arms her infant bathed in her tears.

A single priest, a sub-vicar, a young graduate of Saint-Sulpice, freshly tonsured, bran-new from the seminary, mumbled the prayer of the dead, without organ or incense, cross or banner, the aspergillum not even moist, in front of this blonde widow as beautiful as Mary, at whom he gave covert glances and not with the eyes of Saint John.

The services over, the two coffins were taken out: one by the main door, the other by the side door; one placed in a hearse drawn by six horses, the other on the hearse of the poor with two bearers; the one as it went by forcing the other to give place to it.

The one proceeding pompously to the family vault, a palace of pride for the receipt of stolen goods, which protests by its marble against human equality; the other returning simply to the common grave, to the bosom of natal earth, that equality-loving mother who recalls all her sons, rich or poor, to unity.

The one escorted by a throng of invited guests in dress-coats talking in a worldly way of the late banker Berville; the other followed only by the weeping widow of his collector and a friend in a blouse, a humble person, who had been unwilling to set foot in the church, Jean, the rag-picker.

END OF PART FIRST.

PART SECOND.

THE STRONG-BOX.

CHAPTER I.

THE STUDENTS.

Twelve years have passed since Baron Hoffmann became a partner in the Berville bank and a member of the Berville family.

The strong-box and the hearth have changed their location for the better, from the comfortable Rue du Louvre to the fashionable Faubourg Saint-Honoré, from the Berville mansion to the Hotel Hoffmann.

The bank is no longer simply *bourgeois;* it has become royal.

The citizen king has replaced the legitimate king. The tricolor floats over the Tuileries instead of the white flag. The hammer pawned by the workingman at the Mount of Piety was redeemed in time to crush the royal *punaises* on the escutcheon of the Bourbons. That whose coming the abbé Ventron neither heard nor saw in his *De Profundis* has arrived. At least the reign of the Third Estate is here. The *bourgeois*, thanks to the people, has definitively conquered the priest and the noble and then united with them to hold more firmly at the bottom of the abyss, in the *ergastulum*, the disappointed slave who is now stirring on his own account and claims his sovereignty.

In beginning this second part of our work we are on the way to the democratic revolution of February, as in the first part we were on the way to the *bourgeois* revolution of July. Now the whole financial world is royalist. The opposition has passed to the government, cash and baggage. The strong-box is for and with the throne and altar, with a view to controlling them or at least balancing them. In a word, it is the *constitutional régime.*

At present Baron Hoffmann swims in wealth, a shark of the high seas; one of the greatest financiers in Paris, a representative of the highest monetary circles; the first metallic and political personage on change. His clients are the king, the peers, the deputies, the bishops, and all the merchant-princes of the Rue du Sentier,— client-accomplices. His dupes are all the rest. He is the banker of the Church and of the State, contrives loans, meddles in corporations, is necessary to the Treasury, useful to enterprise, and fatal to labor. In short, he is a high-flying, broad-winged bird of prey, an eagle hovering in the empyrean of the Bourse and plucking all the sparrows within reach of his beak, eating them legally without making them cry.

His hotel is tastefully sumptuous, with none of the coarse ostentation of the *parvenu;* his conduct is as observant of form as Bridoison could wish. In business exact and punctual, marking the hours like a dial; a man of the world undoubtedly, but orderly; proper in his life and correct in his morals; a model husband as well as a model banker; as attentive to his wife as to his cash; irreproachable, in every way admirable.

His predecessor, then, could rest in peace. He had left everything in good hands. All was safe, and Brémont was not mistaken. . . . Hoffmann was worth two Bervilles as the head of the bank ; as the head of the family, in Gertrude's eyes, he was worth many more.

From the first days of her married life this prodigious husband had surrounded Gertrude with attentions and deferences which had outlived the rays of the honeymoon. He seemed always the lover of his wife and courted her like a sweetheart. Bouquets, gifts, new books, boxes on first nights, promenades in the park, he continued all the pleasures, amusements, and surprises which are so delightful to young brides and with which old husbands dispense so quickly for the benefit of their mistresses . . . and the lovers of their wives.

Entering into Gertrude's tastes, he at the outset had her freed from her provincial domestics and attended by grand Parisian livery-servants, those trained Frontins who address their masters only in the third person, serve them only with gloved hands, and offer them their letters, as formerly the keys of Paris were offered to the king, only on silver plates.

He had even gone so far in the way of elegance as to retire—on a pension, of course—the simple cashier from Berri, too co mmon for a baroness, and replace the familiar Brémont by a cashier, if not more honest, at least more modern and more deferent ial.

Thus all things, from top to bottom, were made new in the house and in the best of possible banks, around the former old maid, Mlle. Gertrude *de* Berville, now Mme. the baroness Hoffmann, by the grace of God, whom she thanked evening and morning.

In this general change which time had worked in men and things the baroness had grown old faster than the baron, in spite, or rather perhaps because, of the satisfaction of all her ambitions and pas sions, nobility and devotion, vanity and faith, fortune and power. She had lived too fast, so to speak, in the realization of all her dreams; for all her wishes had been met, save one,—she had had no children; and on this account her health was not all that could be desired.

The human organism has duties, failure in which is accompanied by penalties and the sanction of which is health, just as its pleasure and comfort are proportional to its functions, the joys of feasting being designed for the preservation of the individual, and the delights of love for the reproduction of the race.

Gertrude, then, had suffered the greatest physical and moral privation possible to a woman, the privation of maternal happiness. . . . *matrem filiorum lætantem.*

Had the old maid killed the mother? Was it her husband's fault or her own? In either case she had so far longed in vain for this happiness, and had envied the gift of English queens and codfish,—fecundity. And her repressed passion had altered her humors, though not her temper, which was always even in God.

Fortunately her husband, through a rare solicitude regarding his wife's condition, had made her a present, on one of her birthdays, of a large child, his own natural daughter, six years old, whom he had recognized under the name Claire Hoffmann, and whom Gertrude, for want of a better and despairing of her case, on the advice of her doctor and her spiritual director, had adopted with enthusiasm, love, and piety.

Seeing always the hand of Heaven in everything that came into her life, whether good or evil, she had again thanked it for this new gift, received also from the very man whom she adored next to God. So she had accepted without hesitation. . . . for to do otherwise would have been to blame God himself. Without reserve she had bestowed upon Claire the treasure of love buried in her heart.

Her husband's daughter she had made her own child. She had made up for lost time with a will.

She had reared her with completely maternal affection and application. The child is the mother's doll. She had spoiled it, formed and fashioned it in her own image, nourished it on her faith, imbued it with her ideas, brought it up in her principles, the *good* principles, and educated it in her prejudices in order that in the child she might live again, according to the law of nature. And when the time had come to teach her and the child had grown into a young girl, painfully she parted with her to put her in the principal religious and royalist boarding-school in Paris, the convent-school *des Oiseaux.*

Thence Claire had emerged at the age of eighteen, worthy of her mother by adoption, having profited by the lessons of the pious teachers, aristocratic and devout to the tips of her nails, filled with the false ideal which animated Gertrude and which was to make the daughter similar to the mother and dear to her, the one differing from the other only as Parisian levity differs from provincial solidity.

As for the young Berville, he offered a most perfect contrast to Claire under the same roof. . . . and, if opposites attract each other, Camille and Claire should have been united body and soul. Yet they were the two poles.

The young Camille had grown from a school-boy to a student under the guardian-ship nominally of his cousin but really of the baron, his guardian's guardian, who had been as indulgent with him as Gertrude had been with Claire.

Camille had remained the same, as nature had made him; or rather, he had brought himself up under the surviving and powerful guardianship of his mother, he had developed under this invisible but effective influence the wholesome germ which she had transmitted from her heart to that of her son.

The "stubborn" child was now the free man. Grace and power, gentleness and frankness, he seemed like a Spartan or Athenian youth detached from the metopes of the Parthenon just attaining the age of manhood and transplanted into Paris.

Brought up in the English fashion by the method of toughening introduced by Lord Seymour, nicknamed Lord *Arsouille* * by the effeminate, practised in boxing, rowing, fencing, every branch of gymnastics, his friends called him Iron Arm and Golden Heart.

Too intelligent to be only an athlete, too generous to be only a banker, too moral to be only a voluptuary; in spite of all the stimulants of fortune, the indulgences of his relatives, the examples of his friends; in spite of the faults and follies common at his age; helped rather than hindered by his wealth and the connivance of his guardian; although tempted undoubtedly like others (for the beast always un-derlies the man), he had kept himself pure, stainless, and without reproach. On the verge of a bad action, he stopped short at the recollection of his mother's word: "Remember!"

Like her, in sympathy with the people, he had thrown himself headlong into the Revolution. The Liberal movement had become republican. What good there was left in the upstart *bourgeoisie*, the young element, the student, still fraternised with the workingman; study prepared the way for and always guided labor. It was the heroic age of the Latin Quarter. The tradition was not yet broken, and the union between the head and the arm of France was still in existence. Alas! Why does it exist no longer?

Carbonaro with Mazzini, Jacobin with Carrel, chief of the Students' Group in the secret society La Marianne, and a point of union between the laborers and the medical students, like the Greek Achilles he drove his two coursers abreast, plea-sure and duty, letting neither outstrip the other, jolted sometimes, but never upset, always erect in his chariot in the struggle of life, in a word, balanced.

He went also with the same ardor from the club to the gambling-house, spend-ing the morning with Cujas, the evening with Moliere, the night with Marianne or Lisette, betting on his horse, conspiring for the Republic, applauding Taglioni, and singing: "The kings shall never invade France!"

Nothing human, nothing Parisian, was foreign to him. A man of struggle and

---

* French slang for the type of man which English slang describes as the "tough." — *Translator.*

joy, united with the flower of society, of the press, of thought, of action, leading a four-in-hand life, prodigal of himself and his possessions, of his strength and his purse, pushed on rather than held back by the baron, who did him the excessive favor and doubtful kindness of giving him more money than advice, himself initiating him in the world to take the rust off, as he said, to guide him in case of need, to make him a man in his own image, in short, to make him his son-in-law.

Gertrude had other views in regard to their daughter Claire; and Claire in this matter thought with Gertrude and not with her father.

She had even confided to her mother by adoption that she could never love Camille; that she would refuse to marry him; that she loved another, the brother of a school-friend, the Count de Frinlair, whom she had seen for the first time in the parlor of the convent where he visited his sister.

The title of count had naturally had its usual effect, had exercised its magic power over the mind of the baroness . . . . and Claire, who knew and shared her mother's weakness, had not failed to plead her cousin's aggravating qualities, — his impious republican opinions and corresponding conduct.

After this confidence, the aid of the mother was irreversibly gained by the daughter against the father for the love of God and in the name of the king.

So one morning at the Hotel Hoffmann, when the family was breakfasting, this *tête-à-tête* of three took place.

The baron, wearing an air of pleasantry tinctured with gravity, was seated between his wife, who was growing more and more bloodless and gloomy, and his daughter Claire, in all the brilliancy of her youth and beauty, superb youth and masculine beauty, the oval of her face a little squared, her black eyes a little heavy, her straight eyebrows a little pronounced and having a tendency to meet, her forehead flat but high, her nose arched, her chin pointed, under lips that were pink but full and downy, showing teeth that were white but large, all the signs of a powerful race, all the features of an excessively developed woman or a partially developed man.

"Where is your favorite this morning, my ward, the worthless fellow?" said Gertrude. "If he had the slightest intention or even attention toward Claire, he would be here," she continued, shrewdly; "but no, he takes after his mother, not after the Bervilles, — an atheist, a democrat, and consequently a libertine. In vain do I pray for him; he is incorrigible! It runs in the blood; let him ruin himself alone, it is enough and too much. Claire is right in not wanting him for a husband; and I want him still less for a son-in-law. The young Count de Frinlair, he suits me!"

The baron tossed his head, and the baroness nevertheless continued:

"What a difference! What deportment! What propriety! What exemplary conduct! We see him, Claire and I, every Sunday, accompanying his sister to Saint-Roch. But Camille! Look you, my friend, his opinions and his conduct would surely expose our daughter to a premature widowhood."

"Your solicitude on her account makes you unjust to him."

" No, and it is your fault. You have wished him as he is."

"But, my dear, I could not put Camille in a convent, as you put Claire. His mother would have risen from her grave. I love your cousin as well as you love my daughter, and I have no more desire to play the step-father than have you to play the step-mother. Camille is not a young girl, and the period of youth has to be passed through. Young scamps make good husbands. He will consent to what I want of him because I consent to what he wants; and when he has lived in this way long enough, which will be soon if he keeps up his present rate, then he will rest in the bosom of the family. Where can one be better? See, my dear, I have brought him up as I was brought up myself . . . . and tell me, do you find me so badly reared?"   .

Gertrude, charmed, put her hand over her husband's mouth, who kissed it tenderly to more surely win the cause which again he pleaded:

"Say, then, to our Claire that you are not unhappy at having had a man who sowed his wild oats at the proper time, and consequently has no need to sow them after marriage! See, my beloved Gertrude, I am so happy at being united to the Bervilles that I wish to be thus united again, for the sake of the house and for the sake of the bank, for motives of interest, for motives of prudence, for the dowry, in plain English, for the strong-box. Nothing will leave the family; what do you think of that?"

The baroness, shaken, looked at Claire.

"And you, Claire, what do you say to that?" she asked.

"Yes, answer," said the baron.

But, if the baron seemed obstinate in his purpose, his daughter, who took after him, was no less stubborn in her own. She answered resolutely, with tears in her handsome eyes, but with firmness in her strong voice:

"No, my father, I shall never love Camille."   .

And her mother, moved by Claire's sorrow and also by her courage, again defended her against the father, appealing to his tenderness against his wisdom, pleading the rights of the heart against the strong-box, of nobility, religion, and love against interest; and finally saying to the baron that she would make common cause with Claire, refuse, in her capacity of guardian, her consent to her ward, and, so far as she could, place her veto upon their marriage.

But the strain of her effort to resist her dear baron brought on a frightful reaction, produced one of those nervous crises to which she had become subject soon after her marriage.

Hypochondria, sick headaches, neuralgia, vertigo, nervous attacks, all different forms of one and the same disease, a disease of the cities, ending in hysteria, epilepsy, eclampsy, or madness, — *névrose* in short. . . . ah! the word is found, but the remedy? The incalculable element in the feminine nature is so complicated and delicate that a nervous affection in a woman is a bonanza to the doctor if the patient is rich, and the goal of his science if he is learned.

Diseases, as we know, are dependent upon fashion. Other morals, other maladies! Nosology changes with life. Mucous diseases have given place to nervous diseases; that is, the tissues which suffered from the more animal life of our fathers were the mucous tissues, while the tissues which suffer from our more mental life are the nervous tissues.

As for remedies, fashionable or not, old or new, physical or chemical, all are alike impotent! Indeed, what effect can senna or bismuth have on an andralgic old maid or a mother who mourns a dead child?

In consequence of her morbid state Gertrude had already been for a long time under the care of two physicians, good people! one of the body and one of the soul, Doctor Dubois and the abbé Ventron. Poor woman! To say nothing of her husband, who cared for her more than the two others! What could she be expected to do against three?

"Go for the doctor," cried the baron.

"And Monsieur the abbé," said the baroness.

At that moment Camille entered, seeming less at ease than usual and covered with his *quarago*, a long cloak worn then in memory of the Spanish war, which has left us also the glory of the Trocadéro.

"Pardon me," said Camille to the baron, "if I bring you a friend. . . . of the boulevard, one of the ten of the infernal box, one of those *lions* so singularly coupled with the *biches* of the opera."

Those *lions*, yesterday *crevés*, today *gommeux*. . . . tomorrow what?

"M. Louchard," added Camille; "he desires to be presented to you."

And he bade M. Louchard enter.

The stranger thus presented, doubly decorated on his coat and overcoat, removed his eye-glass from his bleared eye, and made a bow which the baron returned.

"Yes, Monsieur," said he, "I have asked Camille for the honor of an introduction and an interview with you in regard to an affair. . . . worthy of you". . .

Then, perceiving Madame sunk in her easy-chair, he said:

"But it seems to me that I intrude. I find you with your family; and, if you like, we will postpone" . . .

"Not at all, Monsieur, there is time for everything, for business as well as family affairs; and if the heart beats under the pocket, the pocket" . . . .

"Go right ahead without phrases, in spite of the ladies," said Camille, laughing at the baron, who had stopped short; "the pocket stifles the heart; the box takes precedence of everything; that's why it is called the strong-box."

"The madcap! To what affair do you refer, Monsieur?"

"Ah! a colossal, pyramidal affair, a Mont-Blanc," added Camille, laughing. "See the high forehead of the 'straight-haired Corsican' and the imperial lock of the tuft of Brumaire. This is the Napoleon of the press. . . . one idea a day, one victory rather; a great man without principles; a child of love, and consequently without prejudices; a strong friend of the ministry,—a recommendation to you, but not to me; one who has revolutionized the old press by inaugurating cheap journalism, in the interest, he says, of the people and the king, to that end having at his service two journals for and against; in short, a power in your world! Good luck to you!"

"You cover me with confusion, my dear Camille," said the journalist; "thank you!"

"I am at your service, Monsieur," said the banker, with a little more consideration; "I beg you to accompany me to my office."

"Gentlemen, permit me, I remain with these ladies."

The journalist and the banker left the room for the office.

When they were behind closed doors, the writer said to the baron :

"I have. . . . Camille said two. . . but I say three journals at my disposition for reaching the public. Two extremes and a mean. You understand! I speak to all."

"I understand, and I listen."

"I have one idea a day, according to Camille. The fact is that I have two or three, since I have three journals, but today a single affair needs the services of the three,—an affair of gold, a stock company for a coal mine."

"The transmutation of coal into gold. Then you have found the philosopher's stone."

"One need not be a sorcerer for that; coal is the bread of manufactures. France at last has the constitutional *régime* like England, the *régime* and country *par excellence* of manufactures and coal. You see here my prospectus. National manufactures, competition with the foreigner! Great attraction!"

"Excuse me!" said the banker, interrupting him coldly. "Where is this mine?"

"At Saint-Mégrin, Loir-et-Cher."

"In Sologne?"

"Yes."

"Ah! is there any coal in this mine?"

"We will put some there."

"Your reply is somewhat like that of Bonaparte's jailer, who, when his prisoner asked: 'But are there no trees in this island of fire?' answered: 'Sire, we will plant some.'"

"Hudson Lowe planted trees; I will deposit coal."

"But you forget that there are such people as policemen."

"You, too, forget what a certain Greek said of the law: 'It is a spider's web in which the little flies are caught and which the big ones break through.'"

" Yes, but that was a Greek."

" Well, I have for a partner the broker Gripon, one of the sixty of the Bourse, a Jew who is worth all the Greeks. And we Christians, who say so much evil of the entire Levant, though the finest of us was a Jew. . . . we see and calculate after the manner of these Orientals. So Gripon in person has proved to me, as clearly as that two and two make five according to his usual arithmetic, that, if Moses drew water from the rocks, we can draw gold from the coal which is lacking at Saint-Mégrin; that we have the philosopher's *press*, the transmutation of minerals, vegetables, and even animals; in short, that a miracle worked in the desert can readily be repeated in the mine of a saint."

" Leave your plan with me, my dear Nostradamus; I will give it serious study."

He shook hands with the journalist, who went away enchanted, and he returned to his family . . . after business.

" Ah! pardon me," said he as he came back, "but you know. . . . business! What robbery of the affections! The heart after the strong-box, as this disinterested Camille says. Well, my dear, how do you feel now?"

The crisis had returned, and Camille, who had thrown off his cloak, showed the banker his right arm in a bandage.

" What the devil's the matter with you?" said the baron, in surprise and alarm.

" Oh! nothing, as I have told these ladies. An accident, a fall from a horse."

" Take a little better care of yourself, Camille, or you will enable your cousin to prevail against us."

" Against us?"

" Yes, for you to an extent are the cause of the crisis from which Gertrude is suffering, my dear Camille."

" I! Then indeed am I disconsolate."

" Yes; we were discussing your marriage."

" My marriage? Against whom? as Scribe says."

" Oh! do not joke," said the banker, tenderly; "your cousin's bad health makes it important that she should be relieved of her duties, if not by a better, at least by a stronger mistress of the house; and that is why," he added, solemnly, "I have thought of doubling the union of our families. . . . so look you, my dear ward, with a straight blow, as Bertrand would say, full in the breast, I offer you my daughter."

" We cannot be too closely related, Monsieur," stammered Camille, politely.

" You hear him, ladies ". . .

" But first I must at least be able to dispose of my hand," said he, jokingly, showing his right hand in a scarf; "a marriage with the left hand would not suit Claire."

" It is enough to be a cousin," said Claire, dryly, bowing and going out.

As for the baroness, she kept silence, and the crisis increased.

The doctor who had been sent for entered with a jovial air, made inquiries about the case, took the pulse, looked at the tongue, felt of head and heart, and in short went through the entire diagnosis usual with physicians who get twenty dollars a visit; then he talked a great deal about stocks with the banker, and about prospects of rain and fine weather with the baroness; and he was going at last to write his prescription, when the spiritual director entered.

Confessor and physician bowed to each other without laughing, like Roman augurs; and then began between them a clerico-medical or medico-clerical conference, cassia and incense as Molière would say, in which each strove for supremacy.

They agreed on one point, — that Madame was suffering from an indisposition not immediately alarming, but which might become serious, and under certain circumstances dangerous or even fatal.

The baron listened with sympathetic attention.

"What! fatal?" said he.

"Yes," continued the physician, "fatal. But you have her life in your hands; and as death in this case is absolutely dependent upon you, Madame has nothing to fear."

"I do not understand you!"

"Well, I must explain myself. If Madame should become pregnant, she would not survive the birth of her child."

"That is, God must be her heir," said the confessor, betraying himself.

"Not a strictly necessary conclusion, Monsieur abbé," said the baron; "but, doctor, why would pregnancy be fatal? Women do not always die in childbirth."

"Surely not; when the woman is in good condition, it is an act of nature, always painful, but rarely fatal."

"Well, then?"

"It is because Madame is afflicted with a form of nervous disease which does not spare in cases of pregnancy. I should fear albuminuria, or perhaps something worse; confinement, in such cases, so aggravates the disease that it necessarily carries off the patient." •

"But," ventured Gertrude, "may the child survive?"

"Sometimes the mother gives her life to the child."

"Poor dear Gertrude!" exclaimed the baron, embracing her impulsively.

The consultation ended as it began, — upon stocks, rain, and fine weather.

Camille, on seeing the black coats enter, had gone out, threatened with a marriage, glad to evade and postpone the question, having all the morality of his day and time of life, no more.

"No luck!" said he to himself, feeling of his wounded hand, "no more in heroism than in marriage!"

Where was he going?

As his would-be father-in-law said, he was going to finish himself for a good husband by his life as a bachelor.

He was going, then, to Sophie's.

CHAPTER II.

THE STUDENTS. — SOPHIE.

The beauty in the India cashmere, the elegant interloper of the Mount of Piety, who had refused a dollar to her mother, and who had received a hundred dollars which the Hercules of the North claimed, had also grown and ripened, like our other characters.

Endowed with that common beauty which has so many admirers . . . ordinary wine is drunk in larger quantities than super ior Médoc . . . endowed on the other hand with a shrewdness that is far from ordinary, she had ascended the entire scale of prostitution.

She no longer went to the Mount of Piety ; but, from heart or calculation or both, — for these courtesans sometimes have a passion which, intense and strong though low and vile, overcomes everything, even their interest, their security, and their life, — she had kept, perhaps for his physical qualities, as he himself said, her first lover or her champion, the Hercules of the North.

She exhibited him only in extreme circumstances and in cases of necessity.

Established in the locality where her profession is carried on, in a charming villa in the Champs-Elysées, she received there a circle scarcely in keeping with the presence of the Hercules. As an *habitué* of her house, he would have been a hindrance to her business; he had to serve simply as a protector when occasion required. Therefore he never appeared except in case of need, and then only to settle tragic situations, like the God of Horace, *Deus ex machinâ.*

She practised her profession adroitly, prudently; she prospered. She had found out that, to get rich, one must not only work himself, but must make others work . . and still young enough to exploit herself, she was no less shrewd in exploiting her fellows.

It had just struck six in her parlor furnished with divans, sofas, lounges, ottomans, and long chairs of all forms and all countries. One would have said that she had consecrated her furniture to the God of rest.

In the middle of the parlor, however, was another piece of furniture, a large round table, at which were seated not a few blacklegs and young women.

Over the table was spread a doubtful cover, and it was loaded with a suspicious dinner, given evidently for the sake of form and under the name of *table d'hôte.*

Certainly the table must serve for something besides eating, in this house so admirably situated for some other purpos e, in an isolated nook between court and garden, no neighbor able to look over the wall and cast an indiscreet or curious glance at Sophie's double and triple mystery, culinary, erotic, and mercurial, when the real industry of her house was in progress.

The dinner over and the table cleared, an attendant, with the manners and accent of an Italian, brought some cards; and an old woman, resembling the mother who wanted a dollar at the Mount of Piety, brought candles.

Then the friends, of both sexes, all the guests, some standing, others sitting, others more than sitting, according to the Turkish proverb: "Better sitting than standing, and better lying than sitting," took their places at the gaming-table, drew from their pockets larger or smaller piles of gold, silver, and bank-notes, . . . and the game began.

Sophie presided and kept the bank.

Thus, when society is in a morbid condition, the disease which it lops off in one form springs up again in another. The public gambling-houses which it had closed opened again secretly, more dangerous than ever.

The game soon became warm; stakes increasing, losses and gains taking on enormous and suspicious proportions, amid the laughs of the winners, the fury of the losers, the jests and oaths of all; the women looking with favor upon the fortunate, despite the proverb: "Lucky in games, unlucky in love!" Refreshments —pardon me!—stimulants circulating, and the flame of the punch adding to the ardor of the game.

In short, the usual picture of clandestine gambling-houses, worse than the public ones, closed by the government, with which every vice is open and acknowledged, Bacchus as well as Venus, the whole Olympus of evil, except Mercury, except robbery . . . which remains hidden.

At this moment Camille entered, his arm still bandaged.

Honor to whom honor is due! Sophie moved to make room for him at her right. He was welcomed by all, both men and women, for he was the finest gambler of them all; though not the richest, the most free-handed; the least furious when losing and the least inclined to banter when winning; always even-tempered and courteous, whatever his luck; and as generous as he was polite to the conquered, especially of the other sex.

With his uninjured hand he drew from his pocket an enormous package of banknotes and began to play desperately, as if to drive himself to suicide, to ruin himself, to force himself to marry Claire.

With every turn of the cards he won . . . and already the eyes of all his adversaries were turned upon him ill-naturedly. All pupils and all hearts gravitated by the Newtonian law toward his mass in the direct ratio of its weight.

He had taken everybody's pile, among others that of the young cashier who had replaced Brémont at twice his salary and who had lost all; and he had politely handed back to him twelve bank-notes, at the same time making another package for Marraine, as they called Sophie, whose pile was also gone.

All envied this insolent luck; some, trying to pick a quarrel, ventured a suspicion and even an accusation; and things were on the point of taking an untoward turn for the lucky Camille, when suddenly the Italian valet entered, crying: "Police! Police!"

Then there was a general panic. Each one for himself! Men and women rose, ran some to the doors, others to the windows, and the commissary of police entered. He laid hands upon the money and the cards, and meanwhile everybody slipped away except Camille, who, desirous of taking away his pile, had only time to throw himself under a sofa in order to avoid arrest.

The room was thus emptied of the other players.

The commissary, taking off his scarf, straightway sat down beside Sophie, and, taking her in his two strong arms, he cried, laughing: "What a stroke, eh? Ha! ha! Are they plucked? And the little one-armed fellow, too! What luck! Ha! ha! Kiss me again."

And he began to laugh again as if he would split his sides and to kiss Sophie as if she were made of sugar.

During this passionate but ridiculous embrace Camille stole furtively from his hiding-place, and, throwing himself upon his money, seized it and leaped out of the half-open window into the garden.

"Not such a one-armed fellow, after all!" he cried, as he fled.

Sophie and the commissary sat a moment as if petrified.

Then, the first to recover, and crying "Stop thief!" she said to the Hercules: "Why don't you run after him, you stupid? Quick, now, and overtake him! Paolo, Babet, all hands into the garden, and close the street door at once!"

The Italian and the Hercules started with the fury of lashed dogs. Excited by Sophie and the hope of gold and vengeance, they followed Camille, and a terrible chase began through the darkness of the garden.

The fanfaronade continued.

"What! you lazy, clumsy rascals, you are going to let him escape, taking everything with him, cowards that you are!" Sophie shouted after them, with all the fury of Diana the huntress.

They had jumped out of the window, and, being more familiar with the grounds than he, they had already gained on him, and soon had him surrounded; the Italian, nimbler than the Hercules, getting between the fugitive and the door and cutting off his outlet from the garden.

Camille's position was growing critical, and God stood a chance of inheriting the Berville property.

But the Italian being the weaker of the two Curiatii, our young one-armed

Horace, without paying attention to the Hercules in the rear, and having only his left arm at his service, abandoned all reliance on that, and by a stroke known among wrestlers as the ram's stroke (*coup de belier*) rushed head first upon Paolo, bunted him in the belly, and sent him rolling on the ground.

Meanwhile the Hercules had come up and was about to seize Camille and hold him fast in his athlete's arms, when, though not the strongest, the one-armed man showed himself the shrewdest by taking gold pieces from his pocket and scattering them behind him as he ran, as Hippomenes of old threw down the golden apples in the path of Atalanta.

The Hercules stopped, bent over, and picked them up, thus giving Camille a start.

But the Italian, more light of foot and now armed with his national knife, had made a flank movement.

Camille tried the same trick: once more he sowed his gold in order to reap salvation.

"Don't stop to pick them up, imbeciles!" cried Sophie; "collar him first, and we will gather up the coins afterwards."

And they obeyed. Nothing further stopped them, but they were too late in adopting this course, fortunately for Camille.

At last he had gained the door of exit, left open by those who had preceded him in his retreat. He passed out, followed immediately by the two watch-dogs, who nabbed him and began to strangle him. Suddenly Paolo, who had more than one reason for doing so, let go his hold, crying, "Some one comes!" and ran away, leaving Camille to cry "Stop thief!" and struggle in the hands of the Hercules, before whom arose a robust rag-picker armed with his hook.

Hoffman's ward, God's rival for the inheritance of Gertrude's estate, Claire's intended, the student of so much promise, spent an unpleasant quarter of an hour and was indebted for his safety to Jean, who, delivering him from the Hercules, said to him with his sagacious raillery:

"You have made a fine escape, my young man! But if you had not had so much gold in your pockets, you would not have drawn this hornet-drone down upon you."

"Thanks, and pardon me for being unable to reward you better than by offering you this little sum," said Camille, holding out his almost empty purse. "Saved, but robbed! Where can I send you more?"

"It's not worth while," said Jean, with a gesture of refusal. "See, the rascal is running to the right; you go to the left, and good night."

To Camille the words sounded like an echo of the maternal voice; he pressed the rag-picker's hand and started off.

And the rag-picker went about his work again, saying to himself: "Devil take me if I am not decidedly taking the place of the 'cops.' Truly, the police department owes me a salary; and yet it talks of suppre ssing us rag-pickers. What ingrati-tude! It fears competition. Meanwhile we must fill our baskets."

And he worked away a t Sophie's dirt-pile.

Camille, under the pressure of pain, entered a drug-store that was still open, for the purpose of readjusting his bandage, which had been disarranged by the struggle.

What was the origin of this wound in his right hand?

On the morning preceding this fine eve ning he had been at the rooms of the Marianne society to celebrate regici de with a meeting, secret like the gambling-house.

CHAPTER III.

THE STUDENTS. — REGICIDE.

It was the anniversary of January 21.

The students and the workingmen were celebrating the execution of Capet by an extraordinary session, the reception of new members, and a commemorative banquet in the Passage de Génie, situated in the revolutionary faubourg of that period, the Faubourg Antoine, as it was called.

The room was decorated in red, the bust of Louis Philippe occupying a conspicuous position; the meeting was made up of the usual elements, students of all schools, laborers of all trades, the latter led by the workingman of the Mount of Piety with his hammer, the intelligent "typos" being most largely represented.

The session had been opened by the reception of candidates for membership, who swore upon their side-arms and their fire-arms, upon pistol and dagger, hatred of royalty and war upon it, pledging themselves to devote life, possessions, and liberty to the death of the king and the glory of the Republic, to obey the word of command without question, and to keep the secret on pain of death.

Then, by way of symbolism, Camille, who presided, had broken the bust of the king and crowned that of Marianne with oak and olive.

Then the breakfast had begun, the symbolism being kept up by the appearance on all the tables of a big fat calf's head crowned with laurel-sauce as the principal dish, and of Bon-Chrétien pears as the only fruit at dessert.

When the hour for toasts arrived, Camille, as president, had first proposed the toast of honor, the famous toast to the national Convention.

"To that Assembly of Titans who scaled Heaven and the Louvre, dethroned God and the King, and established Reason and the People; to that regicidal Assembly which beheaded the master and crowned the slave; to that patriotic Assembly which delivered the territory and created the nation; to that democratic Assembly which, on the ruin of the three orders, founded the Republic one and indivisible; to that humane Assembly which embodied the three principles of the French Revolution, the three dogmas of Athens, Sparta, and Thebes united, the Hellenic Trinity of modern religion, Liberty, Equality, Fraternity."

After this toast, which was the first and the last, Camille, pouring out his classical knowledge, had added, amid unanimous applause, that to talk was well, but that to act was better; that an ounce of deeds was worth a hundred pounds of words; that the best way to honor the heroes of the Convention was to imitate them; that there was no Capitol without a king's head; that Athens had slain Pisistratus, Rome Tarquin, Lucerne Gessler, London Charles, and Paris Louis; that it was necessary to put principles into practice and restore Reason to Notre-Dame, the Convention to the Tuileries, and the Commune to the Hôtel de Ville; in short, that they must enter upon their work, follow and avenge the ancients and the moderns, avenge Alibaud as well as Robespierre, deliver the People, and reestablish the Republic.

And upon his motion an order of the day had been unanimously voted that, on the first occasion when the king should appear in public, — laughter is mingled with everything in France, even with regicide, — they should rent a window on the Rue de Rivoli, extend a line, with a purse at the end for bait, directly over the royal head, and, at the moment when Philippe would certainly stop and lift his *poire* to this bait, fire at him the liberating shot.

Then they proceded to select by lot the member to whom this duty should be entrusted.

At that epoch police traps were very common, a famous spy, Vidocq, having set the fashion.

His successors have imitated him without replacing him. The young believe that the world was made yesterday because they were born day before yesterday, just as the old believe that the world will end tomorrow because they are to die day after tomorrow.

The truth is that the world is of longer duration than old and young together; that there were strong men before Agamemnon, that there have been some since, and that there are more to come; that men succeed each other and events are constantly repeated; in short, that the world ends and begins again incessantly, with the same bandits and the same heroes, in a perpetual becoming.　•

So just then the police burst into the room. Each one kept silence and his place.

The officer in command of the police asked who was charged with the duty of killing the king.

Silence was the sole response.

The officer then said:

"I arrest all present."

Then a new member, presented by Camille, a student like himself, the young Count de Frinlair, said:

"It is Camille Berville."

"Traitor," cried the officer, "I arrest you!"

"Oh!" exclaimed Frinlair, terrified.

"Yes, you, and you know the sentence! You must die."

Immediately the sham police, which was merely a device to test the fidelity of the members, decided that Camille should carry out the sentence. Then, with shouts of "Down with the king!" "Down with the traitor!" all went out, except Frinlair himself and Camille who was charged with his execution.

It was Camille who had presented Frinlair, his friend, his schoolmate, his fellow-student at the law-school. . . . and his rival for Claire's hand.

Nothing could be more opposite than these two friends, nothing more different than their characters. By birth, by nature, by instinct, by tendency, and by education, they thwarted and combatted each other. They hated each other as naturally as Montaigne and La Boëtie loved each other, and for no other reason than that one was Frinlair and the other Berville.

Camille's well-grounded goodness had overcome the spontaneous repulsion which Gaston de Frinlair had inspired in him.

Camille had often said to himself: "Because he is light and I am dark, because he has a flat nose and I a straight one, must I kill him?"

Frinlair was less scrupulous, and abandoned himself absolutely to his repugnance, his jealousy, his rivalry, and all the passions of race, caste, and class which animated him against Camille.

But duty got the upper hand of pity in Berville, who handed his weapon to Frinlair and said to him, in the manner of a Roman:

"Kill yourself!"

Frinlair was not a coward, but a traitor; his cry did not arise from weakness, it was the cry of an informer.

"Thank you," said he, taking the pistol; whereupon he fired at Camille, wounding him in the right hand and running away.

Camille, surprised and bleeding, had then left also, saying to himself: "I am wrong. The first time a man deceives me, he is wrong; the second, it is I."

And he recalled that the Count de Frinlair, an ambassador's son and an *attache* of the embassy, who had inspired in him an antipathy which it would have been well to have obeyed, had been his first deception and his first duel.

In fact, some months before, smitten with a grisette, — there were still grisettes in the days of Béranger, — and wishing to place her in furnished apartments, like the high-born student that he was, he had called on the handsome Camille and used this diplomatic language:

"Come, do me a friend's service. I am willing to shower extravagances on Mazagran, but first I wish to know if she is worthy of them. Pay court to her yourself; here is her address. If she resists you, you the irresistible, then I establish her. But give me your word of honor that you will tell me the truth."

"A vile errand, my dear; I refuse."

"But, I assure you, Mazagran is charming."

"I know it! I call it a vile errand, not because of her, but because of you and me."

"Not so sure that you would succeed, eh?" said Frinlair, piqued; "but try; friendship before scruples."

"Ah! on the ground of friendship? So be it, then, since you wish it and exact it! I go in search of pleasure through devotion."

After having thus hesitated, he had succumbed to youth, and had accepted. Camille was certainly more seductive than Frinlair, and, above all, more prodigal. Having made the test triumphantly, he was still in doubt whether he should be true with Frinlair. To inform against this good girl, whose only wrong consisted in having been risked by one and tempted by another and in having preferred him to her lover, seemed to him unworthy. But then, to deceive his friend! to violate his word of honor! Where will honor lodge itself next? A lesson, he had said to himself. The mistake lay in having accepted. He should have refused. Finally his promise proved the stronger with him, and, when he next saw Frinlair, he had said to him:

"Be economical!"

"What! It is not true."

"You give me the lie?"

"It is conceit!"

"Conceit and falsehood, two insults! Too many for one service, a bad one, it is true, but still a service asked and rendered. I demand, then, retraction or satisfaction."

The duel had taken place, and Camille had been wounded by a sword-thrust in the same hand. Decidedly this hand was unfortunate.

.   .   .   .

After the second wound made by the pistol, the unlucky Camille went to have it dressed by Doctor Dubois; and that is why he had his right hand in a scarf, neither heroic nor marriageable, powerless to offer a ring to Claire or the purse to Philippe, regretting one more than the other, and certainly owing his life to Jean.

CHAPTER IV.

THE CONFESSIONAL.

If all had changed, and for the better, in the Berville mansion which had become the Hotel Hoffmann, it was different in the Didier mansard. Mansard! the glory of the architect who gave his name to this invention which benefits the poor at the expense of the rats and to the advantage of proprietors! Glory! Be sure that a bad invention brings its author more renown than a good one. The guillotine made Guillotin illustrious; nicotine, Nicot; the bayonet, Bayonne; the plough, nobody. If you kill a hundred men, you have a cross; a thousand, a statue; a million, a column. To great men the world is grateful.

In the Didier mansard nothing had changed, at least for the better; nothing had improved, but, on the contrary, everything had deteriorated; to be sure, there was still and always the same care, the same order, the same cleanliness, Jacques's watch, rescued from the clutches of the Gripon, serving as the household clock. But there was no longer the enthusiasm, the passion, the ardor of former days. It was duty done by habit but wearily; the painful was manifest on every hand, after twelve long years of mourning, privation, and sickness.

What a difference and what a distance! Formerly this poverty was brightened and vivified by the joys of love and the family. The child's cradle, the sun of this poverty, flooded it with light and hope. Louise sang as she waited for her husband. Today this is ended and forever. Hope no longer dwells there. The widow waits for nothing but rest in the grave, her remains mingled with those of her husband. Her existence, like her countenance, is covered with a black veil. Every step in her life is a step towards death.

Seated at her work-table, exhausted by so many trials and sorrows, emaciated and pale, her hair thin and dull, her temples sunken, her eye leaden, her ear pallid, her nose pinched, her red cheek-bones indicative of quick consumption, her hands bony, Louise Didier labored with feverish activity, interrupted by fits of coughing which her bent posture aggravated.

She accomplished her task, the price of her daily bread, but without any heart in her work. That indescribable feeling of privacy, intimacy, belonging, the English home, — the French lack the word if not the thing, — the happiness in short that renders labor light, no longer existed for her. "No more love, hence no more joy," said Lafontaine, the eighth wise man if not the first.

The widow's look wandered for a moment from the table where she was sewing to the bed where Jacques had once lain for three days awaiting burial. Her gloomy thought did not evoke memories of their life together. This bed was no longer the nuptial bed of their lost loves, but the death-bed of Jacques. Misfortune had struck the poor mansard with its black wing and turned it into a tomb; all was mourning now for the widow of the money-bearer. The blow which opened Didier's forehead pierced just as fatally the heart of his companion. She had no further reason to be, to live, to hope. Her soul was killed, but not her conscience.

And, thinking of her daughter, she began again to sew and cough. ˙

"Oh! this cough is breaking me down," she said between two attacks. "Never mind, my neighbor is right. Marie is still so young, thirteen years. . . It would be necessary to take care of me. . . But how, without time or money?"

And she sorrowfully shook her head, absorbed in the fate that pursued her.

A discreet and yet familiar knock, which she recognized, recalled her to herself.

"Come in," said she, trying to put a tone of gayety into her voice.

The rag-picker entered respectfully . . . still robust after these twelve years, but grown old and gray; time spares nobody, not even rag-pickers; a little bent from the habit of carrying his basket, and saddened, like his poor *protégée*, by the very rebound of the evils from which she suffered, brave heart! It was no longer Jean, it was Father Jean.

"Ah! it is you, Father Jean," said the widow, affectionately.

"Yes. I bring you a little work which Madame Brémont handed me from herself and from Madame Gertrude; more than you can do, sick as you are."

And he laid on the table a bundle of materials with a note of explanation.

"And how are you this evening?" he continued.

"Always the same."

"Did you go to the consultation?"

"I have just returned. Again they have told me the same thing."

"Ah, yes, not sick enough to enter the hospital. I am not a doctor, but I say that it is none too soon to take care of you."

And, nothing doubting, he added:

"My heart must be clear. I will go to the doctor of the Board of Charity. They say he is a good man. And what did they prescribe for you?"

"Nothing," said Mme. Didier with a shrug of the shoulder.

"What, nothing! . . . Doctors. . . . impossible!"

"Nothing, I tell you, less than nothing. . . . follies. . . . The open air, the country, a journey to Nice, Bordeaux wine, roast meats."

"A fine prescription! It lacks nothing save the means of following it. A little money would serve the purpose better than their knowledge. And Mam'zelle Marie?"

"She is at confession. . . . for her first communion."
" Hm ! " growled Jean, twisting his beard.
Marie entered.
Time, so damaging to those who are descending, is kind to those who are rising. The little Marie had become Mam'zelle Marie.
The child had grown, charming and clever like her mother, inheriting beauty and goodness. There was no moral deficiency in her poor but healthy education. Precept, lesson, example, and practice, in labor and patience, tenderness and duty, had cultivated all the gifts of her pure, fine nature.
How account for this exceptional flower, which ought to be the rule in a better civilization?
Given the social creature, certainly the most human is that whose type offers the most harmonious *ensemble* of the highest and noblest faculties. We can say logically that the best of beings will be the most beautiful. The beautiful is the form of the good, says Plato. Organs are proportional to exercise, the social as well as the others. The serviceable, devoted, generous being developing more and more the highest organs at the expense of the lowest, by what is called the law of balance, it follows that the Didier species is likely to be more beautiful than ruminants like the Bervilles or carnivora like the Garousses.
The deformation of the race through egoism, pride, and interest is proverbial. The lip of the Hapsburgs, the nose of the Bourbons, and the ugliness of the Spanish grandees are historical.
Marie Didier's youth was of that type which art *par excellence*, Greek art, has characterized and named in its goddess Juno. Her hair of a golden-grain color, her eyes the color of the corn-flower and as brilliant as the corn-poppy, a perfect Ceres in the matter of color. . . . and in form as regular as a Madonna. Marie was to Claire what a Raphael is to a Goya. . . . the beauty of the flower and the goodness of the fruit.
Marie, physiologically, was what her mother was, plus the power given her by her worthy father.
Thus she had inherited the skill and clearness, as well as the elegance and conscience of her mother. She even surpassed Louise. For accumulation by hereditary transmission, as long as the race is not decrepit, is another law of nature; this makes progress. Raphael, the painter, surpassed his father; Charlemagne, the warrior, likewise. It is true that we have the younger Racine and the younger Dumas, but the exception proves the rule.
So Marie promised to be a beautiful girl as well as a good worker. And though she could already aid her mother in toiling for the daily bread of both, unfortunately she could also please the idle who eat bread without earning it for anybody.
Though her cunning hands relieved her mother by sharing her task, her youthful form attracted the looks of the idlers whose only task is pleasure.

Her youth was precocious. It was a beautiful early fruit, such as the Parisian hot-house produces prematurely under the influence peculiar to great cities, the current of ideas, labor, and even want, which rapidly ripens the subject, when it does not rot it, for the thousand and one hands always ready to pluck it.

At thirteen, then, Marie was or seemed sixteen; and already she was called the rose of the faubourg. She already went to the clothing shops to carry patterns and bring back orders which she executed, Louise aiding, successfully.

The mother, who followed, as she had said erewhile at the parish-church, her religion by birth and habit, had wished Marie to make her first communion, and had sent her to catechism and consequently to confession, but at the Church of Saint-Roch, where her husband had been blessed, and not Saint-Paul, her parish-church, where she had been received so badly.

Marie had returned in tears.

Her mother, on seeing her with her white cheeks and red eyes, became alarmed and asked her why she had wept.

Marie did not answer.

" What's the matter? " urged Louise.

"Nothing, mother," said the child.

"It is your first lie."

"Why!" ventured Jean, with a shake of his head, "she comes from confession."

"Is it repentance?" said Louise.

The child, either from shame or from fear of grieving her mother, said nothing, but took her work and labored in silence.

"There is something beneath all this," said Jean to Madame Didier, "and in your place" . . . .

"Has Monsieur the priest sent you away for lack of memory, attention, or obedience? Tell me, I beg of you."

"I will not go back to confession."

"Bah! a false shame. Monsieur the priest has scolded and punished you. But, dear little mule, don't you see that, in refusing to speak and obey your mother, you are committing another fault, a sin, for which you will be obliged to return to confession and get absolution in order to make your communion?"

"Well, then, I will not make it."

"What! at your age? But it is necessary. You are thirteen, and we have no time to lose at catechism; we must work all day long, for I feel that I am growing worse."

"Yes," said Jean, "he who labors prays."

"Come, then, speak! Does Monsieur the priest refuse you? Do you say your prayers badly? If that is why you are sent away, go back to the church and ask pardon of Monsieur the priest; or else I will go myself, sick as I am, to have an explanation with him."

"No, mother, I will go tomorrow to take the sacrament quickly, and then work with you and for you, in order that you may rest and that I may leave you no more."

And they kissed each other effusively.

Jean bade them good night, still shaking his head and repeating:

"There is something beneath all this, and I am going to find it out!"

The next night, her day's work done, Marie, out of filial piety, went to confess. A word before her arrival.

Is there in the world an institution more infamous and an outrage on morals more flagrant than the confessional?

Auricular confession has come with celibacy for the greatest glory of God, the priesthood, and the sanctuary. It is the crowning of the edifice.

Formerly confession was public; it was a delusion rendered by the private conscience to the public conscience, distressing no doubt, but worthy of the remission of sin. Confession, like gambling, has gained nothing by secresy, and this monstrous clerical custom causes the most shameless and pernicious of immoralities to be, not only tolerated, but approved, consecrated, and paid for.

I call this the most fatal injury to the family and to society. It is never good for man to have God for a rival. The priest, representing God, always possesses at least half of woman, if not all of her. Society is strong only through the family, its foundation; in this lies the superiority of Protestant nations. A warning to peoples who confess.

A man and a woman who come too near each other at night on a bench are arrested, convicted of an outrage on modesty, and sentenced. A man and a woman may meet with impunity in a church and, what is more, in a box, — Pandora's box. La Poubelle is nothing!

The greatest prose-writer of the epoch, Paul-Louis Courier, who was murdered partly for this, wrote an admirable page against confession, concluding by saying that, out of many priests whom he had known, he had met only one old one frank enough to say: "I have ended my life without transgression, but I should not like to begin it over again!"

Do we realize indeed that we allow our young wives and even our young daughters to shut themselves up on their knees in a religious niche, on their knees beside a young priest, a bachelor, idle, urged on by high living, excess of force, and privation, both alone in the darkness, head to head, mouth to mouth, and discussing conjugal questions. As well put a match under straw without fearing fire, or bread before a fasting man without fear of his tooth!

Even the soldier, who has made no vow of chastity, would be better than the priest.

Would one expose his wife and daughter to the same risk shut up in a chamber even with a friend?

It would be neither decent nor prudent.

But here again there would be a counterpoise. The man of the world has certain natural reserves through the legitimate satisfaction of his wants, through respect for the family of another, through love of his own,—in a word, through community of duties.

But the priest, picked, chosen, like the conscript, neither infirm nor deformed, young, virgin, and—let us repeat—idle, forced by rich food, idleness, and continence, is in a continuous, endemic, and constitutional state of desire; and if there is a single one among them all, as Pius IX says, who can conquer nature, it is that of Paul-Louis Courier.

So, having eaten a good dinner, very stimulating and, thanks to the *benedicite*, thoroughly digested, assimilated, and converted into chyle, the fat and lusty abbé Ventron, full of the warmest products of the sunshine, wines and viands, in full possession of his animal spirits, was seated in his box in the corner of a chapel of the Virgin, at the back part of the church, in the shadow of the arches and far from the lamp of the chorus, which, moreover, burns but does not light.

All was silence and gloom, profound mystery around him, and he was about to fulfil the sacred duty of the priest, exercise his holy ministry authorized and salaried by the State, lend ear to his flock, counsel them, guide them, give them moral lessons, purify them, absolve some, reprove others, distribute absolution to these, repentance to those,—in short, confess them.

For this rehearsal of the last judgment the representative of God sat indifferently well upon his cramped throne, filled with his digestive apparatus. Then the anointed of the Lord blew his nose, coughed, spat, took snuff, filled his lungs full of air, and at last lent ear to the first of a score of catechised who filed past him indifferently and rapidly, like ordinary offenders in a police court.

Marie, who, through reluctance to take her place, had allowed all the others to pass, still hesitating, but fearing to displease or disappoint her mother, decided at last to kneel.

This catechumen was different. The priest took no more snuff. He no longer gave ear. He applied his lips to the grating that scarcely separated him from Marie's blonde head, until he almost touched, until he even smelt, the child's flesh.

"Say your *Confiteor*."

Marie recited:

"I confess to God the omnipotent, to the blessed Virgin"...

" There, that will do! *Amen!* What do you confess?"

"My disobedience to you."

"A great sin, my child. And why not obey me?"

"Because you have made me cry."

"Ah! it is for your good, Marie. Between you and me, follower and priest, there must be frankness, confidence, and secrecy. God is an enemy of pride and of falsehood, two great sins, two mortal sins, punished with the eternal fires of hell, two blasphemies in fact, for God is truth as well as humility."

The young girl remained silent.

"Ile is love also," continued the priest. "I have already asked you more than once this question: before uniting yourself to God by the holy communion, have you ever thought of this holy alliance? Have you ever dreamed of the sweet Jesus in his human form? At least, have you ever seen your guardian angel cover you with his wings?"

"No, father, never."

"Then I fear you have had visions less pure, desires more earthly; perhaps you have thought of marriage, dreamed of a carnal tie with some lad of your age. Doubtless you have had conversations, readings, caresses, kisses, *oscula viri*," and he spoke the Latin of the "Confessors' Manual," of Monseigneur the bishop Bouvier.

"I do not comprehend you, father," said the poor child, in an agitated voice, fortunately understanding the priest's French scarcely better than his Latin.

"Come with me into the sacristy," said he; "I will exorcise the demon of pride, I will evoke the guardian angel; come into heaven, my dear daughter, I will give you a book illustrated with holy images, and I will explain all this to you. Yesterday you refused."

"No, father, I do not want to," said Marie, instinctively rebelling.

"Obey, rebel," said the theological ogre, "if you wish to make your first communion. I am your spiritual father. You have no other."

"That's where you make your mistake," cried a terrible voice.

Then a man, standing at the corner of the confessional and having heard all, took Marie by the arm, saying to her in a low tone: "Silence!" and then braced himself with all his might between the wall and the box and overturned the confessional upon the confessor.

At the noise of the fall and the cries of the priest enclosed like a turtle in its shell, all the defenders of the sacristy came running up, the Swiss with his cane and the beadles with their maces; and, seeing the box overturned upon its precious contents and then a man escaping with the young girl, they tried to stop them.

But the man, arming himself with a chair and swinging it over his head, in a combat such as is not described in Boileau's *Lutrin*, piled the beadles on top of the Swiss, while the warden called for the police.

The police arrived too late, as usual,—that is, when the man and child had left the church.

Then, fortunately for the avenger of public morality, the incident had gathered a group and a crowd. The man told what he had done and why he had done it; and, the people applauding, the police, who were not the police of Charles X, and who realized, moreover, that they were few in number, either dared not or could not arrest Jean, or even prevent him from going back into the church with the crowd, taking the confessional, carrying it out upon the steps, and setting fire to it.

The confessor, of course, was no longer inside.

The man took the child home to her mother.

"Ah! it is you!" said Louise to Marie; "then you met Father Jean?"

"I beg pardon, excuse me, Madame, I did not meet Mam'zelle Marie; I followed her, and for her good; and I bring her back to you none too soon . . . and I restore her to you safe and sound, but I hope that you will not send her again to confession."

"Why?"

"Why, because it is like sending Little Red Riding Hood to the wolf! because that scoundrel of a priest has said things to your child which she fortunately did not understand, but which would make you blush to hear and me to repeat to you."

"Jean is right, mother; I will never go back there; and I will not make my first communion."

"What?"

"Do you wish her to make it with the priest rather than with God?"

"What do you mean, Father Jean?"

"I mean that your priest would have stolen your child but for me; that, if I had a child, I would rather entrust her to a convict than to a priest; and that it is better to be damned with the devil than saved in the Ventron Paradise. Ah! pardon me, Madame Didier, I swore to poor Jacques that I would watch over her . . . . and over you; and if I had arrived too late to save her from the priest, I would have killed him."

"Ah! my God! in whom can we trust? I will not send her again! Father Jean! thank you! thank you!"

And Jean went to bed, like a good guardian, having done his duty against the confessional and the brothel, having saved Marie's honor as he had saved Camille's life.

CHAPTER V.

THE CHECK.

There was one person in the English quarter, near the Madeleine, who was not happy,—a light-complexioned son of Albion landed in Paris, Master Jack, a jockey who had come expressly to ride Frinlair's horse at the Longchamps races.

The unfortunate Jack was what is called *in training* in the language or slang of the turf, a slang which we have borrowed from the English, as in the case of the word *redingote*, riding coat.

That is to say, Jack was preparing to make the most of his master's horse, not to improve the race of horses, but to damage the purse of men.

It is so little the object of races, or *courses* as we call them in French, to improve the equine race that they have succeeded in making horses without neck enough to feed in pasture or belly enough to digest, and with only such legs as will enable them to run fast, but not long,— which is called progress.

Similarly, always under pretext of improving the race, the makers of meat and fat have manufactured cattle without horns— what will the bull-fighters say?— and without legs, all belly, balls of flesh and suet for John Bull's puddings and roast beef.

Ah! when the English turn their attention to anything, what a creation! what a world! what master-pieces! all for the mouth and the pocket! the last word of civilization.

But if the animal suffers through this British mania which we are beginning to import into France, the human race suffers still more .... in so far as the race can be represented by a jockey.

To an extent he doubtless does represent it; and for this reason we refer to the miseries of poor Jack.

The unfortunate biped had submitted himself for a fortnight to a real martyrdom in order to fit himself as thoroughly as possible to mount a quadruped.

In the first place, he had to be weighed regularly, morning and evening, to detect the slightest increase of weight and stop it as soon as possible.

He was visited by a doctor, who prescribed accordingly.

Neither roast beef nor pudding! Lord! Neither stout nor porter! Only small beer and oatmeal, Great God!

And, coupled with this *régime* of abstinence, a *régime* of continence!
No expenditure without receipts! No Venus without Ceres or Bacchus! Diet
in mensa necessitated diet *in toro*. Forbidden to see his wife!

At last, the day of the races having arrived, ready to mount his horse, with
jacket and cap of Frinlair's colors, he had been weighed for the last time and found
in condition. Good weight, — that is, reduced to two-thirds of his natural weight.
Such is the desire of amelioration . . . and speculation.

Homicide by wholesale is punished, but is permissible by retail. See Merlatti.

Camille, national and patriotic, and out of personal antagonism also, had bet
against Frinlair's English horse and jockey. Perfecting also the equine and
human races of France, he had entered a French horse and jockey who, unfortunately less patriotic than his master, had consented to sell himself to Frinlair,
himself and his horse, which he had drugged; and the traitor allowed himself to
be beaten on the turf, preferring much gold without glory to much glory and little
gold.

Thus Camille and his horse were improved by the Longchamps races.

Frinlair's jockey, or rather his English horse, had beaten by a head the French
horse, dosed and even held in at the end of the race by its treacherous rider.

An enormous stake — these races are only a gambling scheme — had been
wagered by Camille against Frinlair, and Camille had lost.

The bet had been made upon trust, — a debt of honor.

Among those who witnessed the race were the baron, and his daughter in a dazzling toilette, sitting with her father on the back seat of a four-in-hand and applauding Frinlair's triumph.

The victory decided, the four horses, driven at a gallop, took the baron back to
the hotel.

No sooner had he arrived than he went up to Camille's room and placed a paper
on his desk so that he would see it on entering.

And scarcely had he gone out when Camille entered, showing all the signs of
the keenest vexation.

In the first place his pride was involved. He had been beaten both by Frinlair
and in the presence of Mazagran, whom he had definitively taken and at great
cost by way of compensation for the trick played on this good girl. She took her
revenge in her own way, by ruining him.

His love — I beg pardon — his loves cost him the very eyes in his head.

A basket pierced, and with several holes; disputed or rather divided, as Figaro
says, between politics and pleasure; rarely sleeping in his own bed; sober, however, if he ate alone, — his good health held out, but not so his fortune. Gertrude,
tainted by Claire, had ceased giving him advice to which he did not listen. The
baron was too indulgent to say a word, and Camille inherited from his mother a
contempt for money, turning up his nose at it. But every virtue has its vice. She

was generous; he was wasteful, and in every direction. Love, horses, wagers, suppers, he literally ran to his ruin. . . . . and this time, in fact, even honor was compromised.

How pay this debt to Frinlair? he said to himself. Twenty thousand dollars! I have exhausted everything . . . and this week has been a week of disasters. I have bled my guardian at every vein! What's to be done now? Yet by some means or other a way must be found! Not to pay Frinlair is out of the question. To fail him is worse than to fail others. Not pay him! I would rather take the leap and marry!

Suddenly, casting his eyes mechanically on his desk, he saw the paper. "What's that?"

A check for twenty thousand dollars on the bank, payable on demand, to the bearer, with a blank left for the name of the payee and signed. It had only to be filled out. That could be done; the paper lay waiting for it, all ready to be cashed. A frightful temptation seized Camille; the struggle was long and keen. Who had put this paper there? The baron. How? Why? A test? Doubtless a trap? Oh, no, to secure the marriage? And he turned the check over in every direction. At last he took his pen, and was just on the point of writing his name, when he cried:

" Ah! the name that she bore, that she taught me to write on a different sort of checks, bread-checks!"

And he threw down his pen, placed the check on the desk again, rang for Léon who came, and said quickly:

" Ask the baron to come here. Tell him that I am indisposed, and that I desire to speak to him."

The valet bowed and went out, and soon the baron appeared in alarm.

" What's the matter, Camille?" he said.

Camille, taking up the check with the ends of his fingers and showing it to the baron, said:

"You recognize this blank check; you have put it here I know not why; but take it away; it will only be lost or fall into the hands of forgers."

" But, my dear friend ". . .

" I do not want it! Prodigal, yes; but not guilty."

" Ah! guilty . . . with me!"

" I might be impelled to commit a forgery. Decidedly, dear guardian, your kindness will make me distrust you," said the ward.

"But you have twenty thousand dollars to pay this very day," said the baron, vexed and insisting. " It is either money or honor."

" I know it . . . . but since you speak of honor; wait, I will accept this check, but on condition of earning it."

" How?"

"Well, I abandon my life of follies and dangers; I will leave the city of pleasure, Paris, and go to the city of work, London, to manage our branch house. The manager has sent you his resignation; I will take his place at the same pay; then I shall be able to pay my debt of honor without dishonoring myself."

"Separate from us, my dear Camille, leave us! What are you thinking of? What would Claire say? What would become of my dearest wish, your marriage with my daughter? Disturb thus all my wisest as well as dearest plans! Never! No, never will I allow your departure. Exile yourself, deprive yourself of Paris to earn money with which to pay Frinlair? But you are not — I beg pardon — we are not reduced to that point, thank God! I do not calculate in dealing with you, Camille, and if I have thus offended you, I ask you to excuse me. As your guardian I must look out for your fortune, but I can also reassure you as to your resources; and were they insufficient, you could still rely on mine. So frankly keep these twenty thousand dollars to your account and in your name, which I write in plain letters, with my own hand, before your two eyes, scrupulous madcap! Here!"

And he handed him the check made out in his name.

"With that understanding, all right then! Thank you! Frinlair will be honorably paid, and I honestly acquitted."

An hour later Frinlair had his money and Camille his receipt, the latter capable now of marrying gracefully the daughter of so good a guardian, who beat all the American uncles in the plays of Scribe.

Meanwhile Gertrude, worked upon by Claire and the abbé Ventron, still thwarted her husband's plan, favored the young count, and had even invited him to a party given expressly for him, in his honor, and in the interest of his marriage.

CHAPTER VI.

THE PLOT.

With the stubbornness characteristic of a lamb from Berri and a pious one at that, Gertrude persisted in her design of giving her adopted daughter to the Count de Frinlair, in spite of the wish of her husband, who intended her for cousin Camille. She was resolved.

Decidedly God and Claire, to say nothing of the king, were opposed to this lowest of marriages, impious, vulgar, and regicidal.

On the day after the scandal of Saint-Roch the Baroness Hoffmann, her daughter Claire, and their unfailing confessor were together in the parlor, conferring on this subject with mysterious animation.

"My poor child," said Gertrude, "the plan pleases me as much as it frightens me, and really I do not dare ". . .

."Why not?" said the abbé, solemnly. "God is stronger than the baron. His will be done!"

"Ah! your reverence, I shall be Madame Berville . . . . ha! ha!" exclaimed Claire, with a nervous laugh that broke in her throat.

"No," answered her mother, "you shall be Countess de Frinlair or". . .

She did not finish, maintaining a stormy silence, walking back and forth in her excitement as if to give herself, merely by physical motion, the moral strength to combat her husband.

Claire, sitting on the sofa, was no less agitated.

The priest alone preserved the coolness befitting a director of consciences.

The darkness of evening, like a rising tide, little by little invaded the sumptuous parlor.

As the seconds went by, the room became shaded with a deeper tint. This royal luxury, worthy of the first banker of the court, became less loud and gained in grandeur what it lost in brilliancy.

The vast apartment no longer dazzled, it impressed; the ceiling, the mouldings, and all the ornaments seemed to float in a magic atmosphere; the chandelier was more sombre in its gleaming. The golds, too resplendent by daylight, assumed a dead tone which concentrated their richness.

The Boules, master-pieces of a past art, marvels of a dream of the "Thousand

and One Nights," and such as the Louvre itself no longer offered to the king, seemed, in the penumbra, endowed with a fantastic life. The pictures became kaleidoscopes; the family-portraits dissolving views in frames gilded with fairy-like illusions.

All that was fixed seemed to move and change, thus exciting more and more the strained nerves of the two women.

An idea of envy, common and natural to the fortunate of this world who are dying of weariness and idleness in the enchantment of their luxury, then came to Claire's mind:

"There is no one to thwart her in her inclinations. She is very happy, she!"

"Of whom do you speak?" asked Gertrude.

"I am thinking of our little seamstress who goes off so contented with the roll of silk which she takes away for her work. I envy this Marie," continued Claire.

Did the baroness remember that the banker Berville also envied his collector, when the latter was dying in defence of his receipts? . . .

She shuddered.

"Be still," said she; "it is offensive to God thus to censure his designs by ingratitude. It seems to me that his vengeance — pardon me, his justice will visit us with some misfortune."

And the baroness sat down beside Claire, took her forehead in her two hands, thought a minute, and said feverishly:

"Must it be, yes or no?"

"Yes," said the priest, "it is an exceptional case! For great evils great remedies! The end justifies the means. Everything in the interest of heaven and for the glory of God!"

"That or the convent, mother!" cried Claire.

And no longer containing herself, she threw herself back upon the sofa, weeping and sobbing.

Gertrude, moved by this spoiled child's sorrow, bent over toward Claire and took her in her arms, fondling and caressing her.

"There, it is over, isn't it, my pet? Go to your room; I am going to talk with your father. You will be satisfied with me."

"Thank you, good mamma," said Claire, effusively. "Courage!"

And she went out, counting on her mother.

Gertrude at once rang and sent for the baron, who soon arrived, ever attentive and gallant toward his wife.

"Here alone and in the twilight, and with Monsieur the priest," said he, smiling; "a conference. . . . and you call me in. . . . a case of conscience? France is not Spain, and husbands here have a consultative voice. What is the question? Let us see, my dear. I am listening."

And, lighting a candelabrum, he added pleasantly:

"Let there be light. Then my eyes will do service as well as my ears. Now go on," said he at last, in a more serious tone.

Gertrude hesitated:

" Will you be as reasonable as you are charming?"

"What do you mean, my friend?" said the banker, smiling but attentive.

" Well, seriously and finally, what is your last word in regard . . . to your . . to our daughter?"

"Claire?" said the baron, slowly, to give himself time for reflection.

"Yes, since God has not granted me the grace that he granted to Sarah, I must say: Our daughter. . . . Well?"

"I wish her to be happy, nothing more or less."

"So do I. And I know that she does not love Camille."

"She will love him. I have told you repeatedly that I have decided upon this marriage, necessary in our common interest and for the happiness of us all."

"Happiness, no! interest, perhaps! So, then, the gross word is out at last! The strong-box!"

"Pardon me," said he, with an ever-increasing firmness. "I know that figures irritate your nerves, my generous dear. But then a million is a million; it is Claire's dowry . . . and I must look to it. This marriage leaves it in the strong-box, as you say, in our treasury. This marriage therefore is indispensable. Consequently, my dear, send out your invitations for the engagement party."

" And in this account your child's heart figures as an item. I protest, Monsieur, in her behalf and in mine, against this abuse. of paternal and conjugal power, against this marriage objectionable from every standpoint, — character, opinion, and religion."

"And yet indispensable," replied the baron; "that is my last word."

And he bowed and went out, for the first time inflexible before his wife's will.

Gertrude, Ventron, and Claire, who had come back, looked at each other in amazement at first, and then took heart again.

Claire was the first to revolt:

" Gaston nevertheless!"

The priest, more thoughtful, said:

"What inexplicable and mysterious resistance! We shall have much trouble in conquering."

"Have faith, your reverence," said Gertrude. And, more royalist than the king, she cried: "God helping, we will conquer!". . .

Then the *coup d'état* was decided upon.

CHAPTER VII.

Not without difficulty had the baroness been able to obtain the baron's consent to the invitation of Frinlair to Camille's engagement party.

Every time that this name was brought to his hearing in conversation, he became horrified; every time that he heard the young *attaché* of the embassy spoken of, he bristled up, in anger or in consternation. It was more than an ordinary aversion, it was a repulsion as absolute as the attraction which he felt for Camille.

Gertrude, the abbé Ventron, and Claire had used all their strength and strategy to overcome the baron's repugnance.

Claire had shrewdly invoked her boarding-school friendship. She had not said a word of the brother; she had spoken only of the sister. And as the baron had made the mistake, so far as his cause was concerned, of allowing the sister, Claire then had concluded:

"How invite the sister without the brother?"

The abbé Ventron had spoken only of the high royal and papal relations of the Frinlair family, naturally without making the slightest allusion to Claire's love.

As for Gertrude, she, on the contrary, had placed squarely before her husband her prejudices and resolutions against Camille who was only rich and for how long? She could not understand the baron's inexplicable objections to the invitation of so pious a young man, a model of conduct and virtue, whom it was well to cultivate and with whom Camille especially had everything to gain.

"Except his money," the baron had retorted, thinking of the check.

She had finished, as usual, by a charge at full speed upon the democrats, the atheists, the libertines, enemies of God, religion, and society, and against the baron himself, who had disappointed her by his faith in Camille, the worst of all.

And the discussion had become a dispute, and finally the baron, weary of war and even fearing another nervous crisis, had yielded.

Count Gaston de Frinlair, heir of the personage who had supplanted the Duke de Crillon-Garousse in his estate, had the family traits. He inherited from his father the diplomatic genius and profession.

He had at last received the invitation to the rout sent him by the baroness, impelled, as we have seen, to do him this honor by the interest of Claire and the abbé Ventron and by her own inclination.

It was a triple coalition in favor of Frinlair against Berville, who was more than indifferent, and against the baron, who was alone in warmly championing Berville against Frinlair.

Evidently the chances, in spite of paternal and conjugal omnipotence, were in favor of Frinlair. What woman wants, God wants, says the proverb. But what God and woman, and two women, want, the devil himself will want.

Yes, but how to present himself at the house of the baroness, where he ran a risk of meeting Camille? And how face Camille after the treacherous pistol-shot? This was what the young diplomat asked himself.

Camille had not demanded satisfaction of the traitor. One does not fight with Judas; one is content to let him hang himself, provided he have sufficient conscience left.

Conscience and diplomacy are incompatible; remorse did not torment Frinlair, and the spirit of Talleyrand inspired him.

A diplomat is a gentleman who lies in the interest of his country, and who consequently can lie in his own interest also.

Language was given to man — I beg pardon, to the diplomat — to disguise his thought.

Starting from all the axioms of his sixth class, the young *attaché* wrote this letter to Camille:

"Dear victim, — I do not dare to say dear friend, and know not how to write to you after the crime that I have committed against the cause and friendship. My conduct is certainly inexcusable, but not inexplicable.

"That is why, knowing your broad mind, I dare to appeal to it. You know my position; the son of an ambassador, belonging to the Court, and threatened with arrest in company with the others, I yielded to a mad fear which caused me to lose my head and my heart.

"I saw everything compromised, not only for me, but for my father, my sister, and all my relatives destitute of fortune, and — I blush to confess it — I sacrificed you to my family.

"You who so dearly loved your mother perhaps will forgive me for having been so weak in a matter that concerned mine; and I hope that you will not refuse me your pity, until I can find an opportunity to regain your esteem and your friendship."

To this chancellor's letter Camille simply sent the following answer:

"I pity you . . . . . and I hope you will see to it that you get your head broken for the people at the next insurrection."

This reply, in which for the first time and forever he ceased to address Frinlair in the language of intimate friendship, was interpreted by the young diplomat as meaning indulgence and pardon. So he resolved to accept the invitation and go to Gertrude's rout.

The Baroness Hoffmann's party was a splendid affair.   Her husband's refined *bourgeoisie* had raised the style of her receptions; and the abbé Ventron, an accustomed attendant of such worldly festivities, did not complain of them.

This evening, risen from his fall, holier than ever, thanks to a sermon against calumny, and free from certain bruises and occasional allusions in the wicked newspapers to the bruised parts, the abbé showed even more discretion and reserve than at the Berville dinner, not speaking to the ladies, not looking at any in particular, his Tartuffe's handkerchief always in his hand, addressing only the mistress of the house and her daughter, his attention absorbed by the ices and other refreshments incessantly passed around on silver trays.

Gertrude applauded his success, which seemed to her the triumph of God himself over the devil.

The baron was delighted with Camille, who had consented to open the ball with his daughter.

Claire had accepted, making a frightfully wry face at Camille and, behind her fan, sweet eyes at Gaston.

Frinlair was thus avenged for the cold welcome given him by the baron by Claire, who was almost forward in her attentions, and for the still colder salutation of Camille, who had simply bowed, refusing his hand with this bitterly polite excuse:

" Pardon me, Monsieur Count, I cannot; it is impossible for me to use my hand to take yours."

The first quadrille began.

It was really a true rout in the full force of the word, a rush of all Paris, ladies and women, sharpers and nobles, people with nothing and people with everything, hardened in the old privileges or converted — Gertrude said perverted — to modern equality.   Louchard was sounding Ledru-Rollin for political news for his two journals, and Gripon for financial news for everybody; and the young notary, Loiseaux, was talking over the marriage contract with the baron.

Watching the quadrille, the abbé Ventron, more austere than ever, said to Gertrude as he sipped:

" What a frightful thing the ball-room is!   What an example!   What chance has innocence there?   What a denial of the family, what a symbol of our sad morals, adultery and promiscuity!   See these quadrilles, these figures, all temptation and abomination.   First two forward! very well so far; but first three forward! then the gentleman changes his lady and the lady her gentleman!   And balance your ladies.   And the waltz!   O Lord, the sanctity of marriage!"

Gertrude almost crossed herself in assent and contrition.

When the ball was at its height, the abbé, between two rum sherbets, emboldened because he had especially remarked, in spite of his moral reflections upon dancing, Claire's coolness toward her cousin and her ardor toward Frinlair, said to himself: "It is time."

Then, taking advantage of the moment when the baron led Camille away to the card-room, by agreement with Gertrude he made a sign to Claire, who approached the baroness; and he softly spoke a word in her ear.

Claire made a gesture of assent and joy, and quickly started toward her mother's oratory, a sort of boudoir-sanctuary adjoining the very ball-room which so shocked the modesty of the abbé. She entered; and straightway Frinlair, who did not lose sight of her, upon a similar honest and pious instigation from the priest, went in the same direction and entered also.

Here was a fine *tête-à-tête* premeditated and arranged by the abbé acting as a go-between, who watched at the entrance of the holy place to see that these loving devotees should not be disturbed.

Then this pious matchmaker entered with the faithful Gertrude, whose director he was; and there, in presence of the baroness whom he had led to his ends by all means, for the salvation of her soul, the glory of God and of the Church,— in short, that her goods might not become the prey of the devil,— he affianced the two lovers without the father's knowledge and against his will.

Camille meanwhile was playing, and consequently wholly absorbed in his game.

The baron, seeing him engaged in a manner which he so much approved, had returned to the ball-room, casting his eyes about in search of his daughter whom he did not see. Suspecting something, he then looked for his wife, whom he did not see either, and finally for the abbé Ventron, who was likewise not to be seen.

He questioned the servants anxiously.

He was, however, far from suspecting the place and cause of their retreat, when he saw his wife and her confessor coming from the direction of the oratory.

He went straight up to them and said dryly:

"Where is my daughter?"

"She is praying," answered the abbé.

"Praying . . . at this hour?"

"Why not?" said Gertrude.

"Alone?"

"No."

"And with whom?"

"With her affianced."

"Her affianced?" cried the baron.

"Yes," said Gertrude, boldly.

"Her affianced is Camille," said the father.

"No, it is the Count de Frinlair."

"Frinlair!"

"Himself!"

"Never! No, never will I have any other than Camille for my son-in-law. Never shall my daughter marry Frinlair. I am her father . . . . I am the master . . . pardon me, you force me to say it and prove it, and I will". . .

Just then the happy couple, Gaston and Claire, came out of the oratory together, arm in arm, a little rumpled, doubtless from having knelt, but with shining eyes, walking thus attached like two beings henceforth to be but one, sure of being united against all, in spite of father and statute, in the name of heaven, by virtue of the very power and will of God, by an infallible means, by superior force, which would subject the baron, whom they even seemed to defy.

What had passed between them to give them this assurance? God alone had seen and knew. A betrothal at least had been effected, and not that of Camille; God helping, as the baroness had said, God stronger than the baron, as the abbé Ventron had said.

Camille, who had lost at cards, came back to the ball-room with the right to be fortunate in love, and not even looking to see whether Claire was present or not.

The baron reminded him of his duty toward his daughter, saying in a displeased and almost threatening voice:

"But at least think of the dowry; you will need it."

"Cousin, for the next waltz," said Camille, smiling.

"Thank you, Monsieur, I am engaged," and she remained on Frinlair's arm.

Then the baron lost his self-possession, and raised his hand as if to take away his daughter.

The baroness intervened in time to avoid scandal:

"My friend . . . take care!"

And the fright that she had had and the effort that she had made threw her into such a crisis that she had to be carried from the ball-room, followed by Claire, the doctor, the confessor, and her husband.

Camille went back to the gaming-table in search of revenge.

CHAPTER VIII.

THE HOSPITAL.

Louise Didier's sickness grew worse. Unable longer to endure this state of things, Father Jean spruced himself up, as he said, — that is, he put on his best rags and passed his hands through his hair and his thick beard.

He looked at himself in a bit of mirror, and, not difficult to satisfy, hoped that others would see him with his own eyes.

" Upon my word, I have the air of a m'lord," he said to himself; " I lack only a cravat."

And without further reflection, full of confidence, he started for the residence of the celebrated Doctor Dubois.

The elegance of the establishment considerably disconcerted him at first; but he quickly recovered his plebeian assurance, and with perfect self-possession inquired of the janitor regarding the doctor.

" This is where Doctor Dubois lives, of the Charity Hospital? "

" You have an errand with him? " asked the Cerberus, eyeing him disdainfully.

" That's not your business."

The offended janitor, in a voice more supercilious still, pointed to the servants' staircase, which Father Jean quickly ascended.

" This takes the shine off the Rue Marguerite," said he, admiring the clean, light stairway.

He rang, and was introduced without opposition into the kitchen, where a world of cooks, scullions, and kitchen-maids were moving about.

" Oh ! oh ! " he exclaimed, now seriously disturbed.

" What do you want? " asked one of the cooks.

" Is the doctor in ? "

" Yes, why? "

" Because I wish to talk with him on serious business."

" What business ? If you want to consult him, those are not the stairs."

" Where, then, if you please? I do not come for myself, to be sure. I should have no money with which to pay him."

" No matter, come all the same."

Doctor Dubois, as his servants knew, did not turn away the poor, but received them always.

The rag-picker was ushered into the office of the doctor, who had finished his consultations and was counting his fees.

The room was filled with works of art, and paintings by the great masters, ancient and modern, hid the walls to the satisfaction of the doctor and the diversion of his patients.

But what struck Jean especially was a table covered with a pleiad of gold and silver coin, — a firmament, one would have said. Jean was dazzled, if not dumb.

"Pardon me, Monsieur doctor, for taking up your time *gratis*, as I see it is worth a great deal to you; perhaps you have earned enough today, since you have closed your shop to those who pay and receive a beggar like me."

The famous Doctor Dubois, who left his name to a private asylum in Paris, the Baron Dubois, was the great Liberal practitioner of his time, ex-chief physician of the ex-emperor and healer of the ex-nobility, — the opposite, in character and principles, of his no less famous *confrère* in barony and medicine, the avaricious and hard-hearted *savant* who left his name to a museum, Doctor Dupuytren, chief surgeon of the king.

The people called Dubois "the good doctor." He had indeed a democratic temperament, and as a doctor he recognized himself in men.

Consequently the sight of Jean, so frank in look and voice, neither borrowed nor begging, served only to increase the doctor's usual kindness to those who seemed to him worthy of it.

"True," said he fairly and squarely, "time is money. What do you want?"

"Nothing for myself, doctor, as you see; I am well enough, thank God! But I have a lady for a neighbor who". . .

"Interests you, my buck."

"Oh! with the most honorable intentions," exclaimed Jean quickly, "the poor brave lady; and pardon me, Monsieur Dubois, if you give my words a mischievous meaning, that will show that you are not as good as you are said to be."

"To be sure; I was wrong. Come, what is the trouble?"

"Very well, then. You see I have confidence, since I am here. You could easily have deceived me; a doctor must be good! He is not like the lawyer, you know."

"Ah! and why?"

"Why? Because the best lawyer is he who wins the worst case, while the best doctor is he who cures the worst disease."

"Truly," said the doctor, charmed by this good sense, "that is a good definition of the two robes, and is well worth the prescription that I shall give your *protégée*. Go on."

"I was telling you that my neighbor, the widow Didier, wife of a poor collector killed in the service of the banker, M. Berville. . . . You must have read about that in the papers?"

"Yes; what then?"

"Why, this poor lady, mother of a young girl as honest and poor as herself, is dying of consumption. Perhaps you have seen her yourself at the hospital consultation."

"Wait; why, yes, I think so; about forty years old, blonde, from the Rue Sainte-Marguerite, is that the one?"

"Exactly. Well, she has been told by you or some member of the board of physicians, no matter who, that she is not sick enough to enter the hospital, and they advised her to travel for her health — and her revenues? — and thus to wait until she is too sick to enter the hospital. Your remedy is death."

"What would you? The regulations, remember, my brave fellow! There is no room!"

"There'll be room enough in the cemetery; but, Great God! there's no lack of it at the Luxembourg, at the Elysée, at the Louvre, at the Tuileries . . . to say nothing of the suburbs, Saint-Cloud, Meudon, Versailles. What good hospitals, eh?"

The doctor smiled.

"Really, Monsieur doctor, things cannot go on in this way long, good people. She can hold out no longer! She is dying! And if she is not dead already, it is because she frightens death away. I wanted to bring her to you, but, you see, she has no legs left to support her poor body, and not a cent for a carriage!"

"Well! my friend, we will take mine and go to see your neighbor. The hospital is not salvation, but it is better than nothing."

Just then the servant brought him a letter.

"Oh! oh!" said he, as he read; "this letter is from Mme. Hoffmann, the sister of M. Berville of whom you were speaking. Pregnant!" he cried. "Well, that will interest the abbé Ventron!"

"The messenger is waiting for a reply!" said the servant.

"I will go . . . but first your poor neighbor! Come, my old man."

Just as they were about to go out, the servant came back with a card bearing these words:

ISMAEL GRIPON.

Broker.

And in pencil: "Urgent, apoplexy."

"Show him in," said the doctor.

The son of the usurer Gripon, become a "broker," was introduced; he asked the doctor to visit his father, who had had a stroke.

"Where does he live?" asked the doctor.

"Faubourg Saint-Antoine, No. 30; an old man's mania for sticking to his old home."

"Well, I shall pass there, for I am going to the Rue Sainte Marguerite."

A visit to so humble a street aroused Gripon's Judaic disposition.
"How much do you charge for a visit, doctor?" he asked.
"The father of a broker . . . he is valuable; China is right in recognizing only the ascendant nobility; the author of a child like you is worth much. What do you think about it? It will be one hundred dollars."
"The devil! it is dear," exclaimed Gripon, in spite of himself.
"You find it so, M. Gripon? How much do you gain by a stroke in the stock market? A hundred dollars. My plan is to make the rich pay for the poor. Those of your profession do enough to make the poor pay for the rich. Compensation."
"Very well; but at least you will have the kindness to attend my mother at the same time; she is sick also."
"Ah! you want to kill two birds with one stone. Your mother to boot? Doubtless she is less dear, because, having a son of your age, she will have no more. Well, pardon me, Monsieur Gripon, you are celebrated on the floor of the stock-exchange for this variation from arithmetic: 'Two and two make five!' I am content, for my part, with the ordinary rule: 'Two and two make four.' Therefore two visits at a hundred dollars each come to . . . two hundred dollars. Take it or leave it!"

He bowed to the usurer, who returned the bow and went to Dupuytren, who asked him, according to the Gripon rule, three hundred dollars; so that Ismael running hither and thither, seeking paternal salvation at a discount, going from door to door, from the Court physicians to the quacks, lost time enough to inherit from father and mother without having to pay five, or four, or two, but zero to the doctor.

During the economical peregrinations of the younger Gripon in search of inheritance at a cheap rate, the doctor and Jean were rolling away in the direction of the Rue Sainte-Marguerite.

They found Louise Didier in a swoon in her daughter's arms in consequence of a hemorrhage.

The good doctor made her inhale salts, restored her to consciousness, and soon found that she was suffering from pulmonary consumption of an advanced stage; then, carrying humanity to a point not unfrequently reached in his noble profession since the day of the good Ambroise Paré, he took Mme. Didier in his own carriage to the Charity Hospital, after which he started for the residence of the baroness, the Hotel Hoffmann.

Unhappily religion is not always as humane as science. And after the first consultation and prescription, given in the presence of the house-physicians and nurses, Mme. Didier passed from the good doctor's hands into those of a Sister of Charity.

The Charity Hospital was so named doubtless like the Sister, according to the rule *lucus à non lucendo.* . . . it was an antilogy.

In a room containing more holy water than gruel and more crucifixes than *bouillon*, a dozen beds infected each other where there was really room only for six . . . . and even six would have been too many.

The lung, an organ ever active like the heart, needs to be fed continually. It must consume at least twelve hundred cubic feet of air a day in order to oxygenize the blood and furnish the living body its natural heat.

In this cursed common room there was neither a sufficient quantity nor a sufficient quality of air, even for healthy lungs. And the sick woman, in both these respects, had lost by her change of quarters. The hospital was worse than her garret.

If the air of Paris, as analysis has proved, contains more microbes than the country, and the country more than the ocean, how much more than sea, fields, and city does the hospital contain! There Doctor Oxygen becomes Doctor Poison. Hospital fever is the most pernicious of all. It is well known that amputations are more fatal at the hospital than under the tent in camp.

To this must be added the sleepless nights, disturbed by the coughing of the other patients, the death-rattle of the dying, the sight of the dead, and the goings and comings of the nurses as they empty the beds of their corpses and fill them with new patients.

Such are the material conditions offered by official hygiene to the poor, to Mme Didier as well as others.

In all public administration, alas! the administered is a mere package transported to the great cost of the State and to the great profit of the administrator only.

The strictly medical conditions were no better.

Mme. Didier, as she grew sicker and sicker, was less and less carefully attended by the nurse in charge of her health. The Sister's attention was in the nature of an inquisitor's persecution. The religious zeal of the devotee increased with the disease of the patient. With each fit of coughing there was a pious exhortation before the julep! Not a look without a dose of orthodox advice!

"You are sicker than you think," the Sister had charitably remarked on the very first day; "your sickness is incurable without the grace of heaven; and you would do much better to call a confessor who would set your soul at peace, and thus render the body more susceptible to the influence of medicine."

At this word, confessor, Louise shuddered, remembering the abbé Ventron.

Mme. Didier, with her usual straightforwardness, at once told the Sister to speak to her no more of priests, for she no longer believed in confessors or, consequently, confession.

"Unhappy woman," cried the pious nurse, more in anger than in pity, "to whom, then, can you look, I do not say for cure, but for consolation?"

"To my conscience!" and she turned her head toward the wall.

From that time she was disliked, and, as she remained firm to the end, the usual severity changed into cruelty.

The inconveniences of consumption became unpardonable crimes in the poor victim. She was wrong in everything. She spat too much, she spat in the wrong place, she stained the bed-clothes, the carpet, the floor.

One would have said that the nurse was more concerned with the tiles than with her lungs, and that she was more the sister of the bed-curtains than of the patient.

"It is disgusting, you soil everything," she cried every time the sick woman spat blood. "You awaken everybody with your hollow cough."

The worst fanaticism is the son of the worst egoism,—personal salvation for eternity; remember that. Charity became ferocity.

The care, prescriptions, and advice of Doctor Dubois, therefore, were null and ineffective, dead letters, forgotten and unexecuted.

Tortured by omission and commission, she was blamed for everything at the same time that she was deprived of everything.

There was no sweetening in the drinks; sugar, so necessary for the supply of heat in lung diseases, was given out in doses, begged, and stolen. For those who would not eat the consecrated wafer there was no milk.

The nurse became a killer by inches with her stinging words, her pin-pricks; in short, it was a long and atrocious assassination of several months' duration, the victim in such a case as this being fully conscious, seeing that she was being killed and feeling it.

But the moral conditions of the patient were even worse.

This poor, sensitive woman suffered especially in her dignity, her modesty, yes, even more than in all her wants.

Man is at once individual and collective. Though he needs common life, he no less needs private life; and it is especially in suffering that he wants to be alone. The most gregarious beast, a sheep or a hen, once taken sick, separates from the others and goes into a corner to suffer and to die.

It is this need of retirement, of quiet, more necessary still to man, in whom the family instinct is stronger than in the beast,—it is this instinctive repugnance of the people to an unnatural promiscuity which makes them regard it as an insult to be told: "You will die in the hospital!"

All the science and zeal of the best physicians have not been able to overcome this love of home and this hatred of confusion; the hospital, the convent, the barracks, place the same check upon individual sentiment.

Louise Didier had no greater torture to endure than this moral indignity of the cenobitism of the hospital.

Degraded on entering, deprived of name and personality . . . a number, a subject, a case.

Obliged every morning to submit to a public visit, in presence of the other patients, from a band of students, some of them studious, the rest curious, all taking turns in feeling of her, handling her, sounding her, and turning her over in every direction.

Nothing of her own left, not even her skin; treated without respect or decency; made simply a subject of experiment. She really belonged to herself no longer. She was the property of science, of society, which lent her a bed at usury, a bed to die in, on condition that she would die for society, that her agony should be at its service, and then her corpse, provided she could not redeem it from this iniquitous, absurd society, based on the family which it violated, however, by this hospital life.

This mass of misery overwhelmed her courage like a rock of Sisyphus continually falling back on her poor crushed heart. Even the visits of her daughter, whom Jean brought to her, were regulated like everything else, so that she no longer desired them. Instead of soothing her, they embittered her by the separation. Moreover, they took Marie from her work. The little dainties which she brought cost her dear. In short, the mother's heart was torn at the end of every interview; the sorrow which the progress of the disease caused her daughter every week, and which she saw in Marie's eyes however the child might try to conceal it, doubled her own pain. She had reached the point where she desired nothing but death, which finally heard her prayer.

On the second day after one of these visits, foreseeing her end, she wished however, though in vain, to see her daughter and Jean, in order to commend her to his care. It was not visitors' day, but it was death's day, and death was her only visitor.

In the presence of death and his relentless accomplice, the Sister, who tormented the victim to the end, the worthy mother, with her last breath, only murmured three names,—Jacques, Marie, and Jean.

"Good riddance!" said the Sister. "At last! She richly deserved to go where she has gone! May God have pity on her soul! The impious creature! She will stain nothing more."

And sprinkling holy water on a cloth with a branch of box, she threw it over the face.

Number 12 was carried to the dissecting room, where there was an abundance of subjects; and, the season being cold, the body remained there until the next visitors' day.

Then Father Jean came again with Marie, entered the sick-room, and went to the bed.

"Ah!" he cried, terrified, and, turning around quickly, he stopped Marie from advancing.

A man occupied Madame Didier's place.

"Where is Louise Didier?" he asked.

"Who?" said the devotee.

"The lady that occupied this bed."

"Number 12?"

"Madame Didier, I tell you!"

"Too late, good people."

"Where is she?"

"In the dissecting room, Number 12, if she is still there."

"Mam'zelle Marie, stay here!" cried Jean.

And he went out like a thunderbolt, in the direction of the dissecting room. He entered just in time.

Number 12, Madame Didier, was stretched at full length upon a stone table, naked and stiff, without a veil save what was left of her long light hair, scattered over her breasts, her two anatomical arms extended beside her skeleton.

In a hideous tub fragments of human remains were bleaching in cold water, like calves' feet and heads in a slaughter-house.

The Church consecrates only the remains of the rich. To it as to the State the remains of the poor are *detritus*.

Around the funeral table a dozen merry students, with aprons fastened to their necks and scalpels in their hands, laughing, smoking, playing at throwing scraps of flesh in each other's faces, were getting ready to dissect this body, perfect considering its thinness, in order to learn how to cure the rich and become, if not Dubois in the service of the Didiers, at least Dupuytrens in the service of the Hoffmanns.

CHAPTER IX.

THE FAMILY.

Time rolled the twelve months of the year 1847 over our characters, each of whom, as Virgil says, followed his attraction. *Trahit sua quemque.* . . . .

While Louise Didier departed, happy to rejoin Jacques in the ground and content to leave Marie in Jean's charge, Camille ran to his ruin and pushed on the Revolution.

Frinlair and Claire, faithful to their betrothal vows, awaited their marriage by the aid of God and the abbé Ventron.

The baron held stoutly to Camille, and the baroness to Frinlair, when she received her *annunciation.*

Then she felt the first thrill in her maternal organism, the first pulsation of a heart now charged with two lives.

By accident or design, by imprudence or submission to the sovereign of feminine passions, by Monsieur's fault or Madame's, the risk foreseen by Doctor Dubois had been braved and the danger incurred.

The baroness was pregnant.

An immense joy took possession of her at first . . . . to fulfil her destiny, to be at last a real woman, a mother! What happiness! She saw herself sacrificing everything to her child,—sleep, leisure, pleasures, even her religious duties; devoted to him night and day, rocking him, nursing him, bringing him up, sustaining him body and soul on her own substance, breathing only for him, living again wholly in him.

Maternal love, that supreme law of devotion of the present to the future which governs the feminine nature, changing the sheep into a lioness and the lioness into a sheep, and softening and strengthening everything that it controls on earth, dominated Gertrude. Her arm would serve as a bed of rest for her Jesus, her bosom be his source of life. Already she bore him upon her neck like a Madonna, on a level with her, equal to her. She divided her heart between him and God. . . and he was her husband's rival as well as her God's.

Suddenly the memory of death came back to her, and her joy vanished like a flash.

She recollected the fatal danger which science had predicted for her, and the thought took her heart back to Claire, to her adopted daughter, and started her again in a struggle against her husband, fully determined as she was to endow her only for the pious Frinlair.

It was an intestine, constant warfare, secret and open by turns, and to the death.

Poor baron, with a wife both irritable and pregnant! Misfortunes never come singly, but, like policemen, in pairs.

The home, when not harmonious, is worse than the hospital; and the widow Didier dying at the Charity had little reason to envy Gertrude sick in her family.

The doctor, summoned to the house, entered Gertrude's room.

First he assured himself of her pregnancy as carefully as necessary, scolded the couple for their weakness with his familiar but serious good nature, and then prescribed a severe *régime* to prevent the birth from being followed by fatal results.

Her food, whether solid or liquid, was to be carefully selected and weighed, tested both as to quantity and quality; and he gravely warned the couple against any violation of his orders.

The slightest imprudence might be fatal to his patient. Her diet must consist largely of milk, given in small and frequent doses. But nothing too substantial, still less anything stimulating, neither wine nor liquors, neither tea nor coffee, strict abstinence from everything succulent.

Thus the prescription for the rich Gertrude was simpler and less expensive than that for the poor Louise, who was bidden to drink wines and eat generous — and onerous — viands.

But if the poor woman had not been able to follow the too costly directions, scarcely more able was the rich one to follow the meaner prescription.

Gertrude, under the influence of this reduced diet, felt that she was becoming depressed. By nature anæmic, but accustomed to an excellent table, her culinary taste and weak stomach could ill endure privations and agreed in protesting against this fasting *régime*, in violating the sacred commands of science.

She cried of starvation, and wept sometimes like a child, going from disgust to voracity, and then saying:

"I am hungry!"

She bribed her servants and deceived her husband; or rather the former through negligence and the latter through indulgence left at her door some comforting wine and some savory viand with which she satisfied herself in secret, like a glutton, and the more dangerously because she devoured greedily, at varying intervals, without mastication and without regularity, — in all these ways inducing indigestion.

In spite of all the injunctions of her doctor and her husband, something was always lying about under her eyes, under her hand, by chance doubtless, some bit more or less indigestible, forgotten or carelessly put away, meat and wine which she devoured to her destruction.

Sometimes even her husband had not the strength to effectively oppose her, to resist her desires, seeming to feel a guilty sympathy, a conniving goodness, a homicidal tenderness, — a murderer out of pity and killing through love.

So the albuminuria, far from improving under this loosely-followed treatment, grew worse and worse, and the doctor, disappointed and puzzled, unable to calculate on the servants' negligence and the husband's kindness, supposing that he was obeyed and not knowing that he was betrayed, came at last to believe that he did not understand this mystifying disease at all, and despaired of saving his patient.

During the whole course of the sickness all his knowledge struggled thus unsuccessfully and met nothing but reverses until the final defeat.

Chance precipitated it.

Chance is everything.

One day, when the doctor had given stricter orders than ever concerning her diet and milk, the baron had for his breakfast an excellent *languet de Vierzon.* Every winter since she had lived in Paris Gertrude had had this dish from her native Berri.

Summoned on a matter of business, the baron left the table for a moment, no doubt forgetting the tempting *languet.* But scarcely was he out of the room before the poor, famished patient, who, as she drank her milk, had steadily eaten the *languet* with her eyes filled with a look of Tantalus, yielding to her fit of hunger and her provincial taste, had pounced frantically and hungrily upon this pork which was so bad for her, and stuffed herself full, like the monk who invented the dish and died from it.

She washed it down with Sancerre wine, and, when the baron returned, he found nothing but a bare bone and an empty bottle.

The baron scolded, locking the stable-door, as the proverb says, after the horse had been stolen.

A few hours after this imprudence, caused by her husband's chance absence, Gertrude was taken with a terrible crisis, the violent shock of which failed unfortunately to induce the miscarriage which alone could have saved her.

She was seized with cramps and contractions. The convulsions became so frequent and intense that the servants had to be called continually to hold the bent body and the limbs twisted like vine-stocks by a frightful spasm.

Soon the nervous wave, which had begun with the body and arms, invaded the face. Then there was a horrible spectacle, distressing, poignant, even to the indifferent.

Her teeth chattered, shutting and opening like the mechanical jaws in a dentist's show-case. Her mouth frothed and foamed; her eyes rolled and twisted and turned in their sockets till nothing but the whites could be seen; her ears rang; her voice, or rather her strident rattle, was a mingled laugh and wail; a frantic vibration alternated with a corpse-like tension; in short, there were all the symptoms of acute eclampsy at its fatal paroxysm.

The doctor, after having tried in vain all anodynes and all revulsives, the rubbing of legs and hands in warm water, cried:

"Quick, a cork!"

And he placed between her teeth the cork from the fatal bottle of Sancerre, adding to the baron:

"Now take good care that this cork stays there, for she might cut her tongue off with her teeth, and the hemorrhage would be her death."

Then, anxious, he went out to prepare with his own hands a final anæsthetic.

During the doctor's presence the baron had followed the progress of the crisis with a silent anxiety.

Throughout her sickness, between the crises, the inflexible Gertrude always returned to Claire's marriage, like Cato to the destruction of Carthage.

In a moment of calmness, before the insertion of the cork, she had said solemnly to her husband:

"I feel very ill . . . I do not know whether I shall die. . . but if you have loved me, if you love me still, if you wish me to die happy, tranquil, in the hope of going to await you in heaven, swear that you will not sacrifice the heart to the strong-box, our daughter to our treasury, but will marry Claire, not to the scoffer, but to the Christian! It is God's wish."

"Ah! dear friend, what are you thinking of? God does not wish to separate us from our daughter, expatriate her, banish her far away from us, from France, in a foreign land, in the arms of an ambassador-husband! Think only of your sickness, of your recovery, of the happiness of all of us."

And this reply of her husband had unchained the crisis, as we have seen, with all its horrors and all its dangers.

Then, to do his best to quiet her, he placed the patient's hand upon his heart; and Gertrude, electrified by the contact, by the beating of this beloved heart, fell into a delirious ecstasy full of disordered visions and broken words,—strong-box . . . heart . . . interest . . . love . . . God . . . my daughter . . . heaven . . . Bourges!

Then she saw herself in her dear and good old town of Bourges, in the cathedral church, in front of the high altar, amid the fumes of the incense and the tones of the organ, witnessing the marriage of Claire and Frinlair, celebrated by the abbé Ventron made an archbishop-cardinal, primate of the Aquitanias and leading them all into paradise.

"All! all into heaven!" she cried.

"Ah! poor mad darling! dear wife! come back to yourself," cried the baron, as if crazed with grief himself, suddenly placing his face against hers and covering her with sobs and kisses.

Then a heart-rending cry was heard.

In these passionate kisses, by some accident doubtless, the cork had jumped from

Gertrude's lips, and the invalid's convulsive teeth, striking her tongue, had severed it with a cut as clean as a pair of scissors would have made. An irrepressible flow of blood started from the mouth of the unfortunate woman. The baron, in despair, rang and shouted for help and for the doctor; but before the doctor had returned, the baroness, holding the baron's hand so tightly that it seemed as if she would crush it, had breathed her last.

The dead woman's fingers had to be cut off to release her husband's hand.

When death strikes, it is rarely with a single blow. Misfortune is like the policeman; it comes in squads. It caroms like Grévy or Pius IX.

Thus Garousse's hook had been twice fatal to the two families,—the Bervilles and the Didiers.

Thus the descendant of the Frank, continuing the bloody history of his ancestor in our country, had struck twice the *Bourgeoisie* and the Plebeians. He had killed Berville and Jacques. He killed Gertrude and Louise.

Jean claimed Louise's body and saved it from public utility by burying it in the common grave where lay the body of her husband; and Madame the baroness went to await hers in the family vault.

"Now it is for me to marry Claire according to God," said the abbé Ventron to himself, as he blessed Gertrude.

"Now it is for me alone to be both father and mother," said Jean to himself, as he gazed upon Marie.

CHAPTER X.

THE BOUDOIR.

After the secret betrothal effected in the oratory by the grace of God, the baron had hermetically sealed his door against Frinlair, in spite of the tears, prayers, and adjurations of the triple alliance, — Claire, Gertrude, and Ventron.

"But," says Figaro, "if you want to sharpen Rosina's wits, shut her up."

So Claire, in spite of all the precautions and watchfulness of Bartholo, found a way of meeting her affianced here or there, even though at a distance.

For five years thus they had met, not united, exchanging only glances and vain sighs, or at most a word with the holy water at the mass of the priest of Saint-Roch, who, still their ally, had more than once preached before them, if not for them, against sterile pleasures, *Væ soli*, and for the *crescite*, increase and multiply, of the Holy Bible.

Never had Frinlair been more a Christian, more assiduous in his religious duties than during this lustre following his betrothal.

He frequented the church almost as much as the club, neglecting races for vespers and jockeys for preachers.

But God overwhelms with blessings those who vow to be his own. After audacity, patience is the surest weapon of love . . . and perseverance is diabolical.

Finally an opportunity to renew and assure his rights as a lover was afforded him through another medium, less celestial than that of the priest, just as he was beginning to lose hope, as in the sonnet of *Philis*, and to fear the prescription.

Frinlair's sister, Mlle. Berthe, Claire's school-friend at the convent *des Oiseaux*, was about to marry.

She had to go to the fashionable dressmaking establishment of the great Alexis to see her wedding dress. So she had begged her friend Claire, whose good taste she recognized, to be kind enough to accompany her and give her the benefit of her advice.

Before their arrival at Alexis's, a young working-girl in mourning, carrying her box in her hand, knocked at the door of the sales-parlor of the establishment.

"Come in," cried a valet, fat as a prelate.

An *habitué* of the Théâtre-Français, thanks to the tickets given him by an actress who patronized his employer, this original valet had taken the classic name of

Frontin, and put on many airs with the working-girls, whom he called Toinette or Marton. He was dressed in keeping with his name, laced, powdered, breeched, one of the furnishings of this parlor filled with mannikins, patterns, and displays of every sort.

"What do you want?" said he, grandly, to the working-girl; "work? This is not the office; this is the sales-parlor. You do not come to buy, I suppose."

"Pardon me, Monsieur," said she, thoroughly confused by this welcome, "I made a mistake," and she started to withdraw.

Ogling her and succumbing to the young girl's magic charm, he said in a gentler tone:

"What is your name, my dear?"

"Marie Didier."

"What department?"

"Paris."

"What part, I ask you?" said he, with a shrug of the shoulder.

"Faubourg Saint-Antoine."

"That isn't what I mean, you innocent. Are you a milliner or a dressmaker? Do you make waists or skirts? Do you sell or pose?"

"I am a seamstress, and I bring some samples," said she, braving everything through necessity.

"Well, let us look."

"There, Monsieur, sleeves, waists, and skirts; you can choose."

And she timidly showed him three little master-pieces of grace, perfect, like herself.

"Not bad, these . . . but a great deal of work for a little money . . . is it not so? See here, you are pretty, you please me; and, if you will take my advice," he added, giving her a pat on the cheek that made her start, "you will drop the needle for the pose."

"What's that?" asked Marie, surprised.

"Well, for the mannikin."

"The mannikin!" she exclaimed, still more.puzzled.

"Why, yes, simpleton; cloak-wearer, shawl-wearer . . . nice work, much better. than sewing. A dollar a day and your board, to say nothing of gratuities and the pieces. The more I look at you, the better fitted you seem to me for that employment. You have a good figure, and, if you will be amiable, you shall be presented."

"Much obliged," replied Marie, blushing, to this conceited booby; "I prefer to work at home."

Then steps were heard in the vestibule, and, as Marie, wonder-struck, was picking up her box to go, the varlet said to her:

"Stay a little while; if you wish to see some fine dresses for the sake of your own trade, you will look at the *trousseau* of Mlle. Berthe de Frinlair."

Influenced by the love of art, Marie remained.

At that moment Alexis the great, in a dressing-gown, entered with Berthe and Claire, escorted by Friulair and followed by a dressmaker, Mlle. Trompette, carrying a new dress.

A pianist brought up the rear.

Alexis ordered the valet to light the gas, saying to the ladies: "One cannot judge a ball-dress except by gas-light and trial. How else can one tell whether the form and shade suit the figure and complexion? So be kind enough, I pray you," he added, pompously, "to step into the boudoir with Mlle. Trompette."

The three women passed into the dressing-room, and Alexis handed the "Charivari" to Friulair, keeping a fashion journal for himself.

Then, perceiving Marie, he said to the valet:

"Who is this girl?"

"A posing apprentice," answered Frontin.

"Pardon me, Monsieur, a work". . .

"Hush . . . or the door!" said Frontin in a low voice to Marie, who neverthe less was about to reply, when Alexis, like a true employer, hastened to say: "We already have many for that line of work . . . but we will see;" and making a sign to the pianist, he cried: "Quadrille and waltz," whereupon the pianist began a prelude, cutting short the words of Marie, who was gathering up her samples to go.

A large woman then entered, and, bowing awkwardly to Alexis, asked, with a Teutonic accent, to see a cloak of the latest style and largest size for Berlin, she said, German women being taller than Frenchwomen.

"You mean longer," answered Alexis, laughing, and he cried: "A cloak of the largest size."

A posing-woman, Louisa, entered with a cloak on her arm.

"Too small," said Alexis to Louisa. Then, seeing Marie going out, he said: "Ah! you will do. You have a figure. Come here!" And as Marie hesitated, he added: "Come, I say, and stand up straight!"

Taking her by the arm almost by force, he put the cloak upon her back. Then, addressing his customer, he said:

"See, a work of art!"

"It looks very well in the rear. Now turn around, Mademoiselle," said the customer. "Well, Monsieur, that suits me. How much?"

"Two hundred dollars."

"A little dear, considering the material."

"The material! Ah, ah! the material is a consideration for the country, for Germany! Paris, Madame, stands for form. The material is nothing, form is everything . . . and look, it is the latest novelty."

"I see . . . but have you nothing better for the money?"

"No, Madame," exclaimed Alexis, superb in his contempt and indignation, "nothing better than that for you. It is enough that you have seen one, you shall not copy two! Louisa, take away that cloak. And you, Frontin, take Madame's description; we have nothing beautiful enough for her."

"Pardon me," replied the customer, "everything in your establishment is not second-rate, Monsieur Alexis; your insolence at least is of the first quality."

And she went out, bursting with laughter, taking with her in her German memory as revenge a pattern for use in Berlin free of cost.

Frinlair had found the scene quite as amusing as the "Charivari"; and Marie, more and more interested, was nevertheless about to go at last, when Trompette came back to say:

"Mademoiselle de Frinlair is ready."

Then Marie, fascinated by curiosity, stayed longer.

"Wait," said Alexis to Trompette, "till I take my place in order to judge well of the effect."

And he seated himself majestically on his armchair as if it were a throne, the throne of fashion. Then, taking up his eye-glasses, he said:

"Tell her to come in."

And as Berthe entered in her costume, he continued:

"I beg pardon, Mademoiselle, salute me, I beg of you, as you pass, that I may see if the movement disarranges the waist. . . . Good! Correct, not a wrinkle, nothing moves, a cuirass. And now you are going to dance."

"Dance?" exclaimed Berthe, in amazement.

"And waltz."

"Why?"

"That I may see now if the movement will disarrange the skirt."

"Isn't that rather too much? I can hardly walk! But I must submit or resign. Your will be done, great artist! We are your subjects, and you are a real tyrant, the most absolute of all, the tyrant of fashion."

"And the slave of beauty."

"All quarters, all *régimes,* royalty and the republic, nobility and finance, Saint-Honoré and Saint-Germain, all Paris obeys you more than the pope."

"To say nothing of all the crowned heads of Europe, whose hair I dress and whose costumes I make, but at what price! What art!"

"And what expense!"

"To be sure! Master-pieces cost everybody dear, you as well as me. Now, cavalier, come in."

Then entered a young man dressed in a black coat, with a moustache of the same color, white cravat and gloves, and a flower in his buttonhole, — a masculine poser, waxed, polished, glazed, perfect.

"My son, Mademoiselle."

The son bowed.

"Come, give your hand to Mademoiselle; take your place and let the music begin," said Alexis.

The piano started.

"First two forward! Balance! . . . Stop!" said Alexis. "A fold loosened in the skirt, at the right hip, nothing else. Thank you, Mademoiselle, the trial is over. You understand the importance of it now? Such an accident in a ballroom,—what an annoyance to you and what a disgrace to me! I should be ruined! Farewell the throne! Alexis would abdicate like Charles X. . . and unfortunately, though power is hereditary, genius is not, and my son is only a good dancer. Frontin, serve."

Then the valet offered refreshments on trays worthy of the customers.

During all these Parisian follies a serious thing had occurred.

Frinlair and Claire had slipped into the unoccupied boudoir, their absence unnoticed by Alexis and Berthe absorbed in the dress; and they returned equally unobserved, after having confirmed their betrothal under the auspices, this time, of the priest and king of fashion.

The second offenders having partaken of the refreshments with Berthe, all went away contented, especially Frinlair, reflecting upon this modification of Bazile's proverb: "The pitcher goes so often to the well that at last . . ." and upon the morality of Ventron: "The end justifies the means."

Marie, left face to face with Alexis, made bold to say to him then:

"Monsieur, I came to offer you ". . .

"Ah! to be sure! A dollar for the pose. Frontin, take her to the cashier."

Then the employer drank a glass of champagne with his son and went out with him.

Frontin in turn swallowed an ice and offered one to Marie, who refused.

"Well, my beauty," he said to her, "you see you may believe Frontin; did he not tell you so? A dollar a day, with board, washing, and maintenance . . . not much work, and ices to eat . . . and love! Come and get your money and see your room, dear little Marton."

And this airy faun, taking her around the waist, tried to kiss her on account, as he led her along.

"Insolent fellow!" she cried, "let me alone."

And by a sudden effort she released herself from this valet of the boudoir, worthy of being a vicar to the priest of Saint-Roch.

CHAPTER XI.

THE TWENTY-FOURTH OF FEBRUARY.

On the Twenty-Fourth of February, 1848, the municipal guard, composed in great part of the old royal guard of Charles X, which it had replaced under Louis Philippe, sharply defended the Tuileries, but at last was forced to yield by the People.

The soldiers of the line were the first to turn up their gun-stocks and fraternize amid reciprocal cries of "Long live the People!" "Long live the Line!"

It was a decided victory for the insurrection. The battle begun with the cry of "Long live Reform!" ended with the cry of "Long live the Republic!"

For having interfered with the pear and calf's-head banquets, the king of the strong-box, like his cousin, the king of the altar, lost his crown.

For having refused qualified suffrage, he granted universal suffrage, to both the qualified and the unqualified.

And the unfortunate pear-king got into a cab crying in his despair: "Like Charles X. . . . !"

Like him also and with the same madness he said to his Polignac, to Guizot: "The troops will not fire, then fire on the troops!"

In short, like him, he made concessions, and received the same reply: "Too late!"

So the Tuileries were taken by a handful of Republicans, at the head of whom figured Camille and the workman with a hammer.

The workman, with that honesty characteristic of the people, wrote on the door of the palace: "Death to thieves!" and Camille, remembering the bread-tickets, wrote on the front: "For Labor's disabled civilians!"

The rooms overflowed with people singing the "Marseillaise," cutting up the throne, throwing the pieces through the windows, gilded wood and velvet hangings broken and torn into bits. . . . I am writing this story in slippers made from one of those rags.

And all this litter was burned by Camille on the Place du Carrousel, together with the scaffold and the confessional of the royal chapel, amid the cries, a thousand times repeated: "Long live the People!" "Down with the death penalty!" "Long live humanity!"

At the palace of the archbishop the same revenge!

Fire purified at the Tuileries; at the archbishop's palace it was water.

The Seine carried away all the filth that the People found in the palace of the priest, as the flames consumed all the infamies that they found in the palace of the king.

Here crown, charter, and code; there mitre, Bible, and missal, to say nothing of skirts, corsets, and pomatum; in short, the double stables of Augeas, royal and clerical, the Herculean broom of the People thoroughly cleaning them out.

Camille, after taking possession of the castle in the name of the people and dedicating it to Labor, went to the office of the "National," where the list of the provisional government was made up; and he was one of the three delegates who carried it to the Hôtel de Ville.

Camille found there but one of the members-elect, the Chevalier de Lamartine, an old member of the body-guard, a romantic poet, a Legitimist who detested the Orleans family and had become a republican in writing the "History of the Girondists."

He was not, like his fellow-poet, Victor Hugo, a republican of tomorrow, but a republican of yesterday. He was already at the Hôtel de Ville when the other was still at the Rue de Poitiers. Consequently he has had only a statue at Passy, while the other is in the Pantheon. Distributive justice.

Camille caused Lamartine to perform the provisional government's first act of republicanism.

"It is not enough to have driven the Orleans family from Paris," he said to him; "it is necessary to prevent them from returning. The youngest of the princes, the Duke de Montpensier, is still at Vincennes with his artillery. We must bar his passage, and cut him off from the Avenue de Vincennes by a strong barricade. Sign the order, and I will execute it."

Let this troubadour of the coronation be given credit for it, — it was no sooner said than done.

The order executed, Camille came back at night to the Hôtel de Ville, where the government had taken up its quarters. The scramble for the quarry began.

Of all the old personages whom we met at the Berville dinner before the fall of Charles X, but two were left at the fall of Louis Philippe, — Arago, the *savant*, and the venerable Dupont de l'Eure, as they were called. The others were new men, young then, Ledru-Rollin, Louis Blanc, Flocon, Marrast, Albert, etc. The old, fatigued and drowsy, slept lethargically, seated around a table served with a cold bit of that democratic veal forbidden by the king. The young, seated with them, thought neither of sleeping nor of eating, for the People were surging in the square and shouting louder and louder: "Long live the Republic!"

The provisional government, hungrier for office than for veal, constituted itself in its own way, which was not exactly that of the People.

They may be said to have divided the Republic between the men of the "National" and the men of the "Réforme."

Each of these two journals, to the establishment of which Camille had contributed, took and distributed the portfolios.

Louis Blanc, with his child's stature, cramped in his military garb, carrying a cartridge-box, long shoulder-belts and straps, a sword dangling between his legs, and a gun taller than himself, had an appetite that exceeded his stature. He made himself president of the Labor Senate of the Luxembourg, and gave the management of the fine arts to his brother Charles.

Ledru, his extreme opposite, a giant contrasted with a dwarf, but having an equal appetite, became minister of the interior, giving the secretaryship to his friend Jules Favre.

Arago, the *savant*, took the ministry of marine, and gave the office of prefect of Lyons to his son Emmanuel.

It was a dynastic Republic.

Finally Lamartine, minister of foreign affairs, offered the secretaryship to his friend Bastide for the love of the pope, and the Roman embassy to Camille, who, on that sad night of the *bourgeois* Fourth of August, alone refused, saying in a melancholy voice that he was going to be married and wanted nothing — save to make young citizens for the Republic, which seemed to need them.

Each was drawing the cloth toward him and sharing the cake, when the workman of the Mount of Piety, Chaumette Brutus, threw his blood-stained hammer upon the table, shouting: "And labor?"

It was the first false or true note, discordant in any case, to ring out in the *bourgeois* concert.

"Labor!" said the man of the forty-five centimes, another dynastic republican, half-brother of Garnier Pagès; "labor! let it follow Louis Blanc to the Luxembourg or Emile Thomas to the national workshops!"

"One does not live by words alone; he must have bread also! In the land of promises they die of hunger," answered the workman.

" But wait! One cannot reap the same day he sows; patience!"

" Well, we will give the Republic three months' credit."

And, picking up his hammer, he went out with Camille, amid an amazement and even terror that was soon dissipated.

And the scramble for the quarry continued. . . .

Schœlcher got the colonies, Duclerc the finances, Crémieux the department of justice, Marrast the mayoralty of Paris, and the People — the forty-five centimes to pay!

CHAPTER XII.

THE TWENTY-FOURTH OF FEBRUARY. — THE LUXEMBOURG.

The old palace of the Luxembourg, that copy of the Pitti palace which the second Medici, Marie, of but little more worth than the first, brought us from Florence, has sheltered by turns the conservative Senate of the Empire, so called doubtless because it conserved neither the Empire nor the Senate, and the heredi-tary and life peerages of the kingdoms, to say nothing of what it may have to shelter yet; for it has had the good fortune to escape the popular fire which, in the absence of celestial fire, has avenged at least the Gomorrah of the Tuileries, built by Catherine, where queens had mistresses and kings lovers.

On the Twenty-Fourth of February the peers of King Louis Philippe had held their last session under the presidency of the famous Duke Pasquier, who had con-voked them to receive the regent, the Duchess d'Orléans, and her son, the Count de Paris, then heir to the crown and today pretender.

But, with the courageous fidelity of peers and senators devoted by profession and oath to constitutional conservatism, these Newfoundland dogs of the throne and the altar, these saviours of State and Church, had, the most of them, failed of attendance and left the president, the regent, and her minor in the lurch.

The sovereign People had sent their delegates to take the place of the life legis-lators. The Chamber of Peers had become the Senate of workers. Labor sat in the seat of privilege; and for the first time the palace of the Luxembourg was of public utility and national service.

Louis Blanc presided in place of Pasquier.

And the benches emptied by the noble cronies of the duke — barons, marquises, counts, and viscounts, the entire nobility old and new, pure-blooded like Garousse or smuggled like Pasquier, from the prince royal to the *vidames d'espagnolette* — were filled by the real nobility, not that of peers, but that of comrades, that of la-bor and science, that of which it will be the eternal glory of the second Republic to have declared the right and proclaimed the advent.

There all the aspirations of the nineteenth century, ours, all the schools that they have produced, all the theories and utopias that they have promulgated, were worthily represented.

For the first time the world, through its foremost people, France, saw a congress

of workers, a labor council, a parliament composed of laborers for deliberation up‑
on the social future of humanity.

As in every parliament, there were parties. They were called systems. Of these
parties each had its *part* of the truth, for there errors were not contra‑truths, but
parts of truth, each, as the Indian fable says, having picked up only one of the
thousand faces of the mirror fallen from heaven, none having had a hand large
enough to pick up all of them.

Yes, all these parties of the Republic of February followed the law of the division
of labor itself, and, to better bring out all the consequences of a principle, had di‑
vided between them the three great principles of the French Revolution, as reli‑
gious sects divide between themselves the dogmas of the Bible.

The error was simply that . . . . a heresy. Let us throw no stone at them.
They had passion, devotion, and belief, complete republican virtue, but not com‑
plete knowledge. Not in the least were they sceptics, or opportunists, or egoists,
or traitors, and they did not sacrifice "principles to colonies" and the ideal to
results.

The Fourierists represented only liberty without equality.

The Saint-Simonians, equality without liberty.

The third, the Icarians, simply fraternity.

The authoritarians said: Everything through the State. The libertarians:
Everything through the individual.

The truth is that man is at once individual and collective, regulated by two
forces, centripetal and centrifugal, and that the law lies not in the opposition, but
in the composition, of the two forces.

"Mutualism, exchange, no association," said the followers of Proudhon; "each
man to have his own lantern at his own door."

"No individualism," answered the followers of Leroux; "association, solidarity,
the *circulus*, even a common chamber-vessel."

Said these:

"No sentiment, no mysticism, no metaphysics!"

Said those:

"Sensation, sentiment, knowledge, the human trinity, manufacturers, artists,
and scientists . . . the whole crowned by the Comtists with their pope and popess,
the rehabilitation of woman, the worship of great men and anthropotheism."

Certainly, a deep faith in the human ideal; fanaticism for humanity was the
substratum of these contrary theories,— contrary because separated,— of these er‑
rors which required but union to become truths, of these utopias which needed
only fusion to become realities.

So this splitting-up, this cancelment and separation of the principles of '93, were
denounced by the friend of Camille who reflected his ideas, the workman with the
hammer, who, from the height of the tribune, said:

"Citizens:

"You destroy unity, you divide the indivisible. . . No sects! The Revolution! "My name is Chaumette. I am the son of the great Communist. My father was master of Paris, and my child, like the children of Rousseau and so many others, has lived in the hospital.

"I represent the idea for which my father died, and which, dying with him, carried the Revolution to the tomb.

"The Revolution is the Commune, and the Commune is Paris, and Paris is France.

"As long as the Commune of Paris lived, the Revolution lived. As soon as the Commune died, the Revolution died. It was the Commune that cried: 'Cannoneers, to your guns!' and saved the Republic from the Gironde. It was the Commune that declared 'the Country in danger' and saved France from Prussia. It was the Commune, finally, that, killed by Robespierre, was unable to save the Republic from the Empire or France from invasion.

"The Commune alone can save the second Republic as it did the first, and once more save the Revolution and France.

"My system, my school, my especial theory, is revolution. I am not a sectarian, I wish complete revolution, one and indivisible in its three principles, Liberty, Equality, Fraternity, founded on its historical and political basis, the free commune in the nation, like the free nation in humanity; established on the rights of man, of the citizen, and of the laborer; the ballot, the bullet, and the soil universal; each his own soldier, his own king, his own master, in short, the complete sovereignty of the People.

"The sovereign People has replaced the legitimate king and the middle-class king. It is not like any other king. It is a king without subjects. It is the laborer king. It does not reign by force, war, or plunder; it can reign and live only by work, peace, and right. Its civil list is its product, its throne its anvil, its sceptre its tool, its code justice, and its kingdom labor.

"It has no enemies but the elements, no conquests but over matter, no war but labor. This war has its victims, its wounded, and soon its column will replace all the columns of the Cæsars, crowned, as '93 intended, by the statue of the laborer.

"The priest has made labor a penalty, the noble has made it a shame, the *bourgeois* has made it a *favor*, the people makes it its right. And to that end it has other Bastilles to take. After the king's, the jail, it must take the priest's, the church, and the master's, the Bank. It must free itself from the triple tyranny, — servitude, ignorance, and poverty. It has raised the Genius of Liberty on the site of the Bastille, it must raise the statue of Equality at the cross-streets where stands the Bank, and that of Fraternity in the porch of Notre-Dame.

"Then, citizens, the Revolution will be saved, because it will be completed."

Thus these doctors sought, in good faith and in proportion to their knowledge, the best remedy for the second republic, already threatened with a return of imperial eclampsy and all its fatal consequences, — scaffold, throne, altar, and strong-box.

In these days Father Jean never left the Luxembourg,—that is, the door. There were so many bills there, so much waste paper with which to fill his basket! As many constitutions voted as Aristotle wrote, and all lost like his and even like ours, at least fifteen up to the present time.

END OF PART SECOND.

PART THIRD.

THE MASQUERADE.

CHAPTER I.

THE TEMPTATION.

Twenty years to a day have elapsed since the crime of the Quai d'Austerlitz. It is Mardi-Gras, 1848.

The people, sovereign in name but not in fact, has replaced the citizen-king.

The carnival is back again, and misery has remained,—both of them more stable than governments.

The second Republic is founded.

The Revolution has not impoverished the bankers, and consequently has not enriched the rag-pickers. Baron Hoffmann still has his millions, as Father Jean still has his rags.

It was night; alone in her garret, Marie was working on a silk dress trimmed with lace.

"Half past eleven," she whispered, looking at her watch and then sewing again; "my eyes, my hands are weary. I can no longer hold my needle. . . . I am benumbed, and — I know not why — I feel like crying. . . But come! to work! . . I must finish my task, and return this wedding dress. . . My fire is low, my lamp is going out."

She trimmed the wick, which was getting charred, and resumed her reflections.

"How dark it is, how cold it is! Oh! how cold the dead must be under ground! . . . . But I am stupid. They are less uncomfortable than the living. I wish I were dead, like my poor parents. Am I not alone already, as much so as if I were buried? And to that add labor and poverty."

She redoubled her activity.

"What a dress! . . . It is an endless task; it seems to me as if I were sewing my shroud. Ah! if my mother were only with me, I should still have courage. In kissing her morning and evening, I at least regained the strength to work when I worked for two, to earn the daily bread when there were two of us to eat it."

She wiped away a tear.

"But now that I am alone in the world, I have no heart left for anything. I cannot even finish this dress at the appointed hour. Cursed thread that is always breaking."

And again threading her needle, she continued:

" After all, what am I and what is to become of me? What a present and what a future! Fatigue and lack of sleep when work is pressing; hunger and torture in the dull season . . . and always alone. That is my lot! Should I be more alone in the grave than in this room? I should know less want, fatigue, and *ennui*. Ah! I should like to go to join my father and my mother. I should like to die."

She gazed for a moment at the portraits of her parents placed upon the mantle-shelf under the globe of her modest clock.

" It seems as if their dear image gave me new life, as if their eyes were looking at me, as if their lips were calling me. They fill me with hallucination . . . But I have no time to dream when there is such a hurry for this dress."

She went to work again with more fever than attention.

"There!" she cried suddenly, "now I prick myself, to advance matters. I must not spot it at the last moment."

And at last having finished it, she said:

"Ah! it is done, and no damage."

She stuck her needle in her cushion, took off her thimble, rose, and, carrying her lamp to the bureau, undressed to try on the new garment.

" Let me see if it fits," she said, fastening the waist and looking at herself in the little glass. "That's it! Happy woman who will wear it! The pain for me, the joy for her. Married, loved, feted in this dress. It fits me well too," she continued with a sigh. "But what's the use? What good does it do me to be young and beautiful, if I must live thus isolated, in a corner, in abandonment? Shall I not always be poor? Shall I ever have such a dress for myself?"

As she kept on looking at herself, she spoke in a more satisfied tone:

"It is singular; if I continue to look, I shall come to believe it. My mirror says so, the liar! Why, yes, I could wear silk as well as another. What else should I need with this white dress? A pearl necklace and a rose in my hair."

She took a rose from a little vase.

"There! And then, thus dressed up, I should have a carriage, with two horses, to go to an evening party . . . . no, to the play . . . . no, to a ball . . . yes, to a ball!"

She leaped with joy.

"There my admirers would say in low tones: 'What a pretty girl!' I should pass by without seeming to hear and yet hearing everything. . . Then the handsomest invites me to dance. . . . Then he loves me, marries me . . . and we live long, happy, happy. . . . Oh! how silly I am! Yet there are those who have all these joys. . . . Love, family, fortune. . But I shall die without knowing them."

She stopped to listen to the sounds and cries of the carnival rising from the street. Then she continued sadly:

"I should never marry. . . . Oh! the ball-room, the masquerade which I have never seen, the music, the dancing, the pleasures of others! But of what am I thinking tonight? These songs, these noises, make me lose my head. . . No, no, all these joys are not made for me. . . . For me, an old maid, neither wife nor mother, a hospital frock for a wedding dress . . . solitude, labor, and death."

She gave a last look at the glass, and was getting ready to take off the dress, when a swarm of young girls in disguise, acquaintances of the shop, whom she had met in going to get work or to return it, burst noisily into Marie's room.

In front Mazagran and Trompette, the one as a zouave, the other as a hussar of the fancy. Behind them other grisettes, less forward surely, and disguised as *titis* and lumpers.

"Up at this hour!" cried Mazagran, surprising Marie at the mirror, "and in full dress! Gracious!"

Trompette, Louisa, Pauline, and the others came forward also with their exclamations.

"Ah! sly boots, we've caught you!"

"Then you have decided at last?"

"Good! you are coming with us?"

Marie, in confusion, tried to explain and escape from these too noisy friends or rather comrades.

"No," she exclaimed, "I was trying on this dress which I have finished."

But Mazagran would not listen to this.

"You have it on, keep it on!"

And the others approved.

"Yes, just once."

"It fits you so well!"

"Like a glove."

" A little high," observed Mazagran, who had her reasons for liking low-necked dresses.

"Never mind, come just the same," said Louisa.

Marie still refused.

"But it is not mine, as you can plainly see."

Mazagran, demoralized since she had changed Frinlair for Camille, replied:

"Bah! my dear, you have made enough of them for others. You may well wear one yourself. You will make a lady much better than the lady could make a dress. Come."

"The captain is right," approved Trompette.

"Yes, yes," cried the madcaps all together.

"Besides," continued Mazagran, with her democratic philosophy, "it is in the interest of the dress; its faults can be seen better by trying it."

And all applauded.

" 'Tis true."

"Undoubtedly."

"Certainly."

" Bravo!"

"Very good!"

Mazagran enjoyed her popularity for a moment, and then decided in a tone that admitted no reply:

"It is unanimous! Everything is allowable in time of Carnival. Lent is long enough . . . let us go to the Opera."

" To the Opera!" exclaimed Marie, with a mixture of curiosity, fear, and envy, as if a vision of pleasures and festivities had suddenly flashed across her mind.

"To the Opera!" repeated Mazagran, scanning the three magic syllables and exaggerating the effect produced.

"After the ball, a supper," she added, detailing and multiplying the charm. "And at the Gilded House (*Maison-Dorée*) with the gilded youth. . . . Twenty dollars a plate without wine."

"And all the early fruits," said the glutton, Trompette.

Each smacked her lips in advance over her favorite delicacy.

"We shall eat strawberries."

"And pine-apples."

"And melon."

"And Russian caviare!" finished Mazagran, "and English plum pudding, and all sorts of things; an international supper with a universal bill of fare; something for all tastes, rendering a choice embarrassing, among men as well as dishes . . . To the Opera!"

And the mad girls surrounded Marie, shaken, fascinated, won, almost all of them dancing, shouting, and singing:

"To the Opera! To the Opera!"

"Ah! the Opera must be very delightful," murmured Marie, "but I dare not."

"Nonsense, Miss Virtuous!" cried Mazagran, contemptuously. "What is there to hinder you? Poor nun, you are dying of *ennui;* we want to amuse you. You cannot toil forever. One must laugh occasionally. How you will enjoy yourself! The triumph and death of the great Chicard. A hundred musicians, a thousand dancers, galop, gala, green-room, refreshment room, and sherbets, — and supper to conclude. Champagne continually, truffles everywhere, and everything iced. . . . except love. Come, once is not a habit, dear Cinderella. We will take you. Don't be afraid, we will bring you back, and in your dress, I promise you."

"All right as far as the dress is concerned," said Marie, overcome, "but". . .

"No buts,". retorted Mazagran. "Engaged, drafted."

And she began to sing:

Allons enfants de la Courtille,
Le jour de boire est arrivé !

" Enrolled !" concluded Trompette.

" Enrolled !" repeated the chorus.

" But I have nothing to wear on my head," ventured Marie, resisting as a matter of form.

" Ah ! yes," exclaimed Mazagran, who deemed the objection a serious one. " And a woman with nothing on her head is a soldier without arms. But with this remnant of lace we will make you an undress-cap. A careless dress for the head is now the thing. Let us to work at once and with big stitches."

" To work !" again exclaimed the chorus of obstinate inveiglers.

And Mazagran began.

" You shall see how quickly we will fix you out."

" What ardor !" exclaimed Marie, smiling in spite of herself. " There is nothing like working for pleasure."

" Sound, trumpets !" (*trompettes*) exclaimed Mazagran, turning to her comrade and laughing at her pun.

Trompette, without further urging, began in a falsetto voice the popular Carnival song, *La rifla, fla, fla !*

Vive l'Opéra, vive l'Opéra !
La rifla, fla, fla !

And all joined in the chorus :

Vive l'Opéra, vive l'Opéra !
Le bonheur est là !

Trompette sang the verse :

Napoléon Musard
Et son ami Chicard
Commencent sans retard
A minuit moins un quart.

Vive l'Opéra, etc.

Pauline, in turn, sang her verse :

Allons, dépêchons-nous,
Hussards est tourlourous,
Que Musard dise à tous
Je suis content de vous.

Vive l'Opéra, etc.

And Mazagran, while at work on Marie's cap, finished the song :

Au bal de l'Opéra,
Le jour du Mardi-Gras,
Le dernier des soldats
Meurt et ne se rend pas.

Vive l'Opéra, vive l'Opéra !
La rifla, fla, fla !
Vive l'Opéra, vive l'Opéra !
Le bonheur est là !

Mazagran rose.

"D-o-n-e, done," she cried. "There's a cap for you! What *chic!* Isn't she beautiful?"

"The most beautiful of all," said Trompette, who always echoed the opinion of her companion in pleasures.

"Beautiful to exhibit," continued Mazagran, "to beat all women and to set beating all men's hearts. We give her whips with which to lash us. So much the worse; the voice of conscience bids us show her, and it would be a sin to leave her here". . . .

Marie made a last show of resistance; perhaps the memory of her mother or the fear of paining Jean, who had been left to guard and protect her, still held her back.

"Ah! what am I about to do? You infatuate me."

But Mazagran, her leader, would not listen, and, placing her at the head of the others, gave her orders to her troop of merry-makers.

"Fall in! Attention! Quick time! Forward — march !"

And, willy-nilly, Marie, made prisoner by her comrades, suffered herself to be pushed outside, while the mad band again took up the chorus triumphantly:

Vive l'Opéra, vive l'Opéra !

Scarcely were they at the foot of the stairs, when Jean, alone in his loft, situated over Marie's room, was awakened by the tumult and lighted his lantern.

"Oh! oh !" he exclaimed, "the neighborhood is in high glee tonight. What a racket! Come, rag-pickers, lovers, and all other night-birds, our year is composed of three hundred and sixty-five nights. Night is our day, — a day of joy for some, and of pain for others."

He picked up his basket, and, looking at it, continued:

"To work, old girl; let us leave pleasure to the young. The devil! she is a little worn like myself; I shall need another soon. A long time she has served me. . . . . Yes, since the day when I promised that poor Didier to watch over his daughter. Just twenty years today, great Saint Mardi-Gras !"

And flinging his basket over his back, he said:

"There's my domino, made of wicker cashmere. Let us go to work."

On his way down he stopped to listen at Marie's door,

"Dear little neighbor," said he, tenderly, "she is doubtless asleep, for her day ends when mine begins. Softly, that I may not disturb her rest. Good night, Mam'zelle Marie, good night!"

And he descended in his turn.

CHAPTER II.

JOURNALISTIC MASQUERADE.

While Marie thus allowed herself to go with Mazagran and company, a scene no less in keeping with the Carnival was being enacted in the editorial room of Louchard's journal, where were gathered Camille and his usual acquaintances, — Gripon, the broker, Loiseau, the notary, and the future ambassador, Frinlair, who had diplomatically joined Camille in the movement of February.

"Our young ladies do not come," said the journalist, looking at the clock and yawning. "Suppose we put on our costumes while we wait."

"Here?" exclaimed the notary, somewhat amazed.

"Bah! an editorial room is a very proper place for turning one's coat and putting on a mask."

And he sent the office boy to get four costumes, Camille refusing to disguise himself. Costumes of the time, and befitting, moreover, the four persons, — a Robert Macaire, a Harlequin, a Clown, and a Merry Andrew.

Baron Hoffmann's ward looked for a moment at his friends thus dressed, and said, jokingly:

"But you are not so much disguised;" then he added, still laughing: "Stay, I am going to disguise myself too. I want to appear as a journalist . . . and make a fortune doubtless, like you, Louchard. Besides, it is a way of avoiding marriage, for you get rich with your pen, to say nothing of your coal mine."

"Journalist! my poor friend," exclaimed Louchard in astonishment. "Then you think the term synonymous with banker. One has to be strong, you see". . .

"Nowhere in the world does it come amiss to be a Hercules."

"Agreed; but tell us how you, an idealist, would ply the trade."

Camille smiled.

"Look you, masquerade and falsehood prevail everywhere in the journalistic world; everything is false in the newspaper, even to its date; one cannot even be sure of the day of the month from it. If I were a journalist, I should aim at just the contrary; I should try to unite science and conscience, substance and form, art and right; if I had a sheet, truth should take precedence of interest in it, and justice of". . . .

"Poor fellow! you would not make your expenses. You would print five hundred copies."

"So be it, but you, my dear Louchard, — between us be it said, — you may print five thousand, but make no imprint on the world."

"That's ill-natured, but never mind. In return for your witticism, I will give you a word of true truth, as Figaro says. I am going to unveil for you my machinery, my secret as a manager of newspapers."

"I am listening."

"What is a journal? A bit of printed paper to be sold to the public or to the government. The money of the public is as good as the secret funds. Both should be cultivated. The more sheets one has, the more one lives. Thus under royalty I had concurrently the 'Friend of the King' and the 'Friend of the Charter'; now, under the Republic, I manage the 'Social Democracy' and the 'Appeal to the People.'"

"Then you have two consciences?"

"I have two pockets."

"Go on."

"Every evening my editors ask me: 'Whom are we to cut to pieces or deify tomorrow?' And I name the victim or the idol. But all that is nothing, a few thousands, a mere bagatelle, good enough for my old venal teacher, Charles Maurice. But I, Louchard, his pupil, am going to establish a journal which will be the greatest success of the century. We shall reach a million, both in circulation and receipts."

"Oh! oh!" exclaimed Frinlair, "then you will have for buyers all the fools in France and Algeria."

"You have said it," said Louchard with pride. "We shall become of public utility. All the door-tenders, fruit-sellers, and gossips, to say nothing of the clerks and people of leisure, will read and reread the 'Penny Journal.'"

"And suppose some one steals your title and plan," risked Gripon.

"No danger. I appear tomorrow, and I will tell you my programme. Little or no politics; ideas I have renounced; words, words, to content everybody and his father! A journal can be universal only on condition of being like everybody, without opinions. News, ever, always, and at any rate, true or false. *Quid novi?* said the loungers of Rome. 'What's new?' say those of Paris. A journalist is a dealer in news! My news items, astonishing in interest and timeliness; when no dogs get crushed, I will order some crushed; my court reports perfect, — every case a celebrated case. The watchword will be: Sensation carried to the farthest extent. Occasionally an Epinal picture; the children like that. And my serial stories, for the fair sex! It will be the height of art . . . . and of adultery. The ground-floor of the journal will sustain the entire edifice to the skies; never literature, that does not take; pure love and sentiment utterly disregarded; passion carried to the point of lunacy; tears in showers, avalanches of events and incidents, a crime to every line, rape, murder, robbery, fire, and everything trembling;

each instalment ending in this fashion: 'With one hand the husband grasped his dagger, with the other he seized his wife, and with *the other* pointed to her lover on his knees.' (*To be continued in our next.*) That is how I intend to make (*faire*) my journal and take in (*refaire*) the public!"

A general outburst of laughter welcomed this declaration of principles by the great journalist.

"If the public could hear you," exclaimed Camille.

"Bah! if we knew how our food is cooked, we should never eat; but the professional secret lies there, you see! And besides, the subscriber is so stupid. Though he should hear us, he would keep his deep-seated faith and still give us his penny. Every morning he can see that we 'puff' on the fourth page all that we attack on the first.

"In principle, we are against Gripon, Hoffmann, and the rest; in practice, we receive their money and extol their doubtful enterprises.

"In our leading article we say: ' Financiers are the plague of the time. Here is another who has just disappeared, ruining a thousand families,' etc., etc. And in the advertisements we certify 'that the stock of the Company for the Manufacture of Rubber Locomotives calculated to run all alone on gutta-percha rails is the best investment for capital and savings.'

" Why, I who speak to you wrote an article yesterday against the Auvergne Gold Mining Company, which has not advertised in my journals, and today I advertise my Sologne Coal Mining Company, which is no better. Really, if we were to take our trade seriously, it would be neither amusing nor lucrative . . . . and the journal must be both."

" Decidedly, your journalism is too smart for me," said Camille. "It is still more complicated than the bank."

" Not at all," said Louchard, "and here is the simple maxim of the trade: '*Good faith* is the soul of journalism, as *credit* is the soul of commerce.' And upon the strength of that, my friends, let us go to the masquerade. Our ladies must be at the Opera already, since they are not yet here."

And the disguised party descended the stairs of the newspaper establishment and got into Louchard's splendid turn-out, which took them to the Opera ball.

CHAPTER III.

THE OPERA.

Catholic peoples have remained more Pagan than Protestant peoples, who, having no Lent, have no Carnival. We Roman Catholics logically keep Shrove Tuesday and Ash Wednesday.

In '48 the muse of the French dance, called *cancan,* had for an Apollo a frightful fellow pitted like a chestnut pan, as black as a burnt chestnut, and as little as Napoleon the Great, whose name he bore,—Napoleon Musard,—and surname,—Musard the Great.

Absurd fashion had thus christened this emperor of the public ball-room; and the Terpsichore of the Haute-Courtille, the great Opera, leaped only to the rigadoons of this minstrel.

Everything was great, even to the disasters, alas! in our Christian France, after the Concordat of Napoleon I; and, in imitation of the great emperor, *regis ad exempla,* we had the great minstrel, as well as the great tailor, and finally the great *chahuteur* also.

The soul of the orthodox Carnival, the triple God of the tolerated, authorized, and even subsidized bacchanalia, who resembled at the same time Bacchus, Silenus, and Momus, laughing like Momus, drinking like Silenus, and dancing like Bacchus, a personage no less great than Musard himself and rhyming with him moreover, was a dealer in hides, named Chicard, from which name we get the word *chic,* unless *chic* was the origin of Chicard. Which is a question.

This Chicard was the favorite of saturnalian Paris, the lord and master of the masquerade, the tyrant of the Opera. His costume has remained legendary,— flesh-colored tights with a fireman's helmet and a sapper's glove! No less artists than Gavarni and Daumier have consecrated his glory with their pencils.

This dealer in hides—for our clever Paris is so made that it worships folly— governed and charmed his generation, passing almost to posterity, to immortality, and, thanks to the hopeless stupidity of the idle, becoming a candidate for the Pantheon.

For the evening with which we are now concerned, Musard, to draw the crowd and swell the receipts, had promised Chicard to his patrons; and as the great attraction he had devised a sort of bacchic ballet, thus announced on all the walls of Paris:

MARDI-GRAS MASQUERADE.

Triumph and Death of Chicard.

GREAT ENTERTAINMENT.

So, at midnight, there was a line of people at the doors of the Opera, then situated in the Rue Lepelletier, where Orsini's bombs were thrown.

The hall was soon full; the lobby and even the stairs were overflowing with masks and dominos. Musard turned people away, thanks to Chicard, who shared the receipts.

It was a success, even before the opening of the ticket-offices, on the strength of the simple placarded announcement.

Beside those with whom these gross pleasures were habitual, there was an idiotic mass of curious persons, attracted by the reputation of the God of the festival. All political, financial, artistic, and literary Paris, and the *canaille* gilded or wretched, had agreed to meet at this ball announced as the very transfiguration of the great Chicard.

For fine adventures and witty sayings look elsewhere. The meetings and conversations were what they usually are in such a place, stupid or treacherous, egoistic and wanton, sometimes comical, seldom witty, the Jewish spirit of the stock exchange dominating every other. Mercury, on the French Olympus, beating Bacchus, Comus, and Momus, all the revived deities of the Greeks and Romans. In short, the servile customs and bestial recreations which surely lead to the invasion of a people.

The hall was lighted *à giorno*. The floor, raised to a level with the stage, doubled its size; the orchestra was moved to the back of the theatre, and in front a throne under a canopy was raised above a table laid in Pantagruelian fashion with Gargantuan dishes for one person.

Dishes as large as kettles, plates as big as platters, knives as long as swords, and forks as strong as tridents.

Discordant music and dancing in keeping therewith were at their height, when a stroke of the tamtam resounded like a cannon-shot.

Then an heroi-comic march worthy of the hero, to the sound of cowboys' horns playing the famous air of *La rifla fla fla*, and to the cries of "Long live Chicard!" was heard, and the procession entered, entirely suspending the ball.

This procession represented the complete evolution of ancient and modern bacchanalia, in an unconscious picture of the transformation of the species, a natural history of human stupidity, the picturesque zoology of the fashionable biped.

Women of every reign, age, and class, mythological, fantastic, and historical, nymphs, naiads, water-sprites, nereids and mermaids with sea-scales, sphynxes with lionesses' heads and hinds, panthers and *cocottes*, bacchantes and shepherdesses, bacchanals and virgins, columbines and young nuns, *lorettes* and *vivandières*, dragging Chicard with garlands and ribbons, who wore his traditional helmet on his head and his legendary glove on his hand, and sat in a triumphal car escorted by all the fabulous characters of old and young mythology.

Bacchus at the head on his leopard, Silenus on his ass, Pan on his goat, satyrs, fauns, and sylvans, with their thyrses, and tritons with their shells, preceding the extravagant fancies of Gavarni, Daumier, Granville, and Cham, lumpers, *titis*, troubadours, romantic knights, light opera Tyroleans, Nanterre firemen, Lonjumeau postilions, Turks *de la Courtille*, old-fashioned marquises and shepherds, powdered chamberlains, Directory swells, clowns and merry-andrews, Harlequins and Macaires, peers of France in spectacles, academicians in wigs, kings with old umbrellas over their pear heads, queens in old-fashioned carriages, emperors with false noses, popes on crutches, *porte-cotons*, scullions, cooks, *vidangeurs*, all the grotesque figures of the past added to the caricatures and parodies of the present.

Chicard mounted and sat on the throne above the table; chamberlains, carrying the key at the lower part of their backs, decorated him with kitchen utensils; pork-butchers crowned him with blood-pudding; a knight of the Holy Ghost consecrated him with oil and vinegar, proclaiming him, to the sound of horns, Chicard I, king of the land flowing with milk and honey, emperor of the Carnival, and pope of Mardi-Gras, amid cries, a thousand times repeated, of "Long live Chicard and his august family!"

Then cooks served him a monster pancake in a gigantic pan; butlers a bottle of champagne as big as a cask, with a glass as large as a pail, and a cigar of monumental length; pantlers a colossal loaf, and carvers a turkey stuffed with truffles and as big as a fat ox.

During this Rabelaisian repast a general gallop filed past His Majesty, composed of couples authentic and fantastic, loves famous in all poesies and all centuries, showing human evolution, savage, barbarous, and civilized, beginning with the gods, *ab Jove*, Jupiter and Juno, Venus and Mars, Hercules and Omphale, Cupid and Psyche, Pyramus and Thisbe, Hero and Leander, Daphnis and Chloe, Diogenes and Lais, Horace and Lydia, Don Quixote and Dulcinea, Heloise and Abelard, Laura and Petrarch, Beatrice and Dante, Charles VII and Agnes, Ferronnière and Francis I, Gabrielle and Henri IV, Louis XIV and Lavallière, Louis XV and Dubarry, Barras and Mme. Angot, not to leave out Adam and Eve, dressed in modern clothing, disguised in burlesque fashion, women appearing as men and men as women.

A gallop of death, passing in chronological order, first the prehistoric world, then the Græco-Roman, Middle Ages, and Renaissance, royal, imperial, and republican, all shadows saluting their Cæsar in order to die before him.

After the last salutation of the last couple, Chicard, having drank his last glass of champagne, felt sick.

Then Molière's notary, Loyal, appeared with a will which he presented for his signature.

Chicard became perceptibly pale and white. Toinette advanced and placed a nightcap on his head. The physicians of Argan arrived, surrounded him, felt his pulse, looked at his tongue, gave their opinions, and, upon a signal from Doctor Purgon, the Diafoiruses of Pourceaugnac ran up with syringes as big as telescopes. Chicard, frightened, leaped down from his throne and ran away, pursued by the dancers.

The pursuit was conducted to the sound of the horns, which played a lugubrious parody of the *La rifla.*

At last Chicard, who had almost escaped into the wings, was stopped short by a colossal rag-picker rising from the prompter's box before him, with hair and beard cut according to the prevailing fashion, a hook as big as a scythe and a basket the size of a coffin, in face of Lent, covered with ashes and followed by undertakers.

"Halt!" he cried. "I am Ash Wednesday, the rag-picker of Mardi-Gras . . . . into the basket!"

And the rag-picker of Paris took Chicard and tossed him into the basket, the tamtam sounding the knell of Sedan for this society as decrepit as its representative, Chicard.

In the corner of the "lions'" box, called the "infernal box," where her companions had left her, Marie, alone, wearing the wolf-mask which Mazagran had lent her, stood dazzled, stunned, bewildered at all that she had seen and heard.

She said to herself that surely her mother would not have permitted this pleasure party, and that Father Jean would not like it.

Her conscience was not easy. She felt, if not remorse, at least regret; she realized that her conduct was not commendable.

"Well, Marie, isn't it beautiful? What do you think of it?" cried Mazagran, coming back to the box and slapping her on the shoulder.

"I am afraid," answered Marie; "and if you wish to oblige me, you will lend me a dollar to take a carriage and go home."

"Go home! What for? Not at all. And the supper! We will take you home afterwards. That's an idea, — to come to the Opera without a supper! Impossible, my dear! Our gentlemen have gone to order it, and, when wine is drawn, it must be drank."

And as the others also returned to the box, she cried out:

"Say, tell the lambs; this ewe, Marie, is afraid, and the shepherds are no longer here to reassure her. All have gone to the Maison d'Or ahead of us? Let us follow them. We must not make them wait, especially as they would not wait. . . . I know them. Quick time, forward, march!"

And they dragged off Marie Didier, in spite of herself, human after all, unable to resist their high spirits or go back to her garret, and consenting to follow them to supper. A daughter of Eve, she succumbed to temptation.

CHAPTER IV.

THE MAISON-DORÉE.

The attractive programme so well set forth by Mazagran was realized.
From the Opera they had gone to the Maison-Dorée, men and women in separate groups, lest the latter might compromise the former. Prudence and respectability covering up license and corruption. To save appearances is to act like a good *bourgeois.*

So we find these gentlemen again awaiting these ladies in a private dining-room of the Maison-Dorée, facing the boulevard. Chandeliers, gilt decorations, a carpet, carved chairs, a velvet divan to sit or lie upon, a table supplied with fruits and flowers for show, silver-ware and choice dishes, the entire scale of glasses large and small, for wines in decanters and in bottles, warming in their baskets or freezing in ice, in short, all the usual luxury and commonplace elegance of a great fashionable restaurant.

Camille Berville, in a black coat, with a camelia in his buttonhole, a new flower then, was reading a newspaper before the gaily flaming wood fire.

Gripon had just taken his place at a little table, while Louchard and Loiseau were in their seats. Frinlair, very nervous and over-excited, was standing, stealthily eyeing Camille and in anything but a good humor.

"Waiter, the bill of fare," said the notary, breaking the silence.

"Waiter, a pack of cards," demanded the broker.

"Waiter, some paper," requested the journalist, in his turn.

"Waiter, some cigars," added Frinlair.

"There, gentlemen, there," said the waiter, serving them promptly, with a haste proportioned to the fee.

"Absinthe first," said Loiseau.

Louchard approved.

"That's right, make out the supper order, and give me the rest of the paper for my journal."

"Which one?" asked Loiseau.

"For both the 'Democracy' and the 'Appeal to the People.' Let us go to work. Ah! if our ladies of the Musard ball were here, such collaborators would furnish me ideas."

Loiseau consulted the bill of fare.

"On the Charter [*Charte*]?" said he to Louchard.

"No, that's played out . . . on the supper order [*carte*]."

Gripon, with his cards in his hand, made a signal to Frinlair.

"In the meantime, let us have a game of *écarté.*"

But the diplomat returned to his ruling passion.

"I should prefer a game of horse, ha, ha! It is night and freezing; I will bet five hundred dollars that I can go now from Paris to Saint-Cloud backwards in an hour and a half. Monsieur Camille, will you bet?"

"No," answered Camille, wearily.

Gripon tried him, in his turn.

"Do you play, Camille?"

"No," repeated the latter.

"Camille, what wine will you have?" asked Loiseau.

"I am not thirsty."

"What soup?"

"I am not hungry."

"Camille, my good fellow," said the facetious notary, "you are turning into an oyster."

And he wrote:

"Ten dozen!"

Then, after enjoying his joke, he continued:

"We shall be ten, in spite of the old rule: 'Neither less than the Graces, nor more than the Muses.' Is that what vexes you? But you are not a classicist. What ails you, then?"

"*Ennui.*"

Louchard had just finished his writing. He heard Camille's reply.

"Nonsense, crank," he exclaimed. "You are troubled with *ennui.* . . . Listen to this wind-up. It is homœopathic."

And he read:

"The 'Appeal to the People': 'The Republic agitates in vain among the dregs of Paris after having expelled the best of kings. France will not submit to the fanatics of the *bratocracy.* She is already preparing to drive them back into the dens from which they should never have emerged. The People, the real People and not the mob, trust in the future of the Napoleons, who are the logical successors of the excellent, eminent, but too indulgent Louis Philippe. The Pretender is sure of the love of the French. Thanks to him, anarchy will not prevail, and France will follow her progress in order and liberty under the sovereign of her choice.'"

"I will be a bull in stocks," exclaimed Gripon, decidedly.

"Wait," interrupted Louchard. "Hear this."

He took up another sheet and read:

"The 'Social Democracy': 'At last the people can celebrate their deliverance. Citizens have a right to wear at the masquerade the tinsel of kings, priests, and masters, the entire cast-off clothing of a past never to return; for the Republic is definitively established, and more and more tends to become democratic and social. What we have predicted is realized. Before February we danced upon a smoking volcano. Its lava has submerged, in a flood of mud and blood, frivolous sheets, lascivious priests, murderous dukes, and thieving ministers. And it is justice: royalty, as unreasoning as unfeeling, refused reform and offered the guillotine to the people who asked for bread and the ballot. It was a time to say as in 1830: Unhappy king, unhappy France! At last this *régime* is ended . . . . and we shall never see it more except at the carnival.'"

"I will be a bear," said Gripon, shaken.

"The Boulevard will talk of these thunders," concluded Louchard.

"Bah! less than of the masquerade," said Camille, shrugging his shoulders.

"Waiter," called Louchard, vexed. "Take these to the printing-office . . . and don't mix them up."

"What a marmalade!" cried Loiseau.

And he wrote the word on his supper order, while his friends smiled at his sallies.

"How wit becomes notaries!" said Camille, decidedly in an ill humor.

"Pshaw!" said Loiseau, "there is a time for everything. A notary is a Janus . . . . accustomed to play double. Now it is Jean who laughs and now it is Jean who weeps. He has to change his humor according to the acts. Thus this morning I drew up a dying man's will at his bedside. Until noon I was sepulchral. Later I drew up a marriage contract, and I again became gay. Now my barometer indicates fair weather."

But seeing that his remarks were not very successful, he said, pointing to Camille and addressing Frinlair:

"I know no man who takes pleasure more sadly than Camille."

"Oh!" said Frinlair with secret malice, "on the eve of marriage there is good reason for that. You know something about it, you husbands."

"Oh! a little," observed Louchard, "as a matter of form, as Bridoison said."

"Or of horns," added Gripon. "I never take my wife out except when I move."

"And I," said Loiseau, "move when my wife goes out. . . But no matter," he continued, coming back to Camille, to make him the subject of another witticism, "I have always seen our friend . . . *croûte aux champignons.*"

And he wrote down this dish also amid laughter.

"What do you expect?" said Camille; "all your balls bore me; such things amuse you, but they make me as sober as this melon."

And he jestingly designated the object that lay in the direction of the notary.

"Oh! indeed," exclaimed Loiseau, with his notary's merciless wit, "here is Werther, dreaming of a Charlotte . . . russe."

He added this item to the *menu.*

"Well," said Louchard, "we have puns at least. We might eat them."

"And we will eat them," said Loiseau, as gay as if he were drawing up a marriage contract.

Camille continued to dream aloud, talking to himself as well as to his friends.

"Yes, Opera balls, society balls, death dances, insipid or lugubrious farces, all of them bazaars of women and men for sale, where virtuous girls go to seek a husband whom they pay and others a lover who pays them. It is as gay as a fair."

"So be it," retorted Loiseau, "but the supper! Come, Puritan, sit down at the table, and swallow your wisdom. A host may be moral and a victim of *ennui*— all disgusts are natural, — but he must be entertaining."

"Bah!" exclaimed Camille, "I am disgusted with everything, even with your witticisms."

He rose and, throwing his cigar into the fire, said:

"Fortunately I am going to marry. It is a way of committing suicide."

"Why, he is serious, upon my word! he is going to die," chuckled Loiseau. "Waiter, the soup!"

Camille went to sit down at the other end of the room, sober and demoralized.

Gripon, who had succeeded in inducing Frinlair to play with him, threw down his last card, utterly routing his adversary (Jews always win, even against diplomats), and cried, enchanted:

"Now to the supper-table! That will bring the beauties."

Louchard winked his bleared eye.

"Captain Mazagran," said he, becoming aroused in advance, "has recruited a party of grisettes for our entertainment. Diplomats, financiers, notaries, journalists, here we are students again. Nobility, *bourgeoisie*, and plebeians, national unity. . . . What a leveller is love!"

Camille shook his head.

"Love!"

"Woman is only for business or pleasure," declared Gripon. "What do we ask of her? Money or . . . her bed. Half of one . . . or all the other."

"And it is enough for what heart is left us," said Camille again.

The young Berville had reached the last stage of despair. He wished to believe and could not. To such a point had the liberality of his strange guardian carried him.

Frinlair, who seemed to be seeking an opportunity for a quarrel with his old friend, could not repress his impatience.

"Come, come, Monsieur Camille," said he suddenly, in his language of a gentleman of the stables, "change your black horse for a white one, or we drop you."

Louchard intervened and, addressing Berville, said to him in a tone of gentle reproach:

"How can you be so gloomy, you, the darling of the ladies and of the bank, with everything on your side, youth and wealth? . . . . Yours the key of hearts, you the pink of dandies [*fleur des pois*, literally flower of peas]?"

"Stay, I forgot the vegetables," cried Loiseau.

And he began to write again, while the waiter served the soup.

Camille allowed the disgust that filled his heart to overflow.

"Well, yes," said he, "it is true. I have everything, and I have nothing. . . . . because I have done nothing to have everything. I have lived what you call life, richly and vainly, thanks to my guardian, who has thrown the reins upon my neck and made me master of my fate and fortune. I have run, like a madman, as you all have, after happiness, after love, and I have been deceived, as you have been. I have mistaken pleasure for happiness, loves for love, as my future father-in-law, the baron, mistakes honors for honor. Quantity is not quality, friends; and in these matters I prefer the singular to the plural. I would give all women for a woman. The beauties, as you call them, wines, cards, horses, the possible and the impossible, I have used them all, all, even to the duel. I have fought with friends and enemies, at random, sometimes even with reason. . . . . I have drained the glass to the bottom, and found at last only bitterness and dregs, *ennui* and disgust, and even — laugh if you will — remorse. Intoxication has left its after-taste, but without killing desire". . .

Forgetting the sceptical society in which he found himself, carried away by the impulse of his frank and kindly nature, vitiated but not vicious, he smote his breast, saying amid the sneers and mocking exclamations:

"Surfeited as I am, I still feel here, in my heart, a void, a need like that of Tantalus. Yes, yes, I am hungry, I am thirsty still for that love, for that happiness, the shows of which have not satisfied me."

"What an appetite!" exclaimed Loiseau; "waiter, two roasts for one!"

When the laughter had subsided, Louchard resumed his bantering remonstrances.

"How much will you charge for this speech for my journals?" he asked. "These fine things are only to be written, at most, my dear; they are not to be spoken, especially here and today. . . . Pure love in the Maison-Dorée, in the restaurant and on Mardi-Gras! You sing out of tune! Your heart empty? Nonsense. Your stomach? Ah! very well. Thirsty for love, hungry for happiness! What a poet! Come down quickly to prose. Doctor Véron's soup and beef, — those will relieve you."

Camille shook his head.

"No, I am a dead man, I tell you," he continued, slowly. "Oh, of course I can eat and drink and laugh with you at our stupidities. But it is galvanism; death is in my heart. Life, the only real life, is love, and of that there is no more for such perverse persons as ourselves. That is our punishment and its revenge. Like Midas, we change everything into gold. We can no longer find a woman to give us happiness instead of selling it to us. At any rate, not in the ball-room shall I meet such a woman, and that is why the ball makes me sad."

Louchard began to laugh.

"Midas, Tantalus, fabulous . . . these things are out of date, Camille; be a little positive. Do as I do. When I enter the ball-room, I leave my heart in the cloak-room with my cane or my umbrella and take them again as I go out."

"As for me," confessed Gripon, pointing to his purse on the card-table, "there is my heart. And I never open it except knowingly."

"And as for me," said Loiseau in turn, "I put my heart in my glass. Old wines before young girls. Waiter, Madeira!"

"One does not prevent the other," said Frinlair, with a smile that resembled a grimace, "any more than pure love prevents a big dowry, eh, Monsieur Berville?"

And with design, laying emphasis on each of his words, he said to Camille:

"And you, Monsieur philosopher, do you not love the sole heiress of the great banker baron, your noble and rich betrothed, Mlle. Claire Hoffmann?"

"I marry her," answered Camille, simply.

"Ha, ha! he is real as well as ideal."

Camille closed Frinlair's mouth with a word:

"It is doubtless a fine match for those who, like you, Count Frinlair, want grandeurs and big dowrys, a massive million and hopes. I conceive, though not sharing it, the perfect love with which this millionaire goddess, they say, inspires you. Oh! don't be jealous," he exclaimed, repressing a gesture made by Claire's lover, "with me it is as the broker Gripon says, a matter of business and without pleasure . . . an end, not justifying, but justified by my means. Yes, it is to end that I marry; after Mardi-Gras, Ashes. Henceforth I shall live solely for money . . . . a strong-box, the husband of a purse. I marry a capital. I become Hoffmann & Company; I shall be the company, with a belly. I shall be, like these golden louis, a head without a heart, double-chinned, decorated, a deputy, and satisfied . . . with a wife scarcely my own, children altogether hers, and money that is everybody's. . . . Guizot said: 'Let us get rich.' Brothers, it is necessary to die! Let Bréda put on mourning! Let the lions and rats of the infernal box wear crape! Here lies the son of the late banker Berville, a young prodigal, who died or rather was buried prematurely; a victim of marriage, amounting to no more than the rest, having never done any good or earned his own living, regretted by nobody and regretting nothing. . . . Come, my groomsmen, dear undertakers, the prayer of the dead and wine by way of lustral water. Bury me, marry me, eat me in the elements of this stuffed turkey! Drink me, this iced champagne is my blood. . . . It is the devil's communion, my last supper as a bachelor. Let us drink to my death! I die zero to rise again a million!"

All save Frinlair applauded this speech, and, touching glasses, cried in chorus: "To his resurrection! To the health and multiplication of the million!"

Just then the folding-doors opened, and a lackey, broken to his trade, announced in a quasi-familiar voice:

"Those ladies, gentlemen!"

All, rising, added with one accord:

"Ah! Mazagran & Co., at last!"

The young woman appeared with her companions, dragging, almost by main force, Marie blushing behind her black velvet wolf's mask.

"At the table already, and at the Madeira!" exclaimed Mazagran, indignantly; "without waiting for us. That's a fine way to do. Come in! And quickly . . . hurry to your seat," she continued, pushing Marie before her. "The monsters have already swallowed the soup. I protest. Let us catch up with them before the champagne."

She noticed Gripon's money on the card-table, and, throwing a louis out the window, said:

"Louis? For whom? Anything that falls into the ditch is. . . for the soldier."

"Why, what are you about?" exclaimed the broker, non-plussed by this procedure and touched in his Jewish nature. .

"I am amusing myself," said Mazagran, indifferently. "Would you rather have me pocket it?"

Gripon quickly snatched up the stakes.

"That will teach me to leave my winnings lying about another time," said he, with a smile as yellow as the lost louis.

And, an Israelite to the core, he could not help saying:

"You know, you will return it to me. Gambling money is sacred. It is a debt of honor, and whoso pays his debts". . . .

"Impoverishes himself," said Mazagran, decidedly.

"Indeed, you are right," said Gripon, amazed.

But, returning to his louis, he insisted:

"You shall pay me. Money or nature". . .

Mazagran burst out into a frank peal of laughter, singing with all her voice:

Ah! que c'est beau la nature,
Les prés, les bois, la verdure. . . .

Then, with an exclamation and like a flash, she said:

"In fact, I take you at your word; that makes you still owe me four louis. Agreed."

"No, I decidedly prefer to lose but twenty francs," concluded Gripon.

"You are not gallant," said Mazagran. "But I don't care, for between ourselves you are a good enough remedy for love. . . . Come! let each choose her companion. For my part, I take Frinlair."

And amid laughter they placed themselves: Marie apart, at the soberest end of the table; Henri standing against the mantle-shelf.

"I am starving," confessed Trompette.

"I am dying of thirst," said Louisa.

"And I am both," exclaimed Pauline.

"And I then!" cried Mazagran, glancing in the direction of her old admirer, Camille. "I have the appetite of a widow, of the solitary tape-worm!"

"Yes," said Louchard, "eat and drink, my dear. You have reason to drown your sorrow. Decidedly this rascal Camille deceives you; worse than that, he abandons you."

"He would have deceived me much more if he had not abandoned me," said she, carelessly. "He passes to the position of a husband, he dies. I am a widow, and consequently free. After my mourning, in a night I tie myself up for a lease of three, six, nine, at the will and pleasure of the lessee, the last and highest bidder."

And, addressing the journalist, she added:

"With you, if you like. . . . Pass me the pickles."

Louchard held out the plate and declined the offer.

"Three, six, nine," objected Pauline; "that's a little long, my dear."

"Oh! it is dissoluble," observed Louisa.

"And without expense," said Trompette.

"Hang yourself, notary," exclaimed Gripon. "They are stronger than you at your own game."

"To be sure, what notaries these merrymakers are!" approved Loiseau.

"And what merrymakers are these notaries!" said Mazagran, sending back the ball on the bound.

"Too much wit!" said Gripon. "We shall die young."

"Oh! if that's all," retorted Mazagran, "you will live to be as old as Abraham, your father."

"He threatened indeed," said Gripon, "to become the Eternal Father. At last he is dead. God keep his soul, as the earth keeps his dust!"

"And you the inheritance!" concluded Louchard.

The feast continued in this strain. The wine flowed in torrents. The gayety became inebriety. Marie, all trembling, tried to conceal it as much as possible, while Camille, still aloof with folded arms, looked at her with a distracted air.

"Say there, the late Camille," cried Mazagran, suddenly. "Come and pour us something to drink. Because you are dead, my dear, is no reason for letting others die of thirst. Egoist, away with you!"

She rose and passed near Camille, who did not answer.

"What a catafalque!" exclaimed Mazagran, avenging her abandonment by lashing him with her tongue.

And, going toward Marie, she inquired of her:

"What do you say to this supper, little one?"

Marie answered in a low voice:

"Hush, keep still. Oh! how foolish I have been! I am dazed, stunned. . . . . do not question me."

"Who is this unknown beauty?" said Gripon, interested.

"How do you know she is a beauty?" asked Loiseau.

Frinlair took up this doubt:

"I'll bet a hundred dollars she is!"

"I'll bet she isn't," said the notary.

Gripon, Louchard, and Loiseau, exchanging their impressions, looked at poor Marie, who seemed to want to disappear through the floor.

"She doesn't show herself."

"She doesn't eat."

"She doesn't drink."

Frinlair started toward her.

"Are you made of marble or of wax?" said he, teasingly, "an object of art to put in a museum or in a shrine? a Venus or a Virgin, behind your wolf's mask? timid or coquettish? Come, pose less as a master-piece, or we shall be harder to please. If it is a surprise that you have in store for our dessert, give us less cause to pine. Allow us at least to see, if not to touch. I have bet on you, make me a winner. You will not lose by it. Reserve is a good thing, but not too much of it."

Camille could not restrain a movement of pity.

"This young girl seems to me like a saint in the circus," he exclaimed, looking at her with his soft and sympathetic eye; "timid because she is among beasts; sad because she is among madmen; masked because she sees us unmasked, aping the vices if not the graces of our masters, with our appearances of gentleman Jourdains, harlequin diplomats, clown journalists, merry-andrew notaries, and Macaire courtiers."

With a circular gesture he had passed in review the Count de Frinlair, Louchard, Loiseau, and Gripon, all displeased with his sally.

"In short," he added, "because she is afraid of us."

"Oh! we will break her in," said Frinlair, drawing nearer to Marie. "When one has tamed Cabriole, a restive animal does not frighten him. Besides, for taming purposes the Maison-Dorée is as good as a riding-school."

And addressing Marie, who was still masked, he said:

"Come, no trickery, you are to be weighed. Show us your foot, your neck, your head."

With a quick movement he snatched off her mask.

"Sight costs nothing," said he. "Superb! Ha, ha! I have won."

Unanimous applause welcomed this last word.

"My God! where am I?" murmured Marie, in anguish, hiding her face in her hands.

"Poor girl!" Camille could not help saying.
But Mazagran reminded him of his marriage.
"Ah! Camille, you are defunct!"
Frinlair continued his ecstasy over his discovery.
"What a pupil! First prize! A gold medal to Mazagran. Pure blood, upon
my word! Beautiful, fine, as fresh as Suava, a real thoroughbred filly. . . Notary,
my hundred dollars."
And Frinlair held out his hand to Loiseau, who caviled a little about tastes and
colors. All tastes are in nature; the best is your own, etc. . . . . but, pressed by
all, he paid Frinlair.
Camille could no longer contain himself.
"Enough, enough, Monsieur Count," he cried, indignantly. "We are not in a
stable, but you behave here like a jockey."
"And you perhaps like a knight," said Frinlair, provokingly.
And approaching Marie, who sat as if nailed, he took her by the arm and said:
"A kiss for my hundred dollars."
Marie, through horror and instinct, recoiled from Frinlair and sought refuge
near Camille.
"Ah! centaur that you are," said he to the count, who was pursuing Marie. . .
"to maltreat a woman. Then your mother was not a woman. Stop your kicking
and neighing. Respect Mademoiselle!"
He placed himself in front of the young girl, and in this sudden movement tore
the lace of her dress.
Mazagran saw the accident.
"Save the dress," she cried, mocking at Marie, by whose honor she was
condemned.
"Ah!" exclaimed Marie, more and more frightened. "What have I done?
Why, why did I come here?"
And she ran toward the door.
"Marie! Marie!" cried Mazagran, displeased at this flight.
"Ah! let me alone," exclaimed Marie, in terror. "You have ruined me!"
She fled before they could stop her.
"Ruined," sneered Mazagran. "Ah! poor dress!"
They began to laugh at the incident, and the laughter exasperated Berville
still further. Beside himself, he paced the room with long strides, and abruptly
stopped in front of Frinlair.
"Ah! quadruped," said he, with profound contempt, "now you are triumphant.
You make a woman run. Your brutality is your prowess. Your nobility, then,
is incurable?"
"I have him at last," thought Frinlair. "This time all is over,"
And he rejoined haughtily:

" You are going to withdraw these insults, I hope."

" I never take back what I give," said Camille, dryly.

" It is for me, then, to thank you as I must."

" At your pleasure."

" You know to what these words bind you ? "

" To anything you please."

" Insulted, I have the choice of weapons," said Friulair.

" Yes, it is your right and your habit," sneered Camille, alluding to the affair of the banquet. " Do you choose the pistol again ? "

" No, the sword," said Frinlair, now fairly livid.

" Very well," assented Camille.

" At the Porte Maillot, then, at eight o'clock."

Camille bowed slightly.

" I shall await you there," he said, cutting short the interview.

" Oh ! don't be silly," said Loiseau; " see here, Camille, I want to draw up your contract."

" And I to buy your stocks," said Gripon. " A duel, what madness ! "

Camille took his cloak and hat.

" Killed or married, what difference does it make ? " said he, turning his back upon Frinlair.

" I will bet on killed," muttered the latter.   •

" With such an adversary one must expect anything," said Camille, intentionally.

And upon this last word, which increased the count's hatred tenfold, the young Berville went out.

" Ah ! gentlemen," cried Louchard, trying to smooth the matter over. " A duel to the death for a grisette; settle it with champagne rather."

But Camille had closed the door precipitately, cutting off all intervention.

Mazagran had lighted a cigarette.

" What a success ! " said she.

Frinlair took her around the waist.

" Supplanted by your pupil. Vengeance ! One always returns to his first love. Ha, ha. . . . For want of a monk — and what a monk ! — the abbey will not close. We will not let this end our fun."

" End, never ! " said Mazagran, explosively. " That would be too silly. No, never ! "

And all repeated with enthusiasm :

" Never ! "

" And our game ! " said Gripon.

" And the champagne," said Loiseau, filling the glasses to overflowing.

" And my journals," cried Louchard, taking Pauline in his arms and saying to her in a voice thick with wine : " Let us collaborate ! "

Loiseau poured bumper after bumper, meanwhile making notary's puns, stamped. All, carried away by this example and spirit, drunk with wine and tobacco, began to talk and shout, and finally separated into couples, laughing, dancing, leaping, and singing between kisses and hiccoughs: •

Vive l'Opéra, vive l'Opéra!
La rifla, fla, fla!

The waiters had retired respectfully, foreseeing that the smoking-room was to be a scene of orgy, and leaving a free field for the gentlemen and ladies.

When they left the Maison d'Or an hour later, a rag-picker, busily filling his basket with the remains of Mardi-Gras, watched them pass, more or less carried by lackeys and waiters, and murmured:

"To think that once I was like that! Except that I had no valets to put me in my carriage. It's a fine way to behave! Fashionable society, filthy society. . . . But I must fill my basket. Then I can buy a beautiful bouquet of violets for Mam'zelle Marie."

And Father Jean resumed his task, paying no further attention to the revellers.

CHAPTER V.

THE DRESS.

On this night of Mardi-Gras, among other oddities of the Carnival, the curious lingerers upon the boulevards saw, gliding along the sidewalks and spattering herself from the gutters, a young girl dressed as a bride, fleeing in the direction of the Faubourg Saint-Antoine.

It was Marie. She hurried past the pedestrians, doubling her pace, running, flying, without noticing a man covered with a *quiroga*, who was following her, persistently regulating his pace by her own.

Thus, one following the other, they reached the Rue Sainte-Marguerite, where an important scene in our drama was then being enacted.

A woman draped or rather hidden in a large shawl had just climbed the stairs leading to Marie's room. She carried a little basket carefully wrapped under her arm.

She knocked at the young working-girl's door, calling in a smothered voice:

"Mademoiselle Marie, open the door; it is I, your customer, Mme. Potard. I bring you work. And then I want to talk with you on serious business."

And in a still lower voice the nocturnal visitor added:

"She is so good! she will accept for a trifle."

But receiving no reply, she turned the key, which had been left in the lock by mistake, and half opened the door.

"Nobody here!" she exclaimed. "What luck!"

She entered Marie's room as if accustomed to the place, knowing the nooks and corners, and disappeared in a sleeping-room adjoining the chamber, returning empty-handed two seconds later.

"Absent at this hour!" she said as she started off. "So much the better. No one to share with me. I can keep the whole."

She slapped her pocket, felt and fumbled, looked about in agitation, and then began to cry:

"Oh! my God! I have lost, lost all; what a misfortune. Oh! no, it is not possible; I must make a thorough search!"

She went back into the sleeping-room, and then returned in anguish.

"Nothing there, nothing here, nothing anywhere! Quick. . . . I must hurry back over the route by which I came. The package must have fallen in the street or in the doorway. I felt it but a little while ago."

Then, mortally anxious, she continued :

"Perhaps somebody has already found it and fled. People are such rascals in these days. I must find it again. I must start at once."

She was already on the landing, but suddenly she drew back behind the steps leading to Jean's garret.

"Somebody coming!" she exclaimed.

Marie had just entered hastily, closing the door after her and this time taking the key.

The working-girl's mysterious customer went down the stairs like a shadow and disappeared.

Alone in her room, Marie lighted her lamp and saw the dress, torn, soiled, ruined. Then, with dishevelled hair and haggard eyes, in a desperate mood, she fell sobbing upon a chair.

"What a night!" she murmured. "What a sin and what a punishment! Where has this cursed dress taken me? How am I to pay for it? Where can I get the money that it cost?"

She took off the nuptial finery and put on her own poor garments.

"All that I have will not be enough, no !" she continued, beside herself. " An abuse of confidence, almost a theft, prison perhaps. . . . What shame! Never, never. Death rather! . . . Besides, why live? I know what it is now; I have seen the abyss to the bottom. Oh ! these pleasures are crimes; these joys regrets; this happiness remorse. They horrify me. Thank God! I succeeded in getting away. I will never go back. No, no, I do not wish to fall to such a depth again, and remain there as so many do."

For a few moments she said no more, reviewing in her imagination the incidents of this disastrous Carnival night.

" And yet I am afraid," she groaned at last. "Beside the man who insulted me, the one who defended me was so noble and so beautiful". . .

But she immediately reacted against this cry of her heart.

"Ah! if I were to yield again. There, vice and dishonor; here, struggle and despair! Neither the one nor the other : death! I shall die at least virtuous, still worthy of my poor mother."

She rose, possessed by a fixed idea, and continued with a sudden firmness:

"I will rejoin her. It is over."

Then, remembering the only being in the world who was interested in her and whom she loved, the unhappy girl went to her table and said with emotion:

"Ah! a word first to my good old neighbor."

And with a feverish hand she wrote these few words:

"Farewell, Father Jean, I throw off the collar of poverty, I do not wish to put on that of shame; I can live no longer, I want to die. I charge you with the sale of my poor furniture and the payment of the proceeds for the spoiled dress. If the money should be refused, it will serve to bury me beside my mother. To reward you for the trouble I leave you, in memory of me, my father's watch."

And she signed her name, — Marie Didier; then, rising again, she said simply and more resolutely:

"Now then!"

With a firm step she left her room and climbed the steps leading to her old friend's habitation.

Scarcely had she gone out when the man in a cloak who had followed Marie along the boulevard and faubourg pushed into the room after a moment's hesitation

"This dress!" he exclaimed, perceiving the wedding garment. "She lives here, then. Poor girl! she has come home again. I have followed her, and, as it were, in spite of myself. But where is she? Shall I wait for her? Leave some money? Yes, but how much? I will wait."

He sat down, surveyed the room, — something new to him, — and said to himself:

"What neatness, it is fascinating; and what poverty, it is edifying. My heart beats violently. It is strange. I never felt such an emotion. It is not on account of the duel, for I have fought ten of them. It is not love, for I think no more of that. But perhaps I am not as dead as I thought. God grant it! Let us live! I ask nothing better than to love."

He looked again at the dress, with the lace, which his foot had torn, dragging on the floor.

"Lucky awkwardness," he exclaimed.

And trying to recover from this spontaneous impulse, he laughed at it.

"Pshaw! I am having another attack. Love at a masquerade, the ideal at the ball-room of Musard and Chicard! It is absurd. We do not meet angels in hell . . . . unless they go there to save devils."

He shook his head with more of formal scepticism than of conviction.

"No, no," said he, "no more miracles. This girl is as earthly as the others. In spite of her halo . . . I simply come to repair a rent."

He interrupted himself; the door of the room had opened again, and Marie, entering, uttered a cry of fright on perceiving a stranger in her apartment.

Camille rose and bowed with involuntary respect. He was more and more under the influence of her charm. The young girl, in her modest garments, seemed to him as beautiful as in her silk dress, and purer.

"It is I, Mademoiselle," said he, bowing again, "fear nothing. I saw you go away so distressed and offended that I could not help following you. I beg you to be kind enough to accept an apology for our rudeness and the compensation that I owe you for this dress."

Marie made an imperative gesture of refusal; and, in a hurry to end the scene, she said:

"I thank you, Monsieur; you owe me nothing, and I beg you to leave me."

Camille bowed, and surreptitiously leaving his purse, filled with gold, on the table, he said:

"I go, Mademoiselle."

And already he was outside.

Marie, having seen his whole proceeding, recalled him.

"Monsieur, Monsieur, you forget". . . .

She handed him his purse.

Camille shook his head negatively.

"You forget yourself," Marie then said, insisting and forcing him to take back his money.

The young man went out in a sort of enchantment.

"Oh! I am afraid of the duel now," he exclaimed, "of killing or dying. If I live, I will return."

He met Father Jean, whom in his agitation and in the darkness of the stairway he failed to recognize.

The old rag-picker, before going up to his wretched lodgings, placed a bouquet of flowers upon his young *protégée's* door knob, and then climbed to his garret.

Marie bolted her door, saying:

"Now for the end!"

Then, looking at her rose-bush, she added:

"Ah! my poor flowers, they will survive me. Let them not die with me!"

She watered them.

"And you, poor bird, go free!" she added.

She opened the cage and the window for her goldfinch.

"Now I must address this garment."

And she wrote: "Mademoiselle Claire Hoffmann, Hotel Hoffmann, Faubourg Saint-Honoré," folded the dress, wrapped it up, pinned the address upon the bundle, and prepared everything for her suicide. She pulled back the bolt, placed a napkin over the keyhole, stuffed a skirt beneath the door, stopped up every crevice through which air could come in, put some charcoal in the chafing-dish, lighted it, stirred the fire, watched it burn for a moment, and knelt before the portrait of her parents.

Kneeling and already weakened by the fumes of the charcoal, Marie, feeling the approach of suffocation, uttered this prayer:

"O my father, my mother, I rejoin you, receive me! God, forgive me!"

Then a feeble cry fell upon her ear.

Listening in the direction of the sleeping-room, she said:

"What's that? My head swims; I heard a cry there."

She rose quickly, went into the adjoining room, and came back with a basket, saying:

"A child! a child! a poor little child, here, in my room, alive! O heaven! Who can thus have abandoned her babe? The poor little thing is cold!"

Covering him up, she continued:

"He suffers! he groans! Ah! it is the charcoal. . . . Air, air."

She broke a pane of glass, and put out the fire with her water-pitcher.

"What shall I do? Kill him with me?"

Then, as if inspired, she said:

"Oh! I had not the strength to live for myself alone! I will live, I will live for him. Mother, you wish it, do you not? You who toiled so hard for me. I will follow your example; I accept this duty, this happiness. Yes, yes, I accept! henceforth I shall not be alone. Ah! dear child, I will be your mother; for your sake, I take heart and strength again. For you I banish despair and pain. I will work day and night, if need be; and, if I die in the task, God at least will forgive me for this suicide. Linen, linen, my best linen for my baby's swaddling-clothes!"

And taking a new chemise from her bureau, she tore it up and began to sew ardently by the child's side.

CHAPTER VI.

SORTING THE RAGS.

On his return from his night's work, Father Jean had closed his door and dropped his basket with a sigh of relief, saying to himself:

"I will do my sorting. Meanwhile Mam'zelle Marie will rise, and I cannot go to bed without saying good morning to her and hearing her say good night to me."

Twenty years, as we have said, had passed over the head of the rag-picker.

He was an old man already, but of a green old age.

All that is old is not always bad.

Good wines and good people do not lose in growing old. Old wood, old books, old pictures, old friends are the best.

Still there is an end to everything.

There comes a time when old age becomes dryness, when the heart shrivels and wrinkles like the forehead. There comes an age when all illusions are lost, all tears shed, all affections gone; when what are called the *bumps* of the good passions, love, devotion, etc., sink into holes, and when those of the bad rise into mountains; when man relapses into infancy. "This age is pitiless." Second childhood is worse than the first; the senile egoism of reenvelopment is uglier than development; it loves nothing but the past, has no eyes for the good and glasses for evil only, believing everything dead because it is dying. Which caused the poet Anacreon to say: "Whom the gods love die young," and Béranger: "My children, God grant you an early death!"

Jean had escaped to some extent this law of human decrepitude. He was endowed with such vitality that he necessarily remained sound and strong, and, though his head had turned white, his heart was still red.

Jean, like a philosopher worthy of the name, was sociable as well as solitary. He loved to talk to himself in his garret, when he could not talk to Marie, whom he had watched, aided, and protected, as in former days her mother, with honorable intentions, as he said.

So on this night, believing his young friend to be sleeping the sleep of innocence, he busied himself with his rags and old paper, lighting his candle and emptying his basket upon the middle of his garret-floor.

"Let us empty the casket," said he, in his good-natured, jesting way . . . "the basket of silver-ware, the hamper of jewels, the hunt after relics. . . . Let us see if I have done a fine day's work on my Mardi-Gras, if I shall find anything of value in this residue of Paris. It is a small affair, Paris, as seen in the basket of a rag-picker . . . neither good nor beautiful, the balance-sheet."

And folding his arms, he said:

"To think that I have all Paris, all society, in this wicker-basket! My God, yes, everything passes through it, rose-leaves and paper-leaves; everything ends there, sooner or later, in the basket."

He stirred the heap with his foot.

"Love, glory, power, wealth, into the basket! into the basket, refuse of all sorts! Everything comes to it, everything holds to it, everything falls into it. . . What a melting-pot! Everything reduces to rags, tatters, shards, stumps, dish-cloths."

And, sitting down on his stool, between the heap and the basket, with the commercial tranquillity of an expert, testing, judging, and measuring everything by its value, volume, or weight, he said, starting upon his inventory:

"Let us see!"

Thrusting his hook through the first paper within his reach and bringing it under his eyes, he deciphered with difficulty:

"General Union Association for the exploitation of gold mines in Auvergne and railroads in Mexico. Baron Hoffmann & Co. Capital: One hundred millions. Shares, one hundred francs each. A good investment". . .

"Rag!" exclaimed Father Jean, disdainfully throwing the paper back into the basket.

He took a poster and read:

"Concert of the celebrated pianist without hands, given for the benefit of deaf-mutes, in the Hall *des Menus-Plaisirs.*"

"Shard!" said he, throwing the programme together with a broken plate into the basket.

He picked up another poster, still reading with his jocular curiosity:

"Overture of the grand ball of the Opera, with new waltzes and quadrilles."

"Sock!" he sneered, sending it to keep company with an old shoe.

With the end of his hook he lifted a bit of embroidered uniform and threw it after the rest.

"Old clothes!" he exclaimed.

A knot in a buttonhole making a spot of red on the end of a piece of black cloth attracted also his piercing hook as well as his Parisian raillery. He took it and looked at it for a moment.

"Ribbon, tag," he said, sending the Legion of Honor into the basket also.

A big heap of papers bearing the title: "The Knights of the Moon."

"A newspaper novel," said he; "into the basket!"

But reconsidering:

"No, into the lodge! The janitress has asked me for these contrivances. Much good may it do her! . . . Ah! a pamphlet!"

"Reception speech made before the French Academy."

He seized an old wig and threw both into the basket under the same heading: "Grass!"

A new poster appeared. He examined it with the same interest.

"Monseigneur's directions for Lent."

"Holy-water sprinkler!" he cried, joining it with an aspergillum in the hamper.

Another poster which he read more attentively.

"Police ordinance. — Rag-pickers are forbidden to tear down posters."

"Pardon!" he exclaimed.

And passing to a letter written on pink paper:

"Dear angel, my blood, my life, my soul, all for you". . .

He stopped, and for a good reason.

"Ah! a blot . . . and not of ink. . . . Into the basket! into the basket!"

He took next a pamphlet and deciphered:

"Memoir on the civil list, by Timon. Twelve millions."

The pamphlet went to join the rest. But suddenly Father Jean seemed embarrassed.

He had just perceived in the midst of his dirt-pile a crown branded with a flower-de-luce.

"There," said he, shaking his head, "is something that was worth twelve millions when it was in fashion. What a loss!"

He tried it on, and looking at himself complacently in his remnant of mirror, he said with a laugh:

"Father Jean, king of France! A good nightcap."

But wrath followed his irony.

Suddenly the rag-picker tore the royal diadem from his head and hurled it into the filth.

"No," he cried in horror, "I should dream of blood! Into the basket! Into the basket, like the rest."

He remained silent for a moment after this execution.

Good Father Jean, perfect image of the sovereign people . . . . king in name, but slave in fact, a landless subject, like his English namesake, King John, without fireside, without family, having nothing of sovereignty, or even of humanity.

A man by nature, a citizen by law, but in reality a serf, a helot, a pariah, a bastard disinherited by that step-mother who is country only to the eldest, the legitimate, the elect of patrimony, the only sovereigns, those who have all the attributes of royalty, three in number, — the vote that disposes, the soil that feeds, and the weapon that defends.

With his jesting patience and his common sense of the people, Jean resumed the course of his reflections:

"And to think that all that will be made anew, fine glazed paper, stamped, bank bills and *billets doux*, letters of exchange and of love, of birth and of death, books and journals, all the bric-a-brac of civilization . . . . and that it will come back here again and always, even to extermination, in the basket. O cast-off clothing of the late Madame Night-Before! O superb scraps, this is your humiliation, this is the general rendezvous, the common grave, the end of the world, the last judgment! And the rag-picker the supreme judge. . . . Jean, the residuary legatee of Paris. . . . Yes, but held for no debts beyond the assets. And what is left for the inheritance? There! a bone. . . . How it has been cleaned and dissected! It was a ham. The master had it first, then the valet, then the dog . . . and I afterwards . . . consequently there is nothing left. Well! I must eat my dry bread. . . . Obedience to Monseigneur's directions."

He took a piece of brown bread from his pocket, and lifted a newspaper with the end of his hook.

"A piece of bread to eat," said he, " and a piece of newspaper to read: the two nourishments, for one does not live by bread alone. Eating and reading, as at the restaurant. What more? Too happy the rag-picker who finds his bread in the dirt-pile and his knowledge in filth. Good appetite. . . . Waiter, the newspaper. . . . Here, there it is, Monsieur! . . . Thank you . . . ah! no, to be sure, one does not say thank you . . . it is bad form ". . .

After having swallowed his little loaf with his night-tramp's appetite, he began to read the newspaper, using a straw as a tooth-pick.

"Readers whose subscriptions expire are requested ". . .

He stopped.

"They always begin that way," he exclaimed. "But that doesn't concern me; I get my journal free. Let us have a look at the news."

He began to read in a low voice, and soon was sleeping the sleep of the subscriber.

.   .   .   .

Jean slept until his stool slipped from under him, when, his head plunging into his rags, he awoke with a start, his journal in his hand.

He resumed his jocular soliloquy:

"These buffoon newspapers always have that effect upon me. It is with journals as with oysters, they need to be eaten fresh. But I must not speak evil of old papers; they are the best part of my property. Long live the liberty of the press and of the basket! "

He flung the journal into a corner.

"Here I am, at the bottom of the heap," said he, resuming his interrupted task. " The best for the last."

And with a thrust of his hook he lifted a package of bluish paper, saying:

" I found this coming back to the faubourg, almost at the door. What is it ? My sight is dim ". . .

He drew nearer to the candle and read :

" Bank of France. . . One thousand francs ". . . .

Counting :

" One, two, three. . . Ah ! my God, a fortune. . . . Ten bills ! Ten thousand francs. . . Poor devil who lost them ! "

But reflection corrected this spontaneous cry of his noble and honest nature.

" Not so poor, when one can thus lose ten thousand francs at once. . . . Are they good ? . . . They seem to be. They are very ugly ". . .

And then he cried :

" Ah ! if they were all mine . . . what a dowry for Mam'zelle Marie ! "

He shook his head as he concluded :

" Now I must put them carefully away, until I can return them. . . . Suppose some one should take them from me first ! Ah ! but it is unhealthy to have bank bills. Already I have a fever of fear . . . fear lest I may be robbed. Such things happen. I saw much more taken at the Quai d'Austerlitz. I will stuff them into the pocket-book of that poor Didier, which has held many others. Who knows ? Perhaps they have been in it before. Well ! at any rate I will put them in my table. . . . I will lie on them. . . . I shall sleep no more ". . . .

He rose, went to his table, pulled out the drawer, took the pocket-book, and observed a folded letter bearing his name.

" Now what's this ? " he exclaimed, in surprise. " O heaven ! " he cried, mad with despair. " Marie ! foolish child ! to die ! And Father Jean ? Do not die, Marie, live ! Your mother does not want you to die. I want you to live, do you hear ? Wait ! wait for me, we are rich ! ". . .

And he rushed down the steps, the bank-bills in one hand, the letter in the other, and screaming in anguish :

" Oh ! if I am not too late ! "

" Some one comes," exclaimed Marie ; " suppose they want to take him back again."

And she approached the child maternally.

Then Jean, bursting open the closed door and seeing the child, cried :

" A child ! She ! So this is the bottom of the heap ! It is complete."

And he fell upon a chair, overwhelmed with distress and amazement.

CHAPTER VII.

THE DUEL.

This remnant of feudal morals, of the wild justice of Frank chivalry and of barbarian nobility, this right of natural defence which substitutes force and private cunning for the law and public power, this prejudice of an anti-social age when the individual sustained his own cause in the absence of collective power, the duel has outlived the declaration of rights and duties, the principles of the French Revolution; and our *bourgeoisie*, which has inherited the privileges of the nobility, has inherited also its assassinations.

In spite of all the eloquence of Rousseau, the Goddess of Reason of '93, and the sovereignty of the People; in spite even of the wise example of aristocratic England, democratic and social France keeps the duel. Outside of the people, who, I hope, will not inherit this vice, all its *bourgeois* gentlemen, its Jourdains and Dimanches, its republicans even, its citizens of the nineteenth century, still conduct themselves like the knights of the age of judicial combats and judgments of God.

Montesquieu, a feudalist, explains why a blow on the cheek is unpardonable; inasmuch as the knight fought with covered head, none but vassals could be struck on the cheek. Hence, according to this wholly Garoussian theory, the supreme offence, the assault upon a man's cheek, calls for blood. That of the offender we might allow, but that of the offended?

And so it will be until we shall have sufficiently elevated our life and morals to understand the lesson of solidarity that, if one man is offended, all are, and that the offender of one is the offender of all. •

That noble theory, "force before right," still regulates all human relations, individual and collective.

There is even a false code of honor, establishing and containing all the absurd and atrocious laws, usages, and customs of this right of the strongest, civilizing homicide and legalizing murder.

They fight until blood is drawn or to the death, with one or several shots, at the pistol's mouth or at a distance, hand to hand or at sword's length, and with seconds to say *enough* and the doctor near by to repair the *too much*, and in all cases alike honor is satisfied. They equalize weapons, but neither strength nor skill, and in any case honor is satisfied.

They draw lots for advantages of ground and position, but they allow the advantages of fencing and shooting lessons, and still honor is satisfied.

The knave may be the stronger and more skilful of the two,—that is, the conqueror,—and the honest man may be conquered and dead, but always honor is satisfied.

For one of these civilized crimes, then, the two old school friends, the two rivals who had already fought over a love affair, met a second time at the Porte Maillot.

In those days fighting was still allowed in the Bois de Boulogne,

Wood was cut there also; there peaceful labor often met quarrelsome idleness.

On this particular day a poor wood-cutter was there, making his poor fagots, as Piron would say, with his poor child, His pale wife brought him his meagre sustenance, a breakfast of bread and cheese to revictual him, after two hours' work in the morning mist.

Seeing a carriage stop at the crossing of the roads and three persons get out, the wood-cutter said to his wife:

"See, a carriage at this hour! More *bourgeois* about to amuse themselves by killing each other. It is laughable all the same. They come with weapons to kill each other and a doctor to dress the wounds . . . and they call that honor!"

"Yes," said the wife, "they would do better to go to work."

"I do not understand the passion that these idlers have for fighting. After all, they have nothing else to do! Ah! if they had to cut wood all day to earn bread for a family, they would not rise so early in the morning to bleed each other. Whence come they? From the ball-room, and full of truffles and turkey! Ah! if I were the government, I would condemn all these valorous people to support a child of the poor. Children! they give themselves the pain of making them and leave us the pleasure of bringing them up. I hope that the Republic will change all that. I sometimes feel, when I see them, as if I would like to settle all their quarrels with a few blows of the axe and make them into . . . but bah! they are good for nothing, not even for fagots!"

Camille, the first at the rendezvous with his two seconds, of whom one was the workman with the hammer, had advanced during this dialogue between the wood-cutter and his wife.

He was soon joined by his adversary still in his Harlequin costume, and Gaston's seconds, dressed as a Merry Andrew and a Macaire, having had time, after their supper, only to sleep off their wine and get their swords and a doctor.

After having exchanged salutations, Camille said to his adversary:

"This wood-cutter is at work here; let us go a little farther on."

"I am late and fatigued; let him go farther! Say, there, do you hear? The clodhopper does not answer."

"Because the clodhopper could not answer you except with a piece of green wood, and he has no time to correct you."

"Come, get away!" cried Frinlair to the wood-cutter in an imperious tone.
"Get away yourself."

"Insolent wretch," and he lifted his cane.

"How so?" and the wood-cutter lifted his axe.

"Come, my worthy man, here is the price of your day's work," said Camille. And he gave him two dollars.

"This workman is doing his day's work," he added, "and we have no right to disturb him for nothing! Come, my good man, do us the service to go away."

"Very well! but this is too much. You owe me only half of this. Take back the rest, and good luck to you! To give two dollars to kill each other when I earn only one to live. Come, wife, let's be off."

· And the wood-cutter, his child, and his wife, took each a bundle of fagots, big, medium-sized, and little, and made room for the combatants.

Human honor, real honor, is duty, devotion to right, to justice towards one's fellow, one's family, one's country, and humanity.

As soon as the duellists were rid of the wood-cutters, Camille spontaneously offered excuses to Gaston, who did not deign to receive them, and the positions were immediately taken.

The two armed men stood face to face, with that instinctive hatred which animated at least one against the other, a hatred of race, as it were, as well as of interest.

Camille was a pupil of Prévot, a fencing-master whose son, worthy of the father, now gives lessons to the president's guards. Prévot was the assistant of the great Bertrand, whose hall had preserved the classic tradition of the French school, the lightning stroke, the straight stroke to the heart.

But Camille's master had set aside the rules of unity; he was romantic in fencing, saying with reason that there is blood everywhere and not alone in the red heart of the plastron. He had revolutionized the duel.

Camille did not want to kill his adversary, remembering Gaston's mother, his own, and Marie; all these forms of goodness and beauty had driven hatred from his heart. He wanted only to put him *hors de combat*, abandoned the straight stroke, did not cross his sword, but held it low, ready, on the slightest advance of Frinlair, to stop him with a thrust in the leg or in the arm, in such a way as to disarm him.

Frinlair, as supple as a diplomat, as adroit as a monkey, and more cunning than strong at fencing, performed evolutions like those of a cat when its tail gets caught in a door.

He, on the contrary, wanted to kill Camille, through antipathy first, and also through calculation; he hated the man and the rival. Camille was the obstacle to the dowry, the shield before the million. So it was necessary to kill him at any cost, and the best way was to make him lose his guard and coolness.

After having thus dangerously but vainly harassed him by his skirmishing, suddenly he leaped upon him, engaging him hand to hand, and treacherously seized Camille's weapon, though too late, whereupon Camille, taking a step backward, ran Gaston through the body.

The seconds received the victim in their arms.

Two strangers to the duel, who had watched it anxiously from behind a clump of trees, came forth at once to shake hands with Camille.

The baron, ever anxious about his dear ward, had followed him, accompanied by Doctor Dubois, happy to be of no use to the victor.

The police arrived, as usual, after all was over, took the cards of the parties, helped to put Frinlair into his carriage . . . and justice, morality, and honor were once more satisfied in France by the flow of blood.

The duel, war, and the death penalty, to say nothing of wages, three means of the same sort, of the same age, and of the same right, force, which arbitration alone can and must replace immediately for the satisfaction of human honor.

The next day the whole press told the story of the end of Gaston de Frinlair without more comment than as if he had died a natural death.

Gérôme made a portrait of him in his best style.

The Bois de Boulogne, becoming a park, relegated duellists and wood-cutters to the Bois de Meudon.

CHAPTER VIII.

THE BIRTH.

Let us go back a few hours in this evening of Mardi-Gras, 1848.

Mme. Potard, first-class midwife, whose establishment was in the Quartier du Marais, was about to take a little rest at nightfall, when a ring of the bell suddenly made her scold.

"Another nuisance," she exclaimed. "I can do no more, I am tired out. Births, miscarriages, and the rest,—there is no end. Not to mention that the game isn't worth the candle."

In the meantime the servant entered.

"Madame," said she, "a gentleman."

" Ah, indeed! Well dressed or shabby, tell me?"

"Very *chic.* Oh! a swell!" exclaimed the servant, admiringly.

"As much as that?" asked Mme. Potard, smiling contentedly.

"Much more," said the servant, stepping aside to let her mistress pass as the latter ran to see her evening visitor in the ante-room.

She was about to survey and question him when he seized her by the arm and pushed her toward the door.

"Come, start at once," said he, "there is no time to lose."

"But, Monsieur," protested the midwife, "I must first know". . .

"It is useless, time is pressing, the carriage waits, we will talk on the way."

Willy-nilly, Mme. Potard had to go out and follow her customer.

"Well, what is it?" she asked, when they were once settled in the carriage.

The man, who concealed his face under his high collar, explained his business in a few words.

"I am obliged to confide a grave secret to you," said he. "A young woman is about to give birth to a child. How does that happen? That does not concern you. Only thus far are you interested. You are to preside at the delivery. The child will be confided to you and must disappear at once."

"Disappear," exclaimed Mme. Potard.

"I said disappear," repeated the stranger.

"Oh! Monsieur," replied the midwife, "you take me". . .

" For what you are," said the man, drily.

"But"...

"How much do you ask? One thousand dollars"...

"That would be nothing at all," Mme. Potard could not help crying.

"Well, make your own price."

The midwife began to exclaim again.

"At no price," said she. "Disappear! How you talk!"

And becoming suspicious, she went on:

"In the first place, one never knows with whom one is dealing. The police have so many devices for tempting and catching us. If one could only be sure of people. . . . If one knew people . . . perhaps . . . I do not say no. I like to render a service; that's my business . . . but, you see, upon my conscience. . . . Who are you?"

The man remained silent.

"Are you the master of the house?"

The man leaned over toward the midwife and spoke a word in her ear.

"Indeed!" she exclaimed. "Then you"...

"Hush!" said the other. "And now let us come to an understanding."

The midwife still professed reluctance.

"Really, I should like to be accommodating, but you ask an impossibility. A drug, a simple abortion, that's all very well; art has to aid nature. A little spurred rye, etc., and all's done; one does not leave a trade-mark. A fig for the police!"

And coming to the point, she said:

"There are only two of us. If you wish something evil of me, there is no witness; you affirm, I deny. So let us be reasonable. A thousand dollars for such an operation would be no price at all. I should not make my expenses."

"Two thousand," said the man, "and silence, for here we are. There's your money. Is it agreed?"

"Why! since you insist on so much," said the midwife, following her companion with a quick step.

They entered an aristocratic mansion by the back door, and went up stairs and through the halls until they reached a sleeping-room where they found a young woman in the pains of labor.

The midwife took in the situation in no time.

"Oh! she's all right. The birth is a normal one. Only fifteen minutes more of pain. There, bite your handkerchief, my child, struggle as much as you please, and don't be afraid to cry out. We will rid you of that presently."

"Oh!" exclaimed the patient, in horror. "Who is this woman?"

"What!" said the midwife; "then she is not in the secret of Paradise?"

"No," said the man, in a low voice, "you will tell her that the child is dead."

"Agreed," said Mme. Potard.

The time went rapidly. A final spasm drew a last cry from the young woman. "There you are," said the midwife, softly.

The mother raised her voice feebly.

"It is?" she asked.

" A boy," said Mme. Potard.

"Oh! give him to me, the poor little one, and let me kiss him," begged the mother, in a tone of ineffable sweetness.

But the midwife froze the kiss on the lips of the unhappy woman with this single word: "Still-born!" saying which, she placed the child in a basket ready for the purpose.

The mother threw herself back in the bed with a heart-rending cry.

"You are going?" said the man to the midwife. "Is there no danger in leaving Madame alone?"

"No," she answered. "Hers is a strong nature, and she will sleep."

And the midwife bowed and retired.

"Now I must hurry off to the other," exclaimed the man, disappearing in turn, called to another person and another drama which so interested him that he was willing to leave the sick woman to the care of a nurse.

Thus passed several hours.

The dawn lighted the windows of the room.

The man came back.

The sound of his steps aroused the sick woman from her prostration.

"Is he really dead?" she asked.

"Yes, and have courage, Claire; his father has gone straightway to join him."

"His father!"

"Yes; killed in a duel by his rival, caused by a girl. . . . All is over. You must be resigned, my child."

"Oh! I shall go mad," shrieked the sick woman, fainting under this terrible shock.

"Now then," said the unknown, ever imperturbable, "there is no further obstacle to the marriage!"

CHAPTER IX.

THE REVELATION.

A month after Frinlair's death, Baron Hoffmann and his daughter were sitting in the same room, the banker at a round table with an account-book and a pencil in his hand, and Claire at another table giving milk to a kitten. In the middle of the room Laurent, the servant, and Rosine, Mademoiselle's maid, had just arranged a superb array of wedding jewels sent by Camille that Claire might make a selection.

The baron raised his head, saying in an undertone:

"His guardianship account is completed. . . . I hold my madman, hold him in spite of everything, tied hand and foot". . .

And aloud to Claire he said, pointing to the jewels:

"Have you chosen? It is embarrassing. What an array! Camille is eccentric, as usual."

At this name the banker's daughter gave a start of horror, and, without answering, continued her attentions to the kitten, saying gently:

"Poor little orphan, I take the place of your mother, who died in giving birth to you."

And calling, she added:

"Rosine, he is cold; put on his covering, and place him on a cushion near the fire."

"Yes, Mademoiselle," said Rosine, going out with the animal.

"One must love something," sighed Claire, looking pensively at the crosses, amulets, and missals that surrounded her.

"You do not answer me," said the baron again, with a shade of impatience.

Rosine entered with a piece of sculpture in her hand.

"Ah! Mademoiselle," said she, "here is the representation of Minette which the sculptor has brought for her grave in the garden. Does it look like her?"

"All right," interrupted the banker. "Let him be paid, and go away!"

Claire took various articles from a box and handed them to the servant.

"Send these bread-tickets to the poor of this district," said she, "this package of baby's linen to the infant asylum, and these religious books to the prison of St. Lazare."

"Yes, Mademoiselle," said Laurent, who went out with Rosine, saying in her ear: "What an angel!"

The baron rose, and, approaching Claire, said:

"Come, pay a little attention to what I have to say. Let us sit down and talk. My daughter, you are a patroness of St. Lazare, a commissioner of infant asylums, a lady of charity. That's all very well, but it is not enough. You still lack, you know, the title of Madame Camille Berville."

"Ah! never!" said Claire, trembling.

The baron looked in her eyes, and continued in a tone of authority:•

"This last title is needed to assure the others. You must take it at the earliest possible moment. This marriage, announced and published, has been dragging too long already. These delays displease me, and even frighten me, for I am beginning to be alarmed about Camille."

Claire gave a start of joy.

"Is it possible?"

"Yes, since a month, since his last duel."

The unhappy woman felt a mortal shiver.

The baron continued pitilessly:

"Camille is transformed, reformed. No more balls, no more races, no more gambling, no more debts. He is growing orderly. Again I say, that disturbs me. He who all his life has not even calculated his own affairs, spending always without consideration, now has a new skin, and is so changed that one would not recognize him. For the first time, five years after reaching his majority, he calls on me for his guardianship accounts. But to lead him suddenly to become a man of order and good conduct there must be some mystery, and this mystery is very much like love."

Claire felt an immense sensation of happiness in the midst of her pain. She foresaw the possibility of escaping the man whom, since the death of her lover, she had looked upon as worse than an enemy, as the assassin of her happiness.

"Oh! I should escape," she murmured.

And feverishly drawing nearer to her father, she asked:

"Love, did you say?"

"Yes," said he, with a frown, "I have made inquiries. He is enamored of a working-girl."

"Of a working-girl?" repeated Claire, her illusions vanishing.

"Of a dressmaker," explained M. Hoffmann, "and recently, if I am not mistaken, at a masquerade supper, followed by that duel". . .

Claire starting to go away, he had to hold her back.

"Your coldness," he continued, placing himself in front of her, "your delays are the cause. Therefore this caprice must be cut short before it becomes passion. This girl, as I happen to know, is the more dangerous because she resists him. . .

through policy doubtless. You have been desirous of employing her because she was Didier's daughter. You will leave her, I hope. For a little money she will yield, and all will be settled. I know the man and his extravagance. Camille spurned would be capable of anything. He is already capable of order. His love then must be promptly opposed with marriage."

Claire turned away her head with a feeling of repulsion, saying in a low voice: " Always that frightful marriage!"

The maid just then interrupted with the announcement:

"Mademoiselle's dressmaker."

The baron had a sardonic smile.

" Your rival . . . send her away," said he to Claire.

But the latter made haste to break off the interview.

"Bid her enter," she ordered.

Marie, simply dressed as usual, entered timidly, with a pasteboard box under her arm.

"Come in, come in, Mademoiselle Marie," said Claire, looking at her and reflecting.

"She is very beautiful," she said to herself. "Can he then have fallen in love? Oh, no, it is simply another intrigue."

"What do you want?" she asked at last.

"I bring you back my work," said Marie, hesitating.

" Prompt this time," said Claire, alluding to the spoiled dress, "and pardoned."

Rosine intervened.

"Does Mademoiselle wish to try it on?"

"Later," decided the baron, in an imperious tone. " The working-girl will come again."

Marie laid down the box, but before going out she said to Claire:

" Excuse me, Mademoiselle, I know not how to tell you, to ask you . . . . but you have always been so good to me . . . you did not leave me, in spite of the accident to the dress; that encourages me to ask of you another favor now."

"What is it?" asked Claire in surprise.

"Here is my little bill," said Marie, in confusion . . . "and I beg you to make no deduction this time, and to pay me directly; for today I am in need, great need, of money."

Claire started toward the round table, where she kept her money-box.

" Ah! and why?" said she, as she was looking for the money. "You, so economical, so orderly, Marie; have you then changed your habits . . . since the ball? So much the worse."

And she added with design:

" Remember that order is your inheritance, wisdom your only dowry, and that these blessings may be more precious than wealth to a man of heart."

"I make this request of you," answered Marie, candidly, "only because I am no longer alone."

"What!" exclaimed Claire.

"No, Mademoiselle. For a month I have had a little baby in my care."

"A baby!" exclaimed the baron, in turn.

"You!" cried Claire, opening her eyes wide and not believing her ears.

"Yes, Mademoiselle," said Marie, with all the simplicity of her innocence, "a baby that I have adopted". . .

"A fine thing to do at your age," observed the baron, ironically.

"That I found," continued Marie, " a month ago, abandoned, in my room, on the night of Mardi-Gras."

Claire and the baron looked at each other, moved by the same thought, and grew suddenly pale.

"The night of Mardi-Gras?" questioned M. Hoffmann.

"Yes, Monsieur, on returning from the ball, I found in my room, in a basket, a new-born babe, which I have kept."

"Ah!" exclaimed Claire, ready to faint and staggering.

"Claire!" said the baron, sustaining her and signalling her to control herself.

"What is the matter, Mademoiselle?" asked Marie, in a tone of deep sympathy.

"Nothing," cried the baron.

Then, changing his tone and folding his arms, he continued:

"And you have kept this child?"

"To be sure, Monsieur," confessed Marie, "a poor little orphan, good people, and it costs me four dollars a month to support him."

"Beautiful, but expensive," sneered the banker.

"Yes, Monsieur," concluded Marie, "and I need money this very day to pay the nurse who brought me the baby. So I beg you, Mademoiselle, if it is not too much trouble". . .

The baron went straight up to her and said rapidly and sternly:

"A child found in your room on returning from the ball! What sort of a Carnival tale are you telling us? You abuse the interest taken in you on account of your father who died in the service of the house. The money will be withheld from you to pay for the spoiled dress. Dress, ball, duel, baby, your whole conduct is a perfect scandal, and your impudence caps the climax. Go bring up your adopted child as you can. We owe assistance to misfortune only."

Marie turned to Claire.

"Ah, Mademoiselle," she protested.

"Father!" said Claire to the baron.

And she started to pay Marie. The baron caught her hand.

"Go," said he to Marie.

Marie bowed and went away, trembling and anxious.

"Now," she said to herself, "all that remains of my poor inheritance for my child."

The baron watched her departure, and then said, addressing Claire:

"Show a little more strength; what's the matter with you?"

But the young girl could no longer repress her emotion.

"I am stifling. Give me air, air," she articulated painfully.

The banker opened the window a little, and, ever master of himself, went to his table and began to write, after saying to Claire:

"You almost betrayed yourself, and but for me ". . .

Claire walked up to him resolutely.

"You deceived me," she exclaimed. "You told me he was dead . . and he lives!"

The baron went on writing.

"Perhaps," said he. "There is more than one child born in a day."

And, talking to himself, he continued:

"Ah! the wretch! she has deceived me."

He rang.

"He lives," Claire burst out again. "I want to see him."

"How do you know?" said the baron, sealing his letter.

"A voice here tells me," answered Claire, forcibly, laying her hand on her heart. "I am going to take him back."

The baron rang again impatiently.

"Mad girl . . . what are you thinking of?" said he.

"Of helping him at least," said Claire, with a purely maternal impulse.

Laurent entered and saluted his master.

"Silence, imprudent girl," said the baron again to his daughter.

And to the servant:

"Mount a horse directly, and deliver this note to its address."

Laurent went out with alacrity.

The baron continued:

"Let us wait at least until we are sure. Perhaps there is no connection between the two affairs. When we find out, we will see. In any case there is all the more reason for hastening this marriage which saves everything. No more hesitation! Now it is more necessary than ever that you should marry Camille."

"But, my God! I hate him!" implored Claire, in despair.

"And I fear him," said the inflexible baron.

"But he is the murderer of the man I loved". . . .

"And who got himself killed for another woman," said the banker, sure of his effect.

"Ah!" cried Claire, "why did you refuse to unite us?"

"Why?" repeated the baron.

Remembering her love and excited by her hatred, Claire grew bolder.

"Yes," said she, "why? Was not the count rich and noble, worthy of us? My mother chose him on her death-bed. Why did you reject him? Speak!"

"Oh! do not ask it," said the baron, apprehensively. "Remain in ignorance forever for the sake of your peace. And confide in my tenderness and my prudence for the knowledge and fulfilment of our duties. All that you can know, poor Claire, is that fatal word 'necessity.' When I first offered you Berville and you wanted Frinlair, I should have been glad to give you the count, had I been able; but I swear to you that it was impossible."

"And I," said Claire, energetically, "cannot marry the other. That also is impossible."

"It is indispensable," insisted the anxious baron.

"Take care, Monsieur," declared Claire, coldly and firmly. "Your power has limits as well as my duty. I will resist you. Say no more about the matter."

"This marriage is necessary, and immediately."

"Never."

"Foolish girl," exclaimed the baron, in an undertone. "Fortune, honor, life depend upon it."

"How so?" Claire could not help asking.

But her doubt returned.

"No," said she, "you are deceiving me again. I believe you no longer."

The baron, who had made crime an art, now saw success for the plan which the energy of a daughter worthy of him had almost wrecked.

He went resolutely to close the window, and then said solemnly:

"Claire, my only, my beloved child, I am at your mercy. I no longer appeal to your duty, I have not the right. I put my power at your feet. Your old father, on his knees and with clasped hands, implores you in the name of a supreme interest. Do not dishonor me in your eyes. Spare me. Be merciful. . . . Be self-sacrificing. . . . Our safety depends upon you. Be resigned without inquiry as to the cause. Remember that to share confidence is sometimes to share guilt". . . .

"I am no longer to be put off with your reserve," said Claire, obstinately, . . . "and I refuse."

"But we shall have to abandon everything," insisted M. Hoffmann, panting, "everything, — the house, Paris, France, — and fly like malefactors."

"Let us start with my child," said Claire, explosively.

"Where? How?" rejoined her father, overwhelmed, "with all the ties that hold us, the cables to outstrip us, portraits to denounce us, the newspapers to discover us; with all the splendor of our life, all eyes fixed upon us through envy, hope, interest. We are placed under the watchful eye of opinion, the surest of all police. No, I cannot fly from justice; I can only dazzle it . . . . and this marriage!". . . .

Claire interrupted him.

"I do not understand you, Monsieur. I committed a sin to force your consent to an honorable marriage; I will do more to resist an odious marriage. Death rather than this marriage!"

"Well, since you insist upon it," cried the banker, beside himself, "listen then to that which no one but myself knows; which I hoped to carry to the grave; which I wanted to forget, to hide from all, from you especially, and which you force me to reveal to you. Do you not see, then, from my despair, that a mortal secret lies beneath it, and that you will never forgive me for making it known to you?"

"I tremble," she murmured, frightened by the baron's excitement.

She added in a louder voice:

"I am listening."

"Learn then, if you will," said the baron, in a hollow voice, "this terrible secret, the fatal past that engages and governs our future. A youth as reckless as Camille's formerly threw me from the heights of fortune into the depths of misery, and I fell lower yet in trying to save myself and then to lift myself."

"You make me shudder," said Claire, terrified.

The baron continued:

"I rose a guilty man, a criminal."

"Enough," cried Claire, recoiling.

"This is my punishment," said the baron, lowering his head; "I horrify you as well as myself. Now you will not dare to touch my hand. But you wanted to know all, and you shall know all. Poverty, stern teacher, had instructed me."

He stopped to breathe, and then went on:

"With gold found in blood, I gained an entrance under a false name into the house of Camille's father, who, ruined by my crime, took me first as a partner, then as a friend and relative, and finally as guardian of his son. I hoped then that the first crimes would be the last . . . . but alas! crime has its fertility. It became necessary to make my ward, the son of the man whom I had ruined, my own son-in-law in order thus to mingle our destinies and prevent any prosecution. One can stifle remorse, but not fear. To bring my ward to this end, I urged him on in dissipation; I knew from my own experience whither that leads . . . and I have succeeded. He is lost without us, as we are without him."

The baron hesitated again.

"I cannot tell you all. Have mercy! Spare me," he stammered.

And in a lower voice he faltered:

"But it was necessary; Gertrude . . . . she was an obstacle, and her sickness needed only to be aided."

Claire sank down, overwhelmed.

"No more hope!" she exclaimed.

The baron resumed:

"There remained your passion for the count and the cursed fruit of that dis-astrous love. . . . I had to overcome these last obstacles like the others, break your heart, poor Claire, sacrifice you to the same necessity . . . for it was necessary, and it is still necessary, for me to have Camille for a son-in-law."

"It is death," said Claire, crushed by this conclusion.

The baron insisted further, inflexible in his logic of evil.

"Heaven itself has condemned the other marriage. Submit, then, to this one, a marriage of salvation for all. Even though your child should be living, is he of more consequence than your father, than yourself? For you too have a secret to hide, to cover with the nuptial veil, a secret fatal like my own . . . still more so perhaps, for my victims are no more, while yours perhaps still lives, and the count, the count is dead!"

Claire straightened up again, preparatory to going out.

"Oh! unhappy woman that I am!" she said. "For you all that gold can give, the superfluous and the necessary, jewels and a dowry, millions in your hands, dia-monds on your brow, honor, homage, everything in short, except your heart! Love what you hate! Kill what you love! Shed your blood, drink your tears; smile when your heart bleeds in every fibre; make yourself a living sacrifice to so-ciety! Immolate rights and duties, conscie nce and nature, for the monster! For its sake make an infamous holocaust of your holiest passions! Happy, happy the poor girl who went away from here just now! Yes, my God, I envy her. A gar-ret, a woollen dress, a crust earned by toil, humility, and poverty, but at least the liberty of her heart. . . . My father, I resist no longer, you have killed me."

And she went out.

The baron, left alone, was seized by a sort of fit of delirium.

"What a struggle!" he exclaimed; "a woman's conscience dies hard. She re-vives my own. In spite of myself, her terrors take possession of me. I would rather kill a man. . . . And yet what work is that! It is to kill humanity! Im-placable logic of crime! My life is now but one long murder of my own and of myself, perpetuating itself like the tænia. March on, Wandering Jew of crime! Revolve in this circle of blood and tears, without other issue than Clamart. Oh, fortune, how expensive you are when you cost a man his life! When I chose mur-der in preference to suicide, I expected to live rich and happy, to repair the evil by doing good. Miserable fool! Evil breeds evil. I have not wealth, for I have killed repose. I have not happiness, for I have killed my daughter. I have not life, for I am dead, without death's peace. Oh! murder is the great suicide. In killing a man, I have killed myself. . . . Yes, the newspapers told the truth: the Duke de Crillon-Garousse is dead!"

But he heard a knock at a secret door, which he opened, after having secured the door at the back of the room.

Madame Potard entered.

"Ah! here you are, Madame," said the baron, recovering his self-possession.

"Yes, Monsieur, at your service," said the midwife.

"The sight of her restores me to myself," said the baron, aside. "Help yourself, and heaven will help you."

"You have sent for me," said Madame Potard. "Is Mademoiselle indisposed?"

"No, she has only changed her opinion. Woman varies. She would like to see the child again, if possible."

"Ah! so much the better!" exclaimed Madame Potard.

"So, then, Madame," said the baron, in a threatening voice, "you have violated all your agreements. You promised to put it out of the way."

Madame Potard stammered:

"But . . . Monsieur". . .

"To put it out of the way forever," added the baron.

"Ah! Monsieur, forgive me," begged Madame Potard, "I am wrong, I confess. I did not have the strength. . . . And then, doubtless it was not Mademoiselle's wish. I did not know what to do. But be reassured; I have lost the child as much as possible; it is with a poor girl, where it will never be found."

And sobbing, she added:

"Any more than the money that I lost at the same time."

"Capable of anything," sneered the banker; "so dishonest that she even does good when she promises to do evil."

"Ah! I am punished enough by the loss of the notes."

"Lost like the child. . . . I don't believe a word of it, and you must return them to me."

"I haven't them!" cried Mme. Potard; "I haven't them, as true as God hears me!"

"So you have lost them all?"

"Alas! yes, Monsieur, the whole ten."

"Well, I will replace them, if you like."

"What do you mean?"

"If you will do what you have not done."

"But . . . Mademoiselle . . . does she think". . . .

The baron thought the abortionist was trying to blackmail him.

"Then you have these notes still," said he; "you must return them."

"No, no, not one, I swear to you!" affirmed Mme. Potard, with a tone of sorrowful sincerity.

"Then I double them."

"Twenty thousand francs! What! you really wish". . .

"Twenty thousand francs, today, this moment."

"You insist, Monsieur, you force me to it; so be it, then; I can no longer refuse you. You will give me twenty thousand francs this very day?"

"And everything will be done this time?" questioned the baron, distrustfully.

"Yes, Monsieur."

"And you will leave Paris . . . which is not healthy . . . for returned convicts."

"What! you know?"

"Your whole record . . . sentence, breaking of the ban, and false name. You are a relative of Gripon, and free through his protection. Your name is not Potard, but Gavard. Is it not so?"

"I will leave France, if it is necessary," promised Mme. Potard, satisfied. "I carry my country in my pocket," said she, in a low voice; then aloud: "Yes, Monsieur, I will start some moonlight night and never return."

"It is well," said the baron, reflectively. "Misfortune is good for something. . . . Yes, a double stroke . . . the rival and the child."

He took his hat and cane.

"Come along," said he to the midwife, "but this time I watch."

And they went out by the secret door.

CHAPTER X.

FATHER JEAN.

Marie had hurriedly returned to the Rue Sainte-Marguerite. The idea that her adopted child might want milk for lack of money lent her wings. She forgot everything, the insult suffered and Camille, who was to come that day, — for the young man had kept his promise to himself, and had returned. The politeness of the early days had given place to tenderness, compliments to sentiments and oaths. Between the young people, at least on Camille's side, it was no longer a question of friendship and protection, but of love and passion.

Father Jean did not view these attentions favorably, but he had patience, showing himself as discreet as he was attentive and devoted to Marie.

The latter, on reaching home, began to search her drawers with a haste made all the greater by the shrill voice of the new-born infant proceeding from the sleeping-room adjoining the chamber.

"I must be quick," said she, growing excited. "My father's watch and my mother's wedding-ring, my entire inheritance, all for you, dear little ". . .

The child's voice was hushed.

"He sleeps," continued Marie, listening as she looked for her family relics. "This watch which has marked all the hours of my life; this ring with which I hoped never to part, even in death; all that is left of my own, — I must give them up at last, pawn them for the nurse's month's pay."

Just then came a knock at the door.

"Ah! it is you, Father Jean!" exclaimed Marie, opening the door for the old rag-picker, who came in, with a poster in his hand, shouting:

"Good news! I have found the owner of the notes."

"Really! So much the better!" said the young girl.

"Yes," continued Jean; "this morning I picked up a poster a month old; see!" And he read: "Lost, on the night of February 12, in going from the Faubourg Saint-Honoré to the Faubourg Saint-Antoine, ten thousand francs in bank-notes. The finder is requested to return them to the widow Potard, midwife, at No. 4, Rue Saint-Louis, where he will be suitably rewarded."

"At last, then, I can restore them," he said, as he finished reading.

"Good riddance!" approved Marie,

"You are right," said Jean, folding up the poster and putting it in his pocket.

"Madame Potard, you say?" said Marie, suddenly; "why, she is one of my customers. . . . I am very glad for her."

And still hunting, she added:

"Where did I put that watch?"

"Now, to be entirely contented, I should like also to find the owner of the child," ventured Father Jean, who had immediately dismissed his first thought of suspicioh.

"Ah! Father Jean, that's a different matter."

Jean was not disconcerted.

"Now that I think of it," said he, " perhaps this midwife can tell us something. Who knows? It is such a great chance, and among her acquaintances. . . I will speak to her about it. Yes, I am as anxious to see you rid of the child as myself rid of the money."

"Poor little fellow! in fact, perhaps it would be better for him. . . . But no, Father Jean, he was not lost by chance; and those who abandoned him did so because they could not keep him. He is far better off with me than with those who left him here."

Jean shook his head.

"That's all very fine; but no doubt you have spent another night in working for him; it will kill you."

"On the contrary, Father Jean, it keeps me alive; but for him I should be dead, as you well know."

Jean made a movement of affectionate *brusquerie*.

"Oh, yes, I know; it is he who obliges you; it is he who is ruining himself for you. There is no sense in it. He is costing you the eyes in your head. Where is your new shawl? All your poor effects will go the same way. Again you have stripped yourself for him, I am sure. Be seated while I talk to you a little. I have not finished."

Marie, having found the watch, yielded to his desire.

"Ah! here it is! . . . . Well, Father Jean, be quick; what more have you to say?"

Jean sat down beside Marie, and went on with embarrassment.

"Simply that you are too good; you are wrong, Mam'zelle. You know the proverb: 'the wolves devour those who are too good.' Well, you listen only to your heart. You have a passion for doing good to others; you do it secretly, like the good girl that you are; and then, when it is discovered, it turns against you ". . .

Then, with an effort, he added:

"Yes, Mam'zelle, I must tell you at last; they gossip about this child."

"Well, let them talk, Father Jean, cost what it may. It is better to be honest than to pretend to be."

"That is not all, Mam'zelle. I do not know whether I ought to finish. Perhaps it is not my right. . . . Surely it does not concern me ". . . .

Marie gave a start of surprise and annoyance.

"Ah! don't be angry!" said Jean, with growing embarrassment. "It is purely in your interest. And then for some time you have been very dreamy, and a young man comes to see you . . . . a handsome young man . . . . doubtless very honest and very reserved with you, but also too rich for you, Mam'zelle. . . In short, the child on one side, the young man on the other . . . one cannot keep evil tongues from wagging, and I should like to see the young man and the child in their proper places as well as the notes."

"Father Jean, I have nothing to fear," answered Marie, "nothing with which to reproach myself. I did not think it wrong to receive the excuses of this young man after the accident to the dress. If I have done wrong, I will see him no more . . . but as for the child, Father Jean, that is different, I insist. Oh! you do not mean what you say."

"Yes, begging your pardon, Mam'zelle," insisted Jean, "a child of misfortune, superfluous like myself, like all beggars. . . . Beggars! there is no need of being careful of the seed. They will always grow fast enough. So think more of yourself and less of others. Each one for himself!"

"Ah! Father Jean," exclaimed Marie, "how can you talk so? Then you have never loved any one? Did you never have parents? Oh! Father Jean, when one has loved an old mother, one loves little children. If you only knew how good it is to love some one! But say, why then are you interested in me?"

"Why? why?" repeated Jean, disconcerted.

And Marie, affectionately insisting, said:

"Yes, why?"

"Why? Well, I will tell you," said Jean, frankly.

"Ah! that's it; tell me that."

Jean, after a thoughtful pause, began:

"A child of Paris, I was born I know not where, I know not when, I know not of whom, abandoned like the orphan that you have found. My mother, the unknown, cast me, like him, into the arms of misfortune or of crime . . . . into the arms of chance, to grow up as I might. I am of that race of starvelings who, having so hard a life, live nevertheless, willy-nilly. . . . How? Why? No matter! a mushroom from the muck-heap of Paris, a stump from the streets of the capital, one of the offscourings of the old city which time, that master rag-picker, gathers into his huge basket when he sees them. For sixty years, hook in hand, I have thus been dragging about the streets of Paris, which I have never left, where I have always lived, or rather where I have not died, — for really one cannot call it living. Would you believe, Mam'zelle Marie, that I have never seen the fields, the grass, except in the market-squares. . . I don't know why I think of all this just now. . . . Oh, yes, it is to show you that I have never known anything but the pavements and the passers-by."

"Poor Father Jean," said Marie, moved. "How have you managed to live in this way?"

"It is as I tell you, Mam'zelle; as a child, I had neither father nor mother; as a man, I have had neither wife nor child. Nobody has ever loved me; I have never loved anybody. I haven't had the means. It isn't every one that can afford to have a family. It's expensive, you see. I was too poor to have one, and I've gone without. Ah! when I came home all alone to my den, the four walls were very large, and yet my heart felt cramped within them. It was very empty, and I stifled. I turned about like the bear Martin in his cage, and sometimes growled, as he does. I was cruelly tormented. I remember that one day I wished myself in prison that I might not be alone. That day I was thirty years old . . . up to that time I had been called Jean for short . . . . it was quite enough for a single man . . . but after that I was known as Father Jean. This name father put me beside myself. At that time I believe I should have stolen a child but for the necessity of feeding it. . . . Ah! you are better than we! But I could no longer live so; you are right. Then I took to the weed, — pardon me, Mam'zelle, — to tobacco and brandy. Those are friends, those are relatives! They are known as consolation . . . brandy especially. When one is alone, one gets drunk. That makes people; one sees double. Yes, I saw at the bottom of my glass all my imaginations, a household, children around me, and a wife making soup and setting the table for us all. I lived like that, or rather I was killing myself, I was killing myself body and soul, Mam'zelle. Each of us has his suicide. You have charcoal and we three-six. I was always drunk, — yes, that's the word, dead-drunk. But one night a great misfortune, the death of a man . . . of which my wine was to a certain extent the cause . . . one can never foresee the consequences of wine . . . the death of a poor father of a family, Mam'zelle, which I could not prevent, because I was drunk, made me swear to drink no more, to take his place, to look out for his child."

Looking at her with tenderness, he asked:

"Have you ever seen me drunk a single time since I came to live near you? Formerly I could not stand it to go without drinking for a day . . . and now, now I could not stand it to go a day without seeing you. Devil take me, I think now only of you, Mam'zelle Marie; you have broken all the glasses, and I feel something sweet and new which I cannot explain, but which is better than drinking, be sure!"

"Is it not, Father Jean?" said Marie, with feeling.

"Yes," continued Jean, "when I saw you so good, sewing as many hours as there are figures on your watch, caring for your poor mother, bringing up this child, I said to myself what you said just now, that it is good to love some one, and I began by loving you. . . . Indeed I don't know how I love you, whether it is as a daughter or as a sister or otherwise . . . I cannot tell you. I don't know myself in this matter, having never loved or hated anybody. All that I know is that my age is about the same as would have been your father's. Yes, that's it, I love you as my daughter. And when you call me Father Jean, it reconciles me to the name. I take you at your word; my poor heart leaps in my breast. I would give a pint of my blood to save you a tear, and I would weep night and day like the fountains in the public squares to cause you to smile but for a moment."

"A tear! a tear!" said Marie, with emotion.

Jean, laughing and crying at the same time, confessed his weakness.

"Yes, dear child, a tear, a tear of joy, that's what it is! Let it flow; indulge this poor old heart, which has never been able to make up for lost time in all its life with you. It is all pleasure and never enough. When you look at me with your beautiful clear eyes, your pink cheeks, your blooming mouth, and your perfect bouquet of a face, it always seems to me like a celebration of my birthday! And when I can come here like this, sit by your side, talk with you, take your little white hands, and press them gently between my own, yes, I am happy, it intoxicates me. It seems to me that I too have a family, a child, my right, my share, the share of joy, in short, due to every man who has a heart. . . That, Mam'zelle, is why I am interested in you."

Marie leaped upon his neck, and, embracing him with all her grateful heart, cried:

"My good Father Jean!"

"Ah!" said Jean, clasping her joyfully in his arms.

"Well," said Marie abruptly, returning to the subject of her baby, "I love the little one just as you love me, and I am going to try to get the money for his nurse."

She brought in the child.

"See, he has waked; isn't he pretty?" said she to Father Jean, who was conquered.

"I say nothing ill of him," said the latter; "nevertheless I shall speak to Mme. Potard all the same."

"Still!" exclaimed Marie. "Ah! Father Jean, that you may learn, you shall take care of him a little while for me."

Handing him the child, she added:

"Watch him carefully until I return. . . . I shall not be long."

She looked at him pleasantly.

"Now, Father . . . Grandfather Jean, those who have lost him have not wept with joy as we have today," she concluded.

And the charming girl went out, leaving her child with the rag-picker.

He watched her departure with a comical embarrassment.

"Well, well, Mam'zelle," said he. "She does with me as she likes."

Accepting the inevitable, he went on:

"I suppose I must lull the little beggar. Hasn't he a sharp eye?"

He walked up and down the room, cra dling the child in his arms.

"Suppose he should cry? I cannot gi ve him suck. Suppose I try to sing him to sleep! Ah! yes, but my voice is a little rusty."

And he began to sing:

"'Forever wine! forev'. . . . Ah! not that. He will learn that only too soon. 'Rock a-bye, baby, upon the tree-top. ' This is something like work. . . . Father in earnest! or rather grandfather, Gran dfather Jean, as my daughter said. . . Ah! ah! my young rascal, taking a nap at last! I will lay him gently on mamma's bed. . . . It is settled, then. Since she wants him, she shall keep him, watch him, bring him up; she shall pay for his nursing, schooling, and apprenticeship; he is well off, better off than I am; she shall take the bread out of her mouth and her clothes off her back for Monsieur, pro vided he turns out well."

He carried the child into the small room and came back.

"Now," said he, "I will go up and smoke a pipe before she returns."

He went behind his stairs to get some fresh flowers, which he put in the place of the old ones on Marie's bureau, and t hen said, as he left the room:

"I will leave the door ajar, so that I may hear the baby better if he should cry."

And he went up to his lodgings radiant with happiness.

CHAPTER XI.

THE BARON'S DOUBLE STROKE.

Father Jean had scarcely turned his heels when a woman hidden under a black veil emerged from the shadow of the stairs and entered Marie's room.

"She has gone out; I must be quick!" she exclaimed, in a hissing voice.

She crossed the working-girl's room, entered the smaller one, came back with the child concealed under her veil, and disappeared, carrying him away hastily.

In her flight she made the stairs creak, and the noise attracted the attention of the rag-picker, who, coming out of his den, pushed into the room in his turn, listening and saying:

"It seems to me that I hear somebody coming up. It is Mam'zelle Marie, no doubt. I will stay here. If she does not find me at my post, she will scold me. No, nobody, I must have been mistaken."

And he continued to smoke for a few moments.

Then suddenly realizing this impropriety, he quickly put his pipe back in his pocket.

"The devil!" he exclaimed; "one should not smoke here."

He went to look down the stairway.

"Ah! this time there is somebody," said he. "It is she. . . . No, it is the modern."

Camille stood before him.

"Mademoiselle Marie is not at home?" asked the young man, a little embarrassed.

"No, Monsieur, she has just gone out," answered Jean, testily.

"To remain long?"

"I think not."

The rag-picker, after twisting his beard discontentedly, grumbled to himself:

"Come, things cannot go on in this way. I must speak to him."

And aloud:

"If you wish to wait for her, be seated; if not, I will transact your business for you."

"Thank you," Camille hastened to say, "I will wait. It is so comfortable in this little room. It is to me a sort of Jouvence bath. Here I breathe I know not what perfume of virtue that calms the senses and invigorates the heart. I am born again. What a contrast with our world! There proprieties and rights, here nature and duties. Ah! here is real life, that which gives a good conscience . . . here only would I begin mine over again if I had the courage . . . I would find at last what I seek, rest in order, esteem in love, and security in happiness. But am I still worthy of these? . . . And can I be happy? Everything speaks to me of her, — her voice, her gesture, her virgin grace, an omnipotent magic that renews my strength. This pure life, so simple and so full, so useful to others and to self, this vestal lamp, this work-table, this shining thimble, this little needle as smooth as her fairy hand . . . everything enchants me and draws me with a magnet's force."

He took the needle out of the cushion.

"Poor little sword that serves her to conquer her two great enemies, — poverty and temptation. What valor! The moral sense, like the others, grows by exercise. If I may trust appearances, this is the entire support of her chaste and sober life. These are the tools of her toil, the weapons of her struggle, the pledges of her victory, the witnesses of her honor!"

"Oh! yes, indeed, I guarantee you that," said Jean. "It goes from morning till evening and from evening till morning . . . and fast enough to wear the flesh off her bones."

"So much the better!" exclaimed Camille, joyfully.

"You laugh?" asked the rag-picker.

Camille explained himself.

"I laugh and weep at the same time, you give me so much joy and pain at once. Labor is the guardian-angel of her age, Father Jean. It is necessary . . . but. . . not too much! And has she always lived thus by her toil?"

"And on what else, then, if you please? No other bread is eaten here. I tell you so myself."

"Undoubtedly. But though she works always from morning till evening, as you say, she does not always work from evening till morning, as the night of the ball is sufficient to show."

"Ah! yes, once, I know, and only once. The lesson was heeded. That's all I can say."

"Indeed! this girl is an exception, a treasure in a garret."

"Why not? I have found one in my basket. . . Look you, Monsieur, there is good and evil everywhere, in the garret as well as on the first floor."

"Yes, all is not gold that glitters," said Camille.

"And all gold does not glitter," said Father Jean. "There are none better than she anywhere. Good and beautiful without vanity, doing good naturally, as her rose-tree bears its roses. Ah! her husband will not be unhappy."

"Father Jean, you are talking up your goods," observed Camille, smiling.

Jean stopped for a second, and then continued:

"There is no need to sweeten sugar. And if I were young, handsome, and rich . . . But to the point. Monsieur Henri Berville, this very morning I was talking of you with Mlle. Marie."

"And Marie has often spoken to me of you, Father Jean," answered Camille.

"Ah! She has spoken to you of me, dear child," repeated the rag-picker, dis-armed.

"Yes, and as of her second father."

"She did not lie, Monsieur, I answer for it . . . and, you see, that is why I take the liberty . . . the . . . since we are alone . . . to ask you just what you want with her."

Camille looked at him with his clear, straightforward eyes, and frankly answered:

"And because of that respected title which I acknowledge as yours, Father Jean, I shall answer you frankly. . . I saw Mlle. Marie at the ball, I loved her, it is very simple; I have risked death for her sake; I can no longer live without her, and I am going to break off my marriage". . .

"To marry her?" asked Jean, quickly.

"Oh, no, I love her," cried Camille.

"Ah! ah! And you would marry her, if you did not love her?"

"Perhaps, Father Jean; marriage, they say, is the grave of love, and I do not wish to bury mine."

"There you are! the world reversed," laughed the rag-picker; "what is good with us is bad with you."

"As you say. . . I am ready, moreover, to make any sacrifice for her. I am a man of honor. . . . Understand me well. I will make hers an honorable lot, free and happy for the rest of her days."

"That's clear," rejoined Jean. "*It is your will.* The king says: *It is our will.* Now it remains to find out Mlle. Marie's will."

"Undoubtedly," said Camille, "and that is exactly what I have come today to ask her in order to arrive at a conclusion. What I know so far is that she has re-fused all my offers, and that, though I have been her suitor for a month, I am no farther advanced than on the first day. Visits, promises, presents, speeches, and letters,—I have used everything and for nought."

"That astonishes you?" asked Father Jean. "In this I recognize her perfectly."

"Here then at last is one who does not wish to sell herself," murmured Camille, "unless she values herself at a higher figure than has been offered. There have been such cases, hey, old sage?"

"Ah! what's that you say?" muttered the rag-picker. "Pardon me, Monsieur, you mistake white for black. . . And look out that you don't do worse. Without throwing her at your head, she is as good as you are . . . and in your place". . .

He paused, and then resumed with growing force and indignation:

"But you have admitted that you do not want her for a wife. You, in your world, do not marry when you love; you want her, then, simply for pastime, to make her a ruined girl like the others. It would be a pity to make an exception. You call that an honorable lot. Indeed! It is not a virtuous one. Frankly, now, would you make such an offer to a girl of your own station? . . . Good for a working-girl! She cannot rise to you; you descend to her. You do her the honor to dishonor her. Much obliged! Since we have one that is good, let us leave her as she is, if you please. You will not die in consequence. Come, young man, be a little upright! You have carriages, and we have no shoes; you have fine horses, and we have no beds; you have dogs fed on meat, and we have no bread. . . In short, you have everything and we nothing. . . And you want also this nothing that is left to us, our sole and only possession, honor. Do not be so greedy! That will not pass from us, I assure you; it is my right and my duty to keep it, you see. I was unable to save the father, but I swore to guard the daughter, the child of a poor man who died in your service."

Camille started with surprise, while Jean continued:

"Did you ever think of aiding her before you saw her? No. Well, then, do not think of it now in order to ruin her. Far from the eyes, far from the heart. See her no more. There are plenty of others, unfortunately, who ask nothing better than to be yours. I know very well of course that it is what you cannot have that you want. You are all like that. You want her, poverty aiding, for a day, a month, a year. You pay by the hour . . . when you pay at all. And then become what she may! Abandoned, with accounts square . . . with shame . . . and crime to hide it. At that price you are to be guarded. Jean's word for it, the child of your man of toil will not be your 'daughter of joy.' No, Marie Didier cannot be your wife; she shall not be your mistress. I tell you that I will not have it so; that she will not have it so; that neither father nor mother, nor God nor Devil, nor Jean, will have it so. As long as there is any breath left in my body, that shall not be."

"Father Jean, you speak somewhat bitterly," said Camille, not knowing what to answer, and seriously shaken by this revelation of popular honesty.

"Well, what do you expect?" concluded Jean, "I am not all sugar as she is, but ill-tempered enough to defend her. Believe me, Monsieur Camille, change your intentions, or leave her as she is . . . and let us be good friends."

He interrupted himself. Marie had just entered suddenly, without noticing the young man's presence.

"Father Jean! I have the money!" she exclaimed, joyfully. "But I had to pawn everything, — watch and ring."

Then, noticing Camille, she said: "Ah! Monsieur Berville!" and maintained a confused silence.

"Now I am in the way," said Jean, aside. "I must go out, but not relax my watch. They will come to an understanding better alone . . . and I will listen to everything as I smoke my pipe. . . What is said is said," said he to Camille.

He left the room, and remained listening on the landing.

The conversation was taken up again by the young people.

"I was waiting for you, Mademoiselle," said Camille, "for I must speak to you definitively today, and you must give me a final answer. Time presses."

Taking her by the hand and leading her before her mirror, he continued :

"Tell me if this beauty, once seen by a man's eye, can ever be effaced from his heart."

Marie, confused, went away from the mirror.

"Yes, Monsieur, as from this glass," she answered.

"This glass has no heart, and you have given me one which will always retain your image, whatever happens," declared Camille, with fire. "I love you, Marie, as I have often told you already, as I have never loved and shall never love any one else . . . . with a love which one feels but once in his life and which fixes it. To love you as you deserve, Marie, I have sacrificed my tastes, my pleasures; you know it . . . and I want to sacrifice even my marriage in order to be loved."

. "Oh! Monsieur, stop," said Marie, with embarrassment.

"I am frank with you," said the young man, becoming more and more urgent. "Be so with me. I may say that you have restored me my life. I owe it to you, I give it to you. I want to live for you and with you . . . . could I live without you? We are no longer children; we are no longer at the age of twenty, or at least I am not. On your reply depends our whole future. Yes, I will break every tie for you alone, Marie; and though I love you too well to marry you, to be your legal master, at least I swear that I will never marry another. Those are my intentions. What are yours? Answer."

"I shall never be yours," said the young girl, simply and resolutely.

"Never! . . . And why? . . . . Do I, then, inspire you with aversion?" cried Camille.

"You do not think so," said Marie, gently.

"Do you love another more fortunate than I?"

"Oh! you could not believe it."

"Why, then? Tell me," insisted Camille, sorrowfully.

"I will be as frank as you, Monsieur Camille," said Marie; "let us drop the matter forever. You are too far above me . . . and I cannot". . .

Jean upon the landing made a gesture of approval, as he heard this declaration.

"Do not finish. . . I understand," said Camille with a bitterness that was full of scepticism.

And to himself he added:

"Indeed! She would like even more than this old man. . . . Yes, I am mistaken in her when I speak to her only of love and happiness. It is not enough to sacrifice present and future to her, to devote to her my entire life, to renounce every other passion, everything else that I possess, for her. She aspires to something higher. I understand, I understand at last. All this resistance is made from interest and calculation". . .

And carried away by this thought, the product of his *blasé* mind rather than his heart, he concluded:

"You refuse because you wish to be my wife."

"Your wife! I!" cried Marie, trembling.

"Yes, the heart is of little consequence to you," went on Camille, "provided you have the rank. Ah! Marie, my foolish darling, the satisfaction of that ambition will bring you neither esteem nor love."

"Ah! Monsieur Camille, do you believe what you say?" asked Marie.

"I believe it."

"You believe it?"

"Yes, yes," said Camille, becoming excited by his suspicion.

"You believe it! Well, I am yours, Camille! And let your conscience judge me as my own! Neither your name, nor your rank, nor your possessions, Camille, nothing of you but yourself."

Jean made a gesture of despair on his landing, and smashed his pipe against the wall, still listening in alarm and indignation.

"What do you say, Marie?" asked Camille, astounded.

"I say that I love you," answered Marie, passionately, "that I love you for yourself, for yourself alone. . . Forgive me, Monsieur, for preferring your love to my honor!"

She fell upon her knees, her face covered with her hands.

Camille, raising her enthusiastically, gave utterance to his heart in his intoxication:

"Ah! that is your thought, noble girl! Well, no, Marie, it shall not be so. . . . you shall be my wife, my legitimate wife, do you hear? In giving me all rights, you impose upon me all duties. You elevate my heart to the level of your own; you make me worthy of you. I loved you for your beauty, I honor you for your integrity. I unite myself to you, adorably unselfish girl; I restore you the honor which you sacrifice for me. . . . I too am yours now. My father's wealth, and more, my mother's name, are all for you, my betrothed."

Taking her hand, he continued:

"Your hand; no one but you shall have this ring, pledge of my love and of my oath. For you, then, the wedding robes that were being made for the other. Yes, for you, Madame, for henceforth, I swear, Marie Didier shall be Madame Berville."

Jean entered in the meantime, and saw them entwined in each other's arms.

"All right!" he cried. "That's the way to talk. With that understanding I agree; I make no further opposition. Father Jean gives his consent, Monsieur

Camille. Go get that of your relatives. . . You have behaved handsomely. Your intentions are honorable, and happiness will result. Three happy . . . at least I hope so. Ah ! honesty will always be the best policy. For life or death, Monsieur Camille."

Camille gave his hand to Jean, kissed Marie's hands, and went out, escorted by her to the door.

Marie returned to Jean.

" Oh ! how happy I am !" said she. " He makes me believe all that he says and wish all that he wishes. My God ! he makes me mad with joy. I thank you. Father Jean, let me embrace you !"

She embraced Jean, and then turned toward the adjoining room.

" Ah ! poor child, love has caused him to be forgotten. He is only my second thought now. I must return him to the nurse with the money."

She went into the room and returned in bewilderment.

" Ah ! my child ! my child ! where is my child ? Jean, my child ?"

" What ? " exclaimed Jean, in astonishment.

He, in turn, entered the room.

" Nothing ! Stolen ! No, taken back !" he exclaimed.

A loud noise of footsteps was heard on the stairs, approaching Marie's rooms, and soon the door was thrown open violently, revealing officers in citizens' dress and in uniform, preceded by a commissary of police. Camille reappeared behind them in a state of anxiety.

" Marie Didier," said the commissary, extending his arm toward her, " you are accused of infanticide."

Jean too reappeared, entirely upset.

" I !" cried Marie, thunderstruck.

The commissary took her by the arm and pushed her toward his pack of police-men, saying :

" Your child has been found dead in a neighboring well. . . I arrest you."

" Oh !" exclaimed Marie, with a cry of horror and falling backwards.

" Marie !" cried Camille, petrified.

Jean got quickly down beside the fainting young girl and raised her head upon his knees in mortal anguish.

" My daughter," he called.

The commissary made a sign to his subordinates to carry Marie away, which was done in spite of Camille's opposition and Jean's resistance.

CHAPTER XII.

. **THE CROWD.**

When Camille and Jean had been released by the officers who had held them in restraint during the removal of Marie, they in turn rushed out into the neighborhood, which was already in a state of agitation over the arrest.

The commissary of judicial delegations, M. Dubreuil, had taken the arrest upon himself to handsel his recent promotion, for which he was indebted to the government of the Republic.

The news of the infanticide had spread in all directions with the rapidity of a flash of powder. All the neighbors were at their windows or doors. Groups formed, loudly discussing; the women, enraged at the crime and at Marie's beauty, shouting for death, wanting the guilty one straightway cut to pieces; the men, calmer and under the influence of her charm, saying: "Bah! it's not our affair," or else: "Can one ever tell? We shall see later. Justice will inquire into the matter."

Marie, in a semi-swoon, had crossed the Rue Sainte-Marguerite and was going down the Faubourg Saint-Antoine, hurried along at full speed by the officers, who had to defend their prey against the insults and threats of mothers who showed beak and claws, at once taking the accusation for the fact and governed by passion instead of reason.

"She has killed her child!" This phrase flew around her, repeated from mouth to mouth, preceding her, following her, escorting her, causing all heads to turn and all eyes to glare upon her.

"Oh! the coward!" cried a woman; "I have brought up seven, and not my own either."

"I have had five, wretch," shouted another, "all killed by war or hunger, but not one by me!"

Poor Marie! She bent her head under this undeserved cursing, calling death to her aid and not believing it possible to survive this atrocious denunciation by a blinded and pitiless mob.

Lost in the flood of the curious, hidden in the rear of the throng, but raising themselves up now and then in order to lose nothing of the spectacle, a man masked with a comforter and a woman entirely covered with a thick black veil, gliding like shadows by the side of the houses, had witnessed all the circumstances of the arrest, watching police, capture, and people.

Finally they stopped as if by agreement at the corner of a small street.

"Well, are you satisfied now?" said the woman, loftily.

For sole reply the man slipped a small package of bluish papers into her hand and made her a sign to leave him.

"Ah! thank you," said she, with her false smile. "This is the right amount, isn't it? Twenty thousand? Not that I doubt; only an error is easily made with these bits of paper."

Then, after a pause, she continued in a very low voice:

"Saving errors. I am sure that Monsieur the baron would rectify the mistake, if one little blue paper should be lacking. He would not want to ruin a poor woman like myself. . . . Especially as ". . .

She finished her phrase mentally thus:

"I now have the means of defence."

She was about to resume her insinuating remarks.

"Enough," said the man, in a tone of decision. "Verify the amount, pocket it, and be off."

She took the amount for granted, slipped the package into her pocket, and said, to lay stress upon this delicate proceeding:

"One must have confidence in this world. My God! what should we do without it?"

And, bowing very humbly, she disappeared, and the man did the same.

Meanwhile Jean and Camille, who had started at full speed, were drawing near Marie. They caught up with her on the run, as the officers stopped before a blockade of carriages and spectators. The crowd had grown like a rolling snowball as it moved along, turning into an avalanche and raising the old and ever new cry:

"Away with her!"

An empty cab stood a few steps away. The commissary of police, who was walking in advance, summoned it and succeeded with great difficulty in getting in. The crowd closed up behind him, barring the way against Marie and the disbanded officers.

At first the presence of the magistrate had held this furious mob in check, even the women, which is not easy when the maternal instinct is aroused; but now the officers, deprived of their chief, were obliged to release Marie in the middle of a pitiless circle pressing in to stifle her.

Camille, not as strong as Father Jean, but quicker, was the first to penetrate the crowd and shield the young girl.

"Ah! her lover," squeaked a woman's voice. "Mossieu came to see her every day."

This denunciation aggravated the anger of the assailants, and, there being "a Mossieu" in the case, the men too joined in. Insults rained, and even fists were shaken; the officers were submerged in the ever-rising flood.

Already a hand was raised against the victim.

"Touch her not, or I will kill you," suddenly roared a voice of thunder.

And Jean brushed aside, hustled, and upset the men and women in his path, throwing down or trampling upon those who resisted.

"It is her father," said a man. "This is his affair. Leave it to him."

This word *father*, pronounced by the man, neutralized the effect produced by the word *lover* uttered by the woman. Crowds are subject to these abrupt changes of the moral sense.

"Yes, she is my daughter; innocent, and so is he," cried Father Jean.

And after a last push, he seized Marie, carrying her away like a feather in his vigorous arms, and deposited her safely in the carriage, whose doors closed upon her.

"Palace of Justice; Delegations!" cried the commissary, putting his head out of the window and then quickly lifting the glass again.

The carriage started, and was soon moving rapidly.

"Let us follow them," cried Camille, liberated by Father Jean's saving word.

And leaping with him into a cab, he shouted to the driver:

"Follow! You shall have a generous fee."

CHAPTER XIII.

AT THE DELEGATIONS.

The commissary of police, having recovered from the shock of this exciting arrest, reentered his office and began to draw up his official report with the tranquil indifference usual to his function.

Marie was brought in between two officers, while Camille and Jean, at a sign from the magistrate, sat down at the other end of the room as witnesses.

" Well, do you confess?" he first asked the accused.

The young girl made a gesture of horror.

" Indeed, you deny. Of course."

Camille intervened.

" Mademoiselle is not guilty," said he, emphatically.

" Never!" added Jean, in confirmation.

The commissary imposed silence upon them, saying:

" Very well. We will talk together directly. . . . Marie Didier, you have had this child about a month, haven't you ?"

" Yes, Monsieur, at my rooms."

" And he is not yours ?"

" No, Monsieur."

" You deny again; very well; we will pass on."

The commissary consulted his notes.

" You have sent the little one to a nurse. Then, there being no money, he has been returned to you, and you have "". . . .

" Oh! Monsieur "". . . .

Jean and Camille could hardly contain themselves. Nevertheless, confiding in Marie's innocence and the hope of her justification, they mastered their indignation.

The French Themis employs theatrical effects and torture; the magistrate is a combination of actor and inquisitor.

The commissary suddenly straightened up before Marie, and, in the bullying style of a policeman, said to her rudely:

" You lie. The story of the found child is a gross fabrication. You had relations with a young man. This child was born of your misconduct; you placed it with a nurse. Then, finding it a burden, you ceased to pay for the nursing. It .

was returned to you, and you threw it into the well to be rid of it. Your lover, if not your accomplice, is present here. And there lies your victim to accuse you. Stay, look!"

And the magistrate, eyeing her steadily, lifted a napkin which hid the body of a drowned child, with features swollen and blue.

There it lay,—the fresh, pink-cheeked, bright-eyed child which she had adopted as her own.

She could not endure this frightful spectacle.

"Oh! I shall go mad," she cried, covering her eyes with her hands.

"A thousand thunders!" shouted Jean; "and this is justice!"

"Monsieur!" exclaimed Camille, in an almost threatening tone.

"Your terror confesses at last," said the magistrate, pitilessly pursuing his confrontation and mistaking grief for remorse.

"No, no," said Marie, in despair, "I did not do it."

"Still denying! Take her away," ordered the commissary.

The officers obeyed this peremptory order of their chief, who, detaining Jean and Camille, said to them:

"Now we will talk."

And he noted in detail their names, ages, and occupations,—their complete civil status,—and then, in conclusion, asked Jean:

"You are, what shall I call you? . . . the protector of the accused?"

Father Jean, wounded by this equivocal phrase, protested and tried to reply, but the commissary interrupted him in order to question Camille.

"And you are not Marie Didier's lover or the father of this child?" said he, with cold irony.

"Monsieur," cried Camille, "you are wrong, utterly wrong, in this unfortunate affair. I swear to you that Mlle. Didier is innocent, and that I am not her lover."

"Well, here's another," said the commissary, tranquilly. "That will do; you will be summoned if there is occasion and when there is occasion. Good day, gentlemen."

"Here's another!" This last phrase struck Camille to the heart, and a fit of terrible anger lifted him from his bench in rebellion, crying:

"Monsieur! Monsieur! You insult her, you". . .

And he went out, lest he might return the magistrate's words:

"You lie!"

But Father Jean, remaining seated, did not stir, suddenly insensible to what was being done and said around him.

He muttered confused words between his teeth.

"Of what are you thinking?" asked M. Dubreuil. "Go out."

"Eh?" exclaimed the rag-picker, raising his head. "Oh, to be sure! I must go out. Good afternoon, Monsieur."

On the threshold he turned back to say:

"You hold the most honest girl in the world as guilty. But it is only for a short time. You will hear from me soon."

Then he added with emotion:

"Could not her old Father Jean embrace her?"

"No! . . . she will be kept in secret confinement," answered the magistrate.

Jean went out with an air of resignation, and found Camille pacing up and down the street.

"They keep her," said Jean.

"Well," exclaimed he, beside himself, "let us free her by force."

"No, no madness. Leave it to me," answered Jean. "She shall not stay there long, believe me. . . . Come! I have an idea of my own."

CHAPTER XIV.

FATHER JEAN'S IDEA.

In the Quartier du Marais, as it is appropriately named, Mme. Potard, *alias* Gavard, her ban broken but not her patronage, had reestablished her doubtful business as a midwife, committing abortion and presiding at births according to circumstances, with as little conscience as before, but with more science, prudence, and cunning, saying to herself: "One must live," and finding her life in the death of babies, as Jean found his in rags; persuaded that this was really natural, but passing on to each new misdeed between the articles of the Code, with art and without suffering, a first lesson, it is said, being sufficient for the sage . . . . and for the midwife (*sage-femme*). She had gained with age.

Her retirement had borne its fruits. Mme. Gavard, first-class midwife, had become Mme. Potard, "the best of midwives," the height of the art, a difficult art in Paris, where there are as many nurses as mothers, perhaps more; one must live, nevertheless.

Mme. Potard had had a somewhat easier day than usual. She strutted about in her reception-room, furnished with tables, chairs covered with haircloth as hard as herself, a book-case, and a secretary, all looking dismal and doubtful, and completed by a poorly-equipped pharmacy secured with a double lock, a veritable interior of a "maker of angels."

"What a profession is ours!" she murmured, stretching out before her fire with an air of relaxation; "a dog's life, without rest or thanks. One rises, ding! a delivery; one wishes to eat breakfast or dinner, ding! ding! another affair, a virtue to be restored; but one never knows with whom she is dealing, whether the police or a patron. That is the question. And there is no time to reflect; ding! ding! ever the bell is ringing; one hopes to eat supper, not having dined, but never in life; Madame So-and-So believes that she is about to be delivered: Madame Somebody-else that her milk is going to fail; this one says that her baby is getting as red as a lobster; that one that hers is turning as pale as a whiting. A continual nuisance. At last one goes to bed, ding! ding! ding! a miscarriage!"

And poor Mme. Potard, having thus railed against fate, settled down to a rest so well deserved.

Suddenly she drew from her pocket a package of bank-notes and began to count them.

"Twenty . . . that's right. I dreamed of a spider last night. Ah! if I could find the other ten now, that would make thirty . . . a nice competence. . . . I could retire from business straightway."

She rose.

"I must not lose these at any rate," she continued. "These cost me more."

Then, looking at the money, she continued :

"To think that one does everything for this, no matter what his station; that everybody, from the top of the stairs to the bottom, rises for this, struggles, cheats, steals, and kills for this; that all without exception, rich and poor, young and old, men and women, love, serve, and pray to this. Ah! it is the God of us all."

She placed her notes in her secretary, saluting them with pious reverence, and under the impulse of her native devotion she recited her prayer with a fervor worthy of that Paradise of which she was the purveyor.

"Our Father who art in the Bank! certified be thy name; thy profits come; thy notes be legal tender on the Stock Exchange as well as at the Bank! Give us this day our daily interest! Send us our receipts as we send receipts to those who have paid us! Lead us not into prison, and deliver us from the baron! Amen!"

She closed her secretary and rose again precipitately.

Her servant entered.

"Madame," said the latter, "some one wishes to see you on business."

Mme. Potard took the key from her secretary, and said in a loud voice:

"Show him in."

Then aside:

"Business is what one makes it. It is small only with those who have weak heads."

The servant introduced a man of about sixty years, with a gray beard, dressed in his Sunday clothes, and rather shabby at that.

It was Father Jean.

He bowed to the midwife, and inquired :

"Madame Potard, if you please?"

"That is my name, Monsieur," she answered, somewhat disdainfully, in spite of the principle which she had just enunciated.

Jean looked at the servant.

"Madame Potard," he said, "I should like to talk with you privately."

The servant went out.

"Ah! we are alone now," said Mme. Potard. "What service can I do you?"

"I do not come to ask a service of you," said Jean, slowly, weighing each of his words. "On the contrary, I come to render you one."

"Me?" exclaimed Mme. Potard, distrustfully.

"You," affirmed Jean.

The midwife began to reflect, and felt a joy which she suppressed as the thought struck her:

"Ah! the lost notes, perhaps?"

Jean, who did not lose sight of the play of her features, settled her with one question:

"Have you not lost something?"

"Yes," said Mme. Potard, eagerly; "bank-notes, ten, ten thousand francs . . . . recovered? Oh, Lord! you have found them, Monsieur?"

"Yes, Madame."

"What good luck! Where are they? . . . They are mine."

And, seeing that Jean made no move, Mme. Potard added:

"Return them to me."

"One moment," rejoined the rag-picker, with his imperturbable calmness.

Mme. Potard became anxious.

"You have really found them, haven't you?" she asked, stamping with impatience.

"Why, yes," said Jean.

The midwife tapped her forehead and said to herself with profound faith, think-.ing of her dream:

"Ah! the spider, it was sure."

And drawing nearer to Jean, she said:

"Let me see."

"Look!" said the rag-picker, taking the notes from the pocket-book which had formerly belonged to Jacques Didier.

"The very ones," cried Mme. Potard, brightening at the sight of the notes. "I am not bewitched! Oh! upon my word, I recognize them."

And holding out her hand, she continued with beaming eyes: ·

"Return them, then."

"Not so fast, Madame," said Jean.

The midwife replied, with a shade of bitterness:

"They are mine, I tell you, and well-earned. . . I pray you, give them to me.'

"Directly," answered Jean.

Mme. Potard looked at him first in astonishment and then cunningly; at last she cried rudely:

"Ah! I understand; you want to be sure first; I must tell you the place, time, and all. Well, that's right. I lost them on the night of Mardi-Gras, as the poster states. You must have found them in the Rue Sainte-Marguerite, at the corner of the Faubourg Saint-Antoine."

"Precisely."

"Well, then. . . . But my head is fairly swimming with joy. I forgot . . . there is a reward . . . a handsome reward."

"Handsome!" said Jean. "I really hope so."

Mme. Potard went to her secretary to get a purse, and, returning to Jean, she said, with a disappointing gesture:

"But you know, one cannot give as much for ten thousand francs as for a hundred thousand. And besides, in conscience one ought not to profit by another's misfortune."

Then she slowly loosened her purse-strings as if they were her heart-strings.

But again Jean reassured her.

"Hence it is not money that I want," he said.

"Ah! and what do you want, then?" said she, with a joy that was mingled with surprise.

And she quickly replaced her purse in the secretary.

Jean looked her squarely in the face.

"I want to know how you got these notes," said he.

"How?" exclaimed the dumbfounded Mme. Potard.

The rag-picker sat down by the round table in the middle of the room, and explained himself:

"Yes, Madame Potard, you have told me how you lost them; now you will tell me how you obtained them."

"But, Monsieur," cried Mme. Potard, in alarm.

Jean tilted back and forth in his chair, still looking at her attentively.

"There is no Monsieur or Madame about it," said he. "I will return them to you only at that price."

Mme. Potard succeeded by an effort in recovering her self-possession.

"Well, here's a curious fellow, indeed! And what's that to you?"

"Much."

"Ah! And why?"

"I want to know," said Jean, smiling. "An old woman's whim, Madame Potard. You can take it or leave it."

Mme. Potard, recovered from her shock, sat down in her turn and glanced furtively at Jean.

"Why, Monsieur, I earned them by my labor; they are the fruit of my savings."

"Tell that to the marines!" exclaimed the rag-picker, shrugging his shoulders.

And he questioned her as if he were a magistrate.

"You lost these notes in the Faubourg Saint-Antoine, did you not?"

"Undoubtedly."

"At night."

"What then?"

"At four o'clock in the morning."

"What of it?"

Jean folded his arms.

"What were you doing at night, at four o'clock in the morning, with ten thousand francs in your pocket? That is not natural."

Madame Potard was disturbed, seeing herself getting deeper and deeper into the mire.

"Nevertheless it is perfectly true, I swear to you. . . . I was returning from my notary's."

"At that hour," said Jean, bursting out laughing, "notaries' offices are closed. A midwife does not run about the streets at four o'clock in the morning with her pocket full of bank-notes, unless she has a reason for it. There is something beneath all this. . . . Come, out with it . . . or good-bye, Bank!"

The midwife rose, furious at being caught in a lie, and assuming in her turn a threatening tone.

"Ah! but you too are a little queer, yourself. I find you astonishing with your questions . . . and it is very obliging in me to answer them. These notes are mine. They do not concern you, and I shall find a way to force you to return them."

"And I to force you to speak," said Jean, resolutely.

"Yes, that's it," cried Mme. Potard, growing rebellious and running to the bell. "Well, we shall see. I am going to call the police."

Father Jean walked quietly to the fireplace, and said:

"And I am going to throw the notes into the fire."

Mme. Potard was not expecting this straight blow.

She stopped in amazement.

Jean, still smiling, held up the package.

"One for every time that you refuse," he said.

"Ah! don't be idiotic," exclaimed the midwife, coming back to Jean.

"As true as the fire burns," he declared, separating one of the notes from the rest.

"He is mad," cried Mme. Potard, in terror.

"I begin," said Jean, stooping down before the fire. "See? Will you tell?" And receiving no reply, he threw the note into the fire.

"One," said he, simply.

Mme. Potard nearly went crazy.

"But that's a thousand francs, you stupid brute. Don't you know what that is, you savage?"

And seeing the note reduced to ashes, she groaned sorrowfully:

"Burned! Burned! Oh!"

"Have you anything to say?" resumed Jean. "Two!"

He made a taper of a second note, and, lighting it in the fire, let it burn slowly in his fingers, while Mme. Potard threw herself vainly upon him to tear from him the flaming note, burning her hands in the attempt without succeeding in getting it or putting out the flame.

"Oh! monster! demon! sacrilege!" she screamed in horror, her eyes starting from her head in her rage. "So much money! Can it be possible? The good God's money which it is so hard to earn. Rascal, you shall pay me for this!"

And enraged at her powerlessness, she exclaimed:
"Oh! to think that I cannot kill him on the spot!"
Then she shouted in her frenzy:
"Help! fire! thief! murderer!"
Jean bent over toward the fire again.
"Another step, another cry, and I throw in the whole package."
"He would do as he says," said Mme. Potard, crushed. "Oh! I shall die."
And she fell back coldly on her chair.
"Come," said Jean, "let us decide. Three!"
He made a motion to throw in another note.
"Stop!" cried Mme. Potard, seizing his arm.
"At last!" said Jean.
"Well! let us share."
"No, all or nothing."
"All, you say, and all for me?"
"Except the two that are burned, of course."
"Such good notes," sighed Mme. Potard. "It is worse than murder."
"It is your fault. . . . Come."
Reflecting, the midwife said to herself:
"Twenty thousand francs that I have to keep silent, and eight thousand that I shall have to speak. Total". . . .
"Make haste," said Jean, firmly.
"I am calculating," cried Mme. Potard.
And, approaching the rag-picker, she asked:
"But what interest have you in knowing this secret?"
"Ah! you see there is a secret," said Jean, taking her at her word. "Give it up, or else". . . .
And again he made the threatening gesture.
"One minute, forceps!" exclaimed Mme. Potard; "let me breathe! But what do you want, then, if you return me all?"
"The secret or the fire."
But Mme. Potard, suddenly illuminated, cried:
"How stupid I am!"
And tapping him on the shoulder, she said:
"Ah! you sly dog, I see the trick. You want more, a hundred times more. You are right, to be sure. When one has an opportunity, he should profit by it . . . . and this is a good one."
"As you say."
Madame Potard took Father Jean for a blackmailer of the first class, and, bowing in his honor, she said:
"I salute you, my master; I never thought of that, simpleton that I am. Yes, that would be a stroke, and a lucky one; I see, I see."

And, laughing at her perspicacity, she added:

"You want to make the canary sing."*

"Yes, my sly old girl."

"You should have said so, then, and I would have accompanied you directly. It is a familiar air. . . . You have a secret worth more than those, you greedy rascal," said she, pointing to the notes. "You give me the egg for the hen."

"A good layer". . . .

"You are right. Then let us divide. . . . I will tell everything."

And Mme. Potard sat down again.

"Agreed," said Jean, putting the notes back in his pocket.

"There's nothing like coming to an understanding," said the midwife.

"I am listening."

Mme. Potard made Jean sit down beside her, and continued in a familiar tone:
. "Then, partner, let us explain ourselves; let us agree upon our shares. Cards on the table. Eight thousand francs is not enough for such a secret, a treasure, a mine, a California! So we will make an honest and fitting arrangement. First you shall return me my eight notes . . . and after that halves in everything."

"Agreed," said Jean, after a pause.

The midwife gave a final indication of distrust.

"May one have confidence?" she asked.

"It's not to be had for the asking, but I know how to manage the stroke as well as another."

"Oh! that indeed!" she exclaimed.

Then she added:

"Are you honest? That's what I meant to ask."

"You have your notes for security."

"Don't give us the dunce act. You will not sell me out? Do you understand?"

"Oh! the idea!"

To clinch the matter, she concluded:

"Certainly you are not of the security police?"

"Of the salubrity police, suspicious creature. I clean Paris. See where my rake scraped the notes."

"How easy to spoil and burn!"

And drawing nearer to the rag-picker, who sat imperturbable, but all ears despite his air of indifference, she added:

"Then that goes. Listen."

"Go on!"

"Listen carefully," repeated Mme. Potard. "A month ago, at the time of the

---

* A French idiom, signifying the extortion of blackmail.

Carnival, on the night of Mardi-Gras, I was to lose a new-born infant, in consideration of ten notes of a thousand francs each. One must live, you know. The mother did not know about it; perhaps she did not want it done; but her father did. How could I please both? In case of doubt, refrain; isn't that the way? Besides, after getting the notes, my courage failed me. And yet they say that money makes people bad. Oftener the opposite. I wanted to save the child, and I carried it to the lodgings of a working-girl, my seamstress, an accommodating creature whom I knew to be capable of caring for it. Once there, I left the child, lost to the father, but discoverable by his daughter. Thus everybody was satisfied."

"And the working-girl?" asked Jean.

Mme. Potard responded:

"Upon my honor, I meant to give her something for her trouble."

"Ye gods! Hell is paved with good intentions."

"Oh! don't speak of hell," exclaimed the midwife, seriously.

"All right," said Jean, "we will return to Paradise. We were saying then "...

"Why, that I would far rather divide than run into danger. But everything is a matter of luck. I did not find the working-girl, and I lost the notes. Of course I was obliged to leave the child to the mercy of God."

"And of the working-girl, good heart, go on!"

"Too good!" approved the midwife. "For through trying to save the child I lost the money. And they say that a good deed is never lost."

"You see that it is not," observed Jean. "But that isn't all. The names of these mysterious persons of this night of Mardi-Gras?"

Mme. Potard hesitated a minute, and then, making up her mind, answered:

"Oh, yes. Well, Mademoiselle Claire Hoffmann, daughter of Baron Hoffmann is the mother, and Marie Didier is the working-girl."

"Well," said he, "you have dotted the Is; now for the rest."

"What rest?" asked the midwife, her face darkening.

"The end of the story."

"What end?"

"Oh, less mystery! The child that you saved a month ago was killed yesterday."

"Hush!" exclaimed Mme. Potard.

"Come," insisted Jean, "you have made an angel of it."

"Speak lower, wretch," whispered the midwife.

"An angel," repeated Jean, "on account of the devil. . . . . All right! silence in the workshop! And now for the proof of all this?"

This question disconcerted Mme. Potard.

"The proof?" she exclaimed.

"Yes, the proof. I can do nothing without proof."

" To be sure."

" And I must have proof, and good proof, in order to act."

"Of course," said Mme. Potard.

She went to her secretary and got a letter, which she showed to Jean.

"There, read that, if you know how to read."

Then, distrustfully holding back the letter, she said:

"No, listen."

She read:

"Madame, I do not know what bargain has been made with you touching the deposit confided to your care; but if unfortunately it is for your interest to lose it, it is still more for your interest, I swear to you, to keep it. Be kind enough, then, I beg of you, to guard it with maternal care until it shall be claimed; you will be rewarded. — C. H."

"Claire Hoffmann," she explained.

" The daughter of the baron, Mademoiselle Claire Hoffmann?"

" Yes, she sent me that yesterday. She learned my address from the woman who cared for her during child-birth, and to whom I ventured to give my card. One never knows what may happen, eh? What music!"

" Enough said," said Jean, "give and take; there are your notes; count them."

He gave her the notes, put the letter in their place in the Didier pocket-book, and then, putting it back in his pocket, began to get ready to go.

Mme. Potard, having counted the notes, sighed:

"Eight! . . . . no more? Two wanting, you know. . . . . Pardoned, but not quits."

"Bah!" exclaimed Jean, as he started off, "we shall have plenty more."

Mme. Potard retained him by the skirt of his old coat.

" That letter, you know, is worth a hundred times as much. To part with that for eight thousand francs would be to let it go for nothing."

"For nothing at all, in comparison with what I want for it. We will keep our coach and four."

" For the last time, then, it is understood and agreed," said Mme. Potard, "half for me and two besides."

" It has been said again and again, old repeater," said Jean, "half and more. I assure you the best end of the bargain."

" Right away," said the midwife, now decidedly won, "for I am obliged to leave."

" Right away, Madame Potard, right away! I am in a greater hurry than you are."

And he hastened off.

Mme. Potard struck her forehead.

" Say, there!" she shouted.

"Again?" exclaimed Jean.

"Yes, I am thinking," said the midwife, "what the baron will say."

"The baron!" said Jean. "Rest easy on that score. I will not compromise you. I am not so stupid as that. Everything will go like clock-work. You lost the letter with the notes, and I found the whole. See?"

"Let me embrace you," cried Mme. Potard, carried away in spite of herself. "What a man! Ready for everything! It is your affair. Go ahead, you are equal to it. Stay! Instead of sharing, let us marry."

Jean drew back further and further toward the door.

"Thank you, my dear," said he, "I am not free. Too happy already to be your partner."

"That's a pity," sighed Madame Potard. "Well, then, we will share. Good luck! *Au revoir!*"

And Jean went out precipitately.

Madame Potard, left alone, went into ecstasies over her notes, counting them again.

"Eight and twenty, twenty-eight! Thirty with the two burned ones. Oh! he will replace them. I have faith; a pretty little treasure all the same, even though it should make no little ones. . . . But it will. Make some, I beg of you! No matter, thirty at five per cent. will give an income of fifteen hundred francs. I shall not die of hunger. I will retire to the country, far from the Parisian police. Paris is not healthy, as the baron said. I will go to Montrouge and marry the chief of the *gendarmes*."

And, delighted with this charming plan of retirement, Mme. Potard closed her secretary again after a last look of adoration at her "savings."

END OF PART THIRD.

PART FOURTH.

THE STRUGGLE.

CHAPTER I.

FORCED MARRIAGE.

Baron Hoffmann, with anxious brow, entered the superb dining-room of his mansion. The room, always luxurious, wore also, on this evening, an air of festivity. The side-board, a marvel of sculpture and carving, was simply loaded with rare flowers and fruits. A side-table was covered with bottles containing the entire gamut of exquisite and generous wines, not the ordinary richness of every day, but the opulence and elegance of a dinner of ceremony, to precede the making of a contract in due form; for on this evening Camille was to come to conclude the "affair" of marriage, in company with the notary, Loiseau.

The table, dazzling in its whiteness, glittering with silver ware beneath the chandelier lighted with its hundred candles whose flames were multiplied in its thousand crystals of glass, was set for only four people. The banker threw a master's glance at the splendid furniture, the soft carpet, the Sèvres porcelain, the splendid paintings, and all the surroundings, calculated to stimulate good humor and good appetite, and, satisfied with the preparations, turned his thoughts upon the expected guests.

"Seven o'clock," said he, tapping his foot on the floor, "and no one here yet."

Laurent entered with a letter on a silver plate.

"A letter from Monsieur Berville," he announced to his master.

At the same moment Claire appeared, serious and looking at her father with an indescribable expression of horror and pity.

The baron, after reading, muttered in sullen anger:

"The madman!"

Then he said to the servant:

"Go; I will send an answer."

And, turning to his daughter, he continued:

"Camille, whom I expected with his notary, will not come. I had good reason to fear some rash decision. This is what he says: he wishes to break his engagement."

"Seriously?" cried Claire, with joy.

"Quite so," said the baron. "He makes a definitive demand for his accounts. It is no longer you who refuse; it is he. This damned marriage is destined to drag along forever; fortunately the fool is ruined and his sweetheart arrested."

"Arrested!" exclaimed Claire. "For what?"

"For infanticide," responded the baron, brutally.

Claire sank down, uttering a groan.

The baron ran to sustain his daughter.

"How pale she is!" he anxiously exclaimed. "Suppose she should die! Shipwrecked in sight of port!"

But she soon recovered her senses.

"And you dare to accuse her?" she murmured. "Oh! but that is too much, Monsieur."

"I will save her; compose yourself," the banker hastened to say. "I will save her; but no weakness! We must think now of but one object, — your marriage."

"Oh! shall I go as far as that?" said Claire, woefully. "I shall lose my reason, if not my life. I have no will left; nothing but a remnant of dying conscience. I feel nothing but the grief of which I shall be the perpetual prey. Though you hide our crimes from others, I cannot hide them from myself. I am not as strong as you, Monsieur. I can stifle fear, but not remorse."

"Your scruples again!" retorted the baron; "you take everything too much to heart. I will save her, I tell you. It was the only way. Alas! I could not choose. It was necessary to accuse her. It is still necessary, in order to take Camille from her; it is essential to our safety, as you know, and to her own. For now she cannot be saved except after us and by our aid."

"Ah! you have changed my fault into a crime," answered Claire, in despair. "Before, I was your victim; now my guilty weakness makes me your accomplice. Religion, duty, love, — there is nothing left in me of the woman, or of the mother, or of humanity. Oh, God! my nature is ruined!"

"Child, I take everything upon myself."

But Claire solemnly replied:

"Are you, then, tired of waiting for justice? Do you find her too slow that you press her so hard? Do you not see that she comes a step nearer with each of our crimes? For my part, I quake already under the shadow of her hand. Let us stop."

"Coward!" exclaimed the baron. "The world is not the convent whence you came. There are no penalties for the powerful. You belong to the race of masters, Duchess de Crillon-Garousse. Trust then to my experience, and take the law into your own hands. Life is a struggle. Each one for himself, and the devil take the hindmost! It is the law of nature, the right of the strongest . . . . you know, the lamb is for the wolf, the Didiers for the Hoffmanns. A curse upon the weak! Victory to the strong!"

Claire made a gesture of terror.

"Oh! do not justify our infernal egoism by this law of evil. Do not blaspheme! do not tempt God!"

"This law of iron rules us," answered the baron; "let us follow it. We did not make it, we cannot change it; under it we must choose the best course for ourselves and others . . . . and well-ordered charity begins at home. Let us not be more benevolent than the proverb. I will save this girl, I swear to you, but after us . . . as is just, in her turn; I will even reward her; you shall aid me in it, that is your part."

And abandoning himself still further to his grand nobleman's morality, he went on :

"Besides, the evil is not so great. Do not exaggerate. Your sensitive nature makes a monster of everything. Hers is that of her class. A plaster of silver will dress her wound. A generous dowry in her apron with a workingman on her arm when she leaves the prison, and all will be settled. We shall be quits."

Claire lowered her head, conquered.

"Oh! my father," she murmured, "I shudder at your cruel sophistry and your frightful examples. And my cowardly conscience, in yielding, foresees the just penalty which I incur in following them. God will punish me for obeying you."

Just then Laurent entered after first knocking, and she became silent again.

"A man asks to speak to Monsieur the baron," said the servant.

"I am not in," answered the baron.

And, the servant having gone out, he said to his daughter :

"Let us finish. We must promptly answer Camille that he is ruined and she is lost; shame and poverty,—there is no love that can stand against those two remedies. So no more frights! Be bold. The marriage shall take place; that is settled."

Laurent returned with an air of hesitation, and said :

"This man insists, and asks to speak to Monsieur in behalf of Madame Potard."

The baron again became anxious.

"What can it be?" he asked himself.

Then, coming to a decision, he gave the order :

"Let him enter."

Laurent went out.

"What does this mean?" cried Claire, in alarm.

"Leave me; I am going to find out," said the baron, in a tone of authority.

And he waited with a firm foot, ready for anything.

CHAPTER II.

BANKER AND RAG-PICKER.

"Monsieur the baron Hoffmann?" asked Jean, entering abruptly just in time to see Claire go out.

The banker gauged him with his eye for a moment, in anticipation of an enemy, but the man's appearance reassured him.

"I am the baron," said he, disdainfully.

The rag-picker pointed to Laurent, and said in a lower tone:

"I have a word to say in your ear."

"Laurent, go out," ordered the banker.

Left alone, banker and rag-picker surveyed each other, as if to measure their respective strengths before entering upon the struggle.

"We shall play cautiously," said Jean to himself.

The baron passed his hand over his forehead, as if trying to refresh his memory, as he thought:

"I have seen this fellow before . . . What does he want?"

Jean wiped his brow also, saying to himself:

"How he eyes me! The name Potard has had its effect."

The baron looked him suddenly in the face.

"What do you want?"

"To sit down first. . . . I am tired," answered Jean, sitting down without losing sight of his adversary.

The baron was more disturbed than indignant at this lack of ceremony.

"What assurance!" said he to himself, "the insolent fellow!"

"And then to talk with you," continued Jean, still mopping his brow.

"That voice". . . . thought the baron.

And, viewing him with redoubled attention, he inquired:

"But first who are you?"

The rag-picker in turn ransacked his memory.

"I have heard that tone somewhere before . . . where? . . . no matter!"

The baron questioned him more rudely, thinking that he was hesitating.

"Come, be quick; let us finish; who are you?"

"I am Father Jean, rag-picker, at your service."

The whilom Garousse recognized him suddenly and almost betrayed himself. His features contracted. He saw again, as in a nightmare, the Hotel d'Italie, the basket, the crime, and he murmured in his fright :

" Ah ! the drunkard of the Quai. . . . Why is he here?"

And, raising his voice, he responded :

"I do not know you. What do you want?"

Jean, following his nature, went straight to the point.

" I come, recommended by Madame Potard, to talk with you concerning the ar‑ rest of a poor girl."

" Eh?" said the baron, disconcerted by this attack.

"Yes," insisted Jean, " a poor girl accused of infanticide."

" And what have I to do with her?" asked the disconcerted baron.

" Do not pretend to be ignorant, Monsieur baron," said Jean, coldly.

The baron began to reflect anxiously.

"What does he know?"

And he added aloud:

"What girl? Yours, of course."

" To some extent."

"What do you say?"

"Since they call me Father Jean," he answered, "I surely must be to some ex‑ tent the father of somebody . . . especially of her who has lost her own."

"There is no longer any doubt . . . it is he," confessed the banker to himself.

Jean, fixing his eyes upon him, continued:

"I have a father's heart, you see, though I have no child. There are so many others who have children. . . . Well, never mind that, I am for her."

"And what can I do in the matter of the arrest of this girl?" asked the baron, recovering his cunning in the presence of danger.

"Much," said Jean.

"Ah !"

" Yes."

"I?"

" You."

" Well," said M. Hoffmann at last, seeming to yield. "What do you wish me to do about it? Let us see."

"It is not necessary for me to tell you," answered Jean.

"Some money?" ventured the banker.

"Oh ! better than that," sneered Jean. "Madame Potard . . . you know her?"

" The infamous creature !" thought the baron.

Then, determined to deny, he said, haughtily:

" Who is she?"

Jean rose and, standing opposite the baron, explained himself in a tone that breathed a threat.

"The mid-wife whose bank-notes I found told me that the whole thing is in your hands, and I believe her. You have a long arm; you know as well as I what you have to do to secure her justice. . . . That's all I have to say."

"He knows something," thought the banker.

And continuing the same tactics, he added aloud:

"You are mistaken, I am not a judge."

"Much more," said Jean, "you are rich."

"We live in a Republic, you know."

"Bah! money is always king. You are sure that Marie Didier is not guilty; that she even saved the child whom she is accused of killing. . . Come, isu't that enough to merit all your pity, Monsieur baron?"

"He is unwilling to speak," said t he banker to himself.

And trying to sound him, he went on:

"Yes, certainly, that would be quite sufficient to interest me in her . . . . and I shall be able, if only you have some means of justification, some proof of her innocence". . . .

"You have only to tell what you know," answered Jean, ever on his guard. "You know very well that we have not honor enough, we others, to kill our children."

Now the baron fully understood the danger.

"He knows all," thought he; "what proofs has he? He must speak."

The rag-picker cut short his reflections by saying squarely:

"You will speak for her this very day, will you not? I count upon it. In the name of your daughter you will save mine."

The baron then determined on his course.

"Very well," said he, "I understand your sympathy, and, in spite of your reticence, I am willing to take an interest in your *protégée*. So we will consult as to what can be done, and, that I may not be disturbed and may be wholly at your service, I am going to dispatch a pressing matter of business and return. Wait here a moment for me."

"All right," said Jean, " but don't be long,—in your interest as well as my own. A word to the wise is sufficient. . . . I await you."

And aside, as if delighted, he said:

"Ah! Potard told the truth."

The baron went out, saying between his teeth:

"Oh! he shall speak."

CHAPTER III.

FOREVER WINE!

Jean watched the banker go out, and then said, as he shrugged his shoulders:
"So that is Monsieur, with his cross of the Legion of Honor . . . and the Mon-
thyon prize perhaps . . . . a white waistcoat and a soul as black as his coat . . .
and his face ditto, a face that I have already seen I know not where. I have seen
so many of his stamp, decorated or otherwise; and that pale pink of propriety who
was here with him was Mademoiselle. One would give her the good God without
confession and the flower of Nanterre besides. That's the sort of children these
people have. How the devil is it that people capable of killing their children can
have any at all? To be sure, cats who kill their offspring have enough of them.
But then, the poor cats do not always have anything else to eat, whereas these
creatures ". . . .

Looking at the table, he continued:
"What luxury, for one man alone! Just look! Enough for a whole hospital
of orphans and old people. Does this ogre need it all? How many of our shares
does it take to make his?"

He went to the side-table.
"What devices of bottles and flasks of all sizes and shapes, of all prices, of all
flavors, of all growths! It's curious, all the same ". . . .

And he read the labels.
"It's frightful! Champagne, Spain, Germany, the whole earth laid under contri-
bution. What a wine-cellar! A regular seraglio, of brunettes and blondes, slender as brides, fat as fishwives, with pink caps and straw dresses. There's one with
a silver head, and another with gold in her belly. He drinks gold! And we have
not water to drink! . . . What does he eat? Diamonds? Ah! the man and his
wine, the devil and hell distilled, vice and crime sealed and tied up. . . . But it
doesn't dazzle me. I will uncork you, poisons, with a few good strokes of my hook.
All the filth isn't in the street. Oh! the monsters, I will pick them up . . . into
the basket! into the basket! Away with you, gilded debauchery, you shall not
always have so much in your canteen. . . . But he doesn't come back. Is he going to roast me here? I am dying with heat."

He struck heavily upon the table.

Just then his back was turned to the door, and he did not see the baron intro-
duce Laurent into the room and remain behind the curtain himself to listen.
The servant began to fill the stove with wood, saying to Jean:
"Monsieur baron will return presently. He bids me tell you to have a little
patience and to sit down at the table while waiting."
He set the table for one more.
"That's your place," said he.
The rag-picker, walking back and forth in agitation, shouted to the departing
Laurent:
"At the table! He invites me to dinner . . . too polite". . . .
And, left alone, he continued:
"A rag-picker dining with a banker. . . . I see him coming. . . . He surely
means to inveigle me, to offer me his money. They think they can do everything
with money . . . . and they can almost . . . . but Father Jean is not to be taken
that way. Money is not so tempting to us who have none; less tempting than to·
him, who has so much. What ruins these rascals is that they never count on the·
conscience of others. Let him come!"
And he concluded with an explosion:
"Oh! I will save her, in spite of him, in spite of the devil, in spite of his money."·
Laurent returned with a soup tureen, and, pointing Jean to a seat at the table,
said:
"You are served. Wait with your feet under the table."
Jean wiped his brow again. The heat was becoming suffocating.
"Thank you," said he, "I am not hungry."
The servant did not contradict him, but, filling two large glasses on a waiter,
asked:
"You are thirsty at least?"
"Oh, yes," said Jean.
"Well," said Laurent, presenting the waiter.
But, seeing Jean draw back, he said:
"Why prance about in that way? It is not bad. . . . See!"
He drank a glass and filled it again, continuing in a persuasive tone:
"But God forgive me, you are in a perspiration; if you will not eat, at least drink
a little to refresh yourself."
"Indeed, one cannot refuse. I am sweating big drops. I am dying of heat and
thirst; I have run about till I am breathless. It's a long way from Honoré to An-
toine, and on these old pins of mine. . . . Give me some water."
"Water!" exclaimed Laurent; "to make you sick? Water's good for nothing
when one is warm. A little wine, that's the stuff! That refreshes without chill-
ing. . . . Bordeaux! Mademoiselle's wine."
"Yes," said Jean, consenting, yielding to this reasoning and his thirst. "But
only a drop . . . and well baptised."

He took up the decanter.

Laurent held back his arm persuasively.

" There," said he, "as little as you like. Do not get an attack of pleurisy."

This proved the decisive word.

"You are right," said he; "this is no time for that."

He drank with avidity, and set down his glass, which Laurent filled again immediately.

"Enough, thank you," cried Jean. " We should use, but not abuse, — especially with good things."

"Bah!" rejoined the valet, "when one can get *bourgeois* wine. . . . What quality!"

"True, but beware of quantity. Today, you see". . . .

And the rag-picker tried to pour some water into the wine.

Laurent indignantly removed the decanter from his reach.

"Ah! you spoil it," he cried.

Father Jean continued to mop his brow.

"Be seated," advised Laurent; "it makes you still hotter to stand."

"I believe you," said Jean. "This heat is too much for me."

And he turned his head about, looking for a place where he might get a breath of fresh air. The stove was roaring, sending out a torrid heat through every opening.

The valet, decidedly generous, took advantage of this opportunity to refill the glasses.

Jean drank again and threw himself back in his seat, while Laurent emptied his own glass into Jean's, saying :

"Come, old boy, do me the honor. You are still at your first bumper. I am ashamed of you. Just do as I do and quench your thirst . . . . there . . . . tranquilly. How do you like it?"

"Oh! I never drank anything to compare with it," confessed the rag-picker, emptying his glass with one swallow.

"Such wine is not to be had at the first corner (*coin*)" said Laurent, beginning the same game over again, always pouring but not drinking.

"At any rate," answered Jean, good-humoredly, "it is of a good brand (*coin*)."

Laurent emptied the bottle.

" One finger . . . . without water . . . . this time, that you may taste it better. Try that."

Jean tasted.

"Yes," he said, "still better. It does one good."

"Come," said the servant, passing to another. " This is at least its equal. Let's empty the bottle before it gets flat. Upon my word, I am doing all the drinking and you the sweating. Put a little courage in your throat, good old father. Oh! you have no force."

The rag-picker, disturbed and a little humiliated, but resisting the temptation, resolutely shook his head.

"No, no, that will do."

"Oh, yes," said Laurent, "this will completely restore you. Some Bordeaux that has been ripening here for an hour."

"No, I tell you; I've had too much already: I am not accustomed to it."

And Jean pushed back his glass.

Laurent took a third bottle and used colored glasses.

"Ah! to be sure," said he, "you don't get such wine every day. Then make the most of the opportunity when it comes. It is so much taken from the enemy. This is better yet, Monsieur's wine . . . . Beaune-Hospice . . . . the wine of the comet."

And pouring it out freely, he made a pretence of drinking, as he added:

"Do as I do."

"Of the comet," said Jean, under a spell. "Ah! just a sip of the comet."

Then his face became more serious.

"Beaune-Hospice," he repeated, undo ubtedly thinking of the widow Didier, who had died after a few weeks' treatment with watered milk. "Ah! well, many comets will cross the skies before they give such Beaune as that in the hospitals (*hospices*). Why the devil does it bear that name?"

"Why, it is the wine for invalids," said Laurent, pouring it out in floods. "It is balm to the stomach. Each glass adds a year to one's life. Excuse me for helping myself first; this is the foam."

"Oh! the lees are as good as the foam," said Jean, unable to resist. "Besides, I don't wish to be a centenarian."

He continued nevertheless to drink, and with delight.

"Better and better," he cried. "That would revive a dead man."

"It is the milk of old age," approved Laurent, "the joy of man. Another glass to drink your health."

"You are very polite," said Jean, in a thick voice. "A last glass for a hob-nob."

And they touched glasses and drank.

"Here's to you!" said Jean.

A minute passed. He moved about on his chair, sweating big drops and growling:

"Ah! but your master is forgetting me. I am in a hurry."

Baron Hoffmann, who had witnessed this scene from behind the tapestry, made a sign to Laurent, and disappeared without having been noticed by the rag-picker.

Father Jean tried to rise, but, seized with giddiness, fell back again.

"Go and find him," said he.

Laurent picked up the bottle again.

"The rest first," he insinuated. "It is the bottom of the bottle, saving your respect . . . with a biscuit . . . the bread of Beaune."

"Well, to top off with," conceded Jean.

And Laurent went on:

"We must not leave this little bit; it would be wasted."

"That would be a pity," said Jean, drinking and smacking his lips. "It's astonishing how thirsty I am today. The more I drink the more I want, as if I were salted. I am melting with heat, impatience, and rage. This room feels like an oven. My body is on fire. I am burning up."

He seized the empty bottle himself and tried to pour from it.

"There's nothing left in the pump," he exclaimed, looking at Laurent stupidly.

The valet pointed to a bottle in a silver pail full of ice.

"Here's another," said he, "and just what you need to drive away the salt taste. Champagne, champagne *frappé*". . . .

"What do you mean by *frappé?*" asked Jean. "Do you beat it, then? For my part, I would rather kiss it."

"Frozen, iced," explained Laurent, laughing. "Warmed Bordeaux . . . . iced champagne . . . . old novice."

"Iced!" said Jean. "Good! This time I shall be refreshed."

"Yes, yes, this is the thing. So, old boy, you are not acquainted with champagne *frappé?*"

"Why, no, I never drank any. Let us see what it is like."

Laurent made haste to pour some out.

"The devil! how you go at it! Full to the brim. It's easy to see it costs you nothing."

"Bah! what do these glasses hold? A mere thimbleful!"

"That's all right, but I need my head, you see!"

"Oh! this wine does not intoxicate; on the contrary."

"So much the better. For I've got to talk to your boss."

"All the more reason, then; this will inspire you."

And Laurent poured for him abundantly.

"Really?" asked Jean, shaken.

He emptied his glass, and the servant straightway refilled it; then, drinking again, he continued:

"In fact, I've often said that there's nothing like champagne to give one an idea. It's the son of light and the father of wit."

Laurent poured continually, adding:

"Didn't I tell you so? Come, another idea!"

"Yes, yes, the devil take me! it is the *spirituel* wine . . . the blood of France."

The valet nodded his head approvingly.

"With the champagne, take some of the wine of the four beggars."

"Ah!" answered Jean, "why do you call it the wine of the four beggars? Eh, sly dog! Because it asks to be drunk . . . . four times! To make amends, you silly fellow, pour some out."

Laurent hastened to obey.

"Out upon you, old joker! He made up his mouth. . . . He seemed not to touch it. He sipped and moistened his lips, like a sparrow."

And, filling Jean's already emptied glass, he added:

"Now for a bumper! That's the talk!"

"I, youngster," said Jean, piqued, "if I did not restrain myself . . . . I would swallow the whole wine-cellar, to the last drop, and you with. . . . Formerly, twenty years ago, if you had seen me, it was a very different thing; I have fallen off more than a quart a year. . . . Old age! That's what it does for us. Come, pour away, you neglect me, you worry me."

"Ah! what a pity! there is no more here," said Laurent, pretending to refuse in order the more to excite him.

"Well," said Jean, warmly, "turn on the faucet."

Laurent acquiesced.

"Oh, here's some sauterne."

Jean looked at the bottle admiringly.

"See how it sparkles," he cried, in a hoarse voice. "Nothing stupid or dull about that, my boy."

The valet went for a plate.

"And with some oysters," said he.

But Jean, raising himself up, sent them flying in the air with a blow from the back of his hand.

"Oyster yourself!" he articulated, with effort.

He began to drink again, pouring the wine himself and filling the glasses to the brim as he shouted to Laurent:

"But you drink no more. I am just getting a taste for it."

And he continued to swallow, stammering:

"To be sure, you drink every day, and you haven't been running bout'sh I have. . . . . You were right . . . doctor . . . . . this winds up the mainspring; it puts heart in one's stomach. Ah! your rascal of a master can come back when he likes. He has only to behave himself. . . . I am going to talk to him and with his wine. . . . . I am going to rinse him as I do this glass."

He drank again, taking off his cravat, his head on fire, excited, and growing more and more thirsty.

The door opened, and a new lackey appeared.

"Laurent," said he, "Monsieur baron is asking for you. . . . I will serve Monsieur in your place."

"All right, Léon," said the valet, going out.

Jean, swaying from right to left, began to stare and jeer at Léon.

"As many valets as wines," said he; "and what faces! They're in good condition, all these fellows! Ah! they have only this to do. 'Peter, what are you doing?' 'Nothing.' 'And you, Paul?' 'I am helping Peter.' And then, with such an allowance of wine! What nectar!"

Drinking and taking Léon by the arm, he continued:

"What syrup! What a bouquet! Violets and roses! The whole garden of plants! It's better than Niquet. Ah! if Niquet were as good as this and free, I'd drink night and day. . . . Come, finish the glass with a comrade!"

"No, thank you," said Léon, resisting.

Father Jean began to laugh, stammering and stumbling in his speech, and then resumed:

"Is this youngster going to force me to beg him? Come, since you are asked. When wine is poured, it must be drank. Ah! Sainte-Nitouche, you want it full, you hypocrite!"

He refilled Léon's glass and his own, and drank again.

"No, thank you, I tell you," said the valet, pushing back the wine with an air of disdain.

"Don't be afraid," said Jean, "I invite you; I am responsible for everything. I'm the master here. Swallow that down, you booby."

"I never drink wine," answered the valet, dryly.

"No wine," cried the rag-picker. "Ah! poor fellow! You're a Turk, then!"

"I like nothing but brandy . . . and if you will". . . .

Jean started up in his chair.

"Brandy! I'm with you. Oh! I'm not tired yet, my boy."

"Especially of that," said Léon, taking from the side-table a bottle of old cognac, brandy a hundred years old.

"Brandy! Water of life!" cried the rag-picker in a transport of enthusiasm. "What a beautiful name! Do I want brandy, I? Ah! ah! that's my weakness too; shake, old boy, give me your hand; in you I recognize myself. Brandy a hundred years old, older than I am, born at Cognac and before the revolution; let's see it! Pass her to me, this virgin. Isn't she beautiful? Love, away! Still she seems a little small for her soul. Let's see, then, what she has in her soul. Oh! oh! how it shines . . . rays, gleams, as of melted topaz, the entire sun bottled up."

And, turning to the bottle glistening in the light, he said:

"And do you mean to look at me like that with your golden eyes, coquette? Uncork it, my son, uncork it."

Léon opened the bottle.

"There you are," said he.

Jean completely lost possession of himself.

"Come, hurry up, dawdler," he cried, "give it to me! You torture me. I can't resist, because I haven't drank any of it for a century. I am getting dizzy. Ah! dear beauty, my heart beats for you. . . . I am growing sick. . . . I am dying."

"Here it is, passionate old lover that you are," said Léon.

Jean grasped the bottle and said with ardor:

"Ah! darling, a kiss upon your pretty beak, with both hands and full mouth."
He began to drink from the bottle itself.

" Enter the nave," he continued with delight, " they want you in the chorus. . .
and make haste, gurgler. . . . There is a crowd holding high festival. . . . In
clover, deary. . . Buried, the *bourgeois!* F'rever joy! F'rever feasting! F'rever
wine! F'rever brandy! What drives away sorrow? Wine. What gives beauty
to life? Brandy. What warms and revives me when I am dying of cold and
hunger? Wine. What restores me and sets me up when I am falling sick?
Brandy."

And as formerly, at the Quai d'Austerlitz, he sang his refrain:

> F'rever wine!
> F'rever juice divine!

Just then Baron Hoffmann entered, saying in an undertone:

" Now's the time! Let us squeeze the sponge."

" Here, Monsieur!" said Léon to the rag-picker.

But Jean, still drinking, said:

"Who's that? . . . Nothing. . . . What are you talking about? . . . Don't
stir. . . . For my part, when I soak myself, I take root."

And again he began to sing incoherently. Then, after stopping a moment to
take breath, he continued:

" Let's drink the whole vineyard! Let's sing the praises of the entire cellar till
the end of the world!"

" Léon, go out," ordered the baron.

"What? Go out!" exclaimed Jean, swaying before the banker. "What's this
blackbird whistling?"

And he resumed his singing:

> No, friends are not such fools
> That they will part.

Then to Léon:

"Stay, stay, I bid you, and pass him a glass. I treat; he pays."
He hummed with a voice broken with intoxication:

> Fill up your empty glass!

A moment longer he tried to keep Léon, who went out upon a sign from the
baron.

Then, having failed to hold the valet, he approached the master, staggering and
singing:

> The more one stays with fools,
> The more one stays with fools,
> The more one laughs!

"I beg a thousand pardons for my long absence," said the baron, watching him. "At last I come back to talk with you."

Jean stumbled up to him.

"Ah! it's you," he exclaimed. "Entirely forgiven, my dear sir; I have been waiting under the vines."

The baron turned away to avoid his breath.

"Pooh!" he exclaimed, in disgust.

Jean continued:

"You kept me so long that I got thirsty. Been waiting through more than five bottles, but not drunk! I could easily wait to drink the rest. I could swallow the sea and the fish. But here you are! All right, what is it?"

The baron answered evasively:

"I am at your service now. Let us talk of your business."

"My business?" said Jean, bewildered and tapping his forehead.

Then he exclaimed:

"Oh! yes, I remember."

"Did you say that you had a proof?" asked the baron.

Jean answered with great volubility.

"Yes, yes, let's talk of that, and not by four roads either. You've had Marie Didier arrested. You are going to have her released, and that quickly too, immediately and not tomorrow. Tomorrow's a traitor, like yourself, and cannot be depended upon. This very day and even sooner . . . . because you made the child, — that is to say, your daughter did, — and you had it killed, and I have the proof."

Reeling, he tried to lead the baron away.

The baron insisted.

"The proof?"

"Yes, the proof, your daughter's letter, the letter to the midwife; let's be off."

"Oh! the foolish wretched girl!" said the baron to himself.

Jean took the letter from his pocket-book.

"Oh! it's no use. I have that in my pocket which will make you march straight, by rail, by steam, and at high speed. I have the letter, signed . . . . do you understand? I have the proof, and there it is!"

"At last I have him," said the baron aside.

Jean caught hold of the banker.

"Come, let's start!"

The baron stopped him.

"You want to exploit me, do you not?" said he, "to extort money from me? You take me for your milch cow. Well, no scandal! Return that letter to me. I multiply the notes by three."

"Go to! you're a simpleton," exclaimed Jean, shrugging his shoulders.

And he put the pocket-book back in his pocket.

"Your fortune for that letter," continued the baron.

"My fortune!" sneered Jean, who had lost all prudence but not all honesty. "Is that it? Have we come to that? Ha! ha! ha! my fortune! Oh! this brazen-face. I expected it. . . I am on my guard, idiot; proof against gold and silver, baron. How many millions for Jean's daughter? You're too poor, banker! My fortune! And for what? I was already greatly embarrassed with the old woman's ten thousand francs. Fortune for me, Soiffard I, king of the Gonlots? Bah! Just to have a face as ugly as yours, old man, be fed upon bank-notes, have a beast's skin on my hands and death's hairs on my head, and spit in my pocket?"

The baron had just spat in his handkerchief.

"Just to have more wine than one can drink, valets that empty the cellar, daughters that kill their brats and then charge others with the crime . . . the devil and his whole train . . . . never! never! But this is not to the point. We've talked enough. Let's go to the judge!"

Again he tried to drag away the baron.

"Well," said the baron between his teeth, "it must be today as before."

And he added aloud, in a threatening voice:

"You will not give it to me; then I am going to take it."

Jean, unable to defend himself, began to shout:

"Help! help!"

The baron seized him by the collar, as on the night of the Quai d'Austerlitz.

"Will you be silent, rascal?" said he, tightening his grasp and twisting.

Jean uttered a loud cry:

"Ah! the grip of the Quai!"

He had just recognized the murderer of Jacques Didier.

"Proof against gold, but not against wine," exclaimed the baron, taking the pocket-book. "The wine has gone in, the secret comes out."

And, taking out the letter, he cried joyfully:

"I have it!"

Jean struggled on the floor, screaming:

"Oh! robber! murderer! He is killing me, he is robbing me . . . . as he did Didier. He takes, he burns the letter; the proof . . . help, murder, fire!"

The baron was in fact burning his daughter's letter in the flame of a candle. But suddenly, glancing at the pocket-book which he held in his hand, he exclaimed:

"What do I see?"

He read:

Berville Bank. — Jacques Didier, collector.

Straightway he replaced the pocket-book in Jean's pocket.

"Good!" he said to himself.

"Ah! robber!" cried the rag-picker. "Double assassin. My letter! my proof! Stolen! burned! He kills the daughter as he did the father."

The baron rang and called loudly.

"Hello there, somebody!"

Laurent, Léon, and two other valets, one of whom was dressed as a footman, hurried into the room.

"Arrest this drunken man," ordered the baron.   "He is the murderer of Jacques Didier, the collector of the Berville Bank!"

And he went out triumphantly, holding his head high.

Jean, picked up by the valets, struggled like a madman, in a paroxysm of intoxication, and screamed as if the victim of an atrocious nightmare:

"Drunk! assassin. . . . . Who says I'm drunk? No, I am not drunk.   I am mad!"

Releasing himself, he seized a bottle and drove back the valets.

"Oh! my head burns.   Demons! they have poured fire into me; I have been drinking hell! . . . Two against one, the cowards; they have filled me up". . . .

And looking at the valets, he resumed in his frenzy:

"There, there are ten of them now, the traitors.   Murder's wine! the devil's blood! the milk of crime! the water of death!"

Looking in his pocket for the letter, in the height of his fury, he stammered in a frightened yet threatening voice:

"The letter, the Quail! Jacques! Marie! Wine! . . . To the guillotine with wine! . . . I am wine's executioner; I will execute wine! Let there be no more wine upon earth! Where is wine that I may exterminate it?"

With a supreme effort he overturned table, bottles, and glasses, rolling in the heap himself.

Then only could the valets pick him up and carry him off, gesticulating and crying with horror:

> Forever wine!
> Forever juice divine!

˙ CHAPTER IV.

THE CONCIERGERIE.

In prison slang the Conciergerie is called the *Tower* and the great inner court-yard the *Heap*. It is the rag-basket of Paris, the human rag-basket, continually filled up by officers and sorted out by judges, those rag-pickers of the police and the courts. On the day with which we have to do, three hundred Parisian frag-ments were swarming in this pit, open to the sky, but whose high walls, impossi-ble to scale, would have discouraged Latude.

A circular bench fastened to the wall permitted the prisoners to sit down by turns.

On one side a door, on the other a fountain with an iron goblet. The desperate eyes of this wretched crowd were lowered towards the ground. In fact, why look above at free space and thus add the torture of Tantalus to that of the jail?

Laborers out of work, vagabonds, drunkards, keepers of girls, prowlers of the suburbs, old offenders in the courts, superannuated bandits, — this entire world was gloomy, thoughtful, anxious. They jostled without mingling with each other; groups formed and closed up spontaneously, the delinquents of a day separating from the habitual criminals. Like gravitates to like.

A keeper, with his heavy key in his hand, watched the prisoners, imposing silence upon a few youngsters whose buffooneries were continually bursting out, in spite of the posted regulation forbidding loud talking, laughing, singing, whistling, leaping, and running, under penalty of the dungeon, of the *mitard*, to use the word of the prisoners and the jailers, the latter speaking the same tongue as the former, howling not with the wolves, but like the wolves.

Into the "heap" had strayed a young man of scarcely twenty-five, with a smil-ing and honest face, the spruce and natty dress of a prosperous workman, a kind and frank nature, possessing the two beauties, physical and moral, the one reflect-ing the other.

"Ah-ah-ah!" he exclaimed, yawning and stretching. "How badly one sleeps here. What a hotel furnished with bugs! Upon my word, the mattresses are too thickly settled, like the suburbs of Paris. The government doesn't give us enough to eat, but to make up for it delivers us to the beasts to be eaten. Martyrs, well, I should say so!˙ One is pricked, sucked, pumped, reduced to nothing. Oh! the vermin, what officials they would make! They are equal to the *bourgeois*."

The door opened, and some attendants, prisoners helping in the service, appeared, carrying loaves of black bread and a kettle filled with warm water in which a few dry vegetables were swimming.

"Say, I see no beefsteak," said the young man to himself, feeling a good appetite. They distributed the bread and then served the soup in earthen bowls shaped like basins.

It came young Bonnin's turn.

"The devil!" he exclaimed, taking his bowl from the attendant's hands, "am I to wash my hands in this or eat it?"

"You are to swallow it, you joker," said the other.

"Ah! indeed! . . . only I was about to say ". . .

"What?" asked the attendant.

"Why, that it isn't clean enough to wash in; but provided it is for the inner man, I am silent . . . and I introduce your lye into my person. Thank you!"

But the overseer reminded the attendant of his duty.

"Paolo, be quick, gather up the bowls."

"Already!" exclaimed Bonnin, in a vein of gayety. "It was not worth while to pronounce a eulogy of Napoleon in our presence last evening. He ate in a quarter of an hour and we in a quarter of a second. I ask for the demolition of the column."

"Do you want to go into the *mitard!*" cried the keeper.

The workman was not disconcerted.

"If you consult my tastes, I will say no, unless your heart is really set upon it."

Paolo came back to Bonnin to get his bowl, which he had emptied with a gulp to avoid the taste of its contents.

The attendant related his grievance to the workman.

"To think that I should be here, when the last place where I was employed was the Maison d'Or."

"Just imagine that this is a branch establishment," said Bonnin to console him.

"I am ruined," groaned the other, "and yet I am an honest man."

"Retired from business," said Bonnin, laughing. "Come, confess that you have sold your capital of honesty."

"I, never!" denied the Italian; "I am the victim of a fatal resemblance."

"Yes, I see, they have taken you for a canary and put you in a cage."

"I swear to you that they have mistaken me for another," affirmed Paolo.

Bonnin assumed a doubtful air.

"It is you who take me for another. But you know it's useless to serve each other with the sauce of our misfortunes; it doesn't go down."

Paolo, as gentle as a lamb, drew nearer to the workman.

"And it appears that you have been arrested for a political offence," said he.

"Ah! you know that?" said the other, on his guard.

"Yes," answered Paolo; "but, say, what happened at that manifestation of. . . of". . . .

"You are informed, I hope," sneered Bonnin. "You want the explanation of my affair? Well, if any one asks you, you will answer without hesitation that you know nothing about it."

And, as Paolo began his yarns again, the workman doubled his raillery.

"Ah! you know," said he, "with such a face as yours that doesn't go down. Listen to me: on leaving the 'Heap' one generally enters either the *pègre* or the *rousse*, as you say here. One becomes either a robber or a policeman. You lack frankness, and frankness is a necessary qualification for the liberal professions. You were not cut out for a robber. You were a waiter in a restaurant, you say; make yourself a spy. That too is a way of serving society."

But the keeper again called Paolo.

"Well," he cried; "when are you coming?"

The attendant, our old acquaintance of the Hotel d'Italie, resumed his service and stopped before an old workman bent and broken, who viewed this scene with a sombre look of revolt.

When Paolo took his bowl, he saw that it was full.

"Ah! you swallow nothing?" said he, in astonishment.

"I am not hungry," said the old man, without raising his head.

Bonnin took the bowl, saying joyfully:

"Really! Well, you're in luck. I am your successor."

And, after swallowing the soup, he continued his observations:

"To say that that is nourishing perhaps would be an exaggeration, but then it fills one up. Say, of what is this dish-water made? Not easy to say, I fancy. Let's see. Ah! I know; they pick up refuse from the floors of the markets and boil it in the water of the Bièvre. . . . But no; in that case it would be better; that's not it."

The prisoners, interested and amused, formed a circle around Bonnin, who continued:

"Ah! now I have the receipt! They rinse our bowls at night in warm water, don't they? Well, that makes the *bouillon* for the next day. It is the extract of dirty dishes concentrated and perpetuated."

And he returned his bowl to Paolo.

But the latter, who was vexed with Bonnin, killed his success with a joke.

"What stupid nonsense you talk! Don't you know that the dishes are never washed?"

And he finished his service, happy at having driven his nail into the scoffing and impenetrable workman and riveted it.

"Then," said Bonnin, quitting the circle of his hearers, "one is bound to believe that the cook of the Conciergerie is like the good God and makes something out of nothing."

And after this comparison flattering to Providence, he went to sit down on the bench by the side of the old man.

The latter noticed him and looked at him with pleasure, content at finding a sympathetic countenance in the midst of this repulsive herd.

" Tell me, why are you here? " he asked him.

Bonnin, who had no longer the same reasons to distrust, told the story of his arrest with his natural good-humor.

"Ah! This is how it was. The government asked us for three months' credit. Granted. We pinched our bellies; but now it seems that our debtors of the Provisional are insolvent. So I followed the comrades of my section to a meeting of creditors. The friends cried to our debtors: "Bread or lead! Give us bread or lead.' That did not seem to me exactly logical, and I, a little too consistent, as it seems, shouted: 'No! Give us bread, or we will give you lead.' My variation doubtless did not please everybody, for they grabbed me, and here I am!"

The old man shook his head.

"As for me," said he, "I am here because I have worked so hard all my life that I am no longer good for anything . . . not even to enter the national workshops. For worn-out laborers there is nothing but the poor-house or the 'Heap.' I haven't even held out my hand. Having no longer any lodging, I simply slept outside: vagrancy. The prison! Ah! if we have another revolution and if I am free! My name is Brutus Chaumette, young man, and in February for the last time I showed the stuff I am made of . . . the last time, did I say? Who knows? for I left blood there."

And the workman with the hammer straightened up his lofty stature, roaring like an old lion at the story of his life of poverty.

"At your age, my friend, I was like you, gay, laughing, taking life easily. I earned my living as a machinist. Then I got married. Children came and then died. Can one support brats in Paris? The mother died at last, leaving me a little girl. Not a cent left, debts on every hand, and out of work in the bargain."

Chaumette took the young workman by the arm.

"I pawned my hammer to get milk for the child. And then there was nothing left, and I had to carry the child to the Public Charities . . . abandon it, you understand. Poverty has dropped me lower and lower. I have followed all trades, —sweeper, messenger, drudge. At last I became a porter in a refinery, running about naked as a worm with moulds of boiling sugar, carrying them at full speed through rooms as hot as hell, where I had to hold my breath to keep my lungs from burning, and then running to take a shower under the fountain before returning to this task of the damned. All this to earn sixty cents a day. That's why my hide looks as if I were a hundred, my boy. Ah! you'll see, you'll see, you too . . . later."

The old man remained silent a moment and then resumed:

" You see, all that would be nothing, nothing, I swear to you, if I could only find my poor little Marianne again, my daughter, of whom I have never had any news, in consequence of my well-known ideas. . . . 'Wrong-headed fellow!' they have answered me at the office of administration. They owed me no information; they have given me none. Ah! leave me, young man, I need to isolate myself in my trouble; else I shall again become excited, do stupid things, break and smash everything . . . and there is nothing here but walls. Anger loses its rights."

Bonnin, who had become serious with emotion, shook the old man's hand and went away, screwing up his face to suppress a tear.

"Pshaw! I am not going to weep."

The keeper raised his voice and said, addressing the prisoners:

"Attention, all of you! The roll-call is about to begin. He who is strongest in the jaws shall serve as crier today. You, Hercules of the North."

"Yes," answered the latter, detaching himself from the worst group, where he was telling how, in pretending to be a co mmissioner, he had been arrested in earnest, with his dear friend, the beautiful Sophie.

Paolo, who had just swept the yard, m ade ready to pass the call-sheets to the crier, Hercules, muttering aside:

"A spy is as good as a sheep. As well be doing the work and getting the pay of the police, both without and within. I am going to rise in rank. Better the cat than rat. One does not get arrested at least. One arrests! Ah! Bonnin, you shall pay me yet!"

The Hercules of the North mounted the bench by the side of Paolo, who passed him the sheets as fast as he received them from the jailer.

Bonnin, to distract his thoughts from Chaumette's sad story, approached the door to say his word to those coming in and going out.

The Hercules began his work, reading and bawling:

"Maréchal, Auguste, thirty-seven years. For arraignment. With his effects."

Bonnin saw an individual shake hands with the other prisoners and go out with a little bundle."

"On the way to La Force," exclaimed the young workman . . . "no need of a commissioner . . . . in the berlin of the emigrant. All the rascals are not in it; else you would find my employer there."

The Hercules shouted another name, after having deciphered another sheet.

"Bambouli; Bambouli, Ernest. To be photographed."

As Ernest started, Bonnin made this remark:

"That's what it is to be a handsome fellow. You get your portrait free."

The crier continued:

"Grippart, for examination."

And Bonnin shouted:

" For the inquisition."

"Gamord, Antoine," bellowed the Hercules; "Gamord, twenty-five years; For sentence."

A wretched vagabond left the court-yard, dragging himself painfully along. Bonnin stopped him a moment.

"My poor friend, you will say to the judges: 'Ladies,'—of course, since they wear skirts,—'I am roving, you are sitting; let's change, if you please, for our health.'"

The Hercules called another prisoner.

"Charles Bertrand, former employee in the Department of Public Charities, condemned for the Gavard affair, term finished. At liberty, arms and baggage."

The young workman was about to address this Saint Peter of the paradise of angels when Brutus Chaumette, on seeing this liberated prisoner and hearing his name, recalling the greatest sorrow of his life, his exhausted wife and his abandoned child, ran up to him, crying:

"My daughter!"

"What does this crazy old man want?" said the employee, going out hastily.

"Not so fast," cried Bonnin; "the sooner you go, the sooner you will return."

The crier read his last sheet:

"Robert Joguerre, sentenced to hard labor, *en route!*"

The prisoners looked at each other, but not one of them left the groups.

"Come," cried the jailer, "Joguerre, and immediately; otherwise the strait jacket and iron collar!"

"Oh! gentleness!" exclaimed Bonnin. "The iron collar! it was well worth while to take the Bastille, wasn't it, Chaumette?"

But the old man, sunk into a corner, did not answer, thinking of his child.

At last the convict decided to go out.

"To the galleys," said the jailer, striking him on the back several times with his key. "And now, silence and order. Paolo, watch! I am going to receive the new-comers."

Scarcely had the jailer disappeared when the prisoners began to jump, shout, sing, and scream,—in a word, to do all that was forbidden by the regulations and the jailer, just to disobey the administrative tyranny that condemns men to be mute and motionless.

The confusion of noises made an inhuman clamor in which could be distinguished whistles, cries, calls, questions, answers, and threats, a regular dialogue of the Jardin des Plantes, all the growls and grunts of the animal kingdom.

"Hello, Charlot. . . . Is your father arrested? And your brother? And your sister? Hello! Down with the Bourse! Courage to friends and to men! Death to sheep and to spies! To the gallows with *flicks* and *gaffes!* Death to *vaches* and to *bourriques!—Pi-ouitt.* . . . *Youp-ohu!"*

This concert of curses upon judges (*vaches*), police officers (*flicks*), jailers (*gaffes*), etc., had scarcely ended when leap-frog and other games were begun.

"What a menagerie!" exclaimed Bonnin, clasping his hands with a comical air of astonishment.

"Look out," cried Paolo, "the keeper is coming back. Here are the new arrivals."

In fact, under the arches of the prison sounded at intervals this cry: "Into the common room. Receive!"

"Send!" growled the Hercules, raising the shout so familiar in the jails.

Bonnin thought it incumbent on him to do the honors of the "Heap" to the arrivals.

"Take the trouble to come in," said he, humorously. "There's room for everybody . . . and more. Come in, vagabonds, beggars, and starving men; you have been caught in two turns of the arm, you shall be judged in two turns of the law. Justice by steam. Come in, then, I pray you; you don't have to pay until you go out. Here is the rendezvous of workmen out of work and employers out of business. It is the hospital of abandoned childhood, the asylum of invalid old age, the pound for two-footed beasts. . . . Come in, come in! Nobody is refused. This is hell."

Then he pointed up to the windows of the cells and said:

"See, there are the private boxes reserved for the nobility and the clergy, the manufacturers and the financiers. Come in without fear, gentlemen; we do not mix those who have done everything and those who have done nothing. The *bourgeois*, fond of their ease, have rooms apart. Here as everywhere, respect for the wealthy knaves. The barefooted, the bankrupts, the aristocrats, the loafers, elegant and filthy alike, each finds his place and keeps his rank. The 'Heap' is not made for the 'haves,' but for the 'have-nots.'"

And in truth the poorly-dressed prisoners entered the court-yard, while the more distinguished went up to the rooms reserved for them above.

But Bonnin, intent upon his business, received the new-comers with workmanlike frankness, always hard upon robbers, christening them in his own fashion and according to their appearance.

Catching sight of the first, he asked:

"Say, you, Rigolo, what have you done?"

The fellow confessed his offence complacently.

"I almost knocked down my mother-in-law, and she entered a complaint."

Bonnin gave him a friend's advice.

"Another time you will knock her down completely; she will have nothing more to say; at least that's my opinion. You're in for three weeks."

He passed to the second.

"Your crime, Gredinet?"

"Assault in the night-time," answered the other.

"Ah!" said Bonnin, "that's an affair of three months."

Then to the next:

"And you, poor Azor?"

"I thrashed a policeman in broad daylight," was the answer.

"Poor fellow! you'll get three years. Three weeks, that's easy; three months that's endurable; but three years, that comes hard. Keep your courage up!"

A beggar in rags and tatters came through the door.

"Why do you come here, Crœsus?" inquired Bonnin.

"To look for bread. I stole some yesterday in order to have some today."

Bonnin was silent.

A youngster followed, saying in his vicious little voice:

"My parents want me shut up in a house of correction, and I come here to serve my apprenticeship."

"Your parents are right," declared Bonnin; "they wish to show you a good example. Choose your professors. When you leave here, you will have a sure trade, with no danger of ever getting out of work."

The keeper reappeared, shouting again:

"Attention!"

A man rushed into the court-yard, stumbling over the pavements, hitting his head against the walls, and screaming at the top of his voice:

Forever wine!

He sank upon the bench beside Brutus Chaumette, while Bonnin murmured:

"Whoever sold him his liquor didn't cheat him."

"My daughter!" screamed Father Jean, for it was he whom they committed to prison. . . . "My daughter! . . . . Marie! . . . The letter! . . . The Quai! . . . . The wine! . . . The proof! . . . Lost!"

"He is mad," said Bonnin, addressing Chaumette.

"His daughter! . . . His daughter! . . . Yes, mad, as I shall be soon."

Hoots had greeted the entrance of the rag-picker. Several prisoners ran after him, bawling:

"A drunkard! A drunkard!"

And one of them cried:

"To the fountain!"

The old Chaumette stood up in front of Father Jean, covering him with his body.

"Not a step farther, gang of bandits," he growled.

But a burst of laughter answered him.

Bonnin, appealed to by Chaumette, interposed also, and, taking his place beside him, in a pugilistic attitude, he shouted:

"Well! touch him and see!"

His resolute attitude produced an effect upon the leaders, and, no one making up his mind to strike the first blow, the jailer, called back by the noise, had time to intervene and release Father Jean by dealing heavy blows right and left with his key.

Meanwhile the prison bell rang, announcing the hour for returning to the dormitory.

The prisoners formed a procession in pairs, Jean on Chaumette's arm and repeating: "Marie! my daughter!" while Bonnin brought up the rear, saying to himself:

"Really, this old fellow doesn't seem to be any worse than the other. What can he have done? We shall know tomorrow, when he has slept off his wine, — that is, if his head doesn't ache too hard."

Then, his natural disposition coming to the surface, he added:

"Everybody's looking for his daughter today. No wonder there are so many lost girls."

And with this sally he climbed the stairs of Morpheus.

CHAPTER V.

SAINT-LAZARE.

From the men's prison let us go to the women's, from the Conciergerie to Saint Lazare. It has just struck the hour of noon. The gloomy house is gradually becoming animated. It is visitor's day.

The first to send in his name was Camille Berville.

"Some one already," said the sister to herself, introducing the young man into an enclosure set off by railings.

Camille, in great agitation, saluted the nun, saying:

"Please be good enough, Madame, to send for Mademoiselle Marie Didier."

The sister consulted her book and, starting towards a corridor, cried:

"No. 97, the girl Didier."

"Such a call in such a place," thought Camille sorrowfully. "What a pity! Poor saint in hell!"

Again he addressed the nun:

"My sister, Mademoiselle Didier is innocent, the victim of an error. Show her, then, please, all the consideration compatible with your duty."

The nun sulkily acquiesced.

"I will heed your recommendation, Monsieur," she answered, thinking to herself: "Love! either blind or an accomplice!"

And with affectation she added:

"Here, Mademoiselle."

She went out, while Marie, grown thin and pale, made her entrance, clad in the sombre prison garb.

"Ah! Monsieur Camille," she cried, with enthusiasm.

Camille held her in his arms.

"Marie! dear Marie! Good news, you will be free."

Marie sobbed.

"I am not guilty". . . .

"You guilty!" repeated Camille; "as much so as the child they have killed."

"A poor child that I found and kept without saying anything about it," said Marie, sadly. "Must one boast of a good deed? And they killed the innocent while I was out raising the money for his month's nursing."

"I know your devotion. Jean has told me all, dear victim," answered Camille, eagerly.

Marie continued:

"I could not make a merit of my conduct, and they have made it a crime."

"Do not defend yourself," cried Camille, "generous martyr of the rarest and purest love, that of humanity. What are the goodness and the beauty of the saints beside your own, dear Marie, you, whose religion is self-sacrifice?"

"Oh! thank you for those words of esteem!" exclaimed the young girl.

And Camille said passionately:

"Say rather of love, of deep, unchangeable, eternal love."

"Ah! Monsieur, do not use such words to a poor girl accused as I am. You believe in my honor; that is enough."

"Though you should be condemned, I would believe in you as in the light of day, and I would prove it to all. I would raise you up, fallen and branded in the eyes of the world, but all the higher and more noble in mine, heroine of duty. And, in spite of the law, I would still give you what I have promised you, all that I have left, the name borne by my mother, who was as good as you are. I would take you in my arms and say proudly to the world: Marie Didier no more; I present to you Madame Berville. But never fear, I shall have less to do. This is only an eclipse; your innocence will shine out like the sun, and you will go out of here as radiant to all as to me."

"The same after as before imprisonment?" said Marie, joyfully clasping her hands; "ah! I am too well rewarded."

Camille continued with increasing warmth:

"After, before, always, and everywhere; and I come here to tell you so as if you were at home."

Then, after a pause, he added:

"Now it is I who am not worthy of you, Marie, I who have nothing left to offer you, not even wealth with which to pay for so much virtue."

He looked at her steadily.

"Marie, I am as poor as you."

"O happiness!" she cried, with involuntary joy, as she grasped his hands. But, suddenly repressing her impulse, she said:

"Pardon me, Monsieur!"

"I resemble you at least in that," went on Camille. "On leaving you yesterday I wrote to the baron, breaking off my engagement and calling for an account. His reply informs me of my ruin, while leaving me the choice, he says, between poverty with you and a million with Claire."

He smiled and continued:

"Much obliged! Contentment is better than a million. My choice is made; but it is your turn to show your lofty nature. I was sincere, I swear to you, when

I offered you my fortune; I foolishly supposed that I still possessed it; I have it no longer. I have been obliged to confess as much to you; am I still worthy of you?"

"Ah! even more so, but ". . . .

And Marie stopped, seeming to hesitate.

"But what?" asked Camille.

"After what has happened to us," replied Marie, gravely, "I cannot, must not be your wife."

The surprised young man looked at her sorrowfully.

"What do you say, Marie?"

And Marie answered in a tone of deep sadness:

"Camille, dear Camille, I loved you enough to sacrifice myself for you, but I love you too much to sacrifice you for myself. Be free. I give you back your promise."

"And I refuse it," said Camille. "That would convict both of us of calculation and cowardice. Let us not doubt each other, dear Marie; in spite of all that is blind, fortune and justice, we are united, equals. Your pride can no longer reproach my wealth. There is no longer any difference. I shall be the better for it . . . . remade in your image, living by my own efforts, brave in consequence of your example, well sorted, as Jean would say. Count on me. We will work together. My courage shall emulate yours. Your heart shall lend activity to mine. My hands have known how to spend; they shall learn how to save. I have lost; I will regain. My wife, you have restored me; of a drone you have made a man."

"He takes away my reason," said Marie, in delight.

Camille concluded in a fit of exaltation.

"Love, labor, conscience, these are our possessions! We are rich. No more pleasures, be it so! But happiness,—I have it and keep it. I have chosen, I tell you, and I shall tell them also, without delay and without reply. *Au revoir*, dear wife, and patience! Soon I will take you away from here, glorious, to our humble house, grander than than all the palaces in the world, for happiness will dwell within it."

He kissed her hands, started to go, and returned to kiss them again.

"*Au revoir*," said he, and he went away.

Marie whispered in adoration:

"Noble, noble Camille, always the same. Renouncing fortune to marry me, as he risked his life to defend me! How shall I show my gratitude for so much love? What joy amid my pain! My prison is radiant! How happy I am! Too happy, I fear. Trouble has not killed me; I can die of joy!"

"Marie Didier, some one to see you," said the sister, suddenly returning. And again she went out, to introduce this time Baron Hoffmann.

"Monsieur Hoff". . . . exclaimed Marie, with surprise that was mingled with fear.

"Yes, Marie, I come to see you," said the baron, good-naturedly.

"You, Monsieur?"

"Yes, to serve you, if I can," continued the baron, in a paternal tone.

"I did not hope for that," exclaimed Marie, with a last trace of distrust. "Thank you, Monsieur."

"To save you, if you will," continued the baron.

"I am deserving of your protection, Monsieur," declared Marie, touched and confiding; "I am innocent."

"Innocent or not, it doesn't matter," said the baron, in a voice of cajolery; "I am interested in Jacques Didier's daughter."

But Marie answered with dignity:

"If you mingle a doubt with your benevolence, pray keep it!"

The baron, in a more and more wheedling way, calmed her with a gesture.

"Very well, then, innocent. Unfortunately your conscience will not be your judge. Listen to me carefully, my child; and first excuse the somewhat hasty words uttered in my surprise of yesterday and the rather severe ones spoken in my frankness today. Examine your position and listen to reason. To be and to appear are two different things . . . and all appearances are against you and weigh fatally upon you. Such at least is the opinion of the barrister whom I have engaged to defend you. To him the case seems doubtful, the adoption suspicious, and the murder certain. Though the child were not yours, none the less it has been killed; and some may believe that you got rid of it after obtaining the means to bring it up. Poverty, conduct, *liaison*, victim, you have been getting entangled in a net of disagreeable circumstances; beginning with the ball and concluding with the visits of Camille, which still do you harm; and now, to cap the climax, your relations with the murderer of your father, that rag-picker, Jean."

"He, Monsieur!" cried Marie, explosively; "as much a murderer as I am."

"And arrested as you are," said the baron.

"Ah! was not my own misfortune enough?" groaned Marie, falling back on her chair.

The baron resumed:

"All this, to be sure, is not absolute proof, but serious presumption which makes the crime seem real, if not so, and punishment probable, if not sure. Take care! The law is strict, the examination painful, and justice severe."

"You fill me with despair, Monsieur," exclaimed Marie, losing her head.

"Such is not my intention, but the contrary; and if you will believe in my prudent affection for you and aid my influence by a little confidence, I can do something for you, in fact a great deal; but otherwise nothing."

Marie, as if fascinated, drew closer to the railing.

"I am listening, Monsieur," said she.

"In a case so suspicious, the lawyer further said, the better way is not to defy justice, but to soften it."

"What do you mean by that?"

"Justice is indulgent to the repentant, and forgives those who prove their re-pentance by confession. On this condition you can obtain your pardon."

"Monsieur, I ask neither pardon nor indulgence. I have neither confession nor repentance to make, for I have committed no sin."

"I am only telling you what the lawyer says. And he answers for your freedom at that price."

"At the price of my honor and of truth? Never!"

"Unhappy girl! Fatality is stronger than truth . . . and the shame lies in the crime, not in the confession. Believe me, it is the only way you can save yourself. In the flood in which you are sinking, do not refuse the hand that is offered you. It is a question of an afflictive and ignominious punishment, — death perhaps, im-prisonment at least. Confess, and poverty, youth, imprudence, will plead in your favor . . . but against you if you deny. Silence means punishment; confession, salvation; in short, imprisonment for life or liberty and prosperity. . . Choose."

"Thank you, Monsieur, what you offer me is worse than death," said Marie, firmly.

And she bowed as if to retire.

"Well, she will yield nothing for her own sake; let us see if she will for his," said the baron, aside.

"Very well," he continued aloud; "if you will not save yourself, surely you will save Camille?"

"Monsieur Berville?" exclaimed Marie, eagerly.

A gleam of joy flashed through the baron's eye.

"You love him, do you not?"

"More than all the world."

"And you would save him at any cost?"

"At the cost of my life."

"Well, you are ruining him."

"I?"

"You! For your sake he breaks off a marriage that would be his salvation."

"I will release him if necessary, Monsieur."

"Impossible. He will remain yours as long as he believes in you."

"What! you want more?" exclaimed Marie, in terror.

The baron came straight to the point.

"Yes, the noblest sacrifice a woman can make to the man she loves. Make your-self forgotten to save him. He loves you to the point of sacrificing his fortune for you. Equal, surpass his love and devotion. Confession alone can restore his rea-son and liberty. I esteem you enough to ask it of you. But see, Marie, I no longer want a public confession .... no, only a word for him, in time to save him, and then to be destroyed; a private, provisional word, for him and him alone."

"But he, my God, is everything to me," said Marie, wringing her hands. "He is the only man in the world for whose esteem I would give my life. Others may accuse and condemn me, if I remain innocent to him. Guilty in his eyes! Accuse myself in his presence! No, Monsieur, insist no further. It is beyond my strength. Besides, it is useless . . . he would not believe me."

"He loves you, then, so well?" asked the baron, in a hollow voice.

"As I love him," said Marie simply.

The baron rose with these words:

"Then marry in the prison chapel. It is a favor sometimes granted to prisoners . . . . and be happy!"   .

Marie recalled him, saying in a voice of anguish:

"Ah! strike me in all that I love, but do not rail at my suffering."

"I do not rail," declared the baron, very gravely. "He is ruined, dishonored, lost . . . confronted by imprisonment for at least five years for debts so heavy that they will be accounted robberies. Here is the summons. Claire's dowry would save him, but you are ruining him."

"Ah! you torture me," cried Marie, beside herself.

"A doctor is not an executioner," said the baron, coldly, "and you are strong enough to endure a painful remedy, if it be a salutary one. Stronger and more prudent than Camille, weigh well my last words, spoken as a friend in your interest and his own. Let us suppose, taking the most favorable view, that both of you were free, married, happy. How long would it last? Do you suppose that love is eternal? Alas! no more than beauty. Love without bread is short-lived, and his shorter than another's. I do not give Camille six months before he will mourn the loss of property, rank, society; in short, to regret the sacrifice of the marriage of reason to the marriage of folly."

"You slander him, Monsieur, and if you had heard him". . .

"Slander him? Impossible!" exclaimed the baron. "You esteem him too highly; you judge him by yourself. I, his guardian, know him better than you do, this spoiled child of luxury and fashion, a real butterfly, charming in the summer sunshine . . . . but in winter? He is a fickle fellow, as well as a prodigal and a good-for-nothing; his purse is a basket with a hole in the bottom, like his heart. With twenty thousand dollars a year for his life as a young man, he owes even for his shirts. Judge what sort of a husband he would make. He would send Fortune to the hospital. He has two right hands with which to spend, two left hands with which to keep, and not one with which to earn his gloves. He work, and go hungry in the bargain! Ah! ah! a democrat in theory, but an aristocrat in conduct. He, this high-liver, this prodigal, delicate and voluptuous, indefatigable in idleness, insatiable in pleasure, with all the vices of his class and sex, the egoism of the male and the needs of the rich, minus their reason and power,—why! understand what I say, excess is his rule, abuse his order, leisure his labor, and the superfluous his necessity. He live a life like yours! Nonsense! no more than you could live his! You have not the same tastes, the same habits, scarcely the same language. Give up the comforts of his life for the severities of yours! Never! He may say so, but he deceives hi mself and you! Disabuse your mind! You cannot straighten hunch-backs at his a ge. It runs in the blood, from father to son. Ah! you can endure misery, you poor people who are accustomed to it. But with us it is different; we cannot face it with impunity. Our courage does not survive our love, nor our love our prosperi ty. All goes well as long as passion lasts. But some day or other, and before long, too, love takes wings, poverty remains, and hatred comes. Hatred, do you understand, Marie? On that day your paradise will be a hell, your honeymoon a moon of gall, and Camille your enemy. The husband will avenge the lover's decoys. Unhappy, he will blame you for his misalliance and will curse you for having given you everything and received nothing, nothing but an empty love, an ephemeral joy, a perpetual dowry of ruin and shame, a wife who has been dragged through the courts and branded with that horrible publicity which serves as a stigma."

The voice of a newsboy was heard outside.

"Just out. The arrest of Marie Didier". . . .

The baron calmly looked at his watch, and said to himself:

"Punctual!"

Then aloud and solemnly:

"Listen!"

The boy's voice rang out:

"The working-girl of the Faubourg Saint-Antoine, accused of killing her child, with interesting details. One cent."

"Ah! have mercy, my God!" cried Marie, in delirium; "I am going mad."

"It is the red iron," said the baron ; "the mark cannot be effaced."

"You are killing me," she said, in fear.

The baron went to the door, opened it, and introduced his daughter.

"Ah! come and help me to save them," said he.

And in a low voice:

"Apply the finishing stroke."

Claire, as white as a statue, advanced with repugnance.

"Marie, I have come here with my father to advise you. Being a patroness of this establishment, I wanted to inspect your room and do everything in my power to make your position more endurable". . . .

After a pause and upon an encouraging gesture from the baron, she went on:

"I come to console you, or rather to weep with you . . . . and I hope that in following my father's advice" . . . .

"And you too " said Marie overwhelmed; "you believe me guilty?"

"I believe you unfortunate," said Claire, with embarrassment, "and I desire to put an end to your troubles . . . . but I see no other way . . . . Be resigned!"

"I have already told Monsieur that I was not an obstacle to your happiness," answered Marie, gently.

"My happiness," replied Claire, sadly. " Listen to me as I speak to you, with the self-denial that heaven imposes on us both. Do as I do. Be resigned for Camille's sake. It is not a question of my happiness, but of his; do not envy me; I shall not be a happy and triumphant rival, but a victim more unfortunate than your-self. For you love him and I do not."

"Ah!" exclaimed Marie, with surprise mingled with joy.

Claire continued:

"Yes, we both sacrifice ourselves for a man who does not love me and who loves you. Which of us is the more unfortunate? You leave him and I take him. Whose lot is the harder? Yet I obey, I yield to my father, who desires Camille's safety and your own even at such a cost. Let us unite in self-sacrifice. For wo-men on this earth, in France as in India, everywhere and always, there is nothing but sacrifice. Our lot is to immolate ourselves alive for our lords and masters ". . .

Taking her hands, she concluded :

"Poor sister, let us submit."

And Marie answered, in delirious exaltation :

"Yes, Mademoiselle, we will save him, we will save him! Everything for him!"

And she fled in bewilderment.

"Good, good, Marie!" cried the delighted baron; "both of you are saved."

He added in Claire's ear:

"And so are we; come away."

Claire followed him with a feeling of indescribable horror.

"The torture is over," said she. "Let us carry off our forceps."

CHAPTER VI.

THIRTY THOUSAND FRANCS!

The next morning the bells of the Conciergerie awakened Jean, sobered but overwhelmed. With effort he recalled all the incidents that had led to his arrest, and thought a little of the charge against himself and a great deal of that which kept Marie in Saint Lazare.

He had no time to become absorbed in his reflections, for municipal guards came to take him to the Bureau of Judicial Delegations.

Thus the rag-picker again found himself in the office of the commissary who had arrested Marie. Only the secretary was present.

Jean sat down on a bench, muttering to himself and against himself gross insults interrupted by lamentations for Marie.

At last, unable longer to restrain his overflowing heart, he turned to the indifferent and somewhat astounded guards, and said:

"Ah! yes, my braves, worse than a brute! What beast drinks to ruin its young? And I . . . . what have I done? While my daughter was suffering and weeping, I forgot her and got drunk as of old. A hardened offender, incurable, unpardonable! Nothing has availed,—the death of the one, the imprisonment of the other, or my own oath, — the oath of a drunkard. Who has drank will drink. That's what a man is! A vampire. . . . I have drank the daughter's blood as well as the father's, and mine too. . . . Oh! when she finds out! It is her absence too . . . the chagrin, the pain, the trick, a diabolical temptation. Satanic wine! Scarcely can I remember."

And rising:

"To think that I had the proof in my hand, the salvation of my daughter, my life. . . . I had procured it so successfully from the old woman . . . and then to restore it to the old man! It is too much. Wine has stolen everything from me, head and heart, and I have lost everything. . . . Marie as well as Jacques . . . and Jean. As far as I am concerned, it is all right. So much the better, yes, but her! Good people, aid me! What shall I do? What can I say now? Without proof! A man like him accused by a man like me! Rag-picker against banker . . . . a penny against a pound. . . . No weight! But come, come, it's no time to whine. Some way must be found to save the girl who saves others. Where is justice? Where are the police? Where is the good God? She must live or I must die! They cannot tear my chil d from me, my heart. They cannot condemn the innocent for the guilty, whatever the devil may do". . . .

He was interrupted by the sudden ope ning of the door of the private office, The commissary entered and gave his notes to the secretary.

"Ah! Monsieur commissary!" cried Jean.

"Be silent!" said the commissary, sitting down; "speak only in answer to my questions."

But Jean kept on.

"Monsieur commissary, you arrested yesterday a poor innocent."

"Come, no evasions," said the commissary.

Jean continued:

"Marie Didier". . . .

"Speak for yourself," said the commis sary, roughly. "You are accused of having murdered and robbed, on the Quai d'Austerlitz, twenty years ago, Jacques Didier, M. Berville's collector."

"Monsieur, I swear to you that she is innocent."

The commissary grew angry.

"That is not what you are asked. Do not meddle with the affairs of others. It is a question of yourself."

"Innocent as the poor dead child," insisted Jean. "I will prove it."

"Don't you hear what is said to you?" exclaimed the magistrate, rising.

"Yes, yes," said Jean, with his fixed idea.

"You are accused of murder," repeated the commissary.

"All right!" acquiesced Father Jean.

"Followed by robbery". . . .

"All right! all right! my commissa ry, I will justify myself, that's all right! Don't disturb yourself about me; there is no hurry on that score. It's for her that we need to hurry, for her, waiting to be freed."

"You exhaust my patience," cried the commissary, angrily. "It is you, Jean, you alone, who are in question here."

"We will see about that later, my magistrate. Let us go ahead, if you please. They want to ruin her, I want to save her. They accuse me now in order to upset my plans. The old wolf throws off the dogs. . . I know your trick, baron. But I do not lose the scent. It is not a question of me, I tell you, but of her."

And with feeling he added:

"Remember, Monsieur, it is already two d ays, two centuries, that she has been in prison, that I have not seen her, that they prevent me from seeing her, because she is not my daughter. Ah! if I have not the honor to be her father, I have the duty. Children of the heart are well worth the others. They are never abandoned, Monsieur."

"Once more, that is not the question, and ". . .

"Beg pardon, my magistrate; don't get angry. I would not like to fail you in her case or mine. I repeat, I ramble; that I know very well. . . but, see here, I tell you squarely that I will not defend myself until she has been disposed of. If I did not first save my daughter, my family, all that is left to this poor old heart of sixty years, it would not pay to live."

And the rag-picker continued passionately:

"If I do not save her, Monsieur, I have committed all the murders, all the robberies, all the crimes, of the Code. Have no fear, I am guilty; I have done everything, killed, pillaged, what you will. To save her I will suffer myself to be accused, condemned, executed, for then I shall not have robbed her; but I would guillotine myself if I should fail to save her."

"This devil of a man speaks in a tone that moves me in spite of myself," said the commissary, aside.

And, aloud, he added:

"But how can you prove her innocence, since she has confessed?"

"Confessed!" exclaimed Jean.

The commissary exhibited a letter.

"Yes, in this letter written to her protector, M. Hoffmann, and seized in the clerk's office in the prison."

Jean tried to take the letter quickly.

"It is not true," he cried.

"Wretch, what are you doing?" said the commissary, severely, as he drew back the letter out of Jean's reach.   •

"Some new trick!" said Jean, "some sacrifice, some stupidity that I don't understand! But it's false, my magistrate. Her protector, he! Oh! come, come! She is so weak, you see, so good, so simple . . . . a lamb. She has no defender. They have got around her in some way. They have played it well on Father Jean! But, though she confesses, I do not confess. Believe me, hear me, help me, Monsieur. I know the guilty ones. I had the proof, a genuine proof which they have taken from me, the monsters, — an infernal stroke. If I should name them without proof, you wouldn't believe me. I want proof. . . . I will have it."

He stopped a moment, and then suddenly broke out again.

"I have it! I've got them. . . . Yes, I see the way already."

"Really? What is it?" asked the magistrate, in surprise.

"Lend me thirty thousand francs," exclaimed Jean, impetuously.

"What! thirty thousand francs?" repeated the astounded commissary. "Are you mad?"

"Not yet. Can you get them for me?"

"But you are laughing at me?"

"The government can easily find thirty thousand francs for her," said Jean, confidently.

"Enough! We are not here to joke."

"Ah! Monsieur, I do not joke," said Father Jean, sorrowfully; "I have no desire to do so. One doesn't make sport of a child in prison."

"For the last time, speak seriously, or else ". . . .

"But I tell you seriously that I must have thirty thousand francs to save her."

"Well, you are either a lunatic or a knave, and I will teach you". . . .

"Oh! fear nothing," Jean hastened to protest. "I don't want to run away with . . . and her, then?"

And he continued pathetically:

"Once more, Monsieur, if I should not save her, I would ask your permission to die before she. . . . But I would not want the miserable sum of thirty thousand francs for not saving virtue itself. You will not refuse me the money. . . I will not spend it . . . you shall hold it in your hands all the time."

Again the magistrate interrupted him, seeming to be interested.

"But what do you wish to do with the money?"

"Ah! that's my secret, I don't dare to think of it myself. I'm afraid that I may injure it by breathing; for it's the only means left to me. But you shall come with me, you or your agents, as you please; you can have your whole force follow me."

"Decidedly, this is some game, either to escape or to gain time. Let us end the matter."

And, designating Jean to the guards, the commissary said:

"Take this man to prison."

Jean fell on his knees.

"Ah! Monsieur, I never prayed to any one in my life, and I am at your feet. I supplicate you with both hands, on both knees. Hear me! In the name of all that you hold dearest, I am telling you the pure truth. The garment does not make the monk. One is not guilty because he is poor, or innocent because he is rich. She who casts away her child goes to the altar; she who picks it up goes to prison."

The commissary made a sign to the guards, and they seized Jean.

"Ah! these people of justice! Like justice, they are deaf and blind!"

And in a heart-rending voice he added:

"Monsieur, Monsieur, I hold you responsible for any misfortune that may befall two poor innocents."

But suddenly he uttered a cry of joy. Camille had just entered.

"Ah! salvation!" he cried. "You certainly have thirty thousand francs at your disposal, Monsieur?"

"Why?" asked Camille.

"You still love Marie?"

"I forgive her."

"What! Then you believe her guilty?" exclaimed Jean,

And Camille answered, in a voice of anguish:

"I wish I could still doubt, after her confession". . . .

"He too!" said Jean; "love as well as justice. She has only me left. Ah! if I should fail her. . . . No matter, are you willing to save her?"

"Willing? Her confession at least redeems her fault and merits forgiveness."

"Ah! what does he say?" cried Father Jean, with mingled grief and indignation. Camille addressed the commissary.

"Yes, Monsieur," said he, "I come to speak for her. You are one of those just men who cannot be seduced by gold, but by misfortune . . . and what misfortune worthier of pity! For in spite of the confession, I still doubt the crime. Do as I do, Monsieur; doubt also, in spite of this letter, dictated in some moment of madness. Poor girl, her imprisonment has crazed her. . . That's it. Oh! before believing her, I must see her, speak to her, know the solution of this cruel enigma. The baron has visited her; there has been some fraud, some wrongful pressure brought to bear, in view of a certain marriage, upon her, upon her noble heart, her love, and her devotion to me. She has sacrificed herself to release me, to save me from ruin. This will prove the explanation, I am sure. Yes, Monsieur, I swear it; I doubt no longer; I am familiar with guilty natures, with ruined women; and I declare that she is honor itself, incarnate sacrifice; this confession is the best proof of it; she is the worthy daughter of a brave servant of my father, and I cannot tell you all the esteem that she merits. No, she is not guilty. It isn't possible. Day is not night. This old man is right. He alone appreciates her as she deserves. He believes. Ah! pardon me, dear Marie, for having doubted for a moment. Thank you, Father Jean, for having restored my faith, my hope, my love."

Jean, who had devoured Camille's words, embraced him passionately.

"Good! That's it! You are right . . . yes, she is an angel on earth . . . and I will prove it in spite of the letter."

"You, my friend?" exclaimed Camille, with joy.

Jean returned to his queer request.

"Give me . . . no, lend me . . . no, entrust to me thirty thousand francs for a day, an hour, a minute, and I will show her to both of you as white as snow."

"If that's all," exclaimed Camille, enthusiastically; "why, I would give the world for her. I will get the money, I will have it."

"Go after it, then," cried Jean, impatiently, and pacing back and forth.

"Their confidence is telling on me," said the commissary to himself.

Jean led away the departing Camille.

"But not a word there, at the baron's! Keep on in your present course, with a melancholy air, and pretend that you are going to marry the other. Don't let them suspect anything. Consent to everything! And tomorrow I will restore you your wife and recover my daughter . . . provided Monsieur allows me," he added, humbly bowing to the commissary.

"Well, all right!" said the latter, coming to a decision. "I have seen so many odd things in the exercise of my functions. I must reject no method of getting at the truth."

Camille shook hands with the rag-picker, and started off on a run.

"Ah! thank you! thank you! Monsieur commissary," said Jean. "You have done well! Justice for all! But, Monsieur, one more favor. Let me speak and act in my own fashion. Trust to me to the end . . . we have cunning enemies to deal with, you see. You are very sharp, I know.... but, pardon me,—I mean no offence,—in this case I am even sharper than you are. I see this matter more clearly than any one else; I see it from the heart. So promise that you will not interfere with me, and I swear that I will deliver to you three guilty parties for two innocent ones . . . a good bargain for a just man like yourself! My poor daughter, I love her so dearly that I shall succeed. I shall leave Vidocq entirely in the shade."

And kissing the commissary's hands, he added:

"Till tomorrow, Monsieur! And may your kind heart reward you!"

He returned to his place between the two guards, and, taking their arms, at a gesture of the commissary he went out, leading them after him.

CHAPTER VII.

THE GUNS.

. Father Jean went back to the Conciergerie as if he were going home, free from anxiety and alcohol, balanced, solid, full of confidence, — himself again, in a word.

He went to bed and rose, satisfied with what he had done and with what he was going to do, filled only with impatience to finish.

Chaumette and Bonnin, meeting him in the yard again, could not get over their surprise at the change.

"So, it seems that things are going better," cried the young workman making room for him in the sunshine beside the old man.

The latter inquired in his turn.

"Then you have found your daughter again?"

"Indeed I have," said Jean; "found her and saved her, or, at least, as good as that. I am only waiting now for the pleasure of seeing her again. Oh! my heart is big with joy."

"So much the better! . . . But that is not the case with me," said Chaumette.

"Let's hear, what is it?" said the rag-picker, moved. "Who knows? I am having a streak of success. . . . Speak! If I could serve you. I make a specialty of salvations, good and bad; have confidence. We are of the same age". . .

"And have the same misfortune. . . Well," added the old workman, "I too have a daughter . . . but the Public Charities alone know where she is, for I had to abandon her ". . . .

"Abandon her!" said Jean, severely.

"Oh! it was not my fault. It was necessary. Her mother carried away the milk to her grave. If I could have nourished her with my blood.". . .

"I know," murmured Father Jean, softened. "Marie too came near falling into their clutches. . . Yes, those Public Charity people, I know them . . . they are executioners! What's to be done?"

"My poor Marianne," groaned Chaumette, sorrowfully.

"Marianne!" repeated Bonnin; "a famous name, my faith!"

"Yes, Marianne Chaumette," repeated the old man. - "But they must have rechristened her before burying her."

Bonnin, touched by the old man's pain, gave voice to a hope.

" Bah ! it is only mountains that never meet. Perhaps by taking steps . . . to-day, under the Republic ". . . .

" The Republic !" exclaimed Chaumette, bitterly ; " still and always ' the best of Republics.' Yes, I have taken all the steps and been to all the Charity offices. And nothing . . . it is finished . . . I shall never see my child again. And now I have but one idea in my head."

" What's that ?" asked Bonnin.

" I returned to the pawnshop under the Republic as under Royalty ; and once more I was obliged to pawn my hammer and even my two guns ". . . .

" Two guns ? "

" Yes, I had two after February. One I snatched from a royal guard in July, and the other from a municipal in February."

" I understand," answered Bonnin.

" Well, I should like to redeem them before dying and make use of them a last time against those who are starving the people and ruining the Republic. For, at the rate at which we are going, the Empire is not far off. The faubourgs are already full of friends of the pretenders, who are gradually taking from us the consciousness of our rights and duties. The people's heads are as empty as their bellies. Hunger makes one yawn and sleep. . . . Poverty leads to beggary more than to the barricade. . . . Our masters know it well. . . . But never mind ! There are not only the resigned . . . there are also the desperate. Ah ! if I were only out and in possession of my pawned articles."

" You shall have them, be sure of it," exclaimed Bonnin, enthusiastically. " As soon as I am out, I shall go at once to work ; and out of my first fortnight's pay I will redeem your things . . . and share them with you."

Brutus Chaumette looked him in the eye for a moment, and then drew a pawn-ticket from his pocket and handed it to him.

" There," said he, simply.

Bonnin took the paper, put it in his pocket, and observed :

" But say, that's not all. Where and how shall we meet later ? "

" True," said Chaumette ; " I am under arrest as a vagabond. I shall be sentenced to prison, and, after the expiration of my term, I shall be sent to the poor-house."

" I have it," exclaimed Father Jean, who, though thinking of Marie, had heard the father of Marianne ; " you have no abiding-place ; that's the reason of your arrest, isn't it ? "

" Yes ; what then ? "

" Tomorrow I shall be free ; I will give your name instead of mine to my janitor, and abandon my quarters to you. I warn you that they are not very fine."

Chaumette looked at the rag-picker in surprise.

" And you ? " said he.

"I? I?" said Jean; "don't trouble yourself about me. Here, there is your address. You will give it to the judge. They will make inquiry. . . . And that will go as on wheels. You have a residence; then you have committed no offence!"

" Thank you, I refuse," said Chaumette.

" And your guns, my brave old man?"

" True," said Chaumette. "I accept, but not for long."

Jean, for sole reply, pressed his hands.

Just then the voice of the crier was heard.

"Jean, rag-picker!"

" They are calling me. Victory! Very sorry ; . ; no, excuse me, very glad to leave you in order to save you. But I will see you again soon," he cried, as he started off.

Then reconsidering and returning, he said to the old workman:

"Stay, I forgot; there 's the key; it 's the top floor, the attic. Your residence is found; Bonnin will look out for the rest."

The young man applauded.

" Bravo and thank you, old man," he exclaimed.

And turning toward Chaumette as Jean went off, he added:

"I told you that he had something better than wine in his belly. Ah! the worthy man! There you are, saved!"

" Yes," sighed Chaumette. " But she!"

And taking his grey head in his worn hands, he began to dream again of his lost child, thus satisfying in thought his unquenched thirst for paternity; that love so natural, so instinctive, so intense, so human, considering the length of human infancy, so imperious and so tenacious, which tortured old men deprived of posterity by their fault or their poverty, just punishment of the rich bachelor and iniquitous torment of the poor, in a society founded on family and property.

CHAPTER VIII.

PARADISE FOR SALE.

Madame Potard, shaken by the baron's threats and without news from Jean was getting ready to surrender her Paradise to another *maker of angels.*

Seated before her desk, she wrote and soliloquized thus :

"Announcement. Will be sold for cash, because of departure from the city, a midwife's establishment, enjoying a large and fashionable patronage, very profitable, and in a quiet neighborhood. The books alone show a business of 25,000 francs a year, to say nothing of the transactions that do not appear on them. Madame Potard's name may remain on the sign, if desired. Address the Bureau of Small Advertisements."

She rang, and continued her soliloquy :

"Whether the business is sold or not, I have enough to live on, and I save myself without waiting for the rest. Farewell, Paris, rag-picker, and banker !"

The servant entered, announcing :

"Monsieur Jean !"

"Ah ! let him come in," exclaimed Madame Potard, joyfully.

Then, aside :

"What luck ! I was beginning to despair."

She quickly folded up the note, thrust it into her pocket, and rose to receive the rag-picker.

Father Jean entered merrily, accompanied by a person of doubtful aspect, though well kept, — heavy side-whiskers, heavy gold chain, and heavy cane.

"Good day, Madame Potard?" said Jean, amiably.

His companion saluted her more graciously still.

Madame Potard's face darkened a little at sight of the stranger, in spite of his gold chain.

She expected that Jean would come alone.

"Good day, gentlemen," said she, coldly ; "what can I do in your service?"

"It is in your service that I return, Madame," said Jean ; "you see, I am a man of my word."

"Of your word?" repeated Mme. Potard, pretending not to understand.

"Yes, I come to settle," declared Jean.

"To settle?" repeated Mme. Potard, as innocently as if she had just fallen from the moon.

Father Jean resumed:

"Why, yes, the trick is played."

"What trick?"

"Suspicious creature! you can speak before him," said Jean, pointing to the stranger. "He is acquainted with the affair."

His companion, in corroboration, exhibited a pocket-book full of bank-bills.

"What affair?" said Mme. Potard again, still on her guard.

"Oh! not so many airs," exclaimed Jean. "You needn't be afraid, I tell you. Hold out your hand; we bring you your share."

"My share?"

Then Jean said abruptly:

"You refuse? . . . . So much the better! Good evening, Madame."

He turned on his heel, took his comrade by the arm, and started for the door.

Madame Potard ran after them.

"Eh? What is it? What did you say?"

"Nothing! Nothing! We will keep the whole," declared Jean.

Madame Potard was sweating big drops.

"One moment!" she exclaimed. "Just listen; I did not understand, on seeing you two so unexpectedly; I did not know that Monsieur. . . . . Ah! he is connected with the affair?"

"It was necessary, you see," insinuated Jean, retracing his steps. "I was not presentable, in my pitiful costume. For a baron, it requires a *Mossieu*; see, this gentleman is a *Mossieu*, and a substantial one."

"Oh! Madame understands," said the substantial *Mossieu*.

Jean continued:

"So I took a partner . . . . with a black coat, as capital. A black coat and gloves, — with those everything is all right."

"I perceive," said Madame Potard, still anxious.

"We come, then, dear Madame, to make an honest division of the money," said Jean, emphasizing the last word.

The word money had its usual effect upon the midwife.

"All right," said she, thoroughly enlightened. "Better late than never. Be seated, then."

Jean turned to his companion.

"Give her her share."

"Her share and my heart," said the partner, gallantly taking Madame Potard around the waist.

Madame Potard quickly released herself, saying:

"Oh! come, come!"

And seriously:
" How much ? "
Then joyfully :
"And to think I had given you up I May one offer a drop to these gentlemen ? "
" No, thank you," said Jean.
Madame Potard, however, went to her table on which a case of liquors stood,
saying at the same time :
" And the share ? . . . Is it large?"
" Why, yes, it is fat," said Jean ; "but with three of us . . . that cuts the slices
down a bit."
" How much then?" exclaimed Madame Potard, in a disappointed tone and seem-
ing already to regret the three full glasses.
Jean replied emphatically :
" We have drawn from the baron thirty pretty notes like those he paid to you.
Your health, Madame Potard."
He made a pretence of drinking, but, turning around a little, he emptied the
little glass into his hat.
" Thirty thousand francs I " cried Madame Potard, disappointed.
Jean, pretending to misunderstand, repeated the sum, dwelling on each syllable :
" Yes, thir . . . ty . . . thou . . . sand francs I "
" It is little," exclaimed Madame Potard, with an expression of disdain. " Is
that really all you got? You rob me I "
" Ah I Madame Potard, for whom do you take us? Your associates I "
" Then fifteen thousand francs for me," declared Madame Potard in a tone that
seemed final.
" Ten, my good woman; there are three of us," said Jean, by way of correction.
But the midwife would not listen.
" Not at all I Nothing of the kind I I want fifteen thousand francs. I did not
agree to a division into three parts. You said nothing to me about it; it was on
your own responsibility that you took a partner. So much the worse for you.
That's your lookout. I gave the letter for a half, not for a third. I want my
half."
" Greedy creature I And what about us then?"
" Divide with the other; that is your affair."
" But we shall have nothing but the crumbs."
Madame Potard was inflexible.
" It is not my fault, really," said she. " It has not brought enough. You have
managed it badly. I thought you were more cunning. With such a secret you
ought to have broken the bank."
Jean drew nearer, at the same time making to his companion an imperceptible
sign that escaped Madame Potard.

"We did our best," he declared.

And, lowering his voice, he asked:

"Then you really got but twenty thousand francs for putting the child into paradise."

"Hush!" exclaimd the frightened midwife.

"All right, let us say no more about it," said the rag-picker in a conciliatory tone. "I don't wish to argue the point; perhaps I should lose. After all, it is just, and if we were not honest with each other. . . . So no more chicanery. A bargain's a bargain. My friend and I will waive this point, and arrange between ourselves as we can. You must have half," he continued, while the unknown drew the notes from the pocket-book and passed them to him one by one. "There you are!"

"That's all right," said Madame Potard, softening down. "The good friends. Received!"

Nevertheless she counted the notes again.

"Fifteen! That is the account. Minus two, the burned ones. . . . I want those also."

The rag-picker feigned anger.

"Ah! You ask so much! . . . There, glutton, eat the whole and die," said he, taking the rest of the notes and almost cramming them into the midwife's mouth.

"Come, let us not get angry," said she. "In business, profit and loss, you know."

She ran to put the precious papers in her desk, mumbling:

"Twenty-eight and fifteen, forty-three."

Jean, hearing her, said with a laugh:

"What a mathematician! A nice little sum for a rainy day."

"Not enough, all the same," sighed Madame Potard. "Appetite comes with eating."

"And yet it will be all," declared the rag-picker, with an air of regret. "Fare-well, baskets. No way of returning to the plate without a spoon. I had to give up the proof for the cash, the letter against the money. The bird will sing no more."

"How do you know, booby?" said the midwife, nudging him with a mysterious air of superiority. "As well be hanged for an old sheep as a lamb."

Jean pricked up his ears.

"Oh!" said he, "if you still have something left."

"A little, my nephew. I have kept a pear, in case I should be thirsty."

"Far-seeing woman! Seek and you shall find," concluded Father Jean, seeing her start for her desk.

"Yes, prophet, two trumps!" replied Madame Potard, taking a paper from a drawer. "By way of precaution, I had the daughter's letter photographed. I gave the copy to you and kept the original myself. See!"

Jean pretended to succumb.

" Ah I for that stroke I marry you I "

" The original is well worth the copy, isn't it ? "

" Much more I Bravo I A pair royal I Another thirty thousand francs at least. He will sing the entire opera."

" Yes, my orchestra-leader," exclaimed the triumphant midwife. " And always half for me I "

" Ah I this time, my queen, it is different," objected Jean. " Now there are three of us. We must consult the wishes of Monsieur."

And turning to the *associate*, who, during this whole scene, had been dumb but not deaf, he asked:

" What do you say ? "

" Yes, Monsieur, what do you say? " echoed the midwife.

The stranger, laying his hand on her shoulder, answered :

" Madame Potard, in the name of the law I arrest you for the crime of infanticide and as the accomplice of Baron Hoffmann."

Madame Potard fairly leaped, while the officer ran to the door.

" What's this ? I ? "

" Yes, you, who have confessed, proved, given all the proofs," shouted Jean. " For here they are, all in hand and in this drawer, letter and notes, eight of which have the holes made by my hook. See I " he continued, addressing the police agent, who called two other officers and entrusted the midwife to their care.

The agent took possession of the contents of the desk.

" It isn't true I It isn't true I " screamed Madame Potard, struggling. " Ah I my notes, my dear notes I "

" No noise," said the agent. " We will decamp without drums or trumpets. You have only to attenuate your crime by serving justice against your accomplices."

In spite of the officers' hold, Madame Potard rushed at Jean, shaking both her fists at him.

" Ah I traitor I spy I it is you I "

The rag-picker bowed in a unique fashion, saying:

" What, no more love? Yes, rascal, the game is over. You will make no more angels. Paradise for sale I "

And the officers took the woman away.

CHAPTER IX.

THE COUNCIL.

A very big fish for a police commissary's net was the banker, Baron Hoffmann; and, even under the Republic, the magistrate hesitated to arrest a prince of the stock exchange, not daring to treat him like a vulgar assassin without first consulting his superiors.

So he went to notify the prosecuting attorney of the Republic, who in his turn was unwilling to take the responsibility of so important a step and sent him to the Minister of Justice, who referred him to the entire government.

In the same way Barabbas passed from Anne to Caïphas and from Caïphas to Pilate, before being arrested as the Just.

The council was engaged in the discussion of three serious, complex, and connected questions, the combined solutions of which were destined unhappily to bury the Republic.

These questions were :

1. The Roman war.
2. The national workshops.
3. The return of Prince Louis Napoleon Bonaparte.

On the first question the government had decided to send the mayor of Paris, Armand Marrast, to Gaëte to find the Pope and bring him to France, pending his reestablishment at Rome.

Which would favorably dispose the priests toward the Republic.

On the second, it had been decided that the national workshops should be abolished.

Which would favorably dispose the employers toward the Republic.

On the third point, two good friends of the prince, Jules Favre and Louis Blanc, who had Bonapartist leanings from sentiment and even from family, — at least Louis Blanc, — in spite of the secret admission made to them by the prisoner of Ham that he wanted the Empire, spoke in favor of the pretender, guaranteeing his republicanism and saying that his adhesion and return would result in the salvation of the Republic.

At this moment the Minister of Justice introduced the commissary of police, who propounded the fourth great question of the day, the affair of the banker, Baron Hoffmann.

At first the council was half incredulous and half scandalized, but in face of the proofs unfolded one by one by the commissary, it was necessary to come to a decision, solve the question in one way or another, execute the law, or else evade it by conniving at the escape of the accused.

Crémieux, a Jewish lawyer, full of metallic affinities and Minister of Justice, was for connivance.

Goudchaux, another Jew, Minister of Finance, was obliged to hold the same opinion through *esprit de corps.*

The Minister of War, Cavaignac, for several reasons obeyed a similar conscience. A sort of soldier-monk; a Catholic republican; dreaming of the presidency of the Republic by the grace of the Pope, to whom Hoffmann acted as banker through the Abbé Ventron; having married the daughter of a financier, — he was the rising sun, the hope of the bank, the sword of capital against threatening labor, a dictator readier to execute starving laborers than murderous bankers.

But Lamartine, one of the troubadour knights of the Restoration, puritanized also by his " History of the Girondists," had a horror of Turcarets, like the noble spendthrift that he was.

So he preluded against the banker with one of those guitars that he played so well. He sang equality before the law, human conscience, republican justice, etc., — the whole sonata of rights and duties, — concluding democratically that it is not the same with rascalities as with negatives, and that two crimes cannot make an innocent man, even of a banker-baron.

Albert, the workman, Louis Blanc, the Socialist, and the Jacobin, Ledru, formed a chorus with the poet; and in spite of reasons of State, Church, and Bank, in spite of the three-fold interest of strong-box, altar, and throne, in spite of the highest political, religious, and plutocratic considerations, by a majority of one vote the council of the provisional government decided that the banker, Baron Hoffmann, this extraordinary culprit, must submit to the common law, and that justice must take its course.

CHAPTER X.

INTO THE BASKET !

Let us return to the house of the banker, Baron Hoffmann.

Claire has yielded. She has placed her heart upon the altar, sacrificing herself to save her father's bank and honor. Her mind is made up. A victim, if not an accomplice, she will marry Camille.

The day of the wedding, of the holocaust, has arrived.

In an elegant boudoir of the former Hotel Berville, the daughter of the baron is seated before a swinging mirror, while two maids arrange her bridal costume.

All about her exhales a festival perfume. Through the half-drawn portiere at the back, the illuminated greenhouse and garden shine like a firmament.

Claire, resigned and swallowing her tears, abandons herself mechanically to the care of the two *soubrettes*. She will go to the very end.

The baron entered, with a beaming face. He held in his hand a copy of the "Official." Embracing his daughter, and forcing his voice to a caressing tone because of the presence of the maids, though he did so with some difficulty, he said to her :

"So, then, this is the day, dear rebel. How obstinate the female mind! Surrendered, at last!"

He kissed her again.

"Admirable costume," he added.

Then aside :

"Sparkling stone, flaming robe . . . . let us complete the dazzling spectacle."

He opened his journal and said :

"Claire, listen to this! 'Society Gossip: This evening, by privilege, at midnight, will be celebrated at the chapel of the Roman Embassy, by Monseigneur the Archbishop of Paris, the marriage of Mlle. Claire Hoffmann, daughter of Baron Hoffmann, banker to the Papal Court.' What do you say to that? what a festival! It is complete! Hurry your maids, and be ready ; in an hour friends will be here. I will return."

Claire, before her mirror, wearing her dress, crown, and bouquet of marriage, of martyrdom, had listened without hearing.

When her father, having finished his reading, started to go out, she cried anxiously :

" Where are you going. Do not leave me. I don't know why, but I tremble." She rose and ran toward him.

The baron retraced his steps, and, in a low voice and a tone which he intended to be gay, he exclaimed:

" Bah! the emotion of the day, dear sensitive creature! Courage! One last stroke of the oar and . . . in an hour we shall be in port. I have burned your letter, I have the girl's confession, and, to complete the luck, I have her father's pocket-book, a fatal proof against her old knight."

" Ah! my God!" exclaimed Claire, " another victim."

" The last," said the banker.

" When will end this defiance of justice? An accomplice in a new crime! I will not, I cannot. You put too much upon me. . . . I succumb."

" They or we!" declared the baron, implacable in his logic. " It is necessary. Be firm! Audacity to the end. And this time it is the end."

" It is hell!"

" It is the salvation of all, believe your father and friend. I swear to you that I will save them after ourselves. Have I not succeeded in everything? No more risks, no more frights. I am going to make sure of the departure of the midwife. Calm yourself. . . . Make haste. . . . I will return."

And with these words he went out by a side door opening into his private apartments.

Claire remained alone with her maids, nailed to the spot where her father had left her, lost in a mortal presentiment.

" It is salvation," she resumed in a very low voice. " But at what price! Great God! To hide a fault under a crime and pile victims on victims . . . and myself the last one . . . after the others, I decked today for the altar . . . the last sacrifice. Ah! I dare not look myself in the face, I am afraid . . . and these mirrors reflect me everywhere."

She took a few steps, trying to flee from her own image.

" Rosine, my veil!" said she to one of the servants. " Quick! Folded and pulled down."

" Yes, Mademoiselle," answered Rosine, running to find the veil.

Claire walked up and down in agitation and impatience.

" It seems to me," she murmured, " that my secret is written in letters of blood upon my brow, and that it will be less easily seen under these folds ". . . .

Rosine and her companion came to put on the veil.

" Cover me more, I say."

Then suddenly, as if bewildered:

" Is there not a spot on this veil? "

" A spot!" exclaimed Rosine, astonished.

" Yes, a red point there."

"No, Mademoiselle; it is the reflection of the curtains."

"Ah! yes, you are right . . . leave me!"

The attendants obeyed and withdrew.

"I shall betray myself," cried Claire, "my head, my heart, are bursting. . . . . this fatal secret will out in spite of me. It is escaping by force like those poisons that break the glass that contains them. . . . I see it; I hear it cry, ask for a cradle, a grave, change this veil into a shroud, this crown into a pillory."

Then, resolutely;

"Visions! Chimeras! . . . to be forgotten like the others. No more anguish! I must share my father's ferocious delight in struggle, the atrocious intoxication of success. Come! audacity to the end! This secret is under ground. No one knows it . . . can know it. Crime is for the poor! we are rich. . . The Didiers for the Hoffmanns! I am the worthy daughter of my father. We are hunters by race. Let us howl with the wolves! A curse upon the weak! Salvation is for the strong!"

. . . .

In one of the adjoining rooms were exposed to the gaze of a crowd of guests invited to these wedding festivities the numerous bridal presents which the wealthy and vain friends and customers of the banker-baron had made to his daughter.

Water goes always to the river.

It was a dazzling spectacle of luxury and art. One would have said that it was a collection of master-pieces of the goldsmith's art at an international exposition.

Necklaces, bracelets, brooches, and rings, ornaments of all styles and all prices in caskets that were jewels themselves, — all that the great jewelers of the day, the Meurices and the Odiots, all that the rarest stones, cut, set, and mounted in the finest metals, could offer in the way of perfection, with the names of the most illustrious and most august givers.

The Pope had sent the golden rose, — an exceptional honor reserved for queens, — and his blessing, more precious still.

The Nuncio had sent a silver cross studded with diamonds.

And the Abbé Ventron, the dear confessor, a brilliant red ruby, representing the heart of Jesus.

The ex-king of the French had forwarded from London an India cashmere; and the ex-queen what is called a household article, — a tea service.

The English ambassador, a practical man, had presented a silver gilt chamber-vessel.

All the nobility and wealth of Paris were represented there by the entire scale of precious stones, — yellow, blue, green, emeralds, turquoises, topazes, etc.

Then came the gifts of Camille's friends.

Loutchard, among others, had contented himself with presenting his wife. . . . a pearl of friendship, he said.

Loiseau had offered the bouquet of orange-flowers.

As for Gripon, his gift shone by its absence.

There was everything besides, as is the case with those who can want for nothing, from toilet articles to kitchen utensils,—and the smallest lot among them would have been a dowry for a Didier,—each object being surveyed, handled, criticised, and estimated according to the taste of the amateurs. . . .

The last pin had been put in the bride's veil.

Then Laurent entered the *boudoir* and said respectfully:

"They are waiting for Mademoiselle in the grand *salon.*"

Claire turned round, and surfeited though she was with the palatial luxury of the paternal dwelling, she felt a dizziness of pride, and staggered again under the spell.

The *portière* at the back, drawn aside by Laurent, allowed a view of the apartments infinitely multiplied by the reflection of skilfully placed mirrors. Women in full dress and lackeys in livery were streaming with gold, flowers, feathers, and jewels under the chandeliers; here and there the men, sober and stiff in their official dress-coats, offered a contrast of black in this glittering crowd. . . . Claire advanced bravely into the grand *salon* toward the guests, like the goddess of this fashionable Olympus, the millionaire Venus of All-Paris, and received resolutely all the homage that a great lady can desire, the admiration of men and the envy of women.

Everybody smiled and flattered, bowing like a veritable subject. . . . But suddenly there was a movement of recoil and fright.

Rosine came running in, pale, out of breath, and voiceless, approached Claire hastily, and whispered in her ear a word that made her tremble from head to foot.

Suddenly through an open door entered without ceremony the police commissary, with his tri-colored scarf about him and escorted by his agent. Behind them came Father Jean, with his basket on his back and his hook in his hand, carrying his head high; then Madame Potard, with lowered head, and some police officers concealing two other persons, — Camille and Marie.

"Let no one go out, or speak to the master if he comes in," ordered the commissary.

And making a sign to the agent who followed him, he said:

"Watch!"

"Yes, Monsieur."

And the agent went out to watch.

A thunderbolt falling into this *salon* would have produced less effect; a ray of joy shone upon the forehead of more than one woman, and even of more than one man, these sycophants tasting, in the fall of the idol, revenge for their own debasement.

The commissary advanced until face to face with Claire, who stood motionless and overwhelmed.

"Mademoiselle," said he to her, "a painful duty brings me here to effect a confrontation required by justice."

Claire drew back in terror.

"What does this mean, Monsieur?"

Jean, who had advanced, followed by the others, answered her.

"It means that we are invited to your wedding in the name of the law!"

"Just heaven!"

"You did not expect us, I see," continued the terrible Jean, folding his arms in front of her. "Justice is so slow," he sneered, shaking his gray head. "You were going ahead without us . . . all ready . . . bouquet, crown, and veil. You lacked nothing, God forgive me, but the right to carry them". . . .

And, turning to the magistrate, he cried, overwhelming the guilty one with a gesture:

"Yes, Monsieur Commissary, this lady who wears a virgin's bouquet has had a child. This lady who wears this nuptial crown had her child killed by this midwife". . . .

He designated Madame Potard, downcast but affirmative, and then his gesture came back, more threatening than ever, to Claire, bewildered by this inexorable and public execution.

"This lady," screamed Jean, in the paroxysm of his justice, "this lady who wears this white veil of innocence, the Baroness Claire Hoffmann, has suffered this poor and virtuous girl, Marie Didier, to be accused of all these crimes."

Carried away by his own words, with flaming look and fulminating gesture, he thrust his hook into Claire's veil, twirled it in the air a moment, and threw it into his basket, crying with a terrifying laugh:

"Ah! ah! ah! A rag like the rest! Into the basket! Into the basket!"

Claire, crushed with shame, hid her face in her hands.

"Lost!" she groaned feebly.

But Jean, as terrible as the justice of the people, continued:

"Before God and before men you have no right to wear this veil. It will serve as a swaddling-band, or rather as a winding-sheet for your child . . . dead . . . . like your honor."

The rag-picker seemed Olympian, his 'gesture dominated the gathering, his grandeur filled the room. His lifted hook was the thunder-bolt, his basket seemed the gulf. He was no longer Father Jean; he was Jupiter Tonans, risen from the clouds of poverty to hurl gilded crime into the abyss.

"Pardon, pardon," begged Claire.

Marie, unable longer to contain herself, stepped between the guilty woman and her judge.

"Oh! Father Jean," said she, with a prayerful tone that came straight from the heart, "you so good!"

"Yes, there you go," said the rag-picker, confounded. "Defend her . . . queer girl that you are. She or you!"

Claire, more and more bewildered and bending so low that she seemed to wish to disappear in the depths of the earth, stammered in mortal terror.

"Whither to fly? Where to hide myself? In the grave. . . . Death rather than this punishment! . . . . I can no longer contain the remorse that is killing me. . . . Suppose it should become eternal! Ah! I must confess and expiate!"

The commissary seized this opportunity for a confession which he had sought by a stroke of theatrical justice.

"Speak," said he.

Claire fell upon her knees and solemnly declared:

"My God, I recognize thy justice . . . my punishment is even less than my crime . . . may my confession purchase thy pardon!"

And rising again, she said firmly to the commissary:

"Monsieur, I am the guilty party. Yes, I allowed my child to be sacrificed to my honor, and allowed the accusation of this girl who sacrificed her honor to my child."

Then in a feebler voice:

"To her, to her then this crown that tortures me, these ornaments that reproach me, all these signs of purity, love, and happiness!"

As she tore the flowers from her bosom, they fell at Marie's feet.

"It is just," she concluded; "to her my place, to me hers! And it is for us both to reward her, Camille; for me, by dying; for you, by living for her."

Marie sustained her, saying in tears:

"Oh! poor woman. My God, pardon for her! I thank you for myself!"

Jean wiped his moist eyes with the back of his hand.

"What!" he exclaimed, "am I going to soften too?"

Claire uttered a cry of anguish.

"Ah! my heart is breaking. It is the end of the ordeal. . . I die relieved. This saint's tears put out the fires of hell."

She fell into the arms of Marie and Rosine.

Jean, on the alert, heard an officer's whistle, and, turning to the commissary, he said:

"The baron."

"Take me away," begged Claire; "take me away that I may die in peace!"

Rosine, aided by two servants, led the dying woman into her apartments.

"Two," cried Jean, when she had disappeared. "Now for the other, the third and last . . . the worst. . . . And let us strike the iron while it is hot. All hands retire!" he ordered with authority.

The numerous guests withdrew.

"What a piece of news for my journals!" said Louchard, delighted.

"And the contract?" asked Loiseau of Gripon.

"And the bonds?" exclaimed the latter. "Bah! nothing but a change of names."

"You are right," said Loiseau, the last to go out. "They will have need of us again directly. A marriage deferred, but not lost!"

Jean approached the commissary, took him by his overcoat, and said in a persuasive tone:

"Remember your promises, my magistrate. I hold the cards, and you watch the game. . . . Let me finish the job; go in yonder, I pray you."

He made the commissary go into another room. Then he said to Camille and Marie:

"And you go in there."

He pushed them towards another door.

There remained Laurent and Léon, very much flurried and confused.

The rag-picker got rid of them with a few kicks, saying:

"Ha! ha! my brandy-drinking valets, cup-bearers to Mandrin! there you are, then! Well, take that! And that! And dodge this one, if you can. Go look for me in the cellar."

Left alone, he went toward a *portière*, took off his basket, then his blouse, and concealed himself entirely.

"Now it lies between us two," he said. "He or I!"

The private door opened, and the baron walked in.

"Madame Potard has gone," said he, as he entered. "The rascal's house is shut up. All is said. Now to the salon."

"Halt!" cried Jean, revealing himself and barring the way.

"The rag-picker!" cried Baron Hoffmann, starting back in surprise.

Jean placed himself before the door by which the baron had just entered.

"Yes, Monsieur Baron," said he, quietly.

"Here?" questioned the other.

"Waiting for you!"

"And free?"

"A little!"

"You have escaped," said the baron, as he imperiously rang a bell.

"You ring for the deaf," said Jean, not at all disconcerted. "Your daughter is caught, Madame Potard is caught . . . . and you are guarded."

"I!"

"Yes, you, and closely. And I am a witness for the prosecution, with documentary evidence to confront and confound you."

He pointed to the basket and the hook.

"Look," said he, "do you recognize that tool? And this one? Notice the rust of Didier's blood."

The baron tried to go out through the door by which he had entered.

"Let me pass," he growled.

Jean raised the hook and barred the door.

"No thoroughfare," said he. "I have settled Marie's account; now for my own!"

The banker tried to seize Jean by the collar, but the latter released himself with a sudden movement, sneering:

"Ah! yes, the same old fist! A regular screw-twister. I recognize it. Twice goes, but not three times! Every day is not a *fête* day. I am not drunk, as I was at the table and at the quai, when we were only two, two rag-pickers, and when one of us killed Jacques, either you or me."

"I! Baron Hoffmann?"

"Baron of the basket! You, a double knave, a false baron and a false rag-picker, a real robber and a real murderer. You killed the man as surely as you killed the child. The first crime produced the second, and the second proves the first. Madame Potard has spoken, and so has your daughter. . . . All is said, known, understood; and those who have arrested the daughter will soon arrest the father. It is over with the whole race."

"Dead!" exclaimed the baron in despair.

"Not yet," said Jean.

"How so?"

"While there's life, there's hope, and if you wish." . . .

"What? Say on!" asked the baron, ardently.

"If you wish, you can escape," said Jean. "One can give the guard the slip here as well as at the castle of Ham; you are not more difficult to pass than a prince."

Showing his blouse:

"Napoleon's trick, you see."

"Ah! I understand. Well, this full pocket-book, a million, Claire's dowry! . . . my dress-coat for your blouse."

"You are on the scent; but I want more than gold today! You have accused me, save me, I will save you."

"Well! How?"

"A confession that will clear me."

"So be it," acceded the baron, running to a table and writing the confession. Then, after showing it to Jean, he said:

"Take and give."

Jean grasped the paper and gave his garment.

"There!" said he; "fly in that, like a pretender. Honor the blouse!"

The baron put on the blouse over his coat and threw his hat into a corner.

Jean continued sardonically:

"Resume also the basket, which you should never abandon again. Banker, that is your punishment and your salvation. You will pass, like a letter through the mails, under the envelope of the rag-picker."

The baron hesitated and then accepted, saying hopefully:

"Thank you. I will go!"

Then, becoming Garousse again as of old, he went toward the secret exit. As he was about to rush out, he uttered a cry:

"Ah!"

The agent of the commissary who had noted his entrance had anticipated his exit.

He rose before him.

"Derailed!" exclaimed Jean. "So much the worse . . . but for him only!"

The commissary, attracted by the noise, came in again with his men.

"Remain, Monsieur," said he to the baron.

Marie and Camille, called by Jean, entered in their turn.

The banker looked at them savagely, and then, throwing off his basket, tearing off the blouse, and throwing down the hook, he straightened up desperately.

"Well," he cried, "let it end, then,—this long suicide of crime! begun in the blood of another . . . let it end in mine! Today as formerly. . . . Better death than the basket."

He went out, led by the officers.

"Every one to his taste," concluded Jean.

And addressing the commissary, he said:

"Three! Quits, Monsieur! Here is the confession of the father after that of the daughter."

The magistrate took the paper.

"Yes," said he, "quits and free!"

He followed the baron, after a final bow.

Camille, Marie, and Jean threw themselves effusively into each other's arms.

"Ah! my dear wife, what joy!" exclaimed the young man.

"They suffer," exclaimed Marie, sympathetically.

And Jean said to Camille:

"Didn't I tell you that I would restore her to you? Ah! here are your thirty thousand francs!"

He handed him the notes, but Camille refused them.

"O noble friend, our true father, keep them!"

"I have no further need of them," said Jean.

Camille, indicating the mansion with a gesture, responded:

"In fact, all that is ours is yours. We owe everything to you. You shall live with us."

"No, no," said Jean, giving Marie a look of ineffable tenderness, "she is happy. That is all I want. . . . Oh! yes!"

"What is it?" asked Camille.

Jean, giving the baron's old basket a kick, answered simply:

"A new basket."

CHAPTER XI.

THE MARRIAGE.

That evening, as the clock of the Invalides struck half past eleven, the coach of the Roman ambassador at Paris drew up discreetly in front of the archbishop's palace.

Several prelates got out, escorted by lackeys dressed like the Swiss of Notre-Dame, and entered the ecclesiastical residence, the door of which opened immediately for their lordships.

The pope's nuncio, accompanied by his dignitaries, had come to take the archbishop to bless the union of Camille Berville and Claire Hoffmann at his pious embassy. . . .

They slowly traversed the spacious and gloomy apartments of the palace, regardless of the beautiful religious paintings that vainly covered the walls with their monotonous *spirituelle* lust. They had just entered the chapel.

Mgr. Affre was at the other end, buried in a large red velvet arm-chair, in the shadow of the altar.

He gave no sign of life at the approach of his important visitors, and, without stirring, allowed them to approach as near as possible and bow. Then only did he rise, gravely return their salute, and look at them for some moments without laughing, like a Christian augur.

"Is this the hour?" he asked at last.

And without waiting for the reply, he added:

"Let us start."

"We have still a quarter of an hour's grace," said the ultramontane.

"Then let us talk," rejoined the archbishop.

The two illustrious brothers in Jesus Christ walked back and forth beside the communion table, and, while the other prelates listened or conversed in low tones, they held the following colloquy:

"In your opinion what should be our attitude toward the Republic?" began the archbishop.

And he awaited the reply attentively.

"Hostile, very hostile," declared the nuncio. "We must reestablish the monarchy, royalty, or empire, no matter which," he continued, making a threatening gesture under his evangelical robe, "provided we get rid of the government of the *canaille.*"

The archbishop shook his head.

"Then you accept the alliance with the people?" replied the nuncio, firing up.

The other responded sententiously:

"We must accept what we cannot prevent. The Republic, to be sure, is not a good, it is an evil . . . . but it is also a fact. The best way to bury it is to seem to adopt it. As long as we sprinkle holy water over the trees of liberty, their roots will yield neither flowers nor fruit. As long as we continue to be the priests of the Republic, we shall be its masters."

"Then we must bless it to the utmost in order to destroy it?"

"Yes, to flatter the crowd is to capture it. Let us keep its confidence if we wish to impose our will upon it."

"I should prefer frank and open war," said the nuncio, incredulous and proud.

Mgr. Affre began to smile.

"You are an Italian noble," said he to the impetuous prelate; "I am a French *bourgeois.* Hence our divergence of opinion. Believe me, the confessional does its work here, slowly but surely. The priests lead the women, and the women lead the men. The drop of water, falling ever and ever, finally wears away the rock. The population will be disgusted before long with the barren Republic. Let us not treat the democrats as enemies, but as stray lambs. To attack is a great mistake. To pardon is all right. It is shrewder and surer. Let us claim that we are oppressed, receive our budget, make collections for the Holy Father, and bless the republicans, — and my word for it, they will die!"

At that moment a priest of the archbishop's palace announced the pressing visit of the Abbé Ventron.

"A shrewd fellow," said Mgr. Affre to the nuncio in a low tone.

And to the vicar:

"Let him enter and be welcome."

A moment later the Abbé Ventron, all red, out of breath, and gesticulating, made his appearance.

"Well, what?" asked the archbishop.

"Do not disturb yourself, Monseigneur," said the priest, choking with horror and heat; "there will be no marriage! Baron Hoffmann and his daughter have committed a frightful crime, and perhaps more than one."

"Well, and what then?" said the archbishop, without manifesting any emotion.

"He has just been arrested," said the Abbé Ventron.

"What!" cried the nuncio and archbishop together. "He has allowed himself to be caught?"

"Don't speak of it to me," groaned the priest of Saint Roch; "he! Hoffmann! I thought he was smarter than that. I can't get over it."

"What a scandal!" said the prelates, mournfully. "Our Holy Father's banker! And Peter's pence!"

"Then there will be no wedding?" concluded Mgr. Affre.

"Worse than that," exclaimed the Abbé Ventron.

"What then? My God!"

"Claire's affianced is going to marry a poor working girl, Marie Didier."

"A misalliance! Oh! that happens every day," said the archbishop, indulgently. "Calm yourself, my dear abbé."

"But this Camille, if left to himself, will undoubtedly have a civil marriage. The nuptials will pass from under our nose."

"The devil!" the archbishop could not help saying.

"A civil marriage!" repeated all the ecclesiastics in chorus.

"Bah!" exclaimed the nuncio, impetuously; "to marry this low-born Berville to Mlle. Hoffmann was pitiful enough . . . . . but to a Didier, ah! that is impossible. Let them couple like dogs, if they like; so much the better!"

Mgr. Affre could not restrain a movement of impatience as he said to the nuncio:

"I tell you that you will ruin all, you Roman gentlemen who have strayed into our ranks; you have no more diplomacy than the most insignificant country priest."

"Monsieur Affre," cried the nuncio, violently.

"Monsieur!" exclaimed the archbishop, repeating this incredible appellation.

"Yes, or Citizen, if you prefer," said the furious nuncio, aggravating the insult. A deathlike silence prevailed in the chapel.

Mgr. Affre, ever shrewd, mastered his indignation and made no answer, but his lips and hands trembled convulsively.

Suddenly his face lighted up.

"They will not go to the priest," said he; "well, the priest will go to them."

"What?" exclaimed the nuncio, in amazement.

The archbishop took the arm of the Abbé Ventron and said to him:

"Let us go to bless the union of Camille Berville and Marie Didier."

The astonished priest accompanied him, saying rapturously:

"Oh! what a genius! what an archbishop! he ought to be a cardinal . . . and Pope . . . if only the Gallic cock could crow at St. Peter's."

And aloud:

"Yes, it is a master stroke."

"And we remain in our evangelical *rôle*," said M. Affre. "We will have even the atheists on our side."

Then, addressing the nuncio triumphantly, he said:

"You will see this in the papers tomorrow, my dear brother, and you will have no need to carry the news to Rome."

He started quickly for the exit.

" Will you lend me your coach ? " he asked the nuncio, in a tone of raillery.

And receiving an affirmative nod, he said, as he straightened more and more on the Abbé Ventron's arm:

" Faubourg Saint-Honoré."

He went away before the eyes of the nuncio and enjoying his success in advance.

"Oh! how I would laugh if they should send you *ad patres,*" exclaimed the nuncio, with a gleam of contempt and hatred in his Italian eyes.

CHAPTER XII.

RELIGIOUS, CIVIL, OR FREE?

After having resisted his own desires and every effort, prayers, reproaches, and even violences, of his friends to retain him, Marie begging with clasped hands and on her knees and Camille going so far as to close the doors and secretly throw the thirty notes back into the basket, Jean baffled and dominated them all, utterly inflexible, sacrificing his own happiness to that of his child.

"You have no further need of me," he said to them; "adieu!"

"But," said Marie, "you have no right to go away, Father Jean; it is wicked! I no longer recognize you, you so good, so obliging; do you wish to deprive us of the pleasure of being grateful? You leave us the pain of ingratitude, chagrin, regret, the remorse of knowing you as abandoned, poor, old, suffering, sick, without care, without aid, without anything in the world when we have everything, thanks to you! It is cruelty to us! You treat us as enemies."

But Jean was firm; with the delicacy, sagacity, and independence of his nature, he instinctively felt that he would be embarrassing and embarrassed in the world in which Camille moved; he appreciated the incongruity of a rag-picker in a banker's house; he considered his presence in the Berville mansion an impossibility. Accordingly he had made up his mind, and was immovable.

As he left the salon, he met in the ante-room the Abbé Ventron preceding the archbishop in pontifical garb.

Rag-picker and priest ran against and recognized each other, each with a feeling of surprise that fixed them face to face, motionless for a moment like two dogs about to fight.

The Abbé, a *basilate* of Tartuffe, a hypocrite composed of equal doses of impudence and cunning, was the first to recover his self-possession; and, quickly resuming his *sang-froid* and his celestial audacity, he acted as if he had never seen either the confessional or Jean.

The rag-picker, more human, could not suppress a cry:

"Ah! the priest of Saint-Roch."

And, instead of going, he remained, curious to know the object of this suspicious visit.

The imperturbable Abbé Ventron passed by him, without seeming to further notice him.

But Jean stopped him with a question.

"Why the devil do you come here with your laces? Are you one of the married?"

The Abbé stammered:

"I come to speak to Mlle. Marie."

"To confess her again. . . . Oh! if she were still in my care, this time you would not get out of the confessional alive."

Then, restraining himself out of respect for Camille, he added:

"Go in; we shall see how you will come out."

The Abbé and the archbishop, almost disconcerted, hastened to enter with Jean, who said to the young people:

"Pardon me, I had forgotten to relieve you. . . . My basket and hook have no more business here with these gentlemen than I have."

And he pretended to look for his tools.

With unruffled countenance, the priest saluted Camille and even Marie, to whom he introduced Mgr. Affre.

"Permit your old spiritual guide," said he, with haughty respect, "Mademoiselle, and you, Monsieur, to introduce you to Monseigneur the archbishop. He, you know, was to have performed the marriage ceremony for the unfortunate Claire, and he certainly would be disposed to bless your marriage as well."

At first Marie recoiled from this viper, but her natural benevolence, supplemented by her happiness, led her to receive her ex-confessor with an indulgence bordering on pardon, though in silence.

Camille likewise bowed silently, and with an icy coldness.

Then the archbishop took the floor; but, first pointing to the rag-picker, said: "I come here to fulfil a delicate mission. This man. . . ."

"Oh, you may speak before our best friend."

"He!" exclaimed the astonished archbishop.

"Yes. Take a good look at this poor man. I know not whether he believes in God. . . ."

"You shall see," said Jean, shaking his head.

"Well," continued Camille, "I can only hope that the Holy Father, the Pope of Rome, has as clear a conscience as Father Jean, the rag-picker of Paris."

Jean made a wry face at being praised, or compared to the Pope.

"Surely," said he, "it is not religion that has made me more honest than the Abbé Ventron. . . ."

And upon a supplicating sign from Marie he became silent.

The archbishop resumed the floor with that paternal and sanctimonious tone which the Catholic priest affects with his flock, and especially the priest of episcopal rank, bishop meaning ancient, *seigneur*, senior, venerable, reverend, etc.

"Yes, my children," said the pontiff to them, in this unctuous and oily tongue of Holy Church, " God has seen fit, by one of his unfathomable decrees, to restore, in spite of fate, to you, Monsieur Berville, your immense fortune, and to you, Mademoiselle Didier, your good name. It is a great blessing to you, Monsieur, a great honor to you, Mademoiselle. You are engaged to each other."

Camille made a gesture of assent.

The archbishop continued :

" The Church, which condemns pride as the first of mortal sins and the fall of man itself, congratulates you through my ministry. When wealth unites with virtue, it never makes a misalliance. It becomes purified thereby. Be, then, as pious as you are generous. It is for you to prove your gratitude toward God, to thank Providence for his signal goodness to you in uniting you according to his law, his order, and the holy commandments of his church."

Jean was all ears; his mouth wide open with astonishment and indignation, he had entirely forgotten his tools.

The archbishop, having taken breath, after this insinuating exordium, continued to distil his priestly honey, and ended with this serpent's peroration :

" Thus you will deserve the benefits of heaven, and keep its favor upon earth. Upon this depends your common happiness in this world and in the other. For you cannot be happy except you lead a Christian life. The woman who honors God esteems her husband, of whom she is but a half, by the act of the Creator, performed precisely with a view to human unity. If woman does not fulfil her duties toward God, how can she fulfil them toward man? If she believes in nothing, how can she believe in him? If she has no soul to save, what will she care for her body? Lacking divine faith, the seal of all union and the restraint of all dissolution, what will hold her to conjugal faith? Believe me, young people, and marry in the grace of God and under the blessing of his minister."

Camille was the first of the two, with exquisite politeness, to thank the prelate for his advice and his offers, saying to him :

" Monsieur, I thank you for the honor of your visit, which, I confess, I did not expect, and for the good will of your counsel, which I do not deserve. Unfortunately, my convictions are absolutely contrary to yours, and prevent me from accepting that which you condescend to offer me. What you call Providence I call right, and what you call faith I call duty. The innocence of Marie Didier must be manifest like the crime of Hoffmann in the very nature of things, without the direct intervention of God. I do not believe that he disturbs himself about our little affairs."

Camille continued his republican logic against the apostolic eloquence.

" In the matter of our union, alas ! we are no nearer an agreement. I should not like to respond to your advance by an offence, especially in my own house. But though I do not deserve your kindness, I hope at least to deserve your esteem by my frankness. You talk to me of duties toward God. I know no duties save those toward man. You are of Rome, I am of France. You say: ' In the name of the Father, Son, and Holy Ghost ! ' and I say : ' Liberty, Equality, Fraternity,' — a very different trinity, is it not ? You add ' Eternity,' and I : ' Or death.' You call love commands, authority, obedience, force, order, and law ; I call it attraction, passion, devotion, and gift. Every religious or civil law is made only to supply the place of will and liberty. Free thought, free morality, free love, the law of laws, — those are my dogmas, contrary to your own. We cannot, then, agree. Such is my opinion, Monsieur. As for Marie, she will tell you hers. I refer the matter to her, and will do as she wishes. What say you, Marie ? "

" I say," she answered, with charming embarrassment and increasing confidence, " that your opinion is my own, your sentiments my own, that I wish no more than you the honor that is offered us. There is no need of any bond, religious or other, even civil, to make me yours entirely and forever. I am your wife because you desire and I desire it, and not because law and religion desire it, because others than ourselves desire it." . . .

" Permit me, Mademoiselle," said the prelate, interrupting her, " those whom you call others are God and the prince, the sacrament and the code."

" And what is the good," she cried, taking Camille's hand, " of the will of God and men, if you cease.to love me ? The day when I shall no longer please you, of what importance will be codes and sacraments, the laws of earth and the blessings of heaven ? You are earth and heaven to me. No, dear Camille, I do not wish you to be forced to love me. The day when it shall be my misfortune to displease you, palace, fortune, honor, and society, — all will be at an end so far as I am concerned. I shall resume my needle and my attic, beside our Father Jean."

" But your children ? " said the priest.

" Our children," rejoined Camille ; " there we find our sacrament, the bond and the curb. When the human heart is neither forced nor falsified by authority, nature substitutes in it, in an orderly fashion, one passion for another. We shall love each other in the children of our love."

" Ah," said Marie, again pressing Camille's hand, " even though he should no longer love the woman, I know very well that he will still love the mother of his child. Yes, Monseigneur, I wish him to be free, always free to leave me, as he has been free to take me. Believe me, this is, perhaps, more designing, less disinterested than it seems, for it is the surest way of keeping him."

She bowed more profoundly, as if to say a final farewell.

Camille indicated still more emphatically that the interview was at an end.

The two priests, forced to let go their prey in spite of their tenacity, exchanged a look of despair, which directly became a look of malice directed at the young couple, and then went out in a superb and almost threatening fashion.

Suddenly the Abbé came back and said drily :

" But these wedding presents do not belong to you, and the church has its poor. . . . . "

"Possibly," answered Camille, " only Mademoiselle Claire still lives."

" And the pence of Saint Peter, whose banker you are?" retorted the Abbé.

" I am his banker no longer, and tomorrow Saint Peter shall be paid. Be gone!"

"Well said!" exclaimed Father Jean, who had listened to the whole, rubbing his hands with satisfaction.

And he added:

"Now, my children, do you remember," said he, "the day when I broke my pipe, when you *voluntarily* took each other for husband and wife, without priest or notary,—do you remember what I said to you? Well, I repeat it today. ' Well and good! In that case Father Jean gives his consent.' On that day you were married before me, Father Jean, father, priest, and mayor, all, and as long as love wills, Jean wills. Now, my *rôle* finished, I go away content."

And he went out, forcibly tearing himself from their embraces and appeals.

CHAPTER XIII.

MADNESS.

Just then a sharp cry, followed by a piercing laugh, was heard.

"What is that?" said Marie, frightened.

Camille himself was alarmed at this strange noise.

Suddenly a woman half naked, with dishevelled hair and bewildered face, her cheeks flushed and her eyes glowing, came running in, laughing and crying, and followed by Rosine, who was calling:

"Help!"

Claire, attacked by an acute meningitis and suffering from a burning fever, in a fit of delirium had violently jumped from her bed and from the arms of her maids, who had not had strength enough to hold her.

She had lost her reason.

She was more than mad. Because of her strong nature, she had become a raving maniac.

On entering, she perceived the basket which the midwife had brought as proof. She threw herself upon it with frenzy, took it in her two hands, smiled maternally upon its emptiness, cradled it tenderly, kissed it passionately, talked to it as if an infant could have answered her words, her kisses, her smiles, her caresses, walked back and forth with her dear burden, around the room, asking Marie, who was dumb with grief and terror, to see how beautiful the baby was, telling Rosine not to shout, lest she might awaken it, and telling Camille to kiss it.

Rosine tried to take the basket from Claire, who held it with all her strength.

"Oh, the cursed woman! She wants to take away my child, to carry it off, to drown it! Help! Help! My father paid her, the infamous. . . . . What will God say?"

"Calm yourself, Mademoiselle, you have nothing to fear for yourself or for him," said Marie.

Then in a lucid interval, recovering consciousness, Claire cried:

"Where am I?"

"Mademoiselle, for pity's sake," said Marie, clasping her hands, as if she ought to ask pardon for her own happiness and Claire's misfortune, "Mademoiselle, come to yourself and follow me to your own room. You are at home. Rest easy.

This house is still yours, as well as ours. You are our sister, our friend. Forget the past. We will care for you, we will love you, we will console you. Come."

"Ah, ah, good Marie! Take him, care for him, nurse him, you, so kind, so kind! And you, Father Jean, do not awaken him with your heavy voice. And you, Camille, kiss your child. Say nothing to anyone, for my father wants to kill him. Hide him carefully. They are coming to take him. . . Ah, father . . . priest. . . . Religion, family . . . . the oratory . . . . . they have made me mad, guilty. They have killed me!"

It was distressing. All were overwhelmed.

"Yes, dear sister, poor mother, give him to me. I will care for him," said Marie, humoring the mad woman in order to calm her. "Go lie down again, rest, sleep. I will watch over him for you. We will save him, we will bring him up, we will adopt him."

Claire seemed charmed for a moment by the music of Marie's sweet voice, but, on seeing the wedding gifts, her raving became more furious than ever. Rising, with haggard eyes, foam on her lips, and perspiration on her forehead, she cried:

"Ah, ah, the marriage! High society, and its homage, and its presents, — into the basket! into the basket!

She had just seen, also, the basket which Jean had forgotten, and, rushing toward it, she took it in one hand, and before they could stop her or even divine her purpose, with the other she seized all the objects that she could find, saying to each of them:

"Necklace, into the basket! Bracelet, into the basket! Rings, breastpin, and earrings, into the basket!"

And all these marvels of art, luxury, and taste were heaped up like cabbage-stalks in the rag-picker's hamper, which Camille vainly tried to take from her, and which grew so heavy that she could not hold it, and that, in her efforts to keep it, she fell, rolled over and over, struggling in convulsive anguish, crying and foaming, completely covered with gold and silver and precious stones, and saying with a frightful laugh:

"A dowry for the daughters of Saint Anthony who nurse the sons of Saint Honoré!" and always repeating the prophetic cry, with which Jean had fatally struck her reason and her life: "Into the basket! Into the basket! Into the basket!"

She fainted.

"Ah!" cried Marie, throwing herself into Camille's arms, "this house frightens me. Let us follow Father Jean."

The rag-picker had not been a witness of the fainting of Claire, who was piously lifted by Marie and Camille, and carried back to her bed, where Rosine and the other maids watched her until she could be transferred to Doctor Blanche's asylum.

This, together with Jean's retreat, was the dark spot upon the honeymoon of the two young people.

As for Jean, ho had gone away, with the joy of having made the only two beings whom he had loved happy, of having well fulfilled his *rôle* and lived his life as a father.

Foreseeing for the future all his sad existence of the past, thenceforth reduced to himself, having nothing more to protect or cherish, an unconscious and sublime altruist, he could not make up his mind to return to the Rue Sainte-Marguerite, to go back living into his grave. He was seized with a frightful reaction. An immense despair, the very darkness of the tomb, invaded his heart, and took from him all courage to live. The sparkle of the wine again passed before his eyes.

"No," he cried, "death sooner!"

And feeling that he was alone forever upon earth, with all the horrors of solitude, incapable of living without seeing Marie again, and of seeing her again without injuring her, he wished not to end his bitter life in isolation, brutishness, and vice, like the duke Garousse, but to sacrifice to his daughter his moral, human, and paternal life in the very spot where he had begun it, — in short, to leave his conscience where he had found it.

And casting a glance at the splendid mansion in which Marie lived, and contrasting the beautiful summer night with that in which he had saved Garousse at the expense of Didier, — a fault, he thought, that deserved expiation, — on this calm night following one of those hot days that give our Paris an Oriental air, inviting man to rest, and explaining the Turkish proverb: 'Better sitting than standing, lying than sitting, and dead than lying,' he started, this time drunk with pain, for the parapet of the bridge of Austerlitz. . . .

THE END.

www.ingramcontent.com/pod-product-compliance
Lightning Source LLC
Chambersburg PA
CBHW060519030726
47498CB00004B/1000